For those who savor a dash of knowledge with their spice.

CONTENTS

```
CONTENTS ........................ v
PLAYLIST ........................ i
LEVEL ONE ....................... 4
LEVEL TWO ...................... 19
LEVEL THREE .................... 35
LEVEL FOUR ..................... 49
LEVEL FIVE ..................... 56
LEVEL SIX ...................... 67
LEVEL SEVEN .................... 76
LEVEL EIGHT .................... 91
LEVEL NINE .................... 101
LEVEL TEN ..................... 108
LEVEL ELEVEN .................. 122
LEVEL TWELVE .................. 129
LEVEL THIRTEEN ................ 138
LEVEL FOURTEEN ................ 150
LEVEL FIFTEEN ................. 162
LEVEL SIXTEEN ................. 183
THE FINAL BOSS ................ 191
LEVEL SEVENTEEN ............... 193
LEVEL EIGHTEEN ................ 212
LEVEL NINETEEN ................ 220
LEVEL TWENTY .................. 231
LEVEL TWENTY-ONE .............. 237
LEVEL TWENTY-TWO .............. 243
LEVEL TWENTY-THREE ............ 249
LEVEL TWENTY-FOUR ............. 254
LEVEL TWENTY-FIVE ............. 261
LEVEL TWENTY-SIX .............. 272
LEVEL TWENTY-SEVEN ............ 278
END GAME ...................... 289
SPELL ONE ..................... 299
```

PLAYLIST

- **"UNDEAD"** - Hollywood Undead.
- **"BIG BAD WOLF"** – In This Moment.
- **"WARRIOR"** - Steve James Feat. Lights.
- **"GIRLFRIEND"** – Avril Lavigne.
- **"F.O.M.W"** - Ham Sandwich.
- **"RADIOACTIVE"** - Imagine Dragons.
- **"BAD GUY"** - Billie Eilish.
- **"NISSAN ALTIMA"** - Doechii.
- **"SEVEN NATION ARMY"** - The White Stripes.
- **"GLADIATOR"** - Zayde Wølf.

My Valentine's Virus

CONTENT WARNING:

This story contains explicit language, such as violence, stalking, descriptive sexual acts, sexual degradation, blackmailing, mean girls, drowning, cyber-attacks, unwarranted facts about shrimp, and stubborn egoists.

Your mental health is vital. Please understand what might bother you before entering this world. This is a dark romance novel for readers 18 and older. Reader caution is advised.

Author's Note:

Our FMC (female main character), Abbie starts as a caricature of herself. This is how she copes with her crippling anxiety and atychiphobia. Atychiphobia is a severe fear of losing. This is a trauma response she's had from a distressing event when she was a child. It's heightened, and to cope with the overwhelming sensations, Abbie challenges anyone to anything. Fueled by poverty, this has evolved to her trading higher and higher stakes. The phobia has given her an alter ego where she has chosen to challenge dangerous criminals.

Abbie has exercised and troubleshooted her "luck" to a point where she can feel high chances of winning or losing. In conclusion, she's a terrible friend to play games with but the best person to bring with you on a Las Vegas trip.

My Valentine's Virus
can be read as a standalone.

LEVEL ONE

PRINCESS_USER24

Ever wish you had the power to hit Forward in life and skip to the juice already? I do. This shit's exhausting.

I'm in a surreal inner fight with my body to get out of bed. This makes me mull over everything that's gotten me to this point by accident.

Everyone has been in some monotonous rut for a million years with no way out but to wait.

Waiting. Wishing. Wanting. I mean—what else is there to do?

That may be the hole these other walking cadavers want to fall into, but I got tired of being on Pause all the time. *So, so, so tired.*

That's when a violent fire pleading within my soul convinced me to quit my abusive job and move halfway across the country here to Crimson Raven University—my dream college.

That, and a more nefarious purpose—I've been tracking someone down for over six years, *Baiting* them.

And although I don't *need* a degree for what I already do, technology grows. I'm subscribed to Universal Tech News—or UTN for short. It keeps me updated, but it can only take me so far. I needed a secondary goal.

I've been ethically hacking since I was old enough to operate a screen. My code-obsessed brain gravitated to it, and I've spurred a private following larger than *Anonymous*. Okay, maybe not *that* huge, but someday.

Each dollar I saved—if I'm being honest, was *that* week's paycheck—flew me straight to Oregon. I nailed a full-ride scholarship for my cybersecurity major. With this, I receive access to boarding, meals, and the nation's best computers. Buses don't charge us, and honestly, that doesn't sound so bad. What's *really* bad is I know little to nothing about the chirpy state other than from *New Girl*.

My favorite sitcom plays on my TV in the background like a podcast while I convince myself this will all work out in my mind.

I gawk at the ceiling fan. I relate to the boundlessness that is Schmidt while cold tears dive into my eardrums. The tip of my nose tingles as my lungs slowly fill with sticky air.

Classes can't officially start until next week, and even though my stomach does a cha-cha of excitement at the prospect, I don't have a dime to my name.

I've monetized my hacking as a main hustle in the meantime. The checks will take a week to enter my account.

By selling my talents to various corporations that scream out for it, I've been able to make enough cash to afford coffee every day. I rescue files that were swiped from below their noses. It's usually done by other hackers, hired by rivals, or *un*ethical bugs that make easy money. They do it by blackmailing them into giving them millions—or *billions* for their safe return.

Tons of shareholders typically call it quits, leaving thousands of workers jobless. This includes businesses that help communities and all

My Valentine's Virus

to cater to *one* asshole. A violent twist aches in my chest. The same thing happened to my doting dad when no one was hiring.

I remember the agony that withered him away from the inside out while he kept that gleaming smile. The dreadful week after everything went sideways, he grew dense wrinkles within hours. He always smiled even after the night of the storm. Something happened behind Dad's forced expression. The pain underneath it started telling me he expected something new for tomorrow. Even if he knew logically, it was all hopeless. The tomorrows came, but the "new" never did.

I'm slowly winning the battle with my limbs. An image of my father warms behind my eyes, making me turn my head to our framed picture.

On my polished nightstand, the golden frame immortalizes my dad and me. It's a picture of my science fair victory for my artificial intelligence that I named after my pernicious mother, Ana Belle. His proud grin brightens the picture, and I smile, putting a break to my tears.

Younger me is posing beside him—a full yard shorter than the gleaming giant. My emo-phase was being absolutely crushed. I have the most tomboy haircut I've ever seen on a child. Raven-colored bangs coated the entirety of my peripheral, and no one could convince me it wasn't the illest look in all of 2008.

Clearing my throat, I wipe my face and sit up on my own without a cattle prod ready. I face my neon green laptop stationed at my work desk in the lit corner by the window where I study.

I'm reminded of this small-named hacker known as EctoPhantom, who I was hunting on the Dark Web. The rat bastard stole from hundreds of farmers throughout the U.S. in the past few years. He single-handedly became the reason grocery prices skyrocketed, all behind the comfort of a monitor.

Someone of my talent couldn't allow for that to continue. I knew the feds were already on the case, but I surmised they ran into a wall, keeping them from the truth. EctoPhantom was leaving ghost trails in his wake, as his name would suggest.

There was no evidence connecting him to his crimes, so I raced to action like a retired boxer smelling the leathers of old gear again. I issued a virtual challenge to the thief—basic stuff. "*Try* stopping me from notifying authorities of your illegal activities."

No one's topped me before, and in EctoPhantom's case, I made sure of it.

Nothing riles my victims up more than putting their livelihoods on the line. But, if they never wanted to get caught, they shouldn't have fucked with the people of my world to begin with. Karma's a slow bitch with side-quests for days, and I don't subscribe to the romance of patience.

When I fit on my metaphorical fisting gloves, I toyed with my new rival all night long. Psychoanalyzing his next targets, I predicted how he could maneuver around me and turn his chances to zero. The poor baby even tried launching various viruses into my system, making tracking his location easier. I shattered his defenses into pathetic shards, and he only lasted until sunrise.

It made me wonder how government investigators kept losing track of him when *I* didn't even break a sweat. I'm a singular twenty-five-year-old woman running a Linux operating system, and they're the goddamn CIA.

I hauled Ecto's hacker-butt into a dead corner, surrounding him like a drooling hog, ready to *bury* him. Unfortunately, it was all a stab in the neck when I realized he… wasn't even that special.

UTN reported EctoPhantom's arrest on eighteen cybercrime and cyber warfare counts *that* morning. *Un-anonymously.*

This was one of hundreds of cyber bounty hunts I've collected. And I couldn't risk some half-assed keyboard warrior staking claim to my victories. Broadcasters, social media outlets, and news articles all know me as Princess_User24.

My Valentine's Virus

Since the announcement of my alter ego, Princess_User24, six years ago, every cell in my god-like body has hoped for the one I'm hunting for to arise. Mr. Number One himself, Zone_Warden.

Unfortunately, I've remained second on a live online board for a trillion years now. Second.

Second...

I seethe every freaking time. It drills under my skin like an ingrown hair or a shitty nickname. I'm *so* sure most people would be proud of being Number Two in the world, but that mindset is below my understanding.

My dream is to be the best goddamn hacker alive, and I'm so stinking close. The need for it fills my skin with so much heat it's like I'm suffocating in my skin at times. When my plans are set, hankering in the shadows of Number One will be a distant memory.

I uncovered a lead regarding him back in my Senior year of high school. It drew me to Oregon long before I considered Crimson Raven U my college. Life got in the way, filled with dead-end jobs for six years, and I had to push back the burning challenge until now.

EctoPhantom wasn't my Number One, but whoever they may be, I know Zone_Warden's circle of friends and families live in this county. Social media engineering got me this far. It's not even for a moral high anymore. I want that numbered spot. I want to be Ms. Number One. Once that happens, I'll get a tattoo of it around my thigh, and it'll be super true.

After my fun with EctoPhantom, a deep depression snuck up on me. I got used to receiving those in swarms as a teen, and I honestly believed I was passed this. It's a cavernous emotion that plagues me. It's like after you finish an engaging suspense movie, and then you're thrust back into the monotony of life. I mean. How could they do that to you? Just yank the rug like that with no warning and leave you floundering like a fish in the sky. ... *it sucks!* I get this way times a hundred. The adrenaline hangover happens hours after I win something huge.

♥

No. I know what my problem is. It's *other* people. Why can't they stop disappointing me? *You did it again, Abigail. You hyped someone up in your glorious head.*

My eyes skirt across the spartan expanse of my dorm room, and I decide being tucked away indoors over this is for losers. And I'm a winner. Like, I literally won. What's there to be weepy for?

Clearing my voice, I let inner flames guide the rest of my actions like an uplifting possession. For the benefit of my mental health, I zombie-packed my war machine into my laptop bag, along with a pair of noise-canceling headphones and a black allergen mask. I update my beloved virtual assistant before I go, and A.N.A. is up to speed.

My old middle school science project still comes in handy, and I don't have to pay Google my soul's worth of private data.

"Okay, Ana, find me a cute local café, please," I voice into my smartphone while I bike simultaneously. The ache in my voice takes me back. *Ugh, I even sound pathetic.* Some vitamin C should do me good, though.

The sways of my balance lessen from my grip on the crest of control, and the wind roars my hair from my face.

"You got it!" A.N.A. squeaks from my pocket. She reminds me of BMO from Adventure Time when she speaks, forcing my smile. **"Cupid's Café is *three miles* straight!"**

I proceed my wheels down the slope of Main Street. "Thank you," I chant with a smile near her. Being polite with tech is a must. I don't want the object to think I'm a bad person. It comforts me knowing I'll be safe when robots inevitably come for us all in the future. *Hehehe.*

"*Be wary,*" A.N.A. chimes, vibrating in my pocket. **"Police cars are parked on *Stanley Avenue.*"**

I roll my eyes at the "cop detector" update for her. *Aye dios mio.* Now that I'm thinking about it, I could get arrested for what I'm carrying. I sometimes forget these devices are illegal. It's just something I always

My Valentine's Virus

need on me. It's nothing scary. As a joke, I carry a device that helps me lower gas prices from a distance. I got a great deal on it on the Dark Web.

"Don't worry, Ana, I'll protect you," I humor.

"Oh, thank goodness," she sighs in amusement, earning my hearty chuckle.

HONK. HOOOOOOOOONK.

My heart jumps to my throat in a single bound. Yards ahead, a beaten-up purple van skips *its* Stop sign and emerges into my right lane.

Eyes wide, I reject gripping my brakes. My bike is traveling too fast to stop. I'm at an angle on this hill, and if my wheels stop preemptively, I'll do severe damage to myself. "*Shit!*"

My mind searches for every alternative in a matter of heartbeats. Blood gallops to my ears as if deafening my protesting screams. By some miracle, the van brakes, forcing everyone inside to shift forward. Their bodies strain against the seatbelts as I narrowly swerve and miss a would-be collision.

Breathing hard, I slow down. Glimpsing at the windshield, I check if the driver and passengers are conscious and at least safe. They raise their shoulders at me with thick guilt in their eyes, igniting my disgust. My jaw tightens, and my frown cuts through my forehead.

Fuck those people! I could have broken my neck. I push a wavy strand from my eyes in a heated huff and pedal on. In heaves and ankle pains, I school my features and face back toward my destination.

Hot adrenaline cools from me finally until an engine's rev threatens my heart rate and shatters my eardrums.

With my nerves spiking and my patience lacking, I glare with burning hatred at a motorcycle's howl, demanding my attention.

His clean visor helmet shines as I brake to cover my ears. With a sour expression, the rider slows to approach me. I didn't know Neanderthals would make their return in my lifetime.

He's a breathless tower of a man with alluring broad arms and shoulders wrapped snugly under his leather hoodie.

A. DARANG

The visor covering his face has a white skull imprint of Elysium's logo. I raise my brow high enough it might give me muscle cramps. Elysium is such a *niche* brand. It's the leading security software of the four largest banks nationwide. I bet no one's even thought about that on a regular basis. Don't ask me how *I* know that's even a thing.

I struggle to catch my breath as panic spills out of me. Maybe he works there advertising the company. My hazing eyes narrow tight, checking out the label like it's the answer to all my riddles. Maybe— *Maybe*, I'm overthinking about a hottie on a motorcycle. I shake my thirst away, remembering the jump scare. Who does he think he is making all this racket in the morning?

Eying his form, I raise my fingers in a square, with him locked inside to mentally photograph him in my Asshole Journal.

There's something furry on the side of his motorcycle. The fuzzy black-and-silver creature, squirreling around from view is searching for something.

Whatever.

I smack my cheeks a little, bringing me out of my delirious haze. The coppery taste of panic cools to sugary fury.

Gripping the handles of my ride, my knuckles whiten, and I chase his bike like it's a triathlon. Keeping up with the cyclist's speed, my legs grow numb to the movement.

He turns his head. "R. U. O.K.?" He signs one-handed while drifting before a red light.

I stop near him and thrust an offensive sign at his face. Not a second sooner, the red light of about three seconds mysteriously blares green again. My brows lift a foot as he speeds by, cocking his head back in a humorous tilt. He then makes a heart sign with both hands in his drive. And I hate how a chunk of me melts for him.

It's my knees. My knees are fluttering, and my heart is whispering obscenities. *I'd like to trade places with that motorcycle… have him hold my handles and steer me where he wants.*

My Valentine's Virus

He's the kind of guy absorbed with so much confidence that he leaves puddles of it on the floor for others to lick. Judging by the black matte coating of his vehicle, he appears well-off—you know, *rich*. The breeze he's giving off smells of pine, like his ride is fresh off the lot too.

A warm blush dances to my face, forcing my smile. Struggling to calm my hormones, I fix my hair behind an ear, silently regretting not stealing his number. Not that it's too late.

I can't stop thinking about that logo. I'll look into Elysium on my way to Cupid's Café. It'll be my evil lair this evening. Locking up my bike, I hike the rest of the way. With my laptop tucked soundly in my shoulder bag, a cool autumn breeze plays with the strands of my black hair.

While I stride down Main Street, a wobbled *"Stop! Thief"* makes my heart skip, and my head whirls toward thundering steps.

"There's too much going on today," I huff.

A man several inches over me in a blue ski mask, gray hoodie, and jeans shuffles around the corner like his ass caught fire.

The voices in my head unanimously agree how funny it'll be if I trip him. And I do.

His body skips and plops across the emptied crosswalk like a pathetic hockey puck. Fistfuls of money descend into the air with the grace of confetti. Blinding me from the man's violent scowl temporarily, I snort as I set my laptop bag against a brick wall.

What do you know? It *was* funny.

During my giggles, a grunt later, he scrambles to his feet, reaching for his right side and revealing a dark glint from his holster.

My throat tightens as he draws a gun, and I examine… the pitiful way he's holding it. He points his nine-millimeter in my face like a show-and-tell prop he's super proud of. I almost want to get his parents on the phone and vent about how disappointing their son is.

Spit froths at the curve of his lips through the hole in his mask. "Are you trying to die, bitch?!" His voice pitches in rage like it's his first day. His hands quiver as he steadies his grip. "Hands up! You're gonna learn what fear is today! And empty your pockets!"

It takes everything in me not to roll my eyes at the polite request. Fucker thinks he's staring in a bank-heist movie when *I'm* the main character. He's also stupid since I'm in the pocket-less skirt I planned to wear out before next week's classes.

I cock a brow. "Is that really your go-to, sweetheart?" I taunt. My hands raise in a mock surrender. A smirk plays behind my lips as I glimpse at his weapon again—It's some second-hand relic from last century.

I'm gonna choke. *Is this a fucking gag?* I'm half expecting some *Tiktuker* to appear with cameras, but there aren't any other footsteps around.

The weight of his wrist tells me everything in a millisecond. For one, I'm not in any danger, and the only one who should be scared is him.

I've seen more than my fair share of weapons in my face. Instinct takes hold before he can register my tact. My body weight shifts, and my hands move in a blur before snatching his pistol for myself and clocking him hard enough to the side of his skull with it.

His form shrinks before me, but it doesn't prevent him from fleeing. I love seeing people cower before me. It's a high like no other. Their eyes grow wide with panic, and you physically watch as their lives flash. I'm not a bad person, but I am a villain in someone's story.

My self-defense lessons are second nature to me. They need to be for what I do for a living. I've been stalked, assaulted, and kidnapped most of my life, but half of which I can't trace back to my hacking endeavors. I don't let it bother me much since those life experiences

My Valentine's Virus

have taught me that even a young woman can unarm a grown man if she's lethally trained in hand-to-hand combat.

I veer toward the coffee shop sandwiched ahead between two other restaurants. It is a warm and inviting haven for my caffeine-deprived spirits. Through the large windows, I scan the chaotic scene my robber friend left behind.

Two men in navy blue aprons—the baristas, I take it—clean up broken glass and various spills. The masked man scurries back inside for some reason, and a chorus of police sirens pierces the air.

A small swarm of officers round the corner and park a few blocks down. The moment they exit their vehicles, their badges glint in the passive sunlight. I trust they have everything else under control—*that*, and I've already done my fair share for free today.

I return to fetch my bag while the baristas—now waiting outside the building collect the remaining scattered bills.

They've seen everything. I hope they can fill in the gaps of events while I set up my equipment in the corner of their café.

Following the scent of baked sweets and coffee, I ignore the shaken employee's attempt to block me from entering the café. I refuse to halt, and he lowers his arm before I plow through him like snow.

He recalls the inner protest and returns to the questioning officer to recount the tale.

The café is astoundingly larger on the inside, like an alien's police box. It's still cute. Fuzzy warmth blossoms through me despite everything being a complete wreck. The separation glass by the registers is shattered into a half-foot pile against a broom and dust tray. Steaming coffee pools against the stone-tiled floor. Everything on the counter by the registers litters the floor—sugar packets, complimentary tea bags, those little red straws, and baby-sized creamer cartons.

The jig is up. I don't actually drink coffee, but I find the warm scent of it in the air sparks my productivity. Luckily, their counter has free orange juice available.

I reclaim my spot near my laptop, and as the adrenaline rush leaves my body, I remove my headset from the pocket of my bag and work while the rest of the chaos continues in the background.

Freshly squeezed orange juice blankets my tongue. Red and blue lights from the cop cars reflect on my laptop as an annoying distraction. My eyes unbind from my screen to notice the flashing atmosphere has been tamed.

The pair of chatty baristas lean against the counter, exchanging tattoo compliments and work politics I never asked to audience for.

Following a few shouts, scuffles, and objects falling against the hard ground, the few cops take their time grappling with the dirtbag I had the pleasure of meeting.

It just isn't his day. Any other moment and he probably would have gotten away with it.

Setting down my paper cup, we try ignoring the harsh swears hurled at me by the delightful terrorist. I really don't care what he says, I just want a drink and to torture strangers on the internet.

I take another sip of my orange juice, my middle finger holding the weight as I offer him a glance while he's hauled out.

It earns me a snarl and a chuckle from one of the officers shoving him. He looks better fashioning a pair of handcuffs and the black eye I gifted him.

The door of the police car slams shut, and his shouts and obscenities muffle behind it. I raise my hand beside my ear to exaggerate how much I'm listening. Ahh, the sweet tune of a random victory.

Maybe now I can get back to work. Right when I plug in my charger, one of the officers strides to my table.

"Ma'am, we're going to need your statement as well," he says.

"Oh, come on," I bemoan, my shoulders sulking. Gesturing to the baristas in the corner, I raise a brow when one of them braces a mop

My Valentine's Virus

in defense. "Those two already told you what happened. I've handled my part, now kindly let me get online." You know. Before I scream.

The officer narrows his eyes with a raised brow, spinning to his supervisor, I'm assuming.

Strutting over, the higher-ranked official pats the other man on his shoulder to have him leave me be. With the situation managed, they exit with their capture.

Seconds later, the relieved baristas bombard me with praise and promises of free breakfast as their token of gratitude. I remind the kind souls I want to work, but I'm not guarded enough to reject a free breakfast offering.

This is my spot now. I can't trust the internet back at Crimson Raven University's dorms at the moment. Not with what I plan on doing with the access.

My eyelids get heavy, and my arms limp against my table. In my private grieving party, I mourn EctoPhantom.

He was my plaything, and now he's not going to have internet for at least two years. He began his crime spree at seventeen. I was oddly proud of him. EctoPhantom didn't rise to the occasion to stand up to my cyber-attacks. I suppose it was *my* fault for expecting some effort.

Getting into computer hacking is like no other, but involving yourself in a high-stakes war with notorious crooks puts everything on the line. It's nothing short of playing chess with God in an eight-dimensional hell.

Adrenaline in its purest form.

You fire all synapses to your fingers against time, heart racing in and out like a fire alarm, betting it all—your family, your loved ones, all to prove you surpassed them. You have power and lives under your fingertips, like a God weighing the outcomes of their hell.

Once I got into hacking, I realized technology's hold on us and how vulnerable we make ourselves with it. Our phones, computers, tablets, and gaming systems are all susceptible to an attack. Most screened devices nowadays have cameras that can be accessed even if we haven't authorized them.

I use tech to fight tech, while some use it to numb the passage of time like a drug. Most of us would look to suicide if the world decided to ban screens, ushering us into the lamest apocalypse.

I don't have social media. It's a buffet for hackers to steal your identity or worse. I rarely answer my phone, even when it's family, and I'm wary of what I say while in front of a device's mic. Not to mention, my laptop camera is duct-taped shut.

Sure, saving small businesses from cyber-attacks might be seen as heroic. I get rewarded for my efforts, but it's been leaving me unsatisfied. I need *more*.

EctoPhantom was at least good for something. When digging up dirt on his illegal activities, one of his online ventures sparked my curiosity—prompting me to delve further.

As it turns out, my rival was only a bench warmer for the real thing. He's Mr. Number One's *student*. And through this, his online name was revealed to me. Zone_Warden, this so-called *"King of Hackers."*

I grin, rubbing my chin at my monitor. How amusing. I'm going to spread some malware to see what I'm dealing with. With my creative methods, I managed to break into his bizarre online message board filled with others like him. Apparently, they're *all* his students, and it's full of filth.

It's a mosh pit of the worst online scum you can fathom. Everything from illegal traders to fatherless shitheads making nefarious *"Share this post or your grandma will die"*—bullshit.

"Ma'am?" A delicate voice breaks my concentration, and I lower my headset. A tatted-up woman with blond hair raises her cute pierced brow at me.

I didn't even notice the employees changed shifts. Hours have passed, losing myself in lines of code and encryptions. The sun dips

My Valentine's Virus

below the horizon as I peer behind her for the window. The café's interior grew cozy with the warm glow of dimming hung lights.

"We're closing soon. You may need to pack up," she advises in a soft tone. I smile and nod as she spins back to the safety of the back room.

I do a quick sweep of any recent hacking attempts in here and it checks out fine. I *tsk* at the last report, then lock my war machine into my bag and zip up.

Crisp autumn air hints at the impending rainstorm. My body shivers like I'm an old lady, and I tense even in the cozy confines.

A certain breeze hits me through the cracks of the café doors, and my face reddens. I struggle to swallow. The nerves in my face ache while I grip my bag to fight back a cry. The cornered edges of my laptop sting my fingers as I pound back memories. The nightmares. The tiring evenings. The pain of forgetting what my mother looks like.

Fatigue settles in my dropping shoulders, and I exhale. I feel eyes burrow into my right side, held by the P.M. baristas.

I turn to ask if I can wait out the storm for a bit, and they nod. It's been a long day.

LEVEL TWO

ZONE_WARDEN

Alone in my home office, I monitor my sexy computer screen. The beeps from the servers fill the silence with The Nightmare Before Christmas' *This Is Halloween*. The shadows from my servers blanket me, stacking each other like guardians of my little secrets.

The sun sets a perfect orange shade over the lush untamed forest of a typical Maine backyard. Chimes of cicadas fill the crisp summer air near my window.

No, I wouldn't recommend this routine to anyone. It demands I stay a full-time introvert—which I love—but… I'm not inclined to believe it's healthy. Not that anyone would notice by looking at me. Sure, I have dark circles beneath my eyes, but I get asked for gym advice weekly.

My Valentine's Virus

    Rubbing the back of my neck, I groan from the barrage of students messaging me. Some of it's praise, reaching out for help, or informing me of who my next hit should be. I don't mean to have them waiting, but I need to maintain a calisthenics regimen when I'm not making victims out of suspicious CEOs.

    It's the only workout that staves off the pains and aches that accompany endless hours of leering at a screen all night.

    A conservationist group in my inbox explains their dedication to raccoons and other wildlife aid. Melting my heart like a candle, their strategic logo of *Marvel's* Rocket Raccoon prevents me from focusing on anything else.

    Before I know it, I'm gripping my bank card.

    I stop, drop, and roll over to their website, but my head tilts at the declined notification. My payment isn't going through. That's never happened to me before. I could look into it, but it's already eleven. If I needed to contact someone directly, I'd have a happier chance of it around nine to five—human hours.

    It's a minor inconvenience, but I trust Elysium. It's my bank's security system and my personal software. Until it fixes itself, the funds for the little masked devils will have to wait.

    My dry eyes pin at the email from Dad I've been ignoring. It's been hanging in my inbox for days, joined by the knots in my stomach that form when he *emails* instead of calling me.

    Figures.

    I yank open the drawer on my left, rifling for my lighter and medicinal herb to get ready. I rest the blessed cigarette between my lips before lighting the end. The soothing plant fills my lungs, and my Fight-or-Flight meter lowers.

♥

A. DARANG

"Bring a friend or find a date for February 14th." The subject of his message simply ordered.

My eyebrows hike against my forehead in a series of irritations. Already knowing what the body holds, a tired sigh finds its escape from me as everything goes red.

He clearly couldn't be bothered when I nearly died from his meddling. The scars under my shirt throb, the wound chaining me to my regrets. My heart aches with every pulse, and the only thing grounding me is a long drag of my cigarette. My breathing settles, and I can almost see in color again.

It's beyond me why he wants to focus on his bloodline suddenly. I'm unsure how to break to him that ends with me. But I'm a good son, so I'll skim the stupid letter. I've already reached the limits of my disgust when it comes to him. The first line of his letter suggests he doesn't even remember my name.

Dear son,

I hope you are doing well. It's been over a decade since we last caught up. I have an important matter to discuss.

A grand business celebration approaches. Powerful individuals are gathering to commemorate triumphs and create new opportunities. I've been waiting for this occasion to showcase your success. You've become my second greatest achievement, and introducing you as Speaker would bring me immeasurable joy.

I understand that finding a date may not be easy, but attending with someone would show your social prowess and contribute to your image of being a well-rounded man. Bringing a friend who can share this experience with you would be equally delightful. I hear you're visiting Oregon. Perhaps you can reach out and invite

My Valentine's Virus

your old friend, Jean-Pierre? Even if she is from that third-world island, attending with nobody is inexcusable.

This event may bridge the gap between us after all these years. Your presence would mean the world to your mother and me. We are excited to hear back from you in writing.

With love,

Lawrence K.

My hand trembles over my keys.

Nah, I can't fucking do this. It overwhelms my head to the point of expanding nausea.

He only reaches out when he needs something—*like my fucking dignity*. And for what? To boost his image by showing me off to his flesh-eating business partners. He's constantly left me to play the role of a dutiful son worthy of his legacy while reeking of desperation.

His latest message does a great job of reiterating how little he cares for me. He doesn't ask how I've been since the accident nor offer me an apology for how horrific he handled what came after it.

My fingers can hold still again, but I can't bring myself to engage. But if it's bothering me this much, I'll just pretend it never existed.

I hit delete, then double-wiped its history, leaving zero traces of it ever hitting my inbox. Now it can't come back to haunt me. Heh, heh, *heh*.

What's he going to do about it? Call? *That'll be the day.*

My gaze relaxes as I return to my satisfying distraction. One of my students insisted I investigate this fraudulent vitamin company founded in Eastern Europe. With flawless expertise, I navigate through Big Oval's website.

My target glows on my screen while I bypass their half-assed security system and firewalls. Breaking into their folders, I channel the spirit of what Gollum must have felt like with the Ring. But instead of chanting *"precious,"* I hum *"profitable."*

I "borrow" the most scandalous data from them to use as blackmail later.

Big Oval is only *one* of thousands like it I've left in my wake. My ego and bank accounts have swelled so much that the only things standing between me and the Pentagon are a VPN server and a fake mustache.

The sinister CEOs of this world *deserve* the backlash for the sins they commit. And I never have to go hungry, knowing the world has an endless supply for me to extort. They love pretending they don't know any better. It used to taint me with vibrating rage until I accepted that some people are just evil.

The records I often find unveil everything from embezzlement, tax fraud, money laundering, and sexual harassment claims in their trash to outright murder. Most of which makes my stomach clench. Not that I'm claiming to be a hero punishing the unpunishable. There's a sick satisfaction that comes with watching the "elites" beg and crumble like complete toddlers. Especially when threatened by the consequences of their actions. It's more euphoric than any drug on or off the market.

My dark gaze flashes as I come across Big Oval's well-kept secret, and *fuck* is it dark.

My Valentine's Virus

Lo and behold, Big Oval has numerous consumer complaints explaining in clear black and white how their "tested products" have been turning body parts fucking *green*.

Four hours after being ingested, everyone reported rapidly spreading cancer cells. Not many of us guinea pigs know this, but "FDA Cleared" doesn't mean "FDA Approved."

Somehow their informative reviews have mysteriously been wiped off the website and their partner's affiliate sites.

How bizarre. I better hurry and let them know.

Big Oval *will* deny the claims with whatever bullshit they have concocted to keep their investors happy and their wallets fat. So, I copy those files, their images, and even the subpoenas from various law firms. I store the deets onto an external hard drive and exit their system with no trace of my intrusion.

Now for the fun part.

Before I cozy up down the hall, I tuck a burner laptop under my arm with a *Minecraft* Creeper mug one of my students gifted to me.

My place is a testament to my solitude, a den untouched by warmth. The matte pine-colored walls are devoid of designs or pictures of my handsome family. Instead, a sparse collection of framed video game franchise posters and relics of my youth that adorn the otherwise desolate expanse. Their vibrant colors don't appear in the dark, though.

The space breathes darkness at this hour, a testament to the void surrounding me as I haunt it. Moonlight infiltrates through the wall-length curtains. The rays reveal the hollowness defining my haven. The shadows are unyielding and unbroken and cloak the room in a shroud of quiet desolation.

I inhale a deep breath, savoring the best color the universe was born in—complete blackness.

Though new, the dark sofa already bears scratch marks from the tiny raccoon that tricked me into caring for him.

The carpet moans beneath my slippers as I traverse to the couch. Propped in my other arm is Dice, a snoozing raccoon I've homed. Dice struggles to remember he's supposed to be nocturnal from time to time. His gurgling snores bring my smile from retirement as I rest the little thief on my sofa.

He paces around in circles before his tiny stomps make the already comfy couch comfier. Laying down, he hugs his tail between his Muppet-like hands as if it were his security blanket.

Opening my monitor, a sip of bitter coffee soothes my gullet, and I upload the collection of files to email Big Oval's team.

In it are the basics. Everything I discovered goes in the body of the email with a sprinkle of direct threats. I'll leak the files to the press unless they pay me a sizable percentage.

This is a high-risk game, but it's outright addictive. I always hold the upper hand in these scenarios. Companies like these are quick responders after their Spidey senses go a-tingling.

Now. Will they cave and pay the ransom? Or stand firm and risk total annihilation? Maybe one day, I'll slip up, but they'd have to either be on my level or above it, which I'm doubting possible. I'm Number One for good reason.

I set down my mug and log onto one of my favorite places: my homemade message board. It's filled with like-minded specialists I've taught in the past gathering online across the world to gloat about our feats in a ranking system. I'm at the international top of

My Valentine's Virus

the *top* and have been for over ten years. The king himself: *Zone_Warden*.

The alias came to me back in middle school, and though I cringe a bit whenever I look at it, it's a piece of my younger renegade soul I'd rather not see changed. It's a good living. My work ensures I don't depend on a job for as long as I live. This is how I choose to survive, and I wear my reputation like a suit of armor.

While skimming a heated response from Big Oval's cronies, something else catches my eye, diverting all my attention. My chest freezes, squinting at an urgent email from Elysium laid unread and ominous above. The roof of my eyes simmer, latching onto the word *Urgent*.

Heat pumps to my ears, causing them to cramp the moment I open the email. The string of sentences in the email has enough power to bring the toughest of men to their knees. My sweating hand can't hold still as I scroll to expose the rest.

My bank accounts have been *frozen* and drained until further notice.

"What the hell...?" I muster as the coffee in my stomach resurfaces in the back of my throat. Re-reading the lines again constricts my airways.

I trace each word as if it were an illusion caused by my lack of sleep. But no. I triple-checked—this is real, and it's way too sudden and way too irritating to dissect at 1 a.m.

A visceral blow pulls my breath, changing its calm with white-hot mania. Coherent thought blinks out of range until all that remains is pressure beneath my lungs. I hold my head, buckling under the weight of anxiety, drilling into every corner of my skin. *Frozen. Drained.*

The very earth tilts. My vision blackens as the screen swims in front of me with every word thrown at my eyes like a fucking taunt. Disbelief grips every muscle. Each penny I've earned over decades of work is gone in seconds, leaving me floundering and gasping for air.

I clench my fists tightly. My fingernails dig into my palms as the pain grounds me the moment panic replaces it.

"It'll take years to recover from this..." I rasp. My heart pounds a symphony of rage against my rib cage as I try piecing together what the *fuck* happened.

Dice wakes and scurries down the hall. A pained grunt wrings at my guts as I lash out, hurling the laptop into the wall.

The crash echoes through the silence leaving only the gratings of my heaving form. Darkness consumes all remnants of me. My chest holds a rumbling, threatening its escape again with every second. I bite it back, and the flames replacing my blood settle long enough for me to get to my feet.

Marching back to my office, I ignore Dice, who is taking refuge in the hole I created in my wall.

I don't remember returning here under this possession. Before I know it, I'm scrolling past every news outlet dragging my name through the mud.

The words reverberate and set in my head until a guttural shout shreds through my ribcage. "How did this happen?!" More importantly, "How did this happen to fucking *me?!*" I grip the base of my hairline, the harsh sting of my cigarette not soothing enough in my illegal search of who the fuck did this.

The clock ticks into the night, and my fingers burn across the keys, scouring with tireless madness for a loophole—my ticket out.

My Valentine's Virus

But no matter how innovative my search, my efforts, or my pulls, I hit a wall at every turn.

My throat pinches as I struggle to breathe, and then, as if fate itself intervenes, a Universal Tech News article appears on my browser, catching my red eyes. *"Princess_User24: The New Face of Hacking."*

My vision latches onto each line where my name is mentioned in the article, and it becomes clear: Another hacker has targeted me. Bested me.

I dig deeper into the aftermath of my bank's securities, it's not evident how someone unleashed a devastating virus, but this looks like a copy of EctoPhantom's handy work. It explained why my accounts were frozen too.

My leg shakes, pinning the lines of letters on my screen.

Princess_User24 did this? That fucking joker. Why now?

What's lost to me is there wasn't a warning. No blackmail request or negotiation. Just a blog post by UTN about what this wannabe did to my reputation overnight.

After the past few months of deflecting this troll, she's finally managed to grab my attention.

Scrolling through the countless blog posts on her, it's evident she's taken the world by storm.

An editorial column praises her as a *"hacktivist goddess"* of all things. Ugh. I could vomit. Her "talents" expose corruption all in the name of protecting "innocent" victims.

The details state how she not only stole billions from under me but has been pinning to challenge me for my rank as Number One for years.

♥

Trying to calm down before giving myself an aneurysm, I lean back in my chair and wipe sweat on my face.

Princess has been a thorn in my side since she managed to infiltrate my message board. We exchanged some friendly remarks. I threatened the well-being of her family, and she fired back by threatening my balls. The way she instigated me made me feel like a kid again, so I let her play around. She's gone too far. *Some*how, the little miscreant stole *back* the data I had on a construction company in Florida too. My hubris kept me believing it was dumb luck.

In my deep dive, I find she's taken down networks harder to break into than Fort Knox—systems *I've* personally helped secure.

Well, that sucks. Another article on her has me forgetting I need to breathe. Princess had poor EctoPhantom arrested for about everything *I've* been getting away with. It's like an invasion with her.

I'll see how he's doing the minute I can.

She's certainly earned herself an impressive track record. Despite her lame username, she's more skilled than I pictured, but she's made the mistake of messing with my raccoons.

I take my outrage to my message board and check up on my students. My frown creases tighter at the dastardly name glaring on my screen. *Princess_User24*.

I rub my forehead to ease the burn. This goddamn lunatic keeps finding her way back after I've blocked her IP addresses multiple times.

My students rally behind me, but I honestly wish they wouldn't provoke her and go the way of EctoPhantom.

My Valentine's Virus

That_Matt69: This the annoying cunt that got EctoPhantom canned?

Princess_User24: The one and the same. But don't be sad, you'll all be joining him when I'm through with you ;)

CrowWrangler420: Not unless the king finds you first. Then your ass belongs to us, Princess.

Princess_User24: Ur so-called "King" has abandoned you, peasants. If he were as legit as you preach, he is, he could have stopped my virus's hold on Elysium. But he didn't :)

That_Matt69: He's only waiting for you to slip up, and when that happens...

Princess_User24: Yeah, when that happens, he'll be united with those other fools I put away. Ya' scared, Zone? I know you're reading these ;)

This bitch.

CrowWrangler420: Zone, where TF are you? Log in already and put the twat in her place.

I study the way she deflects and picks out information from the thieves I've raised in their little ramblings and debates. As far as I see, they're only embarrassing themselves, and by extension, embarrassing *me*.

♡

From her online mannerisms, I surmise she's not some teenager with unsupervised access to the Dark Web or a government agent. No, she's a rogue operator who knows how to manipulate answers out of people all through her screen. It's like a contest to her.

She's something more... evolved. Something entirely annoying and should be stomped out.

More heat fills my head with thoughts that aren't my own. They're demonic and unhinged, which drives my next actions. As I wait and watch how she communicates, I picture her blood on my hands. With everything at my disposal, finding where she is will be a walk in the park.

One way or another, I'll douse this rampage of hatred she's left to rot inside me, even if her IP is untraceable.

My jaw tics, eyeing a pattern. She's been following me, using my affiliates like Target Practice until she can coax me out--even learning from them.

I'm not *un*impressed with it. Hell, a fraction of me is flattered. She's gone to such lengths for my attention, and despite her lame username, she's more skilled than I envisioned.

Before a tinge of sound thought revives in my throbbing head, I hunt down her cyber footprint. The shadows behind me disappear in way of morning rays.

With a few key pushes, her entire life can be discovered and sold to the highest bidder within the week. No matter how pristine or unexposed her digital footprint may be. I'll find her. The dark web would have a holiday for obtaining the hidden info of the whore who's been ruining them by making a show of it.

Visions of the faceless woman being locked in misery, kidnapped by the shadow government, blacklisted, or stalked by

My Valentine's Virus

corrupt authority have me descending further into villainous madness. My blood cools a degree, and something abnormal happens. A rational idea breeches in my mind. *Why not accept her challenge?*

The premise of competing in a *hacker* war feels all flavors of stupid, but this girl has unearthed a disturbance in my core I didn't even know slept there.

It's competitive sin—being in the aftermath of someone operating on a playing field more advanced than others. It's not just about the money or the power anymore; this is about something raw. Something primal. Especially when it comes to her.

I make my presence known in her chat, and all hell breaks loose from my following. They spam a hundred messages like rapid fire while we both wait for the cheers, threats, and "finallys" to settle before Princess lists her demand.

[Princess_User24]: I invite u to find my true identity before I find urs. The winner is free to dox the information to whomever they choose. Mine, being the federal authorities for your involvement in blackmail. If you win, I will release Elysium in return for deletion of my information.

Princess has a twisted mindset for such a life-shattering pursuit while also wrapped in a cloud of might and mystery. She has my rage veering and spurring my erection.

A strange chill marches throughout my body, and I can't will it away or identify it.

"...Cute," I sigh, mocking her efforts and leaning on a mad smirk against my seat. "I have a *little rival.*"

♡

With every prick of static bouncing off my skin from the vision board of articles on her, I make peace with not sleeping tonight. No, not after this.

I want to win.

Zone Warden: I'll do you one better, little rival. I'm going to find you.

Zone Warden: Can't wait to see you tomorrow, Princess. It's been a long time coming.

Princess User24: I'm shaking in my Converse. Y'know ur not going to win, right?

Zone Warden: You dunno who you're playing with, but I'll prove it to you shortly.

Princess User24: Sure, I do. A sad, cowardly man who gets off on blackmailing for his own gain. I think that sums u up.

Zone Warden: You're playing with fire. Don't say I didn't warn you.

Princess User24: And ur about to get BURNED, Zone. I hope ur ready for the HEAT.

My Valentine's Virus

Zone Warden: Wear something extra cute for me when I find you.

Princess User24: U couldn't find ur way out of a sack.

Zone Warden: Giving me ideas, Princess? Let's see how you find your way out of the sack I stuff you in. After I pin and fck the wit out of you.

Princess User24: You think I'm witty? 😊

Zone Warden: I think you're a disease.

Princess User24: Oh rawrr :p

Princess User24: Tell ya what, Zone. If u can find me, u can do whatever u want to me. I wonder if u can handle what comes next.

Zone Warden: Don't care. I'll make you regret contesting me.

Princess User24: U promise? ;0

*Technical note from Professor Kaiser: a **VPN server** is like a secret tunnel that lets you connect to the internet from a different location, hiding your identity and whereabouts.*

♡

LEVEL THREE
PRINCESS_USER24

Heart pounding, I sprint through Crimson Raven University's auditorium doors. This college is only for the wealthiest sons and daughters of stock market tycoons and CEO trust fund types. I stem from a single father who works in construction, and they failed to stop me from bypassing their heavy doors.

A beam of light from the projector cuts through the darkness of the auditorium, and my eyes scan the room for an empty seat. There's over a thousand of us here. Students settle in plush red chairs, training their eyes on the blaring screen ahead. The leather smell of the new auditorium seats mixes with expensive colognes and perfumes.

Despite the curious glances and surrounding whispers, I push down the aisle. My dark hair clings to my neck, causing a cringe to ripple through me, yet even as the AC air brushes my skin, the inferno blazing in me shows no signs of relenting. I'm practically frothing, I can't wait to show them all up.

I spot an empty seat near the center and try not to stick out much while shuffling for it. I've been such a mess lately since last night.

My Valentine's Virus

Several sneers follow me down the aisle like swarms of wasps and seem to escalate the minute I sit down. These bougied-up clowns and their overcompensating school. They have yet to learn I feed off opportunities to prove myself against adversity. That's how I made it this far.

Bouncing my leg, I study the room. Wincing from a cold stain under my palm, I glare down at my grandmother's sweater. My stomach drops to my butt after finding sprinkles of bacon bits, and what I'm hoping is orange juice all over it. It's practically rancid.

I didn't think it was this bad.

The scent clings to the air like an unwanted guest, overpowering perfumes or colognes in the area. A small group of girls from behind me continue their teases long after I've gotten the fucking point already. But even as embarrassment stings my cheeks, I can't concentrate on them or anything else.

Shaking my head at it, my gaze tilts up at the bright projection screen in the darkness. Everything around me mutes, and it's like I'm elsewhere, entirely in my mind. Unfocused on what's in front, behind, or next to me, all I can think of is *him*.

I think about the crazy shit I did last week on my computer, and my teeth chatter. Biting my lip, the bitter coppery taste provides little comfort to the adrenaline streaming through me like an unrelenting river.

Leaning forward, I adjust my skirt beneath my thighs. More pompous eyes burn holes near me, and my cheeks pale. I still when I realize, hey, I forgot underwear too. *Great job, Abbie.*

I close my eyes before sinking into the seat with a tired sigh, allowing the ol' mind to wander.

A week ago, I issued a challenge to the world's most merciless hacker but was left on Read. That's when I cracked my fingers and sent out my virus to drain his bank accounts. I've been keeping the funds somewhere he could never reach without my knowing.

The encryption code guarding Zone's bank accounts was some of the toughest I've ever seen. But I made my way past his bitch of a firewall in record timing.

A proud smile tugs at the corners of my lips, imagining the absolute shock he must have had when he realized it was *me. Pussy~*♪

I let out a giggle in my chair like a mad woman. If only Mom could see me now, bringing the most intelligent man alive to his knees. Speaking of the glorious woman—it's my responsibility to honor her legacy.

She was *an* IT expert in her medical field. When she wasn't helping those in need, she'd show me the true powers technology held. Her dedication made such an impact and inspired me to pursue a career in IT too. Dad praised my gift for developing my codes at age six, but he'd get disturbed by my cutthroat approaches the older I got. He'd always say he doesn't know where it came from.

I've outgrown all of my "competition." So far, Mr. Number One is the only person who's been matching my growth. It's not my fault he ignored me. My chance to make a mark on the world leads through the fall of his empire.

His response to my recent attack was swift, but something unexpected took hold of him at the last minute. This led me to believe I awoke a beast in him—the same warring dark flame I carry, growing as a forest fire fed heavily from destroying others.

Though I don't know *what* he'll do, I'd be lying if this toxic side of me isn't thrilled to find out. There's no turning back now.

Out of nowhere, something in the atmosphere feels off. The front projection announces the seminar will continue soon. Sweat beads on my forehead from the heat of another's gaze.

This one's different.

It tears into my skin and causes the hairs on the back of my neck to stand up in warning. Veering, I scan the crowd of jerks in the audience around me, and my shoulders tense more when I find nothing out of the

My Valentine's Virus

ordinary. Other students chat away at the latest celebrity to hate, making their evil little connections and exchanging their info.

The prickling sensation still won't shove off.

I can't explain the sixth sense of danger or how the moon oversees the tides, but I do know someone in the auditorium is watching me with ill intent.

I'm forced to recall Abuela's witchy warnings about this ambiance and how it *needs* to be heeded no matter the cost, but I can't bring myself to move. Invisible pins of—I think pride? Stubbornness? Grit? All of that keeps my thighs glued in my seat.

The seminar begins with the increasing glow of the projection screen. The crowds of students and officials quiet before the speaker even introduces himself.

My mind wanders and comes to an odd connection with this sense. This *thrilling* weight of danger. It only arises when I communicate with dumb Zone online.

I might just be anxious about how exposed I feel under this short skirt. I didn't think I'd hate such a cute uniform, but they were not made with busty women in mind.

Run, my body shouts in the pit of my stomach.

It grows more apparent in each tic and each toc. A presence looms over my body like a thundercloud, threatening to strike unpredictably. I gulp as a spike of fear and excitement mingle in the back of my throat. Though I don't know his real name or face, I've often danced with this fiery sensation.

The only thing I'm afraid of is my heart thumping so hard it might burst through my chest. And I should be scared. I should take the rest of the day off. I should tell somebody, but... he's already here.

Shortly, a man in all black struts on stage, oozing with a slumped confidence an experienced orator would embody.

My nerves from before vanish as soon as he emerges. He's irritatingly tall. Black hair radiating sheen amidst the spotlight arises from the shadows. And those eyes of his, sharp and green like cactus thorns that spear and pin me deeper in my seat. The spotlight doesn't reach his eyes as he sweeps them over the heads of the crowd—as if searching for something.

When the light exposes his face to us, my eyeballs nearly pop out of my head. I get to my feet without realizing it.

It's Xalton *fucking* Kaiser!

My mouth parts, but I'm old enough to hold in the fanatic scream threatening to surface with the rest of the audience.

Rumbling cheers cause the room to vibrate with excitement like a concert until they lower to murmurs and whispers as the rest of the crowd struggles to identify the mysterious guest.

They quiet after the echo of his steps. His taut muscles tense under his dark gray suit as he strides to the stage, demanding focus.

"Good evening, my script kittens," his deep voice penetrates the air, leaving the crowd speechless. The rasp in his voice sends a shivering heat up my spine and *holy hormones, Batman.*

A grin takes hold of his sculpted face at the effect he instantly has on the audience. The chill of perversion skips lower and reminds me why panties are a necessity for keeping seats dry.

He runs his fingers through his dark hair, the slight stroke from the distance advertising how soft his locs are. "Yes, I *am* that Xalton Kaiser," he purrs as a self-assured smile teases on his lips. His voice is deep and sultry without even trying. It's like a sharpened blade gliding against the devil's wings, sending shivers of seductive between my legs. Wild strays of cheers and applauses follow while I still.

Struggling to process his existence here, I remember I need oxygen sometimes to breathe. This man is an absolute *titan* in the IT industry.

After graduating at only sixteen, he cemented his name as an innovative mastermind behind groundbreaking software and revolutionizing cyber security.

My Valentine's Virus

With a legion of fierce, passionate followers, he's a true maverick whose creations have helped reshape the world and the only man to slay my fucking heart. By some stroke of fate, he graces the stage of *my* university.

My heart flutters as my celebrity crush walks among us with his electrifying presence. Maybe one day, after my graduation, I'll bask in his brilliance as an intern.

I let my mind wander, picturing us getting drunk at a holiday venue and getting close. Maybe that hand of his gliding through that perfect smooth black hair can slide up my thigh. I give my cheek a little smack to check if this was still real and not one of my recurring dreams of him. The sting doesn't register, but even if this is a dream, I don't care.

He parts his dangerously tan lips, and I can't stop focusing on how smoky his tone is.

An overwhelmed swoon by one of the ladies in the front row breaks the powerful silence he brings about.

A mischievous half-smirk plays on his lips as if remembering the effect he has on everyone in that instance.

My heartstrings violently pull as he gives a sultry glance to the girl with great taste. A thick pang of jealousy stings throughout my chest like a bullet, and I'm tempted to write poetry about how envious I am of her. An aggressive knot forms in my stomach, and I wish I could trade places with her so badly—to be the one catching his eye at that moment. The mix of desire and frustration wells in me, watching him with longing from the distance. I cup my heart in the shadow, losing myself in his eyes when the room fades to darkness.

Fuck. I'm drowning in the bittersweetness of it all, knowing I'm just a bystander in this.

Extra lights shine over him like dessert in a bakery window. The muscles in his jaw clench before he continues. "I'm honored to be back here at the prestigious Crimson Raven University."

The world around me blurs as I remain locked on him. My mind races with heated thoughts I didn't expect to have so early in the morning. Like, the way his perfect black hair pours over his forehead when he cocks his head toward us.

I can stare into those sleepy, focused green eyes for decades. His bulging biceps give the impression that he chops wood for a living and has my knees threatening to melt. My eyes draw to the way his large hand grips around his mic, and my cheeks heat, trying to envision if he'd grasp his dick that way. My gaze drifts lower, and my face runs even warmer, struggling to picture it through his pants.

He goes on to explain how hackers don't just use pre-made tools but have the creativity and skill to create their own or something. He then mentions how outdated and overused the term "hacker" is in the IT community.

I roll my eyes in agreement. The 90s ruined the word way before it even sprouted legs.

His presence in person pulls at my soul like a magnet, drawing me closer yet keeping me at arm's length. Each stolen glance at the row of people, each confident smile he shares with them, fuels newer flames of envy in me. It's tormenting.

He continues to drawl on about tracking methods he used to help police and the Federal Bureau of Investigation in his younger freelancing stages.

His history in the field is admirable, and I'm not at all surprised the school asked him to start the semester like this. I wouldn't put it past them to be seduced by his dark charm, either, since his entire aesthetic matches the school's black and red theme.

Just then, my phone buzzes, alerting me of a text message taking my attention away from his speech. Before I raise it to check, the speaker's sudden pause causes me to hesitate.

My eyes snap back to the stage, leading my heart to thud with an intensity threatening to consume me.

My Valentine's Virus

He's looking directly into my eyes, way in the center of the audience.

The familiar sensation I pushed aside before returns in devastating waves as it yanks my breath from me. My throat constricts, and I work to swallow through the weight of his stare lingering on me, charging the air between us.

Was this because I was checking my phone? No—everyone else has theirs out recording him and tweeting about him.

No words are exchanged. No gestures were made, but the intensity of our quiet encounter speaks volumes to me.

"It's amazing what you can find with so *little* information," he hums, the words caressing the ears of the captivated crowd. Moistening his lips, he causes a shiver to ripple through my core.

The corners of his lips curl into a smile, but there's a predatory glimmer in his eyes as his gaze roams my distant form, tracing every contour with a precision that mirrors a leopard stalking its prey.

The weight of his words hangs in the air, laden with a sense of intrigue and a hint of menace. His subject change has me frozen in place. My phone is glued in my hand under the shadows of the seats the longer he watches me.

"For example…" His voice trails off, drawing out the words with deliberate slowness. "…by finding a three-second video, I was able to track someone down who considered themselves *un*touchable." His last word hangs in the air, elongated and purposeful, causing a surge of anxiety to wash over my body.

Why is he looking this way? Are his words directed at me?

His eyes penetrate my defenses. But before fear grips hold of my throat, I work a swallow, brushing off the idea. Let's chalk this up to my inflated ego trying to find significance where there isn't any. *Still…*

A sultry chuckle rumbles from his lips, at the visual denial I make, it seems. His seductive vibrations permeate the air and has me drenched in arousal.

Just when I thought I finally moved on from my crush, he yanks me back under his clutches by simply being... *him*.

His observation jerks from me to the rest of the students, granting me a semblance of mercy. Continuing his spell on the masses, he continues, "But of course, I wouldn't want to give away my secrets in case a *rival* university member *is* in the crowd *here today*," he says. The words are clever enough for me to decipher.

In response, the audience erupts in a chorus of boos, showcasing their support and shared rivalries.

A mischievous glint dances in Xalton's eyes, and laughter ripples through the room, creating a wave of mirth that washes over the audience.

It's the kind of chuckle that makes you feel like laughing yourself. The closest could be that of actor Robert Downey Jr.

Meanwhile, my cheeks cramp from straining the hold of a hard blush. Once again, caught in the uncomfortable spotlight of his attention, I shrink internally, my hardened peaks friction against my blouse.

He's not even funny. Why are they devouring his every word like chocolate? Sure, he's cute, smart, and possesses a voice I want to replace my thoughts with, but that's where it ends.

Don't fall for him again, bitch, I scold myself, attempting to regain control. *He's beneath you—meat to be devoured... and Mama is starving—stop.*

But despite my inner conflict and self-admonishments, the persistent crush I have for Xalton threatens to resurface.

In his command on stage, with flawless effort, my palms dampen. I catch myself eyeing the girth of his arms, outlined by that tight black Armani suit.

Even from this distance, the intensity in his eyes pierce through me once more.

Determined to break free from his spell, I quickly raise my phone, using it as a shield to resist the hold his eyes have on me. I need to snap

My Valentine's Virus

out of it, get a grip, and remind myself he's just a person on that stage. A beautiful, sleepy-eyed giant in a suit barely containing his muscles.

[Unknown]: Enjoying the show, Princess?

My brows crease at the text from an unspecified sender. I know Zone is lurking somewhere close by. I can practically *feel* the little nerd I've been tormenting hiss down my neck. But apparently, he's too much of a *coward* to reveal himself.

When I picture Zone, I imagine some acne-coated cave dweller with an overhanging gut, terrible posture, and even worse breath.

I refuse to give him the satisfaction of watching me lift my head and scan the room for his presence again—like some alerted bird. *Ugh*.

Still, I can't shake off the heat of his eyes fixed on me from some hidden vantage point.

Instead, I let my imagination take over. I'm predicting him hacking into the seminar from the projection screen ahead. I can bet on his type of revenge based on our chats. He'll probably hide behind some stupid mask, relishing in his fake accomplishment of "finding" me at my own school, and maybe give some vague threat to my life. *Fucking geekwad.*

I cross my arms over my chest to raise my head and find Xalton staring right at me once again, but this time for a longer beat.

Then it all clicks.

My eyes widen in an instant, and my jaw drops. On instinct, I cover my mouth to regain composure, clenching it shut as the realization hits me like a freight train.

No way.

Is it fucking *him?!*

My life unfurls like a scene from a horror movie, and my heart punches my chest at the thought.

A wicked grin stretches across his lips once more, casting a malevolent aura that has me gasping. His thick, dark eyebrows lift, confirming my questioning face.

My smug smile betrays any control I have, grappling with dread and intrigue as I lower my hand.

There's a dense ping going off in my ears as if a grenade detonated throughout the field of people—but I'm good. Everything's still here. I just need a minute to understand my new reality and how it all led to this.

Slowly, I open my phone and shoot a text back to the mysterious sender with Xalton's conceited gaze on me stilling. No doubt his text was sent on a timer just for this moment.

My boiling face tightens again as others try following his line of sight in my direction amongst the crowd. I bet he thinks he's the cleverest fuck in the world.

Xalton tilts his head back, closing his eyes, as an arrogant smirk teases his lips again. On cue, a vibration from his right pocket causes his shoulders to loosen.

Fuck! I didn't want to be right. But there it is. My entire body shakes as he careens toward the sea of crimson-vested students, their eager eyes fixated, ready to inhale more of him.

He slowly squats. "For those of you who've been following the news of a new hacker, Princess_User24, you're likely aware the *mysterious* Zone_Warden accepted her challenge. Not only to defend his title but to meet her in person," he explains, his eyes lingering on me.

Is he going to rat me out in front of all these people? Does he have the balls?

My heart somersaults in my throat.

"Do it," I mouth, daring him. A wider grin etches across my face as our eyes lock. "Pussy."

The tension in the room heightens as he inches closer to the crowd, matching my crazed smile. "Her father posted a short video of his renovated backyard," he prompts. "Just three seconds of blurry silence, but it turns out to be Zone's golden ticket to finding her."

My Valentine's Virus

I wait in trembling impatience for him to continue. My heart can't catch a break at this moment. He really believes I slipped up. Proving him wrong is going to taste so fucking sweet.

Xalton rotates the microphone in his hand, easing the tension in his wrist while maintaining an unwavering gaze on my face. "Zone did himself a favor, flipping Mr. Nuñez's video first. Smartphone cameras are often mirrored," he states deliberately as if measuring our reactions. The crowd responds with murmurs of agreement, encouraging him to resume his revelation.

"There were oranges in the corner of his yard, but no orange tree," he reveals, his tone slowing for dramatic effect. "Just a stump where one used to be. The *brilliant* hacker focused on the direction of the setting sun, right where the tree once stood. By utilizing data mining and analyzing the context of the background, told Zone *everything* he had to know."

The murmurs from the crowd grow more agreeable, their eagerness driving Xalton to divulge further. The chitter-chatter subsides gradually but replaces it with silence. A dark quiet allows his words to travel with a hammering impact making my throat parch with each minute and my leg tremble. It's like I'm waiting for the conclusion of a suspense movie to unfold in real-time. Where is this going? *Stop waiting, you asshole.*

He rubs his clean-shaven chin in contemplation. "There was a corner piece of a popular food chain at the fork in the road and a lighthouse," he continues, his voice resolute. "Bingo Bango, baby. That's all Zone needed to discover the tree was removed due to damages caused by Hurricane Orion years ago, which also destroyed *poor* Princess's home," his words cut through the silence while he paces at the front of the stage, "How tragic it was," he muses, tone laced with a touch of derision. "I remember *my* father going on non-stop about the devastation in Maine. And now, fate has brought the wretched daughter here to Oregon, to *this* very school."

He wouldn't!

The audience erupts into frayed boos as he references me. Each jeer pierces my ears with a mix of pain and a strange satisfaction intensifying my core as I fixate on his dumb perfect face.

He rolls his jaw before gesturing at the bright screen behind him.

A video displays his progress and the exact footage Dad captured.

"Using compass math, Zone deduced Princess's old address and dived right into the history of its inhabitants. Only two families were listed, so he narrowed his focus to the most recent. It unveiled the names of the occupants: Randall Nuñez and Abigail Belle-Nuñez. Your public records are now under Zone_Warden's fingertips, *Princess...*"

He must think he's a goddamn anime villain, but I can't stop smiling from his cheesy theatrics.

White panic overwhelms my tensing body from my very identity being at risk.

I curse under my breath for trapping myself here. If I leave now, I'm certain to be exposed. The weight of his revelation hangs, compacting through the space, threatening to suffocate me. But amidst this cocktail of danger and arousal, it dampens my senses the longer his eyes burn on mine.

"Oh, *Abbie...?*" He croons, darkening his eyes over the audience.

My eyes grow keen to the sound of my name flowing off his tongue like sugary venom. I know no one's caught on yet, but the weight of converging eyes on me, searching for hints, has my heart drumming in violent rhythms.

Only a prescription drug can help soothe it right now, but this wasn't how I expected my day to go. Zone announcing himself to me like *this*. It's... it's some parts unnerving, but... *sweet*, how he did all of this from his hate for me.

I'm all shades of fucked right now.

He smirks as the crowd cheers him on. "I believe Zone withdrew from his house for the first time in four *long* months just to track you down. So, tell me, Princess... You *scared?*"

My Valentine's Virus

A grin spreads across his face as the students murmur in gasping disbelief. Their attention shifts away from him, engrossed in their whispered speculations, as he lets out a quiet laugh.

"Could he be Zone_Warden?"

"Impossible. He must be working for him. The Zone doesn't show himself in public."

"Using Xalton Kaiser as a decoy is cool as fuck though."

"Should we be worried? Zone's no joke."

"I wonder what he wants with Princess."

With a tap of his heel against the rim of the stage, he silences their excited commotions. "Relax, kittens…" The attention from everyone fires back to him, his flexed core and posture relaxing.

He concludes his speech and exits the stage to a round of applause. Deliberately avoiding eye contact with the headmaster as he hands it to her, she reclaims the microphone.

Her elegant platinum hair is rounded in a neat bun, and her brown eyes narrow at him as he proceeds without exchanging words.

The stakes are high and soaring to newer peaks as I planned. Most people would fear for their lives, but the arrogant ass didn't even consider I *wanted* to be found. I never imagined he'd put his own identity at risk this way. It was grandiose and nothing I could have expected from the introvert.

A vision of him handcuffed, with me as the last one standing, becomes increasingly clear in my mind.

I'm drooling, just waiting for the final ball to drop. With trembling fingers, I compose a response to his text, ready to embark on the next stage of our dangerous game.

Me: You'll find, I'm not so easy to impress, Xalton.

LEVEL FOUR

ZONE_WARDEN

The typical nerves of stage fright don't hinder me as much as they used to. I've honed my skills in addressing and manipulating an audience of this magnitude since I was a kid.

Opal Mayor, my father's friend and headmaster of this school, hands me her mic. I keep my gaze forward in my stride, holding my breath so as not to inhale her dusted magnolia perfume.

I begin my speech with a sarcastic tone. "Greetings, my fellow script kittens."

I stalk the stage, and my eyes fall on a young woman with unkempt dark hair snuggled in a black cardigan covered in lint, who sauntered in at the last minute.

After my speech left the audience frothing, I presume my hidden message to Abigail in the crowd hit from my timed message.

I'm not sure what I expected. Maybe a nerdy-looking girl fleeing from the auditorium in tears, standing up to reveal herself in a martyr-like

My Valentine's Virus

fashion, or something between the two. Right on cue, I observe the one I suspect in the shadows of the crowd, peeking at her phone.

This is her. I know it is.

My prey gifts me a reply from a hidden number in my presentation. A satisfied grin stretches over my face when I stride off the platform.

Applause follows as I head to my dressing room. She reclaims her microphone, avoiding the headmaster's glare, and I glance at Princess's reply on my watch.

Unknown: You'll find, I'm not so easy to impress, Xalton.

The girl's got nerves built from steel. Her reply spreads through my mind like a virus. I'm in her goddamn home base drinking tea, and all I get is a line translating to *"try harder, butt munch."*

I need to make my intentions clear. I plan on hurting her—torture her for thinking she has the mettle to contest me.

Concentrated fury turns time as I change attire. I face the wall-length mirror, barely able to recognize myself in the shadows of my hood.

I'll be the last face she sees before taking her life. I grab the switchblade from the compartment at my waist and test the blade's point with a finger.

Blood pebbles from the immediate prick, and I retract the edge, return it, and zip up my jacket.

I'm used to ruining lives from the comfort of my home, but what difference would it make if I ended one in person? I don't care what shedding her blood turns me into—she made me this way, and there's not much stopping me from executing her.

Descending the steps, I navigate the shadows of the audience for a better view of my little rival amidst the sea of bobbing heads. The moron remains in the dusk of the auditorium.

That spark of superiority emanating from her is so thick that no one else can possess it—the same intangible scent that wafts off my computer screen whenever she logs in. But she can't hide behind it here anymore. We've spared online like a pair of conceited thirteen-year-olds. But this is reality, Princess, and I hold reign here, too.

The headmaster drills on about the school's illustrious history, and I sit two rows behind her in the thick darkness.

Her little classmates in front of me attempt to provoke her about her appearance and... aroma. I inhale the orange juice and bacon scent even from way over here, and a smile tugs on the corner of my lips. It's not a bad smell per se, just unexpected.

Some of the comments I overhear are harsh, and these Chanel-raised brats aren't the type to hold back their punches.

I don't have sympathy for her, but I don't have a desire to join in either. I lean to get a better look at her since... I'm curious to know what she looks like in person. I study how she reacts from her backside. The blanket of darkness doesn't help one bit, but I can examine each micro-expression during the ceremony.

She starts tying her hair into a ponytail. Some parts wavey, some straight, like she lost a fight with a curling iron. I find a tan scar above her eyebrow there, making me wonder what she's doing picking bar fights at her age.

The discord of chatter among the students fades into the background as I grow attuned to the subtle movements she makes.

The projection light increases ahead, revealing something more delicate than the monster my mind painted. Time stills as her features soften before my eyes. My jaw unclenches.

She rises to adjust her skirt, and my face is struck with heat. The deep sinful curves of her shadowy figure turn my knees static. A figure of seduction and bewitchment makes me still. I work a swallow, the *calculative* rage that possesses me flickers like a defective light bulb.

My Valentine's Virus

Her long voluminous ponytail swings like a hypnotic pendulum. She exposes the perverseness of a small neck, and my mind deviates. I imagine my fingers wrapping around them, squeezing until light fades from her eyes. My cock squeezes against my waistline at the thought of her pulse warming my palms while she gasps over my tongue.

Big smoldering eyes lock onto mine like she's reading my thoughts. I'm tugged out of my daydream to face Princess_User24 in the flesh.

I can only make out the shape of her face in this lighting, but whether she recognizes *me* in the crowd doesn't affect either of us.

In this halted moment, time ceases to exist until a glitter of defiance in her stare skips over the heads of her bullies. She smirks at them. Fucking *smirks*.

My temper skips again. *She's just as smug in real life.* A chuckle rolls from me.

In that fleeting moment, the bitchy whispers, the headmaster's plummy accent, and the bourbon I wolfed down to calm my nerves all wither away.

Everything around us becomes insignificant, so I can absorb more detail of her, committing every inch of her to memory.

My first victim.

I'm reminded of my brief internship with the CIA. I was trained to dissect everything about someone at first glance. Princess reveals... a mask.

The negative attention tossed her way doesn't bother her, but her stiffening shoulders exhibit her true emotions.

"Brave girl," I wipe my face in annoyance at myself. I'm afraid I might continue humanizing her. The stab of pain I received from my bank's email re-ignites the flames of hatred in me.

All I get from this is she'll be easiest to break in person without the security of her computer.

I squint, glaring daggers at her backside, and bounce my leg as the minutes tick.

I'll bring her to her knees the minute she's alone, pleading for mercy.

She sprouts from her seat to excuse herself, and my chest thumps for action. Fury holds me like a second skin.

I stalk her to the empty corridor.

Natural lighting spies through circular gothic windows and vivid mosaics of the ceiling. The rest of the ceremony plays on in the background, and thanks to my watch doubling as an EMP device, surveillance cameras within a hundred-meter radius shut down. The red blinking lights cease along with the other hall lights the closer I approach Princess's sweet citrus scent.

My mind replays each attack I launched at her over the past few weeks. Each sleepless night, an embarrassment of failures.

I round the corner, and my fists clench.

She stands fully bathed in the rainbow of assortment lighting that streams in from the windows overhead.

Before I take another step, my breath catches in my throat.

Her dark hair glows like pristine marble basking in these rays. She wanders the hall, seeming to enjoy herself, her maple-colored eyes filling with unspecified curiosity at a knight statue catching her intense focus.

I catch my heart fluttering like she's the centerpiece of a regal art gala. She kisses her fingertips and delicately brushes them against the knight piece displayed by the wall—so slowly.

The closer I step, my hard-on wrestles against my zipper. Undiscernible burns trickle in my chest, watching her. She doesn't notice me. She's too absorbed in that bastard of metal. *It isn't even that cool.*

I crane my head back for a hard exhale and squeeze my eyes shut. I'm not seriously *jealous* over a statue. No, no—it's got to be something entirely killer.

She is *breathtaking*, with more beauty stacked in her like a Russian doll. But I know at the center lies a demon who gets off on her victories.

My Valentine's Virus

I should be offended she's aware of my presence but still glides through space like I'm a figment of her imagination. I should be consuming her every thought like a nightmare.

The school is a marvel, so I can't fault her for the distraction. Everything from the elegant and grim atmosphere of deep crimson and rich black hues to the sharp-angled art and medieval knight decor in every corner adds to the university's haunting allure.

My heart continues to race, fueled by a volatile vengeful mix. Yet, there's something else dark and overpowering clouding my mind.

It takes all my strength not to wrap my hands around her throat after I force my knee between her pillowy thighs.

My vision returns, and I'm towered over her.

She's pinned against the wall under me. Her big doe eyes take in my form bouncing back a heat I didn't expect.

I swallow, taking a moment to hide in our gazes, every tremble in her cherry-stained lips begging to be bitten.

The smallest of her whimper drives straight to my cock like a curse. I'm losing focus again. The impact of her cat-like smile has my chest swelling with a craving.

With little sleep, less patience, and even smaller restraint, I breathe down her neck. She doesn't fight back. Her flushed skin vibrates beneath my entrapment of her. A dark whisper reminds me of what she told me I could do when I found her.

At this moment, she's alone and all *mine*.

Technical note from Professor Kaiser: An **EMP or Electro Magnetic Pulse** *device—if you're annoying—can disrupt and destroy any electronic devices. They... can occur naturally, but some hackers can design man-made EMP devices for their own means. Typically, nefarious. Just a heads-up: messing with EMPs is frowned upon by the law. Making, possessing, and using them for shady shit can lead to a legal dance only I can afford tangoing with.*

A. DARANG

LEVEL FIVE

PRINCESS_USER24

In the hallway, I scour for the restroom. There, I'm hoping I can scrub the damn orange juice smell off my sweater and not hear another word about it. Back-up is also requested. A hard chill skirts up my spine, and my head whips around to meet a wall of a man. His dark masculine form has my heart skipping.

He saunters toward me. I squint to find a face beneath his hoodie, but the shade covers him well. *That's got to be on purpose.* I swallow.

The cold stain sticks against my right hip and becomes an afterthought while I try recalling him from somewhere.

The onyx brick interior acts as his personal backdrop for mischief. That's when I knew he was *him*.

My nostrils flare as long legs consume the distance protecting me. His sculpted face appears under mosaic lighting like some pornographic light show. As he passes, darkness leaves and reappears around him. I make out his translucent face, but the light doesn't touch his eyes. They're a pair of hooded masculine orbs that most people couldn't find in common crowds. His dark green eyes form a paradox, like a hedge maze at night. It's breathtaking and entirely fantasy.

My vision heats, finding tremendous focus in them—on *me*. He reminds me of a prowling panther in the shade. Even if he's already been spotted, he doesn't care. He's happening.

The smell of bourbon is penetrating even in this distance. I fight to keep my expression trained as he raises his hands to shape a heart.

Time freezes, but he comes closer.

My muscles clench, and I remember the jackass on his black *Ducati Panigale* motorbike that Saturday. The white skull Elysium print on his helmet surfaces behind my eyes, and my shoulders sag.

Violence twists in my spleen, ragging on myself in drowning waves. Even if the rapid traffic light change and his logo were a *minor* suspicion, I should have investigated the driver as soon as I got home! My teeth grate, hoping he doesn't notice.

How screwed am I?

"*Zone is no joke.*" The rumbles from the audience clash back into my head.

I mean—this was what I wanted, right? What I *planned*?

I massage the growing tension in my neck as if winding my gears. My nerves need to *fucking* chill. I hesitate at the sweat accumulating in my palm.

Intrigue meets the hard scowl of my walking doom, and his fingers brush against the brick wall like an enchantment. My body numbs, I struggle to swallow, and my eyes can't shift from him.

The closer he gets, the more stifling his size is, even in the echoing expanse of the gothic ceiling.

Air-conditioned space heats, warmed by his disguised rage. A vein pulsates near his forehead and neckline as if he's on the verge of bursting.

Oh, he's *pissed*—no. That word doesn't even scratch the surface of his murderous expression.

My Valentine's Virus

I inhale more of him, and my knees weaken. *I've finally got him! Mr. Number One.* An inhibited grin builds behind my features.

This is… reviving. It's overwhelming in bounds.

Is he really Mr. Number One? My entire body betrays the chill exterior I've cultivated. But in my defense, Xalton gives me no time to adjust to his God-like presence.

Everything he had on stage follows him here. I'm still stuck on how he's *this* huge in person.

Glimpsing away, I recall his Wiki page. *Six ft. Six in.* Xalton's a full foot taller than me with his gravity too. It siphons oxygen from the space, replacing it with his own.

I need concrete proof Zone is *him* and not paid Xalton Kaiser in his place to fuck with me. It'd certainly be a great way to. I've looked up to him since high school.

Confidence sways in and out of me like turbulent weather.

"Oh, Mr. Kaiser!" I perk, channeling my inner fangirl. "It's such a *slam* meeting your heroes. *Ha ha.*" I shoot him a single finger-gun while my other hand hides a clenching fist. The submission in my voice is so jarring to me that I want to claw at my own throat.

He gives me a look to say, "Aw, I'm her hero," but then barrels over me until my back presses the wall.

I miss a breath, my head bobs back from the tap, and my gaze yanks to his. I hold onto the threads of my conviction when a flame ignites in his sleepless eyes. With an inch of space between us, my heart crashes against my ears.

Xalton's hands are as big as my head. He shifts them on each side, caging me in his broad arms. The hairs on the back of my neck ascend to the top of my scalp, urging me to flee.

Before he devours me whole under his shade, I refuse to blink. My glare clings to his' like I'm drowning in a vortex. But I reject showing how he affects me.

He takes his beautiful time, toying with my examining gaze while roaming over me like a curious serpent.

"The novelty must feel similar to meeting your *foes* too," he croons near my flushed ear. "I found you, *Princess.*"

The deep erotic timbre of his voice rumbles through my muscles. My alias rolling off his tongue sounds like a curse. It's difficult to breathe in. The little oxygen he gives turns to gas—any flicker threatening destruction.

His wicked smile brushes my ear, and a crescendo of goosebumps coats my skin. Joy never radiated from his smile. Even when he was on that stage, there was a shadow of force, as if the notion had been beaten into him since birth. But this one is genuine. Sure, it's an evil grin, but… he wears it well.

I don't hate this. A shiver skates through me again as I struggle to reject the effects he's causing me.

He was giving me *serial killer* vibes a minute ago. Now, he's relishing the way I quiver beneath his warm shade.

"If you find me, you can do whatever you want to me."

At the time, it made sense to goad him. I sent him on a worldwide puzzle, but it only took him a few sleepless nights. I figured, *"Hey. If he does meet me in person, he's guaranteed to kill me. I may as well lose my virginity to the ultimate hacker first."*

"Anything I want, right?" He inches close as if stealing my thoughts.

A bashfully willing smile cramps my face. "What?" I chuckle to ease the breath I've held. If I feign naivety, he might doubt himself for a second, and in that time, I can bolt and reassess the situation.

This is too surreal. *Xalton Kaiser was Zone—this entire time?*

He ghosts his thumb parting my lip, and my breath shudders. I inhale his leather and bourbon musk, only for a moan to flee from me. Under the weight of our penetrating gaze, his length digs hard between us through his clothes. I shove against his chest, and my lips flatten in dismay when he doesn't budge.

My Valentine's Virus

Great. Trapped between a wall and a hot celebrity psycho.

"I want to know what my little rival tastes like when she's been bested." His knee plunges between my bare thighs, and heat slaps my face from how exposed I am in this uniform.

"H-Hey—*"* I jolt in protest.

"Shut your fucking mouth," he cuts me off, growling through clenched teeth.

I wince when his knee rides to my cunt beneath my skirt. Regulated panic surges in my ears like a river. I heave a breath while air brushes my pussy, the vulnerability causing my back to arch.

"Make me," I dare. Pools of violence, heat, and something else churn in his gaze. I reach out from his blind spot and grab his balls. I ignore my blush from the firmness of him, and I shamelessly double-take, second-guessing if I'm clutching his crown and jewels or some mutilated third leg.

His eyes don't leave mine, and he didn't even flinch at my grab,

So, here we are.

Two adults threatening each other's undoing in a hall of prestigious architecture. I didn't see this in my twenty-year plan.

Once the heat settles, I cock a smile at my dance partner. Stuck in the void of his glaring inferno, he tilts his head for a better look at me. *All* of me.

"What a *filthy* thing you are." He cups my chin to face him. His grip is rough enough to cause me harm, but instead, he *laughs*. "You're… getting off to this."

His knee begins stroking my slit, and bliss flings within me.

I glance at the shadow of a stain I'm leaving as he swipes his knee, and my embarrassed soul leaks from my ears. I gasp, and he chuckles deeply. The rumble vibrates all around my body, making my chest loosen.

"Your pussy wants it so bad, it's fucking sobbing for me," he taunts. Craning his face down to mine, I practically taste the bourbon on his breath. "Why *is* that?"

"Look who's talking," I retort with as much smoke in my voice as his. "Your introvert-ass always this packing when you leave home?"

The muscle in his jaw bulges as I clasp his testicles harder. I savor the pained groan in his voice. If he doesn't let go of my face right now, I'll fist his balls like they owe me money.

He hikes his knee firm against my slit, and my lips press together to conceal a shudder. My grip lessens with our words whirling through us, enticing each other for submission. My instincts clash between competitive nature and temptations. So, I decide between the two and die a little inside at my decision.

"I think you're mistaking me for someone else, Mr. Kaiser," I whimper. The mischievous spark in my eyes flickers away.

"Zone Warden," he clarifies. "That name ring any bells for you, *Abbie?*" With an amused smirk, he cocks his brow, his sculpted charm persisting even while probing to verify further.

His hand releases my chin, and I release his trousers.

"...*who?*"

The rage in his breath rakes over my ear. He reels back an inch before the friction of his knee strokes my clit.

Oh, fuck.

His thick thigh forces my legs further apart, stealing a sharp gasp from me. He grips my jaw again, his examining eyes burning. "You can *try* denying it, Princess, but you're as transparent to me as a fucking snow globe." He strokes his knee against my crotch, pacing his words deliberately. "If you want me to shake you up and coat you in my *white Christmas*, that can easily be arranged."

My eyes careen back from the jolt of pleasure coiling in my guts. The instant he lowers it, my hips spring forward on their own for more. I gasp so hard I can't form words.

My Valentine's Virus

"Who knew you'd have such a cute needy voice?" He leans into my ear. "So… I know where you stay, where you eat, and where you sleep now. You can run, but there's *no* hiding anymore." He bites the shell of my ear, and a grunt teases in my throat.

I cough out a laugh, breaking his hold on me. My grin grants him the verification he needs. "Zone Warden. Huh…?" I hum jerkily as his knee inches toward me again. "That sounds like the name of someone who doesn't know when to give up… even after he's lost *so* much."

A smile curls on his lips as I continue.

Unable to brace in time, I wince when his knee returns. He rubs my pussy until I'm forced to sit on him.

The heat and friction of his lap brings a wail of pleasure blinding my senses, and I can't stop it. I don't think I want to. *Oh my god.*

How does this feel so good? I'm not me anymore, but a starving creature possessing me, grinding until I'm satiated. With each firm thrust of his knee, tension gathers like a coil, ready to spring throughout my core.

Xalton stifles a grunt when I press against him, humping his thigh to chase that sweet spot he found.

The shivers of my body make his bulge strain against the seam of his pants. His lips brush against mine, and I pant.

"For the record," he rasps. "I *am* embracing what's between us here today. So, I'm giving you a chance. Once I'm finished punishing you, you'll dismiss the hold you've implemented on Elysium. Threatening *you* doesn't work, but I have your dad's information to sell if you continue testing me."

Classic Zone, going for the people around me if all else fails. My father's details are disguised. I planted them to lead him to me, but that's the furthest thing on my mind currently.

His threat is muted to me when my climax crests. My gaze heats into his, begging for him not to move away.

We've forged a sliver of unspoken trust for the sake of getting off, and my need intensifies.

The sensation is blazing, and just when I can't take it anymore, his hands snake around the base of my throat. Conceding to my wordless plea, his lips collide against mine. His pedal-soft lips burst the bourbon taste across my cheeks, and I share his high.

Our kiss is nothing short of chaos and explosive. His teeth brush mine, following an aggressive tongue, challenging my own. My moan frees in his mouth and senses his cock stiffen from my whimpers.

My clit swells as I nip him, and he squeezes my throat in response. He grips so tight a piece of me reconsiders our temporary truce. I'm lost in his eyes, mine pleading in return. Dancing on the edges of surrender and domination, the world around us fades. Spots of white delight drift into my vision as I crane my head back to the rush of bliss.

He lowers his knee, denying me, and something feral replaces it, shooting up my spine. My lip curls in a sneer, and I grab his shoulders.

His expression grows indifferent, awaiting my answer.

"I…" I sigh. "…*want* your punishment."

The pulse in his jaw twitches, swiping the moisture on his knee against my dewy thighs.

"Then you'll get it, you goddamn cock tease," he grunts before forcing my thighs further apart.

Raising my skirt, he thrusts his fingers into my mouth before I fully register it. He strokes my tongue in rough swipes, removes them, and leaves a line of drool webbing on my chin. Xalton caresses my tortured bud with his fingers, and the heat of them disperses to my chest. His eyes narrow, and I find a faint shimmer in them, like a haunted swamp meeting morning. "I'll give you *five* days to revert it," he says. "That should give you enough time and… I can torture you the entire time." His palm smooths up the valley of my chest before cupping my breast.

I suck air when he removes his hand from off the wall and circles the hard peak, molding it like an artisan of clay. A moan slips from me at his definitive clockwise motions. My pussy clenches his swiping fingers, and I tremble for more.

Someone could easily stumble into the hall, but they'd also be my evidence that this isn't some really good dream.

With his other hand, he thrusts his middle finger into my pussy without hesitation. His expression strains again as if he's holding something back. "Your cunt is so tight," he grunts knowingly. "Saving yourself to get railed by your *'hero…?'*" He curls his finger, aiming straight into a spot that has me hearing singing angels.

"Fuck…!" I gasp sharply, unable to contain it.

His thrusts stroke in that region, gauging my reaction like he's tuning a guitar. Amusement props his brow while he troubleshoots the strokes that make me shout the loudest.

My soaked flesh swallows his finger so tight I memorize the sensation of the ripples of his fingerprint.

"Look at the mighty Princess User24," his wicked chuckle lands against my ear as I melt all over his palm. "Coming undone only by my finger?" Xalton dives his knuckle deeper, circling, punishing my walls, and juicing more cries out from me. My hips buck in haggard motions. He pushes his thumb tight against my clit like he's struggling to fuse with it.

Lightning shoots through me when he tries, and my ached moan echoes throughout the hallways. *"Fuck…!"*

Xalton strokes the side of my face, his broad chest pressing into me. I grow dizzy coming down from cold bliss.

My legs shake, riding out waves straining to keep my balance.

"I *wondered* what you'd sound like once I got my hands on you… I didn't think your whimpers would be this *pathetic*," Xalton teases with a warm smirk. His fingers slow, but they don't stop after my release, stimulating another one. He adopts a more sensual rhythm, helping me balance again.

"Fuck you," I hush.

His fingers increased their fervor, teetering me on the verge of another fatter climax. "No, fuck *you.*"

I bite a moan in half, fighting off the urge to lose myself again. *"Fuck! Oh, fuck!"*

He slaps my pussy with his other hand while continuing his assault. The vulgar echoes of my wetness reverberates in my ears. My eyes roll back. The impact of something new threatens to overpower me, and I don't know if I'm prepared for it. As if reading my thoughts, Xalton thrust a second finger, pumping at inhuman speeds.

Hearing, seeing, tastes, smells—all those senses leave me as frenzied vibrations surge in my rapture.

Too fucking good. I can't hold back my voice. "Xalt... *Xalton,"* my weary wails ache in my throat.

His concentrated eyes press against mine, his crazed pumps showing me no mercy and no signs of fatigue to stop.

My eyes dip back, unable to take him abusing the fuck out of my g-spot.

Large white specks engulf the rest of my vision.

He presses his warm lips to my ear again. "Cum on my fingers like the bitch in heat you are," Xalton groans.

"Fuck! Xahhhlton...!" I whimper.

"That's it, Abbie," he praises.

My muscles tighten, and my toes curl in my shoes. Muffling my cries burns my throat, unable to stop it from echoing across the school.

"Such a thirsty slut you are," he breathes. "Look how *deep* you swallow me. Your sopping pussy can't get enough, can it? Do you hear how loud you're being, Princess?"

I break into a million pieces. With a release so thick, my grip digs into his shoulders. Pulsating aftershocks give me savory glimpses of space and the heavens. A moan sputters through me, my breath hitching, and I shudder as the sensation becomes too much. My head rocks back in surrender with my release.

My Valentine's Virus

Heavy breaths spill around me as I return from my orgasm.

My legs glisten with moisture. I struggle to recapture my breath when I find a glow of amusement filling his expression.

My legs tremble on their own, and the moment I shift footing, my eyebrows knit into a frown.

D... Did I just *pee* on this man? No. I *squirted?* Well, that's new. *Dear, God.* What do I even do now?

I shut my eyes tight, letting waves of humiliation ride through me.

"...had enough?" He hums, rubbing his flooded knee against me again. He doesn't even comment on it like he's used to this sort of thing. I'm grateful for the deflection, at least.

Xalton pulls his fingers out of me, parts his lips, and slurps his fingers. His eyes roll to the back of his head, sucking and licking my arousal off his fingers like it's rare frosting.

My womanhood vibrates in astoundment, and I memorize the act for a private time.

Fuck, I can't anymore. My head falls to the side, and I realize for the first time I've eaten more than I can chew.

I'm not experienced enough to deal with this level of freakiness.

"You taste as good as you feel," he croons. "Your body belongs to me from now on. Your trembling pussy is my favorite new treat."

LEVEL SIX

PRINCESS_USER24

When I was in high school, I wrote fanfiction about Xalton and me. I know, *cringe*—but it was only once. Even in my wildest fantasies, nothing could have topped this.

I've peaked.

The only man I admired from my screen *fingerbanged* me so good and in *public*. I mean, curtain call, baby. There's no topping that.

With that in mind, I don't have to wonder what his touch feels like anymore. It's irreplicable. Powerful. If he asked me to get on my knees and suck him off, I would. Right here.

Xalton's hands rake through my hair, and I groan, returning from space. I grit my teeth when he fists my hair back. I moan from the feel of hot velvety lips licking and sucking my neck. He tastes it before sinking his teeth into me. I wince and writhe, but he wraps his overpowering body tight against mine. My breasts squeeze flush with his chest as I thrash from his mark. Hot stings bloom into pleasure. His rough bulge presses my clit through his clothing.

My Valentine's Virus

"It's too soon," I mutter, not understanding the tremble in my voice.

A hunger in his dilated pupils makes me still. The air between us does as well. A smile breaks on my lips as I sense an opening. Trained panic takes hold of my motions before I move. Shifting footing, I spin on my heel and grab his wrist with both hands.

Before my next action, he releases his grip, and I use that momentum to hightail it away to find the restroom.

I race to gather my thoughts as my heart pounds in my chest. I'm met with four other ladies inside. My shoulders ease, and I take in the gorgeous room. It isn't as massive or overwhelming as the rest of the school, but that doesn't deter it from making it as lavish as Buckingham Palace.

Pressing my back against the door for support, I huff. The movement pushes the strands of hair from my eyes, and I catch a whiff of something... intimate.

Instead of the cursed citrus scent, there's Xalton's honey bourbon and sex.

My face heats with each identifying inhale.

Before recovering from the high of *Xalton Kaiser*'s legendary finger-fucking, I focus on a girl keeping a maroon stare over me by the mirrors.

Stunning platinum blond hair waves down to her waist in two tendrils by heavily pierced ears. Her dark eye makeup looks professionally applied and is an opposite contrast to her porcelain skin.

With an air of confidence, her perfectly manicured hand rests flat over her uniformed chest.

"Is everything fine, my dear?" she asks with a sharpness cutting through the air. Her accent reminds me of my Queen's-English-bred grandmother on my mother's side.

"Uh... yes, why?" I race a reply. My smile must have given my first impression as ditzy. But it's not directed at her. Every part of me still shakes with humiliation... and bliss.

She cocks her head, studying me with a narrowed glare. It's like she'd scoop out every detail of my face to memorize. "*Because*... you smell like one of those little *piggies*," she giggles. "You know. The ones that fled from the big bad wolf about to blow their house down." Her words drip with malice, and her venomous smile twists upward.

The other girls leaning by the wall next to her burst into laughter. Their taunts ricochet off the stone walls, making my organs churn. A pang of hurt causes me to recall they were the ones trying to get under my skin in the auditorium—well, trying to.

I gather my composure, refusing to let their projecting words affect me.

My ego wouldn't stand for it.

Wetting my lips, I meet the rude girl's siren-shaped gaze. "Aw, and what house did you seek asylum from? One made out of boring lines? How about you head back to *Gossip Girl*, sweetheart? I'm *sure* they're missing you."

Knowing I can break her six-ways to Sunday comforts me, so I don't care what this chick's problem is with me. Because seriously, we're not in middle school. Be direct, or keep me out of the circus you call ahead.

My ears perk at a snorted giggle from the last stall.

"Girl, you *tell* her!" A melodic voice cheers to me in support.

Evil goth Barbie stares me down. I cross my arms over my chest, doubling her efforts. I also try not to picture unscrewing her head like all my actual Barbies growing up.

My new fan emerges, flinging open her door with a crash. Our eyes shift from each other and land on her. My cold heart unthaws, watching her wince from her unintended racket. She offers us a half-smirk, but it ends into something more threatening when it lands over my adversary.

She's the first of her kind with her twisted aesthetic. Long chocolate and caramel-colored braids curve her blessed frame. Her warm bronze complexion glows amidst the cool-toned room and compliments her

My Valentine's Virus

uniform. The scent of strawberry lotion follows her and floods the entire restroom.

Moments after her presence, the snooty chick and her henchwomen graciously meander toward the exit. I refuse to move aside in time, and a silver-haired shorty with a pretty rat face brushes my shoulder, managing to knock my bag off my arm. Blondie side-eyes me longer than I can stand, and I return the gesture by throwing them the bird upon their leave.

A gleam from the pair of pins tying her bun together blinds me as she exits.

I adjust my bag strap and face the approachable one. I adore chicks with her gothy, earthy, boho, goblin vibe. She looks like she sells tonics and predicts the future for bones or something involving tarot cards and magic.

She works her dimples as I approach the sink offering a contagious smile.

The glimmering onyx marble countertops reflect us in the shine better than mirrors do. A familiar textbook cover is propped on the cover, and I assume it belongs to the model next to me.

"I'm glad I'm not the only one avoiding the 'wolves' out there," Braids hums as she runs the sink and soaps her hands.

It's disarming to find at least one other person of color at this school, though the ladder has taught me that they think differently. Not only that, but she fits the rest of the dark theme better than most.

"Tell me about it," I sigh. I tug off the sweater wrapped around my waist, and she dries her hands. While I flatten the fabric over the counter, she checks her hair in the mirror. I get down to scrub Caribbean style in the sink, and I find one positive thing about not wearing panties today. I don't have to scrub them here too. My nose scrunches at the thought.

The vanilla hand soap lathers the orange juice spots, and the sweet scent is so permeating that I can taste it.

A gentle gaze tickles my shoulder, and I glance at the girl stilling beside me. She hesitates for words as I give her an awkward glare.

"I didn't mean to gawk," she grins. "May I ask who taught you how to hand wash like that?"

I return to the task but sincerely think back on it. "My grandmother. She was Puerto Rican," I answer without gauging her motive.

Her posture melts at my answer with a deep exhale. *"Beautiful* country. My parents are from an island very near it—neighboring Haiti and more similar to it. I'm Fraixian."

I cock a brow identifying her reddish-brown skin tone. "I don't want to sound like a bumpkin, but what's *Fray*-she-in?" I slow the word I've never heard before this moment.

She nods. "Don't stress over it—it's an *itty*-bitty island that emerged from volcanic activity," she sings the last word while playfully pinching the air. "Fraixia's only about two hundred and five years old and a well-kept secret from the U.S."

"Well, your secret's not safe with me. I'm going to let the volcano know of your escape," I joke with a straight face.

Bubbling laughter riles from her as she hugs her stomach. The childish giggles bounce throughout the space, causing a smile to reach my eyes. This chick is seriously cute, and she laughs with her whole body. I may as well make nice.

"I'm Abbie, a first year. You?"

Her warm brown eyes light up. Wiping a tear, she covers her ruby ring-coated fingers with her mouth. "I'm Psyra Jean-Pierre, but call me Psy. I'm a first year too!" She jumps before bumping shoulders with me like we're bros.

"I gotta tell you before the mood passes—I *love* your whole aura," she adds. Swinging her pin-coated shoulder bag around, she unpacks a smaller red bag packed with organized makeup and brushes. "Don't freak out, but I sense the flames of a God surging inside of you. You're

My Valentine's Virus

one in a million," she casually remarks before leaning at the mirror to apply mascara.

Oh, she's fucking weird. I already can't get enough.

"Thanks... I think?" I respond with a humble smirk and continue massaging my sweater. A blush tickles my chest. Can't say anyone's ever complimented my *'aura'* before.

Rendering a serious expression, she circles the apples of her cheeks with a brush. "No, seriously," her tone grows, almost annoyed by my dismissal. "You're a *badass*," she says with genuine admiration lining each syllable.

My smile widens at the unnecessary surge to my ego. "Well, I *try* not to brag, but..." I sigh, leaning on a pose against the wall.

Psy lets out another colorful giggle. "*Arugh!* Can we be friends? At least before Melanie Mayor decides she wants to swallow you whole?"

Okay. I'll bite.

"Mayor, *who?*" I ask, pushing up my brow in annoyance at the word. I kept hearing that name throughout the headmaster's speech and in the hall speakers.

Psy grabs my arm and pulls me further into the shadow of the room. "Melanie *Mayor*," she hushes before unhanding me. A grim shift in her round eyes urges me to pay attention. "The headmaster's *daughter,*" she explains.

My eyes roll so deep in the back of my head that I think I just found the tiny goblin operating my body—because, *of course,* she is.

Psyra reels back and fishes through her bag with nostrils flaring, retrieving a keychain from her collection of other jangling knickknacks. I lean closely, trying to identify each of them.

My girl came *prepared.* I spot a toolkit with an array of tiny pink screwdrivers, a matching small hammer, measuring tape, a level, crystals in every color, lotions, a goddamn almanac, earbud case—what *isn't* here?

"Jesus Money Christ, Psy," I mutter. "You holding a Fraixian armory in there or—?"

I cough at the sudden cloud of blue mist fires, targeting my sweater.

She averts her gaze from mine, refusing to acknowledge fault. "Yeah, girl. You're *not* lucky. It's coming off you in waves like a curse," she teases. "But my *handy*-dandy Luck Spray will do the trick." She releases her silly little spray, and it swings back to join the rest of her family of keychains. Psy pats my back as I continue hacking a lung.

"I didn't." Cough. "Need." Cough. "Luck." Cough. "What if I wanted to keep my misfortune?"

She ignores me, but I don't really think she heard through the wheezing. "I'm a Mystic. Don't fret."

Ayo, what? "Oh, how *foolish* of me," my counter laces in sarcasm.

Is that a level up from being a Witch or—you know what? I-I don't care. She's hot. She can spray whatever "enchantments" she wants on me, as long as I stop reeking like an IHOP Sunday morning special.

"Listen," Psyra sighs, her eyes narrowing into slits beneath her full lashes. "Not to be a *'word around campus'* kind-a guy, but word around campus is anyone who crosses Melanie regrets it later. She just *looks* your way and decides you're expelled."

An untamed scoff escapes me. "As if a—"

"Source," she bemoans, like she's in my head. Psy already has an article pulled up on her smartphone to show me. "You *see...?*"

"Oh..." I bite my tongue at the screen. Quickly scanning CRU's Campus News headline, it names the twenty students who were expelled last semester.

According to the article, there was little to no evidence showing *how* they were guilty of trashing an entire computer lab. The case was open until Ms. Melanie Mayor pointed out video surveillance of their comings and goings to campus police.

If I'm to follow Psyra's conspiratory tone, my guess is, evil spoiled Barbie must have framed them.

My Valentine's Virus

"I know them from my old school, and they all told me she's full of it," Psy huffs, her vision drifting to the ground as she folds her phone away. "Those boys and girls used to manage a robotics team with her. When deciding the 'look' of their project, they got into a huge fight—a brawl." Psy swings back to the counter and pushes to complete her look with a navy-colored gloss. With a pop of her lips, she organizes her bag.

I exhale the knot forming in my throat and massage my eyebrows to ease pity merging with concern. "As if some dark Regina George is gonna expel me," I mutter.

I really shouldn't direct my attention away from my stalker issues by being in both of their creative ranges. My well-being and homework could suffer.

Glancing at the ajar door, I'm half-waiting for my stalker to enter and pull me out so he can drown me blind in ecstasy again. I could have broken his hold three ways to June, but I was heavily distracted.

Xalton is hotter than the sun, and if I hadn't left as soon as I did, I can't trust that I wouldn't have caved. I might have given him everything back.

I robbed that man of billions worth of stolen data from big-name corporations. Those companies hired me to steal back their secrets. How he got through their defenses is a feat I'm unable to grasp... *yet*.

Having him close by will help me study his tactics, and I may even absorb new ones to mold with my own.

Fucking Xalton Kaiser, of all people. I love how I finally got under Zone_Warden's skin. But *this* much? Mmm. It's an opportunity I can't let slip away.

Shaking my head, I bring myself back to the present and turn to Psy, who is adjusting her braids to a higher ponytail. My eyes gloss to her block-chaining textbook again, shadowed on the counter. Putting two and two together, I figure we might be sharing some classes. During my rush, I forgot that exact cover back in my dorm room.

"Psy?" I test her nickname. "Do you know anything about that well-known hacker from the ceremony Mr. Kaiser was going on about? Zone Warden?"

"Not really, but..." Psy pauses after a beat, freezing in her little makeup pats. "Xalton and I go way back."

A smile peels on my face, inviting *my* new friend to the party.

I freaking got him.

LEVEL SEVEN
ZONE_WARDEN

It's taken much for me to grow and realize I'm anything but a finished project. Just like every other jabroni on this planet, I'm weak. A vessel for impotence I can't understand and much less tolerate. I'm aware of the way Abbie elbows the worst out of me, but this was… surreal.

My mission today was to scare the piss out of her—didn't foresee that in a literal sense. If things didn't go my way, I would have kidnapped and tortured her for fucking with me.

Risking poetry, I let darkness as pure as the deep take reign but without understanding what might happen if it interacted with hers.

I wipe my face, her intoxicating scent remaining on my fingers, begging the question, *why the hell wasn't she wearing underwear?* My little rival has a hedonistic side. I wonder what else I can find out about her.

Raising my head, the ornately carved lights flicker on. As I stand in statuesque awe, absorbing what happened, the large double doors of the auditorium open. Expensive shoes worn by students and faculty clap in the distance conveying the end of Opal Mayor's lecture.

The serene hall and heavenly silence are short-lived, overlapped by rumbles, people jabbering on about their classes and which professors to hate.

I remain, breathing the tailor-made perfumes, annoyingly pushing Abbie's sweet *citr-ussy* one away.

Her evil pussy had no right tasting that good. Fuck her sexy body and the way her mouth trembled for me. I still feel the phantom memory of how tight her walls engulfed my fingers. My dick was so hard it was plotting ways to knock me out for a jailbreak.

As a cutthroat hacker myself, I can relate to using dirty tricks to achieve what's needed. So, I can't be too angry with my little rival for escaping doom. For now.

Straight out of a *Marvel* flick, she pulled some Black Widow maneuver before high-tailing it down the hall. But not before treating me to the full moon reveal under her uniform. My gift for her first squirt session, I suppose. At least, by the surprise on her face when it happened, it was her first. I scowl on the outside, but after making a splash appear from nowhere, my heart's been singing show tunes. I ignore the blue balls I didn't come in with to focus on how I to fit my head between her olive thighs. They ran slick with nectar as she flipped me off. My knees nearly buckled from the show.

Very uncalled for. It most definitely will work on me again.

Seconds later, a sea of raised heads traverse by me, taking up space as I disassociate. An alert from my watch disrupts my smile and pulls me out of my trance. I swipe it open in the crowd of bustling students and press against a wall, allowing everyone to flood through.

My live security cam footage reveals my living room being ransacked by my masked *rat*.

My Valentine's Virus

"Dammit, Dice…" I seethe at the pocket-sized raccoon who conned his way into my life. He makes it rain stuffing before sticking his face into the cushion and wiggling his tail into the air.

It'd be precious if it weren't so frustrating. I bonded with that couch even if I was for a short time. Dice isn't used to me leaving home, so I understand him acting out for my attention.

That and he's a goddamn raccoon.

I care for him more than I care for most people, but attempting to protect my shit from his destructive habits is like trying to keep a tornado on a leash.

I know the legal ramifications of keeping a wild animal, but Oregon doesn't know Dice the way I do.

Still.

It's gotten so bad I had to move my valuables into spare rooms, giving him free rein.

I suck my teeth, scouring for options. With a definitive sigh, I leave the chaotic scene for future-me to deal with.

The sudden scent of marigolds overpowers my senses. Inexplicable darkness shrouds my heart, and there's a tap on my back. Schooling my expression, I force a modicum of a smile and shield the rest of my soul from the annoyance that is Opal Mayor's voice.

"Xalton Kaiser!" she snaps, recognizing me in the crowd. I guess it never mattered if I changed clothes. The old bat always finds me when I don't want to be seen.

Opal Mayor is a friend of my father's. They've been in contact my whole life, and she knows my parents better than I do.

"Headmaster," I respond smugly to the festering manifestation of evil in a blazer.

Her angular nose crinkles up to me, and my height over hers is comical. She still has to face up to scowl at me even in her high heels.

How do women even wear these things? It looks like medieval torture to force yourselves in for hours. They're already beautiful when they're in comfort. Unlike this haunting specter.

Her manicured hands prop to her waist. "Don't *'Headmaster'* me. What was all that about?"

I delivered her opening ceremony with a slap, and she still wasn't satisfied. It's not like I was even given a script of direction. I was informed to greet the students, talk about my experiences in the CIA, and then hand the mic over.

I give her a patient look, urging her to provide more information, and she scoffs.

Opal massages her frown and then points to me. "You *snubbed* me on stage." She clarifies.

Ah. Could it be because you instigated a betrothal of your unhinged daughter to me, who doesn't understand the word "no?" Could it be because you forced the idea into my father's and her head since I was a goddamn toddler? Or maybe it's your entitlement over everyone's time. Gee, Mrs. Mayor, I don't know. I bite back the response burning in my chest. Resting my hand over my heart, I offer a sympathetic brow. "Forgiveness, please. It was dark. I couldn't have seen you," I lie on cue. "You were a *silhouette* in a myriad of moving shadows. The moment you announced yourself on stage behind me, I already had to use the little boy's room."

"Is—"

I cut her off. "I figured we'd find ourselves another time," I smile, but her hesitance makes her silver brows knit tighter.

"Is that alcohol on your breath, Kaiser? In *my* school?" She sounds like she's seconds away from pulling my ear and hauling me to detention like I'm not a thirty-one-year-old. And she'll do it without a moment's thought.

"I ate some bad bread earlier. I don't mean to worry you."

"Mhm," she taps her foot, visually debating whether to believe me or not. "Well," she huffs before quickly surveying her surroundings. "I

My Valentine's Virus

wanted to apologize to you in person regarding the circumstances with my daughter. I heard from your father you made a substantial amount from that lawsuit."

A sneer strikes through me, and like lightning, it vanishes before her notice.

She frowns, checking out one of the shoes a student has on while striding by us. "I don't see why you still can't be together after everything. It could make a cute story to tell your kids someday."

Out of necessity, I face away from her and wipe the cringe filling my face. Without finding the bead of discomfort I'm giving off; she doesn't stop talking.

"She's seeking psychological help and meeting the best therapists—"

"No," I interrupt and swallow. Darkness hazes the sides of my vision, and every cell in my body screams for me to pull my knife out and slit her throat. Then my rationality bleeds in like cold rain on my skin. *Deep breath.*

I give her a quick smile. "I don't want to hear another thing about that person, Mrs. Mayor. With respect. Most importantly, I can't have her knowing I'm back in town—"

She rolls her eyes at my plea, the irritating gesture putting out the legs from her apology. "What?" She blinks rapidly, and it takes everything in me not to sneer.

The hag's already told her. I mean, in her defense, I gave her too much credit. Her daughter's famous ex is representing the school in a ceremony. How could she keep her cakehole shut?

The more she stands without combusting into flames, I contemplate sneaking shit into her breakfast cereal.

I take another breath and rest a used blunt in my mouth. Mrs. Mayor's demonic hazel eyes bulge before I reach to take her hand in my mines for a long uncomfortable hold. I smear the remaining moisture of Abbie's juices in her palm.

♥

The memory of defiling her lavish halls with Abbie's needy cries keeps my demons at bay.

Mrs. Mayor stammers after I release her, and I smile. Turning on my heel, I light my joint. It's time I revisit the cafeteria. I've developed a craving for vitamin C.

After a quick breakfast, I make my way to a Blockchain tech laboratory. My eyes immediately find Princess, and my eyes narrow into slits at Jean-Pierre.

You've got to be joking. How did Abbie find someone in my family's circle out of everyone infesting the planet?

Our parents used to work together long ago and left us together for play dates. She was this emo freshman whose father worked as an agricultural businessman from Fraixia. Word around my circle says Magnus Jean Pierre's been running for president on that island, and his odds are good. Deep down, I've envied JP for having a loving father—her entire family, really. They were once my second home as a teen, but that's all been behind me.

Princess must have done some digging and targeted her for information on me. That's what I'd like to believe, but the two behave like they've been girlfriends for lifetimes, chortling through the space and sharing inside jokes with each other.

I'm here for one thing: to solidify my presence near Princess. I'm going to lurk in every shadow the same way she's been lurking in my head.

My heart fists beneath my chest at the sight of her. Blue hues from the mosaic sky strike her hair, and my face heats.

The second those deep maple-brown eyes meet mine, I sneer.

She sticks out her tongue, and my erection revives, but I advance toward their small group. I take in the Blockchain tech lab in my

My Valentine's Virus

periphery. It's as familiar as my own home. The rows of high-end computer hardware line the walls skirting contentment through me. It's a ramped mini auditorium that I admit helps make learning more *theatrical*.

I nod my head down to JP as a greeting in my approach. A dark smile plays on my face, eager to interrupt their dumb conversation.

JP lifts her bright expression, exposing her face craters to me. "Xalton!"

"Jean-Pierre," I susurrate. "How's the family? Dad's business going well?"

If I know my target like I think I do, Princess has probably gathered as much as she could from the girl next door. *Like my fucking address.*

I fold my lips as a peel of irritation wrings at my spine. Whatever. Being doxed is the least of my issues with her. It's not even my main home.

"I'm glad you asked," JP supplies. "My folks are great. We just finished signing a contract with a big client. And, for the umpteenth time, it's just *Psy*. Thank you," JP corrects.

I roll my eyes. "S'no way, I'm calling you that… it's pretentious."

Jean-Pierre scoffs. "The only pretentious thing here is you…" She delays, swaying her ring-decorated fingers. "With your whole *'Bad-boy'* get-up here. We were *just* talking about you, by the way." She side-eyes Abbie for a time, then glances at me and then at her.

Princess turns, blushing at thin air, and my attention on her holds.

What *were* they talking about exactly? There's a wrinkle in her nose when I'm mentioned, and it makes me grin.

"Good things, I can only hope," I add.

The air around Princess's crooked smile grows ever-so-thickly. She hides it as if remembering this is real life. Not protected behind some screen, Abbie stifles her arrogance, but it ebbs off of her in waves, like heat over an active flame.

Though I've been obsessed with tracking her down, I'll try not to let her know how much she's captured my attention here today.

The truth is, since I found her breathtaking silhouette, *every* movement she makes places me in a trance.

I spent sleepless nights filled with fits of rage, but I couldn't get enough of her or her ego. I didn't expect meeting her in person to amplify the sensation in bounds. I shouldn't even be having them. I *want* to kill her.

Time peters on, and my mind wanders. The more I observe her annoying tomboy-like charm, my mind floods with depravity. Warm images of touching her supple skin and exploring every inch of her squirming cause my pants to tent.

I massage my scalp, forcing my libido to remember how I need to tear her limb from limb. Not romance her.

"Alright, I get it," Abbie interrupts my banter with her new friend. "You two *know* each other." There's a sarcastic punch in her line I can't dissect. It sounds… envious.

"You pick up on things quick, *Princess,*" I hiss, mocking her online persona. "Having fun living the life off of my work?" I cock a brow as she physically restrains herself from grinning like a psychopath.

"Like you're in any position to speak," she retorts before crossing her bare legs over the corner of her desk.

My trachea tightens the moment my eyes trace the surface of her smooth skin, leading down to the skirt I surveyed. I'm tempted to trap her again if it means I get to bury my face between them.

JP's jaw drops, sensing the tension between us but not fully understanding it. She covers her navy-blue maw with her fingers before muttering, *"You're* Princess_User24?" She faces her with a new air as though she were a hidden celebrity. "I should have known! You speak just like her."

The accused verifies by erasing her societal mask. Easing her posture back in her chair, Abbie bares her teeth in a sly grin.

My Valentine's Virus

"You're in a hacker war against Zone right *now?*" JP presses as she leans toward her. JP's oblivious to me being the online persona, but it's not like I could even tell her if I wanted to. I've done a lot of bad things. She wouldn't look at me with admiration the same way anymore—not that I care… I hope.

Princess narrows her dark eyes over her shoulder. "I wouldn't call it anything less than a *total* takeover," she replies, her voice purposefully sultry.

Unable to ignore her heated glare, I moisten my lips and bend closely. I revel in the way she shivers at my response. "The only one doing any taking over here is *me,*" I declare. "You may have one once, but don't let it get to your head. I'll have your maneuvers read eventually."

Princess's glance flickers at my mouth before pulling away, her maple-colored eyes darkening. "It sure is trashy of you to get *that* high on a Tuesday," she snaps, her voice matching mine, colder than the Arctic.

Heat paints my scowl, swirling straight to my erection. I'm not getting under her skin with my words—no. I never have. Not *yet*. That's the thought alone keeping me coming back.

"Ahh, you think me delusional?" I smirk, playfulness evident in my voice.

"The numbers don't lie, my guy." She eases back in her chair in a patient simmer.

I shoot the shit with JP for a few minutes now that I know it bothers her. I then move on a few rows behind the girls as more students begin filling the empty seats, oblivious of the battle in the air between Princess and Zone Warden.

Her eyebrows shoot up as she jerks around to snarl up at me. She huffs, turning back around, and whips out her phone to pat furiously.

My phone vibrates, and I swipe the screen to check. I wonder who this might be. I grin at the three bumps, indicating she hasn't finished flirting with me.

[Unknown]: Get out! U r NOT a student!

[Me]: Oh, I am. As of today.

[Unknown]: The class is full and entry is barred for more students. The professor will notice and that'll waste everyone's time.

[Me]: Well, it's a good thing only ONE of us in this room is the world's #1 hacker.

[Unknown]: I HATE you.

A ball of heat rumbles in my belly from her last text. I conceal a wide grin beneath my hand, knowing I'm getting under her skin at last. It was worth relocating just to make that easier.

[Unknown]: How'd u do it? U take advantage of some driven kid and boot them? Just to enact some petty revenge??

She's giving me so much credit, I could blush.

[Me]: There's nothing petty about getting 3 billion bucks back.

[Unknown]: Whatevr. Only a prim asshole like u would ruin someone else's life to justify ur own gain.

[Me]: This how you speak? To the man who made you cum so hard, your eyes rolled into your skull like a slot machine? Are your legs still trembling with need for me, Princess? Or should I remind you how good I feel inside of you?

My Valentine's Virus

[Unknown]: What happened to not letting luck get to ur head? Any moron could tell I was just ovulating. Obviously. I hardly call that an accomplishment. You sound so proud of it too. It's really sad.

I smirk. *That's not the insult she thinks it is,*

[Me]: Brat.

[Unknown]: STFU! What happened to that missing student??

[Me]: Early graduation. The school's system has a completed list of every student accounted for who's signed up. They also always have at least a "John Doe" or "Student X" hidden in their code in case one of the faculty misses a student. Sometimes paperwork gets lost, files get stuck in between cabinets, and some student's histories just disappear. So, to prevent lawsuits when brought up by the Student X's of the school, they just replace that hidden name with theirs and say they've graduated.

[Unknown]: Ur full of it. Do u honestly expect me to believe that the people in charge wouldn't check with the professors?

[Me]: You expect a single professor to remember the exact names and faces of four hundred students? Half of these geriatric dinosaurs can't recall what they had for breakfast that morning, Abigail.

[Unknown]: Is that how you graduated? How else would u know about this unless you were snooping around?

[Me]: Precocious little rival, aren't you? But no. Am I still the asshole?

Silence stretches on her end, and I glance down at her, frozen in place. She huffs before resting her phone in her sweater pocket, bringing out my smile. *Super transparent.* The cutest thing is how she thinks she's hiding it. What a fucking dork.

As several students arrive, I offer the ones who greet me with an inspecting glance. A few familiar faces offer small waves and nods of respect before staking claim to their seats. I return their starstruck gestures with fist bumps and forced smirks.

The rest of the room falls silent except for the claps of rummaging of notes and birds cawing outside. Princess and JP continue their exchanges until the professor enters the lab room.

My little rival shoots me cautious glimpses now and then as if carefully choosing which questions to ask Psyra. Following her around, I'm getting to see just how conniving she is. I didn't account for the fact that she even knew how to find JP.

She may not know everything about me, but JP's family and mine have roots. Her mother helped design my parents' mansion, and they've been in contact ever since.

I knew her daughter had an interest in computer science but not enough to think she'd finally go through with the education. Horrible timing.

Entering the hall is Professor Saito—another familiar face. Long dark hair knots behind his head, and he appears as though he hasn't aged since I graduated at sixteen. He's strict but fair, always demanding excellence from his students. He was the only one who wasn't a pain in the ass.

After his introduction to the course and what's expected, he introduces Melanie Mayor moments later. My eyes narrow into slits. I was so lost in space on what Abbie's next moves were that I didn't notice the headmaster's spawn ogling me the entire time.

My chest tightens, and I brace myself not to let her bland expression take me back to that dark place a year ago. Her icy gaze pins at my skin,

My Valentine's Virus

forcing my face to run cold. Opting for my focus, my eyes drift back to Abbie while she snickers like a mischievous little ant.

Her curious pupils search for me in the crowd, unsure if I've left yet. The moment Abbie finds my stare on her, her body shrinks, and she yanks the sweater on her head.

A warm laugh trickles from me, and I lean over my desk to adore her. It's hard not to. My pulse races when I reminisce on her terrified whimpers echoing in my mind and forcing my balls to ache.

Melanie drags on about her involvement with the school, but I can't help but grow annoyed by how she and her mother share strong similarities. They love hearing themselves talk and torturing others to hear them.

During the brief lecture, my mind wanders again. I can't help but be proud of the disconnect from her in a short period. I overhear Princess and JP mock her openly, mimicking her lines and ad-libbing the rest in their little world.

Abbie shows her a more open gesture when she finishes stroking her ego. "Hey, Melanie, it's nice to meet you. I heard you're a big fan of classical music?" Abbie inquires. The last thing I want is for those two to team up in some way.

Melanie looks at Abbie with a haunted taut face, nearly taken back by her existence here. It takes her a moment longer to respond. "Actually, I prefer more *refined* selections, like opera," she replies in a superior tone.

JP snickers, and Abbie appears to be fighting back a chuckle herself. She fans JP. "I told you she—" the bubblier of the three mutters.

"Ssh," Abbie grins before facing Melanie again. "You're... *sure* opera is your favorite?"

Melanie's brows point upward. "What nonsensical game are you playing?"

Abbie scoffs, "Opera-*deez nuts.*" She crosses her arms behind her head before arching back in her chair. JP dabs and rests her giggling head on her desk like a drunk. Their stupidity makes me lose control of a laugh, and my core tightens from the act.

Most of the class finds amusement in her childish joke except Melanie. Rolling her eyes, Princess gives away her stance on the humor, but a semblance of a smile pokes at her lips.

The professor tries redirecting the conversation, but the tension is already thick in the space.

Abbie's subtle giggles hum in my ears, making my shoulders ease. The laugh she has is so fucking weird. It's like a cross between a donkey and a choking puppet.

I hide my grin behind my hand as Melanie glares up at me. I'm giggling. We're giggling. The rest of the posse, I gathered giggles, too.

While at odds with the other students, she displays herself like the perfect little doll she's known for on the outside. But beneath her calculated facade lies a vile wolf waiting for the hunt.

The professor opens his mouth to speak on Melanie's behalf, but we all seem to hate Melanie for different reasons.

I agree; the headmaster's daughter did not deserve that. I wouldn't put it passed her to make everyone pay attention to the lack of attention.

Princess and I snicker together from afar. The warmth of our distant bond overpowers me. Her cat-like smile deserves to be a tattoo design, immortalizing her smug power.

I can only guess what a girl like Melanie would do to you, Princess. But rest assured, the only one that'll be your undoing is me.

[Me]: I hope your swimming is better than your sense of humor.

[Unknown]: Eat a mile of dicks.

Technical note from Professor Kaiser: Doxing is when someone (an enemy) searches for your sensitive information and advertises it to the universe for anyone

My Valentine's Virus

and everyone to see. It's done without the victim's consent *and is seen as a filthy form of illegal revenge.*

LEVEL EIGHT
PRINCESS_USER24

When I was a little girl, a single thunderclap taught me how fragile our universe is.

We had a forestscape of a backyard that held the most beautiful orange fruit tree in the world. She had shiny leaves, attracted flocks of rainbow-colored birds, and the fattest squirrels you can imagine.

I'd spend every afternoon playing on the swing Dad installed on a branch. When those intense summers gave their worst, she'd provide cool shade, and I'd catch its fallen fruit. The sweet stings of orange juice quenched my mouth, and I can still remember its unique flavor to this day.

After Hurricane Orion plowed through, everything changed. The bastard uprooted our tree and left our beloved house in ruins. In the aftermath, I awoke to the heart-wrenching cries of my father. Damp, chilly air left me numb as I found Mom's lifeless body, her tangled raven hair matted with the rain spilling in from the giant hole in the roof. The tragic loss left a gaping hole in our family. I don't remember much, but

My Valentine's Virus

I always admired how, even then, my father placed my needs above his grief.

I drift deep into my memory of the time we spent in the motel. It was a mildew-scented room with yellow-brown walls and old furniture. The vending machines contributed to my stomach aches after having free reign of them outside.

Sitting me down in our run-down motel room, Dad made us a promise after the tragedy.

"Listen, Abuelita," Dad's voice choked with emotion. He always called me his *little grandma,* swearing I looked exactly like the woman who raised him. "I'm going to be working more hours from now on." His brown eyes soften before looking at me in mine. "I need you to do the same with your schoolwork. We must try making it without... making it without Ana."

I nodded, wrapping my good arm around him to provide what little comfort I could. "I promise."

"Bueno," he praised, giving me a warm kiss on my hairline. "My brave, strong girl." His red eyes were full of sorrow and depleted whenever they landed on the stitchwork on my forehead. They then shifted toward the neon-pink arm cast I got to choose at the hospital that day.

I can't remember a time I felt so respected at that age. My father and I were a team. He wasn't going to let our tragedies define us. He knew what had to be done for us to survive, and he was going to try. That was all I could have asked for.

There I was, with a magic marker and colorful paper I swiped from school the next morning. I created a twenty-year plan for myself as if I could look directly into the future and picture it like a reel.

I was so proud of it. The minute I finished, I'd wait for my dad to come home from work, and we would compare notes.

I swayed back and forth on one of the motel chairs, watching Dad flip through the papers. Rubbing his dark beard, I found a break in his stoic expression as he handed me back the papers. "You can't get married at *seventeen,* Abuelita. How about fifty when I'm dead and don't know them?" Dad joked, passing me a red crayon.

His honest smile returned a little more each day, and that's how I knew we were going to make it.

Then, one day, news reporters swarmed in to film the remains of our home. The most devastated house in the city. That's when Dad broke down on live television.

The backlash triggered everyone in the community's generosity, and in little time at all, our neighbors and absolute strangers helped raise money to bring our heads out of homelessness.

We got a brand-new house in the town over. I got to go to the best schools in the state. We gave Mom an amazing, elegant funeral, and it all felt like things were moving faster than I expected, and I needed to revise my script.

We were moving on. Everything was fine without her. But something dark festered in me the moment things got better. A strange… annoyance with my father grew.

I don't think I could have verbalized it at my age then. Maybe not even now, but I was the only one who kept our promise.

He accepted the cash—other people's hard work. There's been a rock at the pit of my stomach for even feeling this way for years. I don't know if it's guilt tearing into me. Disgust maybe? Trust issues? Whatever it is, it feels gross.

I know being a single-grieving father is a challenge. I know anybody would have accepted as many handouts as they could because, well… he needed it.

But the disappointment lingered on for years, and I didn't know how to deal with it. It fueled a deep-rooted spree of competitiveness, and that spring of crazy got me to absolutely crush the educational system. Everything I could turn into a contest, I did. I excelled in martial arts and clubs—everything I was passionate about. I didn't care if it meant I

My Valentine's Virus

skipped out on having friends. They couldn't compete with me anyway. So why would I?

I was driven not only by Mom's memory but also by the desire to prove I could hold the weight of both promises. Most importantly, I wanted to establish my capabilities to the universe that dared take her away from us.

Now, I face a new challenge today.

I've dealt with a handful of annoying stalkers before, but this is ridiculous. I grit my teeth as I fight the urge to glare back at my newest one.

I mean—did he really need to enroll in my fucking class? What does he have to earn by doing this? I don't care. But from *his* perspective, I can't see how this benefits him at all.

As he and Psy catch up on lost time, his voice softens, and his smile is pursed, making my throat dry up. It's not just his looks that always catch my eye. It's the way he laces each of his lines with an icy husk that surges to my core.

I need to lose my V-card before I succumb to *his* type. For heaven's sake. Why couldn't the nerd just *look* like a nerd?

Professor Saito continues his boring lesson about the history of block chaining and the basics before getting to the juice. I find myself tuning out. I've already brushed up on most of what he's saying, but it's at least a revitalizing refresher knowing what I've learned on my own is still pertinent.

I sigh after scanning each student's head in accidental admiration as they hurry, jotting down every word.

Psy is stroking her lapis choker to my right, giving her studies 110%. Given how fast she's scripting, I doubt she can even read her handwriting.

I came in today expecting to find newer rivals to break, but it's been pretty mellow besides everything from earlier. Fighting off the urge to look over my shoulder at my actual threat, I pout in my chair.

♡

He *would* sit where I can't spy on him spying on me. Taking out my phone, I cover the glass with my hand so the dark screen can show me what Xalton's up to from behind.

To my surprise, his reflection is equally as bored and disengaged as I am. *Of course.* I'm not sure if I expected him to rub his hands together like a villainous fly, snickering, or whatever.

I break and look over my shoulder to see him give me his resigned glare. He raises his thumb over his neck and swipes the air, signaling he's going to end me.

I scoff in my seat, showcasing my middle finger to him.

Professor Saito asks the class about the potential vulnerabilities of a new blockchain network, and my hand emerges high to answer.

Before the jerk in the back row is even called on, he answers instead. "Well, it's obvious the consensus mechanism could be compromised through a Sybil attack," Xalton answers, winking my way and triggering my frown. "And don't even get me started on the potential for 51% strikes."

His fans applaud him, and I nearly snap my pen in half.

"Puh-*lease,*" I blurt out at the risk of looking feral. Turning toward him seated, I tilt my chair back in a harsh lean. "Xalton gave us a *basic* answer. It's the equivalent of training wheels."

He rolls his eyes smoothly. "Well, I highly doubt *you* could even execute one properly."

"Oh really? I expected something more advanced coming from the world's largest innovator of software tech," I shoot back with a thick laugh. "Because last I checked, I *successfully* infiltrated EctoPhantom's network using an *advanced* Sybil attack, bypassing his security system." That's the short version of how I did it, but he doesn't need to know my artistry. "Now he shares a toilet with a thousand other men," I add, twisting the knife.

Xalton's homeboys tense up beside him, exchanging a series of revelated looks and whispers.

My Valentine's Virus

Xalton himself, to my confusion, wears a small smirk in the crux of his mouth. "I'm so sure you're still riding on the high of that victory. It couldn't happen a second time." He crosses his arms, and my brow hikes in response.

"Oh, you want me to prove it? I'll show you just how easily I can take down any network you throw my way."

The eyes of everyone in class pounce from Xalton to me like a ping-pong match. We continue debating various techniques and strategies, each one more complex than the next.

Professor Saito tries to interject, but neither of us can stop. We want to prove our superiority over each other just like we're in front of a computer.

Before I know it, I'm panting. He sure as hell looks cooler than me in his seat back there. I must admit, as silly as we seem, this is a great way to burn stress.

I cut to the professor. "Professor, would you mind if we borrowed the projection screen for a minute?" I ask, already approaching the board. "I need to prove a point."

Professor Saito shrugs meekly. "Uh—sure." He steps back, motioning his hand where he stands.

Bending over to the professor's setup, my eyebrows push up in admiration. These computers are sent from heaven or maybe hell, considering the cost of even holding these babies.

It wastes no time loading. After a crescendo of hurried keyboard play, I present the screen to shove Zone's stupid face in it.

"Xalton, if you would please address the board." I cock my head with elegant superiority. Using an alternative line of code, I bypass others for what's needed. I'm careful not to showcase my methods in case someone else steals the idea.

The atmosphere is ripe with heat. Both our fat heads soak up the oxygen in the space. Scribbles from other students jotting down what we say escalate as background music to our fight.

My heart pounds against my sternum as I witness Xalton's cold face twist with exertion. I swear I spot a glimmer of pride shining in them, and my face heats.

"It hurts, doesn't it? Being *wrong*," I sprinkle in the tease, the corners of my grin nearly damaging my cheekbones.

A vein appears in Xalton's neck. Rolling his jaw, he saunters out of his seat to approach the front with me.

As if Professor Saito can sense the heated tension coming off Xalton's body—whether it's violence, passion, or mirth, he gets in between us. "L-let me go over what you did to the class for a minute, eh?" The professor raises his hand in front of Xalton's torso as my pinning glare weighs on him, my smug grin refusing to wane.

Xalton's shoulders ease as he tilts his head back. *"You* haven't won anything." He voices tightly. Facing our professor, he tries to appear less like a nuclear reactor. "Professor, I appreciate your patience. Taking a few more minutes of your time would be beneficial for everyone involved. You have my word."

Professor Saito nods thankfully at him before stepping aside with me.

Xalton gives me a look as he assesses me. I can't translate, but it's fiery and inhuman. I've been waiting for moments like this forever— that energy of not giving in to defeat.

While a part of me feels a twinge of guilt for turning Professor Saito's class into a battleground for our egos, his intrigued smirk suggests he doesn't mind.

Judging the students' visions engage with each of Xalton's explanations and jabs, it's clear everyone's eager to watch our clash unfold too. And even though my hands tremble when Xalton double-checks the networks I traveled to, I'm going to give him and everyone else a great show.

Zone_Warden's third defeat against me is right around the corner.

My Valentine's Virus

Our butting nature drives us to push our limits, but before either of us submits—not *me*, of course, the noon bell chimes, echoing through our ears to dismiss us.

What absolute nonsense. We were only going at it for five freaking minutes. Pausing, my eyes narrowed tightly at the clock in the center of the room. *It is indeed noon.* That sucks.

There's no clear winner, but that doesn't prevent Xalty-boy from shooting me an ironic salute in the end.

When we each depart from the classroom, he brushes past me, making me lose the grip of my bag strap. He glances over his broad shoulder with his motions, half out of revulsion and parts playful.

I adjust a piece of hair behind my ear before fighting back the fluttering gathering in my abs. His sultry stare should be illegal.

A pale hand emerges from nowhere and grabs my wrist.

Melanie approaches me outside the room and loosens her grip after seeing me wince. "Abbie, I apologize about our first meeting in the powder room. It was childish of me to take my irritations out on a stranger. I only hope we can put all that behind us."

Oh? That was... oddly pleasant. Remorse for mocking her earlier settles in my stomach like rotting soup. However, I didn't expect everyone to find my stupid joke funny. I wasn't even loud.

Xalton and his goon squad clearly didn't help with his laughter. I don't know if I could have stopped them, but there's just something about his laugh. It's the kind you only hear in video games, usually by the attractive villain. It's wasted on him.

Melanie stares at me in my daze. "What is your... relationship with Xalton, if you don't mind?"

I grimace. "Ew... relationship? We don't *have* a relationship. There's no relationship. I met the loser to*day*. Thinks he's above me when it's the other way around. I only want to help him see it." I pout, aiming not to look as smug as I sound.

"Look. Just watch yourself around him," Melanie snaps. "He may seem charming on the outside, but you don't want to cross him."

Oh, hon. I've *since* known.

I rolled my eyes heavily. "You're funny. I'm *eight* times as charming and more of a threat to him than he is to me. But thanks, Mels. I appreciate the talk. I'm sorry about before, by the way. It was awkward, and I didn't plan to have everyone laughing at us like that. So yeah, I'm looking forward to our semester together or whatever. I'll see you around." I pat her on the shoulder and wave as I pass her, excited to be reunited with the beauty of this school again.

Sashaying through the hall, I brake and turn my feet to admire the world I'm in, collecting every distraction.

Stealing my ebbing nerves away is the design of a bustling Crimson Raven University Hall.

The stonework of the dark walls is intricately carved with Gothic details of a gargoyle battle. As my pace slows, my soul takes in the glistening grotesques peering out of each crevice. The hall is vast, with high ceilings and stained-glass windows that are clear and colorful like candy.

The walls are lined with black knight suits of armor, and the marble floors are polished with swirls of obsidian and ruby pooling around like cyclones under my feet. It's a sharp contrast to the normal schools I'm accustomed to.

The reflection of my bare ass says hi to me, and I'm hoping no one else.

There's no way I was going to let Xalton or Melanie scare me. Mel's words *are* nagging at me a bit as I walk inside the locker room. Xalton's voice echoes in my ear.

"I now know where you stay, where you eat… and where you sleep."

What the hell's he gonna do? If he tries to ruin my food *or* my dreams, I'll punch him in the stones. I don't care if his biceps removed the function of my knees.

My Valentine's Virus

[Unknown]: URGENT: Skip ur P.E. course tomorrow. U have a target on you.

I raise a brow at the message appearing on my screen. This isn't how Xalton texts. I know him well enough to discern that at this point.

Who is this? I glance at the hallway for anyone whose eyes lock with mine, but no one does. An eerie sensation looms against my shoulders. I don't know what's going down, but one thing's for sure. I'm definitely not going to do that.

LEVEL NINE
PRINCESS_USER24

After *Xalton* took up the sweet professor's time, Psy and I arranged to share boardrooms through our campus app.

She complained about being alone in hers, and I figured someone else could help remove me from my introverted slumps.

I packed up my things, and she made room for me in a sizeable space that puts basic NYC apartments to shame. Psy has more things, and her place is in a better position than my old room. It'll also trip up a certain stalker of mine.

We had to go through Melanie, though, since I found out she's the board chairwoman.

I carry the last of my things and say goodbye. I'm still unsure what I need with a box of spare computer wires and upgrades, so I rest it on my side of our room. Psy and I hike toward the mess hall. I'm sure it will be anything but sloppy. I bet the food served on campus is to die for. Since I get paranoid in crowds, I haven't had the chance to indulge in them.

My Valentine's Virus

Having caught up from her phone call, Psy nudges me with her elbow. "Yo, babe. So, what *was* stopping you and Xalton from tearing each other's clothes off back there?" she brings up now that she has me trapped.

I cringe away from her knowing gaze and flirting brow raises. *"Ah. Stop it."* Covering my face, I race down the hall.

I admit I'm in a good mood after watching Zone get all worked up in real-time. The way his jaw muscles clench, the murderous rage in the depths of his eyes. That tight expression of restraint on his face when all he wants to do is strangle me—it's so soul-quenching.

Giggling in her jog, Psy catches up to me and yanks my bag strap. She hugs her stomach, whether from laughter or the mild exercise. "Listen. Hear me out. If this ends up being an enemies-to-lovers situation, can you promise you won't break poor Xalt's heart?"

"Ex-squeeze me?" I blurt out before thinking.

This is borderline treachery.

I massage my face. The overwhelming ache in them begging to be stopped. What makes her think he's even into me that way? He thinks I'm his plaything, and I barely mind it. It's not that I *don't* see myself with him long-term. I just don't see myself with anybody at this stage in my life. Even if he is the only man I'd want. Also, I'm half-certain he wants to kill me. Something about that gravitates me to that flame more than anything, and I don't know why. It may just be because it's a challenge.

"I'm not here for rom*ances*. I'm here for *adv*ances," I enunciate as she awaits my response.

Psy returns an odd look with her brow arched at me. "Eh. Couldn't hurt," she dismisses and hugs my arm like we're dating.

While promenading along the darkened halls, I have a content sigh. It's sweet being in Psyra's presence. She's warm and smells like a cherry blossom festival blew up. I'm usually prickly when it comes to other people, but she makes me feel like I'm a teddy bear prize she won at a carnival.

♥

It's hard for me to admit, but I've never had a friendship I've looked forward to before, even if I'm sort of using her to get dirt on Xalton.

Psy sucks her teeth. "His last relationship... well. It's not my place to say, but it didn't end as he imagined."

I scoff. "What many do?"

Melting in the moment, we're surrounded by gorgeous ruby glass windows in honeycomb shapes of our stroll.

Entering the cafeteria feels like entering the gates of a Valhalla hub. The mosaic-styled ceiling soars overhead too high, and with little details carved into it, I might hurt my neck.

Psyra smiles at my face gluing to it, and she has to pull me further inside before I fall backward.

There aren't a lot of students eating at this hour—some are here just to study in an open space that isn't as deafeningly quiet as a library. The echoes of feet clapping along and simmering dishes from random cultures take up the space.

Crimson and onyx marble tables align the reflective floors, and every part of me becomes an art enthusiast to the pieces I find catching me off guard. Knight statues and gargoyles dance along the ceiling of colorful mosaics. *Ugh.* I'd marry this campus if I could.

After lunch, Psy and I head back to the women's dormitory, and my feet halt in their tracks at the end of the hall. Psy bumps into my back and searches my line of sight.

Xalton Kaiser leans against the wall like he isn't Xalton goddamn Kaiser. His hood hides his face from sight as his eyes are glued to his phone screen. People traverse by him left and right and wave without him returning the gesture.

His eyes tighten on his screen, and I'm half curious to know what he's looking at. He found my new place a little too quickly.

I squint, trying to think of an alternative route without letting him confirm I live here.

My Valentine's Virus

Psy continues toward our room while I remain in place. "I'll catch you inside. I gotta study." She waves to Xalton out of courtesy, and he barely raises his face to greet her.

He waves after she closes the door behind her and raises his head when I vacate.

I speed around the hall, careful enough that I can slip away. My throat dries the moment combat boots pound after me.

"Abbie," the masculine voice calls out.

I hurry my steps, sprinting around the hallway.

With cautious and quick footing, I leap over someone's move-in box littering the corner of the second hall I scurry into. My palms sweat as I dig for my keys and yank them out to open our door.

Xalton's footsteps are on top of mine, and my heart pounds in my ears. Adrenaline shoots up my spine the moment I unlock and barge into my new room.

Psy, already deep in her studies, waves over her shoulder as I grasp my bed sheets.

I tie a confident knot at the end of her heavy antique dresser with the sheet and hurry to open the large window of our room in the center. Climbing out from the third second-story window, the autumnal breeze caresses my hair. Using the bedsheet as a makeshift rope, I put my skills to the test and scaled down the exterior wall. The door opens from above, and I grin because I'm only a leap away from the ground floor.

I snicker, looking up at Xalton and glaring down at me. Raising my middle fingers, I secure my bag strap and stride away. I can study at Cupid Café while I'm out. It's only a two-mile walk and—"

"You think you're so clever," a deep voice tsks from behind.

My eyes fly open, and I spin, finding Xalton already on my tail.

What the fuck?! How did he get to me this quickly?!

He grins wide, that damning expression stunning me before I'm hurled from his tackle. He fumbles against the ground, and I grunt while his body absorbs the butt of our fall.

♡

I'm more concerned over the well-being of my war machine in my bag, but his arms bound me like a rubber band on lobster claws. Facing the blue sky, I wrestle against his bear hug.

"Get off!" I growl and hurl both legs, Halasana yoga style. He arches his head from my landing before pulling me back against him. I gasp hard while his lips stroke the shell of my ear from under me. Heat flutters up my skin as a blush pinches my face. *He's zapped my strength just from that?*

"Which dojo did you train in? I might know your sensei. Do you mind giving me their number?" He casually sparks.

"1-800-UP-YOURS!" I reel my head back to strike his face and grit my teeth at the harsh crack of cartilage.

He physically winces, but not enough to lower his strengths. When I go for a second headbutt, he yanks me under him.

I grunt, kicking, pulling, but before I realize it, he has my hands pinned above my head. A hot drip triggers my panicked haze, and it clears once I find his face coated in blood. Did I break Zone's nose? My breath hitches, and he takes that moment to smile down at me, crimson flooding his teeth.

"What's that face you're making?" he lowers his head over me. "Are you worried about me, Princess?" he purrs.

Does he not feel pain? "Well, yeah. It's not exactly comforting," I counter. I shouldn't even care this much. Yeah, he's hot, but he's also trying to murder me. I focus on my breathing, but it's easier said than done, however. He's a man made of stone. His ability to overpower me makes me feel small, and I hate it.

Gritting my teeth, I reflect on how I've always been bigger than everyone on the inside. I stand up to bullies and those small-minded losers who rally to defend their actions. I view people as individuals and not by the bodies they inhabit. It's the ones with character, minds, and ambition that are scarce in many circles—none to rival me. It's eaten me up inside and made me feel like an outcast for it.

My Valentine's Virus

I'm like the sun, and I burn up anything that can't handle my rays. I am an inferno of *me*. I am Princess_User24, and this is not the end of my story.

Finding the glint in my eye, Xalton releases my wrist. "You're thinking of fifty different ways to grind my balls into dust, aren't you?" he queries. "Are you *that* mad?"

"You won't even get to *see* me mad," I bite.

He laughs like I'm joking, and I huff to settle the raging flames circling within me. "You're so mean to me. I thought you said I was your hero. It touched my heart."

"Fuck you!"

He shakes his head near mine. "Oh, Princess. You know how hard your voice gets me. What do you think swearing does?"

Before he finishes his sentence, something hard grows between us.

"Maybe I should remind you again, but with my cock. I'd love tearing right through that virgin pussy of yours."

My calm breath stalls. "H-How do you even *know* that—?" I squeak. *Fucking kill me.*

He snickers. "I didn't."

"*Arugh!*" My face heats to my ears, and I find the power to wrestle him around. Tilting my posture, I have Zone under me in a second. His tired pupils roam over me as I heave labored breaths.

He leans back, crossing his arms behind his head like he's waiting to be entertained.

My brows crease tighter when he cocks his brow as if to say, "Well, I'm waiting?"

I pout, somehow the creepy crawlies of insecurity filling itself into me. His erection throbs under my hips, and I avoid the eyes of passersby shooting us uncomfortable stares.

I bet this looks bad, but it's not like anyone lifted a finger when they saw him tackle me to the grass.

Raising my middle fingers, I swing around like a lawn sprinkler as Xalton rumbles in hysterics under me. The density of his abdominal muscles clenches, and I focus on his heated gaze.

I grip the collar of his shirt and lean into his face. Our lips don't touch but escalating heat bounces from his to mine as our noses touch.

A touch of red paints his face as he works a swallow.

Verifying what my body does to him, a devious smile adorns my face, and I release my hold. With confidence flooding back to me, I get into a stand and give him both middle fingers as I walk away.

"Enjoy your blue balls!" I begin sprinting.

"I won't…" he mutters.

LEVEL TEN
PRINCESS_USER24

[Unknown]: URGENT: Skip ur P.E. course tomorrow. U have a target on you.

I spent all night using every ounce of expertise to track down who sent this message, but to my luck, it was untraceable. My frown pinches, and my jaw unclenches. I bet Zone could've figured it out if I asked him, him being Mr. Number One and all. *The jackass would probably have me beg.*

I shove my phone on my nightstand and roll over into my crisp covers for some sleep. Hours into the night, I wake from a nightmare involving my mom. What's worse is I can't remember any of it. All I have to go on are shivers, sweat, and tears staining my pillow.

I painfully glance at Psyra's side of the room. She slept with her pillow covering her face and ears. A pit of guilt drills deep into my abdomen,

She groans from her side. I lift my pillow over my head and throw it at her. She catches it in mid-air and lets it fall flat against the floor. *"Yes, I'm awake.* Can't you masturbate quietly?"

"Pfft! Is that what you thought I was doing—?"

"Girl, I don't know," she interrupts. "I was too afraid to ask."

"But not enough to accuse?"

"That's right. I went with the *lazier* option," she bemoans into her pillow. "What is it?"

"I was having a nightmare. Like... an intense one."

"Mercy me," she sighs before sitting up and I squint from the blinding sheen off her black robe. "That makes so much more sense. You were moaning and groaning about your 'mommy' all night. I was debating to find a hotel room." Unfolding her duvet cover, she wipes her eyes awake. Psy slumps from her bed like a zombie and reaches for her electric candle lighter on her nightstand. "Okay, let's perform a quick seance while we're up," she yawns, gesturing for me to hurry.

Who just has seances? Who just nonchalantly brings up calling the dead like we're making a long-distance call?

"Psy." I raise my palms to her, but she keeps lighting candles in a semi-circle. Setting them in the center on the hardwood floor, she then fixes her yoga mat at a cautious distance. *"Psyra,"* I whine. Psy saunters to her dresser and removes a small wooden bowl. She then piles jewels, flowers, and other offerings I can't identify in the dark.

"Psyra," I plead. "Normal people don't do seances. That's spooky shit. I've seen too many movies about this *exact* thing going wrong—"

She scoffs exaggeratedly at me as if I'm a scruffy child. "Girl, if you don't sit your dump truck ass down here, I'm going to be haunting *you*." She closes her eyes and gets into her meditative pose on her mat. "...Ruining my sleep. ...Nightmare-having bitch," she grumbles under her voice.

My Valentine's Virus

My head cocks back in laughter at her irritated babbles. "Please don't summon anything from *The Nun*. I've already got enemies on this plain of existence."

"Shut *uup*," she groans.

"Fine." I am too tired to argue, and she's already set up. I cast another once-over at her intricate placements. I'll trust she knows what she's doing—I owe her that much after everything I put her through. My shoulders sag, and I mirror her position on the floor.

Psyra starts her hums and chants, and I try to humble myself to the powers of the universe. I could totally take it on, though.

An hour into the ceremony, she advises I shut my eyes in case I haven't already, and then she chants my mom's name.

We wait. All supernatural and common sense aside, this is pretty fun. *I understand why some people do this.* At least, that's what I think until the air around us grows colder and heavy. As Psyra continues her chants for her summon, it's as though several people are in the same room with us.

It's odd to explain.

The otherworldly sensation curls up my spine, but something tells me not to open my eyes yet. My body refuses to.

The moment her candles all flick out by a sudden gust, my eyes fly open to check the window. I already know it's locked tight, but the draft is so dense in here, it has me second-guessing. Swallowing hard, my neck hairs raise, but the waves vanish before it stays, like a cooling mist.

Psyra opens her eyes, lowering her shoulders and tilting her head with an apologetic look as she gathers her words. "I don't know how to say this, Abbie. But your mom's not… picking up."

I roll my eyes after wasting an hour of sleep on this. "That's what I get for believing," I quip, getting to my feet and turning my back to her.

Psyra shoots a less-than-bubbly glare at my *Invader Zim* PJs. "You're just cranky. You don't mean that."

"Yeah? Well, you're goofy," I grumble and yank my covers over my face.

I catch her smirk before she continues the end of her meditation practice in silence.

An hour and a half in, and I still can't sleep.

[Unknown]: URGENT: Skip your P.E. course tomorrow. You have a target on you.

This message has been digging a hole in my brain ever since I received it.

I don't know anyone else at this school who would go out of their way to warn me. It wouldn't be Psyra. She would just be straight up with me.

With that logic, it's definitely not from Xalton either.

I bring up my issue with Psyra, and she offers to walk with me to our early morning course. After that, she finds me for a quick meal, and we make our way toward P.E.

Psy pauses a few feet away from the women's locker room entrance. "Listen, don't take this the wrong way. You… remind me of this kid named Tex I'd babysit. She felt like a little sister to me. For some reason, she couldn't admit when she needed help with anything. She was bullied a lot because of who her dad was and…"

Psy winces while immersed in her tale. "Tex shouldered the brunt of the abuse meant for *him*," she finishes, leaving my heart writhing.

The idea of anyone harming an innocent child makes me want to set the world on fire and have the Earth start over again.

Psy's eyes glance into the distance, replacing the glow in them with something so deep in the past that she leaves me behind in the present. She then hides that gaze in me. "If you ever need help with anything, I'm a text away, 'kay?"

My Valentine's Virus

"Christ." I stare at her for a beat, then adjust the strap of my bag back on my shoulder. "*Ominous*, much?"

She lightly punches my arm in retort and removes her phone to tap away frantically. "C'mon, you can do it. Say, *'Okay, Psy.'*"

"Okay, Psy! I'll reach out more, but I'm not Tex. You can ease up." My face sours from being compared to a kid, but I shake it away since it came from a place of love.

A withering smirk crosses her pouting lips. Waving at me, still engaged in her device, she massages the purple gem of her choker. Psy's worried brows shift to a stoic state. "Hey, go ahead without me," she groans as her lips pull in. "My dad's been worried sick about his business contract. I need to touch base with him ASAP, but I'll catch up with you on the way," she explains as urgency spikes in her purposefully rushed tone.

Seeing her depart from this girly ball of giggles to a full-blown business monarch is a reality shake for a bit.

"Sure thing," I respond. My shoulders lower as my attention sways back in our direction. "I'll see you inside—*Wait.*"

Psy answers a phone call before walking off.

"Is Tex still alive?" I ask, growing aware she didn't finish her tale. Accepting how her small figure was too far to hear me, I let it go and stumble into the pool's corridor. An immaculate view of the CRU pool grounds demands my attention.

And my god, this place continues to be a fairytale.

The faint scent of chlorine in the air heightens the more I proceed. I traverse a walkway of onyx and red tile crafted by someone's meticulous obsession. My path beckons me into this realm of gothic decadence, immersing me in an atmosphere of grandeur.

Soft rays of light filter through stained glass panels, casting kaleidoscopic patterns onto the stone pavement. The vibrant hues dance, forming a tapestry, captivating my every step.

The closer I draw, the more my heart sings at a wall-length window, that showcases where my next class will take place.

Beyond the windowpane to my right, that unveils to me like an aquarium, lies an enormous black swimming pool. Beneath the lights, it glistens like liquid charcoal.

Intricate stone carvings adorn its borders, with more mythical creatures frozen in stone. Pure beauty and refinement are wrapped up here in harmonious excellence.

As I fall more in love with the school, someone tries to steal my attention. "Hey, Abigail?" a tall, self-assured blond with effortlessly tousled hair approaches.

The weight of Xalton's intense stare, even without looking directly at him, sends a prickling sensation that glides up my spine. My eyes fix on my rival's torso above the water, praying my expression stays unamused.

With his piercing gaze locked onto me, Zone leans against the pool's edge, waiting for me, it seems. With the muscles of freaking Hercules, Xalton's arms fold over the ledge.

"I'm Augustus Astor," the stranger introduces, veering my line of sight from him. "Gus, for short." Gus' smile reveals a set of perfect teeth that add more to his charm. At first glance, Gu seems comfortable in his skin, and he exudes an air of self-assurance that's hard to ignore. There's no denying he's a looker, but as I've learned, it's not enough to grade a person's intentions.

"You heading to the pool too?" he asks, trying to keep up with me.

I nod. "Why?"

"Do you mind if I walk with you? I could use the exercise and the *company*," he winks, showing off his dimple as a last resort to melt my stone expression.

It worked.

"Sure," I shrug nonchalantly. Maybe I have been on edge lately, but I can make more friends.

My Valentine's Virus

We stroll toward the pool, and Gus nudges me. "Have you heard the one about the mathematician who's afraid of negative numbers and winter?"

"What?" I raise an eyebrow at his attempt to set up a joke. "Can't say I have. Go ahead, impress me."

"Well, he'd yell, *'Stop! I refuse to go below zero!'*"

I give him a courtesy snicker. "Clever, but not blowing my mind."

"Fair. Fair. Okay. Last one. How about the scientist who tried making a soul-sucking vacuum?"

I shake my head as he struggles to keep up with my pace. "Go for it, bro."

"He gave it his best shot, but all it did was suck up the dirt and leave behind a bunch of dirty *souls!*"

God, his jokes are fucking awful. I love them.

"I was in the last class where you crushed Kaiser. You're exceptionally bright, you know? Passionate too. Stealing the lecture just to prove a point? Alpha moves," Gus flatters.

"Yeah, it's a curse," I hide a strand of hair behind my ear, looking down at my feet, of all things.

Gus walks closer to me, but I keep my distance, growing overwhelmed by the attention.

"You're *really* beautiful too," he went on.

"Yeah, it's a curse," I repeat. I break my steps. "Listen. I appreciate the company, but I'm not interested in you that way." I finally say. "Are we cool?"

He nods acceptingly. "Of course. Thanks for breaking that out early. Any reason in particular? If you don't mind me asking—"

"I don't date," I bluntly state. "But I'm rooting for you, bruh." I raise my hand for a casual high five.

As the light in my eyes fades, Gus snorts before missing my hand and running his fingers down the back of his head.

♥

"Rooting for *me?*" He repeats, then brings up his white t-shirt, unveiling his tan six-pack. I hardly buffer with how naked he got. "There's no need, doll." Whipping the fabric over his shoulder, he flexes his perfect torso muscles, with his grin growing the more frozen I become. "Not with *these* pecks."

My eyes identify his silver dog tags bouncing against his built chest and the etching of his red uniformed bathing shorts. They tell me he's on duty as a lifeguard.

"Good luck today. And don't drown on my watch. I only volunteered to pick up babes. 'kay, *bruh?*" He retorts.

"I fucking hope you're still joking." I frown at his disgusting sculpted back parading away from me.

Stripping off my top and pleated skirt in the corner, I stuff my belongings there too.

Xalton scans me from head to toe. I've never been shy about showing skin before, but how his roving eyes quickly shift from impatient to a ravenous tame has me flush.

The sinful part of me is disappointed in his choice of attire, though. It's intended to conceal rather than reveal what's obviously a core worthy of envy. His sleek black bathing suit covers his upper half, extending to his wrists, leaving little to the imagination.

From my two-minute conversation with the *other* guy with a ripped physique, Xalton's modesty doesn't make much sense in my mind.

As I reach the pool, my knees lock up.

Holy fuck, he's in the deep end, and I only now remember how bad I am at this. I can only swim as long as my feet or my hands are touching the bottom of the rim.

Most will argue that that's not what swimming is, but what else would you call it? *Spider-Man-ing?* I dunno.

I—I can't be here. Not with him—

The minute I turn my back to join the other ten students in the four-foot section, Xalton points at me.

My Valentine's Virus

"Abbie." Floating like he's the next Michael Phelps, Xalton's eyes darken with vengeance. "Get your ass in the water before I *throw* you in," he orders at my hesitation.

I wince from the idea, and my throat squeezes.

He keeps his prying glare on me. "We're finishing that match here. Race me. Best two out of three," he shivers.

"You're going to do this *now...?*" I sneer, marching closer to find that he's just as alarmingly handsome wet as he is dry.

The water droplets clinging to his chiseled jawline trace a path down to his strong neck. His dark hair clings to his forehead in damp tendrils until he wipes them back, revealing his intense green eyes.

My heartbeat crawls into my esophagus, and the sparkles of the water below are of no comfort. "No... it looks cold."

"You're supposed to dive in before the little shock gets to you. S'not hard." The asshole splashes me with the zero fucking degree water, and it takes all of my focus not to jump in to strangle him. Fury climbs to my throat. I fist my towel and launch it at the floor while spouting a cornucopia of Spanish swears at him.

He smirks, maneuvering back as I lean forward. I gulp, and my footing wobbles as I stare into the depths.

"You're scared," he studies, but my ears mistake it for mockery. "You can't swim?" He gives me a grim brow while analyzing my expression. The words muffle against my ears, and I steel my face. "Abbie," he repeats, with more depth to his tone.

His sharp, jade eyes expand, focusing on something behind me.

"What?" My face jerks to his. "I'm... preparing—"

His eyes bounce back to me, wide and analyzing. "Abbie, if you can't swim, get away from the—"

A loud splash later, and I'm submerged in the infinite waters. I can't tell if I jumped in out of resentment or if I tripped.

A whistle from above pierces the silence of the brisk waters as it laces my skin with sharp ice. *It's fucking freezing!* Aren't these pools supposed to be heated before the students can use them?

Another flop happens above, and a floating ring overhead from the lifeguard seat is launched.

I kick vigorously for it as my heart races. Seconds thump by with the little air I have left to hold before I can seize it.

With only a second of breath remaining, my lungs cramp. I graze the lifesaver as my vision grows white with panic.

My body is cast above the surface. Gasping for life, bringing oxygen, I'm encased in a warm grasp. Xalton's broad arms wrap around me possessively, and I've never been so relieved he's here.

His gaze searches mine in erratic sweeps with an expression I can't make out. His eyes then harden prompting them up at Melanie. "Couldn't control yourself, could you?" Xalton mocks in a low voice, his breathing unusually labored. He adjusts the soaked hair from my face as he guides my hand to the edge of the pool so I can manage.

The long-haired blond crosses her arms over her red and black laced bikini. "What?" Melanie scorns him with double the ice in her vision. "You *said* you'd throw her in."

"You... *menace!*" I cough, my calm restraint slowly slipping.

She snickers from my response like we're friends and we're fucking *not*. "I did you a favor, Abbs," she urges with her voice poised.

"A *favor?*" I frown at her.

I mean, I am in the water, and it's not as cold as before. I give her a more patient glare, finding it hard to get a read on her.

Xalton's arms block me and maneuver me into the corner where I can't flee. His dense glance roams over my body for another beat, and my eyes are still on his.

"What is it?" I nip at the air, my heart hammering in my ears. My face heats knowing he's finding me going haywire beneath my skin.

My Valentine's Virus

"You can't race me," he plainly states, loitering closer and removing the distance between us.

His proximity is disorienting but warm while he teeters on the edge of genuine concern and insult. I can't tell what his actual demeanor is, but he has my heart doing uncoordinated backflips of uncertainty.

Melanie reaches to retrieve the floatation ring and plops it beside us. "Ugh, just use *this* for now," she spouts with a voice lined with annoyance.

"I'll... race circles around you... *bitch*," I mumble in a shiver while pulling the floaty to my chest.

He grins at my less-than-convincing grumbles. "Alright, Princess." He pushes off the wall and into a casual backstroke. "Better hurry before your coach gets here." Xalton effortlessly glides through the water, leaving me with a bereft ache.

Preparing my mind, I take a deep breath to murder my fears. I kick off the wall, clinging to the floatation ring, and give it my all to get used to the water.

Xalton takes the lead in the first round while I focus on my technique and propel forward with each stroke. His fans cheer from the sidelines, and I glance at Psy on the bleachers, rotating her arm above her head in frothing support for me.

"Woo *woo!*" Psyra praises, still unable to pry away from her phone call.

My fan of one is all I need. Smiling, determination ignites in my lungs, and as we reach the finish line, I touch the wall after Xalton.

He wins the first round, but he's not as breathless as I am. He wears a related smile, but it vanishes the minute I face him. "Giving up?" He laughs.

I scoff, splashing him from the pool's dividers. "You wish. I've only just started. Wipe that arrogant look off your face."

He grins, pumping more power into it, and my stomach flutters, threatening a swoon.

In the next round, my competitive spirit kicks me into high gear, and I showcase true swimming prowess—despite my assist. Xalton is *speeds* ahead, but I refuse to let him out of my sight. My arm slices through the water with increased intensity. Despite his victory in the last round, I finish a close second, leaving no doubt that I can keep up with him.

This time, he's panting, and victory ensures in my bones from that sign.

I cover my hand over my mouth as I take a breather too. "Look at that, I won."

"You can't be cocky while holding onto a handicap," he bemoans. I sure *can*.

"You mad, Xalty-boy?"

His laugh drenches in mischief from my counter. He wets his lips, his eyes traversing down to my dripping heaving chest. "As a hatter."

In-between chit-chat gets my attention on the other end. Gus gets his flirt on, impressing the other first years with his flexing biceps. Stealing my cave-woman gaze longer than I care to admit.

"Abbie." Xalton's tight voice near my ear makes me jump. "*Beta-bod* back there isn't going to help you." He faces ahead, the muscle in his defined jaw ticking.

My cheeks ripen to a sting, but before I can respond coherently, he pushes off the wall. "You didn't say *'start!'*" I call after him.

"Start," he waves while completing a stroke a quarter-way.

Prick.

No matter. Gripping the lifesaver, I pace after. We're tied halfway toward the other end. The pool water surrounds me. It's refreshing embrace urges me on. Adrenaline pumps through my body, heightening my senses and sharpening my concentration. My mind fixes on one thing: catching up to Xalton's perfect butt.

In the final round, we lock eyes. A silent understanding passes between us, knowing that whoever wins this gets to take home the tasty

My Valentine's Virus

bragging rights. With a nod, he dives back into the crisp water, giving it his all.

Xalton's strokes are robust but precise. I match the intensity in my adapted style, pushing my limits with every ounce of strength I can conjure.

As we battle for the finish, the race becomes a blur of splashes and effort. The cheers and encouragement from our classmates fade into the background. My muscles strain and sore, but I refuse to let fatigue hinder my progress so far.

Every fiber of my being assembles for me to increase my speed the minute I finally pass him.

Faster. Faster. Faster.

I kick harder, propelling myself forward with every stroke. He closes the gap, but I can almost taste victory.

But as I whip for that final burst of velocity, my fingers slip from the lifesaver that helps me stay afloat.

The battle between Xalton and I immediately switches to a fight against the water's resistance. The float slides further from my grasp, slipping away—the lifeline I desperately need.

Panic rushes through me. The flickers of uncertainty don't even set in this time. My lungs breathe the chlorinated water. I choke, coughing harshly as the liquid burns my chest while I struggle to keep my buoyancy.

The stability I relied on falters. I'm losing my balance, and I can't relax. My heart pounds against my ears as my mind races throughout my existence for solutions.

The water mercilessly pulls me under, and all light in the room diminishes faster than I can adjust to. My consciousness struggles not to fade in my rough kicks and lashes.

My circumstance dawns on me as time slows down in this very real moment. My body tenses. My muscles strain against the opposition of the water, keeping me awake. Cold fear revives and abandons me quicker than it came and is replaced with a grim acceptance that I fucked up.

The only thing that manages to pry my eyes open again is the idea of seeing my mom in the afterlife.

Fuck no!

My eyelids stiffen against my face, and my vision forces light where there isn't any.

I can't face her if I die like *this!* A blaze of emotion threatens to destroy my soul if I don't keep going. I refuse to let this overpower me. Digging deep within, I find a reserve of strength I didn't know existed. At the impossible bottom where light doesn't exist, I thrash and flail, combating Poseidon's bitch-ass again for round four.

My lungs scream for precious air, and my body craves respite, but I advance up, boosted by an unyielding resolve to finish what I fucking started.

But before I can reach the halfway point toward the surface, the fire inside me is put out by the waves and I'm gone before I can be aware of my absence.

LEVEL ELEVEN

ZONE_WARDEN

I slap my hand against the poolside, marking the end to the realm of our competition. Winded in the attempt, I fix my hair from my eyes, no doubt expecting the pouting twenty-five-year-old to proposition me for another round.

I whip my head for her, and a cold shiver shoots down my spine, mingling with the beads of sweat on my forehead. I scan the pool's wave-like surface, desperate for the sight of her. Panic grips my chest like a vice, squeezing tighter with each second. I don't see her.

Her float is there. But no Abbie.

A barreled pang strikes at my ribs. The minor thought of Abbie *drowning* claws in my mind, filling me with pure dread. Horror flashes in my eyes as I frantically pace. The pounding of blood in my ears

I ascend, breaching for air, and it's rough in my lungs as I shout, "Where is Abbie?!" With pain evident in my voice, everyone's awareness seizes.

A hush falls over the pool grounds as everyone becomes aware of the missing swimmer. Above, Psyra drops her phone over her shoulder and stalks anyone who may have seen her friend, my expressive howl conveying what we fear.

Diving straight back to the depths, I free the forces I held back from our race to scour its shadowy bottom.

It's too fucking dark down here. Aesthetics aside, making a swimming pool pitch-black is the most absurd design choice possible.

"Kaiser! We could lose *you* too!" Astor, our lifeguard, decides now's the best time to convey that tidbit. My mind races, vowing to drag his head under and keep his ass there if Abbie isn't safe.

She was right beside me—*she was right fucking beside me and gaining momentum.*

As much as I can't stand the fuckboy right now, Gus's right. My heart is pounding at near-light speed, and it's not helping her if *I* can't get it together.

As heat consumes every inch of my body, I burst up for air and slam my fist at the pool's surface. I draw in a deep breath before diving back in. My hands thrash through the depths, creating a whirlpool. My throat dries in the darkening waters, but the lights beneath turn on, assuredly from JP's intervention above.

Time stands as fear threatens to restrain me. The minute I find her silhouette, my stomach plummets to my feet. Images of her shadowed form from the auditorium and our encounter flash behind my eyes. Heart-shattering devastation pierces my soul. My blood runs cold, and it takes everything in me not to break into a wail in the depths.

Abbie, no! Fuck no! Not her!

My Valentine's Virus

Abbie's hand is stretching up toward her lifesaver. Her once lustrous black hair tangles with the water, and the vibrant glow that adorned her face has faded.

My chest squeezes from her eyes—the light that danced within those big mischievous brown orbs drew me in like a moth to a flame. They're extinguished, leaving a hollowness that sends a hard shiver through my spine.

Moments later, Melanie and Grace, one of her friends, yank us both up, but not without a fight from me.

Grace's movements are efficient enough for me to believe that she'll reach Abbie's unconscious form. She's faster and hauls her up within seconds.

Without another thought, I avoided Melanie's grab and cut through the water to the girls with renewed urgency.

Nearly above, my arms scarf around Abbie's limp shoulders, pulling her close. Waves crash against us as I fight against the water's resistance, refusing to let it claim her.

On the poolside, I close in on Astor, hovering over Abbie as Grace helps gently set her on her back. His stupid face contorts with uselessness.

My focus narrows on the woman I can't bear to witness, and my glare ices at Melanie, assessing her as I charge over.

The minute Astor decides to do his job, something demonic switches in me, engulfing my muscles like a storm.

"Get your greasy hands off her!" I shove him back, and he loses balance falling tailbone-first into the deep end. As if I was going to let an incompetent buffoon give *his* diagnosis.

"Help!" Astor whines, his voice high-pitched as he flounders like he can't see up from down. "I *can't* swim!"

Grace dives in to retrieve him while everyone else quietly shares the same line of questioning in their eyes at once. *Who. The. Fuck. Made. Him.* Lifeguard?

JP sails beside me, her gaze pained and wet as I check Abbie's pulse against the floor.

My face runs cold as more dread washes over me. There's no hint of her heartbeat, and breathing becomes an afterthought to take in for me. The weight of her cold body in my arms shatters me into billions of shards. I have only *milliseconds* to bring her back before she succumbs entirely.

Compressing her chest with locked fingers, I go with the recommended beats over her heart. "One. Two. Three."

I arch her head, lift her chin to open her airway, and pinch her nose before crashing my lips against hers. Delivering air, I alternate between them and my chest compressions in appropriate ratios. My frown creases, aching against my face over hers. Panic rises through me like a fever, but I can't lose it here—not yet.

JP covers her face, suppressing her anguish as another minute passes. She alerts me an ambulance is on its way, but I can't hear.

"Come on, Abigail!" I plead. "Our match isn't over!"

With my voice breaking, Melanie reaches out to place her hand on my side as if for me to call it in—and if she does, I'll fucking lose it. I'll break her in *half* with my bare hands.

But JP is quick in my periphery before that happens. JP intercepts, positioning herself between us, her nostrils red and flaring like a goddamn dragon she's wronged. Her accusatory finger points high toward Melanie in her pants, but the words don't leave her trembling lips. JP shakes her head in a mix of loss and disbelief.

As if reading her unspoken thoughts, Melanie crosses her arms over her chest in defiance. She lifts an eyebrow in a challenging manner before huffing and storming off toward the women's locker room.

A faint moan trickles from Abbie's lips, and I reel back in time for her to expel vomit and water. Her gasps for air sing in my ears.

My Valentine's Virus

JP fumbles back to us, bringing her to sit up in my momentary rest. Facing JP, we share a heave of relief. She lifts her eyebrows in a not-so-subtle smirk, hinting at me in a way I'm not ready to discern in my state.

I let out a shaking lungful, my arm rising to cover my face laying against the concrete as I try sorting the remnants of my sanity together.

JP pats Abbie's back as she coughs more, and she rolls against her, losing consciousness for the second time. The rest of the onlookers watch in awe and relief as Abbie breathes in and out on her own.

I reach to cradle her in my arms, bringing her up to hurry out.

The chill of water clings to our bodies. Breathless, grief threatens hold of my chest toward the infirmary as I carry her. My gaze fixes on Abbie, unwilling to let her out of my sight, while JP guides us in the corner of my eye down the outstretched halls.

Meeting her drifting eyes, I know the connection between us here has shifted. The bond hits me like a throat punch, and god-fucking-dammit, how scared I was to see her that way.

"I'm aware this isn't the best time for this, Xalton," JP gives a self-deprecating sigh. "But Melanie had two hairpins before one went missing." She signs, bringing up her fingers. "Before she gave Abbie the float she was using. *She* caused… what happened."

Of-fucking course, she caused what happened.

My snarl emits a heat that vibrates throughout my cold skin, heating me.

Melanie tries to ruin everything I… hold dear. It's been half a year since we broke up, but to go as far as to *murder* Abbie?

The scars under my bathing suit serve as my intense reminder of exactly what the headmaster's daughter is capable of. A shudder roars through me as hatred manifests into a separate thing scraping at my stomach.

A soft snore from my little rival brings me back, and my chest aches in ways foreign to me.

I close my eyes for a second, and before I'm fully aware, we've reached the infirmary. Resting her on one of the open beds, I turn my back to leave without a second glance.

JP's about to chase after me, but the doctor wheels around in her chair, arguing that Abbie is about to wake.

I slide my fingers through my hair for the millionth time today. *I saved her.*

I saved the life of someone who was trying to ruin me. I think back to the nightmare that seized me when I gave CPR. The prime terror of losing her is fresh in my mind. How did I let myself get this close? How did this *infuriating* woman worm into my head while simultaneously forcing loose my darkest thoughts?

I press my trembling palms against the rough wall of the corridor. My teeth grind, fighting against the torrent of anguish overtaking me.

Whatever that was and whatever *this* is, I can't let her weaken my resolve any more than she already has. In this stupid twist of fate, I was her protector. Not only did I bring her back—a death that would have *benefited* me, if I failed to revive her, nothing would have stopped me from diving back in and following her to the afterlife.

My body rises and falls, preventing the chaos from surging within. It's like I'm in a maze of my own making without seeing how to escape it. A veil lifts in me, exposing warm threads that weave the makings of my aching heart. She was so cold—I couldn't bear it.

The weight of finding her like that crushed me harder than anything I could interpret. I grip the collar of my chest, slamming the side of my fist against the wall.

An uncharted wilderness of pain forces me to come to terms with what she means to me.

What she's always meant.

I love her.

My hands remain trembling. Every piece of her I've come to know peels back the layers of a mask I didn't know existed. I had to count off

My Valentine's Virus

prime numbers during her little strip tease, revealing her tiny orange bikini.

What I have for her is starting to surpass her wrongs.

I swallow as the pain welling inside me threatens to engulf my rationality again.

I've prided myself on my ability to be detached and maintain control in any situation. But from the moment we met online, she's captivated my every thought. Keeping me awake each night, I anticipated her next moves until I'd pass out with her jammed in my mind.

But deep down, I know better. I can't afford to go through this turmoil again. I take a breath, fighting to regain what's remained of my composure. I have goals to achieve and a challenge to win. No matter how my body reacts to her, I need to resist it.

Pushing myself off the wall, my fist throbs as I rest it in my pocket. If I want to survive her, I need to remind myself of the pain loving someone causes.

Memories of the many nights I spent in tears live behind my gaze as I stride down the campus corridor. I'd stay up late, questioning why my mother even had me if she was going to abandon me all alone in that big house.

Love or anything near it has no place in my world. I came to that conclusion long ago, and nothing's ever going to change it.

The large part of me that's curious about Abbie's effect on me is purged from now on. I won't let it dictate my actions anymore. With a final shake of my head, I vow to bury those emotions deep, locking them away for good.

This event changes nothing. She's my *prey* and nothing more. Just like all the others.

LEVEL TWELVE

ZONE_WARDEN

The charges against EctoPhantom has him imprisoned for five years with a fine of $250,000. The news headline flashes across my screen, hitting me with a force I didn't anticipate.

The weight of my guilt and pity has me leaning back in my computer chair. Maybe it's the genuine possibility that I could face similar charges once Princess recovers, adding to the weight of the impactful news. She might hold off on it now, considering I brought her back to the land of the living. But with that girl, you never know.

Despite not knowing how to swim, she still adapted, nearly besting me in our race and risking her life just to prove she could. As charming as her obsession with victory is, she's a major security risk—a risk I can't afford to play with anymore.

My Valentine's Virus

her, and it scares me. I've been obsessed since she gunned me down online, and I was forced to look into her. Rage aside, there's no one else like her.

I recline, assessing my inner battle since Abbie's incident. I'd prefer handling Melanie on my own, but that's easier said than done, considering our history.

Whatever we had wasn't real—no. Not like those lovey-dovey ones romantics fawn over in movies or books. It was a placeholder to impress my father's business crowd.

He orchestrated it behind my back with her mother, Opal, leaving no room for disagreement. Dad was blessed with the opportunity to introduce his beloved son, who had a shiny blonde at his side.

I still remember the meeting at a previous gala. The younger me picked up everything there was to know about her at first glance. Over the years, her company had as much spice to it as milk.

She clung to me like a shower curtain. I'm not saying her unhinged grippy sock mentality wasn't cute, but she had no substance beyond her narrow obsession with her looks and tendency to judge strangers' bodies every other minute. It got old.

I didn't tell my father beforehand how I was going to break up with her. I knew exactly what his reaction would be—he'd disown me. And that's exactly what he did. But foolish me had a sliver of hope that he'd get it.

Recalling the nightmarish moment that keeps me up at night, the scars on my chest throb. I exhale a drag from my cigarette, allowing the wonderful plant to do its thing and soothe my nerves.

In hindsight, maybe breaking up with Melanie during a couple's cooking lesson wasn't the brightest idea.

We were stirring pots side by side in silence, and I struggled to explain how she was draining the life out of me. You know that old saying? *It's like ripping off a Band-Aid.*

"Don't forget to add the oregano—" she whispered, barely audible, before I interrupted her.

"We should break up," I affirm, my jaw tightening to secure my tone's seriousness.

"...Because of the oregano...?" Her face paled, and she kept a long gaze on me as if pressing me for an explanation that didn't need further analysis.

The air was otherworldly dense, and it felt like all eyes were on us. I didn't care. I was miserable and hated every second with her. It was like breathing in poison, but I took the reins of my life back and broke the curse.

"No. I'm just done," I uttered.

I'm good at reading people before they open their mouths. Only 30% of what we say is verbal; the rest is conveyed through body language and expressions. So, I wasn't surprised when her entire body stiffened. Hurt filled her piercing red eyes, a sight I wouldn't want on my worst enemy. But I was drowning in misery with only one way out.

The rest of the lesson was spent in tense silence as she avoided eye contact with the other couple we were grouped with. An ideal pair. So in sync with one another, trading smoldering eyes and whispering inside jokes. They barely kept their hands off each other while kneading dough, as if mocking whatever it was Melanie and I had the table over. Envy for what they had would be an understatement. They showcased pure, unfiltered love solidifying what I already knew: we weren't ever right for each other.

There's no way I'd ever be that way with her or *any*one.

I decided to cut the lesson short by grabbing my bag to leave. That's when she clutched the closest thing within reach: a knife still stained with tomato juice, and aimed it straight for my jugular.

At first, I thought it was a mistake. I was doing both of us a favor, but she attacked me with a fucking knife like she was possessed by the spirit of Jack the Ripper.

My Valentine's Virus

I stumbled backward, narrowly avoiding hitting the back of my head on the table.

She lunged at me, gripping the weapon like a Viking ready for a kill. My life flashed before my eyes as the knife pierced my chest. She raised it again, testing my fortitude and adjusting her wrist for a killing blow.

The couple beside us sprang into action as they witnessed the horror unfolding before them. The woman emptied her pot to throw at Melanie's head, knocking her off me. Her partner then ran in and grabbed her wrist while grappling for control. She screamed and writhed in tears over the fact she couldn't finish her assault.

The woman rushed to my side to apply pressure on my pouring chest like a seasoned professional. I couldn't make heads or tails of what happened. I was dizzy, overwhelmed, scared, and breaking.

Paramedics and police were called. I was rushed to the nearest hospital and needed emergency heart surgery. Melanie faced attempted murder charges, but her mother somehow got them all dismissed before they could go to trial.

My father filed a lawsuit—a lawsuit I had to press him to help me file while I had to focus on recovery in the ICU. I'm not sure which hurt more.

After the disbursement of my sizeable personal injury settlement, my parents insisted I forgive her. The psycho still walks amongst the sane, but I was lucky I left Oregon when I did. My scars still pound from the aftermath, and I had a lot of growing up to do between them.

Abbie's become her target now. I don't even know why that is. Something has me believing it's her twisted attempt at helping me, which is even more sickening.

Over three hours pass when I find myself staring blankly at my message board in my home office.

I wait for Abbie to log in and pester us all as usual, but I know she might not tonight. My knee bounces, unable to focus on any work until I know she's behind a screen somewhere.

♥

Time slows to the agony of my impatience. *Tick. Tick. Tick.*

I cave and pull out one of my burner phones from the box beneath my desk and send her a text message.

[Me]: You hiding from me, coward?

That would warrant a response from her but not tonight. My heart squeezes in my chest, and the agonizing burn fills it until I'm grabbing my jacket, helmet, and keys to leave my home.

I bid Dice farewell before taking my motorcycle straight to the CRU campus. Abbie's changed her room to board with JP, and I can't even be mad at that. Psyra's family is still in touch with mine, and she could send one little text to have my parents disown me. Abbie, you conniving smartass. There's no way in hell those two just bumped into each other and became friends.

She must have tracked her down on purpose just to get to me. That's what I get for having acquaintances.

I swivel off my motorcycle as I arrive in front of the women's boardroom. There's an air of mystery at night. Its red and black elegance matches the overall theme. I enter with ease.

High dark mahogany walls with intricate engravings fill the space. Vintage chandeliers cast a soft, dimmed glow, and stained-glass windows depict the enchanting scenes that set the ethereal atmosphere. It's a refined space filled with history and artistry with every step. Opal's never been one to lack taste, I suppose. I only wish she could channel that energy within.

The hall is dark, and motion censored. Breaking into the system, I disable them with my specialty wristwatch. Maybe don't have everything running on Wi-Fi if you don't want it getting hacked. The easier it is to access, the more offended I get. I can make a motherboard from scratch, but they didn't think to ask me to secure their college.

My Valentine's Virus

Pacing the halls, I count down the numbers of Abbie's room. Her orange scent makes it all the simpler.

I use the keychain lock pick Psy still doesn't know I swiped from her yesterday. Honestly, I was looking to nab that stupid necklace she fiddles with so much and toss it into a river.

The door clicks open, and I push it inward. It takes me a minute to remember how this is also JP's room.

In the shadows, I raise an eyebrow at JP herself, clutching a laptop brick charger by the cables like it's a Morningstar. I suppress a laugh from her ridiculous stance and expression.

Relieved, she exhales, lowering her "weapon" as I disarm her.

Physically shaken, she watches me raise the wires in front of her in a mocking motion.

"What were you planning to do with this? *Charge* me to death?" I tease.

"I was grabbing the closest thing, intruder." Psy protests with unhindered disgust in her voice. "What are you *doing?*"

I sidestep her complaints to make my way over to Abbie's side of the spacious quarters.

I intercepted their texts and, through the conversation, found out when she returned from the hospital.

I still from the sight of her gently snoozing in her bed. She looks so delicate sleeping at a reasonable hour.

"What the *fuck* are you doing?" Psy repeats firmer, breaking the silence with her harsh whisper.

I absorb my little rival's features like nutrients as her chest rises and falls under her comforter to the fading sounds of Psy's complaints in the background.

I adjust the thick strand of hair from her face revealing the scar across her eyebrow. She shudders below my fingertip and mutters a soft cry, making me freeze.

"M… mom…my," Abbie whimpers, shifting in her sleep.

A nightmare? I contemplate waking her, but I can't stop enjoying her sleep more than I care to admit. She's delicate this way, but so is a bomb.

JP huffs behind me and crosses her arms. "She's been talking in her dreams every other night. Her mom visits her in her sleep, so don't freaking wake her."

I straighten without moving my gaze from Abbie's lips. "You know I don't believe in your wizardry bullshit," I dismiss.

JP shrugs, undeterred by my skepticism. "Whenever I bring it up, she changes the topic before I even realize it."

I turn to JP as I head to the door. "Take care of her for me?" I find myself asking.

Psyra rolls her eyes before giving me that look she gave me at the pool before. "I thought you *hated* her," she mocks in a half-smirk.

I still can't dissect where she's going with that face. "Of course I do. I can't have her dying before she realizes who the better one is. You slow?"

I remove my jacket as Psyra snickers with a forgiving eye-roll. I place my jacket over Abbie's body, and her shiver slowly ends. Warmth fills my chest the moment she stops shivering, and time stills for a beat.

"I can wing-man for you. Just give me back my lock pick, and we're square."

I take Psyra's hand and surrender the useful keychain I picked up. "Borrowed," I add with an irritated huff.

She pinches her brow as I face the doorway. "How are you this whipped without knowing it? I—"

Before she finishes her sentence, I shut the door behind me, leaving her words hanging in the air.

The next day, I leave the administrative office and somehow bump into my little rival in the pathway. My shoulders ease, seeing her hair

My Valentine's Virus

down. The mist of dawn highlights the tantalizing waves of her long black hair surrounding her frame. She wears my jacket over her uniform, revealing her bare shoulders. Her expression flushes brightly from my heated gaze. She adjusts her hair behind her ear, making my cock swell. I inhale that sweet orange scent that follows her like a shadow. The visceral reaction my body has to hers should be studied.

"X-Xalton, hi. I..." Abbie stammers, her eyes softening up to mine. "I've been looking for you."

I love how my name sounds from those lips. All the sensations I vowed to keep at bay resurface, but pride flashes its way, and my throat dries.

I clear my voice. "Keep the jacket," I interject, my voice faltering. "It looks nice on you." Someone shoot me. Seeing her flustered in my clothes is still taking my goddamn breath away. My thoughts are clouded with desires I really shouldn't entertain.

She smiles sweetly, and my heart swoons. I love her. I can't deny that, but I need to be in control. She's capable of doing so much damage, and all I want to do is run my hands through her hair, brush my lips over hers, and whisper vile things in her ear to make her writhe with need.

"Listen," we both chime in unison.

"Go ahead." I shake my head, urging her to continue.

"I want to thank you for—"

I raise my hand, cutting her off. It trembles before I put it to rest in my pocket. "Don't," I reply, suppressing the emotions that threatened to spill out the moment I saw her.

If she thanks me for this moment, I don't think I'm strong enough to manage what I might do to her.

A gleam of discomfort flickers in her autumn-colored eyes. "Don't *thank* you for saving my life?" she questions.

If I hadn't egged her on, it would never have happened. "I want to make something clear to you, Abbie," I assert, steadying my voice and swallowing the lump in my throat.

Hearing the base in my tone, she steels her expression.

"We're not friends," I clarify in a curt tone. "I don't even like you. Or did you forget that? Keep my jacket, burn it, throw it away, or sell it but don't parade around in it like I'm your boyfriend. It's disgusting." I'm not even sure if I'm convincing myself but I keep going. "Rescuing you meant we could settle our score until I've picked your brain and inevitably crushed you. Is. That. Understood?" I emphasize each syllable.

I needed to say it more for me than to wound her.

The angelic smile of hers vanishes. Abbie's eyes glisten with hurt until swapping it with fading apathy. Then her expression merges into something more corrupt I've never seen. Both terrifying… and exciting.

She cocks her head back, fixing me with a direct stare. "What's understood here is you're *mine* to crush," she retorts, her voice almost nonchalant. "I'll fucking devour you before you can even match my speed."

It takes all of me not to crack a smile at her nerve alone. That ripe insanity.

"I've already accessed your primary servers. You'll be in handcuffs before you can bow your head in defeat," she attaches with unwavering confidence.

I keep my expression stoic before I graze by her. Her jacket falls off her arm, and she glares daggers into my back.

"Fat chance I'll let that happen."

Our clash for supremacy has shown me how unnerved she is as I am. I eagerly anticipate what she has planned to stop me from revealing her data when her days are up. I know it'll hurt, but it wouldn't have happened if she hadn't hurt first.

LEVEL THIRTEEN

PRINCESS_USER24

I've since pushed back the pain manifesting in my chest when I approached Xalton earlier.

I'm not heartbroken—just confused and rightfully pissed off from all of his mixed signals. I thought there was something *more* going on with us.

When I woke from the hospital, Psy was at my side, regaling about how I ended up there.

Going into graphic detail, she told me how Xalton threatened Gus with a *"touch her, and I'll end you" and* then got into this huge fight over my honor. Then he shouted into the heavens, cursing at God to bring me back before breaking into tears.

I couldn't believe it. I didn't. I've picked up on how Psy loves exaggerating events, but I do remember one part. If it wasn't for Xalton's shout reaching me from my subconscious, I don't know if I could've come back.

The way he cried out for me when I was tiptoeing between realms like a prisoner of my own body was surreal. I felt like I owed him for that. The aching panic in his voice wasn't fake like what he just said to me.

There's no way he doesn't feel more beyond our rivalry, right? Not after that. Xalton cares. He may even... *like* me.

Even with that in mind, the fire swirling in my stomach yearns for me to break him for making me second-guess myself.

Pouting, I charge through the doors of the women's locker room for my second class today.

It's a different P.E. course—not that I'm a quitter. We were barred from swimming after using the pool without the instructor on site, which led to me being rushed to the hospital. The only available one left was a team-based class.

Striding down the halls, I'm greeted by Psy. She spoke to me about my sleep-talking, I'm sure she's been making up. Last night they were calmer than usual. Since the drowning, they've been getting more memorable.

My own mom. Haunting me. I can't even recall what the dream was about, but I wake up every morning in tears. Wet, just like the day she was taken from us.

I never felt as close to her as the night of my drowning. Honestly, I rarely think about her unless she comes up naturally in conversation or around her birthday and Mother's Day.

Images of her beautiful dark hair tangled in the rain, her pale skin running cold, and her eyes glazed over cause my hands to tremble each time. I know it's not how she would have wanted me to remember her, but it's always been what my brain goes back to whenever I think about her.

My Valentine's Virus

Psy, being a self-proclaimed spiritual expert, gave me some insight into what it could mean. While we were getting ready in the locker room, she was vague, but her support helped. Telling me my mother is always watching over me pushed our bond even more, to say the least.

Of course, our gymnasium exudes an air of timeless elegance. Towering arches and ornate carvings adorn the walls. The high vaulted ceilings give an impression of grandeur, while the polished wood floors could be mistaken for mirrors under my feet.

It's filled with everything any other auditorium would have except, wherever appropriate, it's painted with black and red colors.

The gymnasium echoes with the faint whispers of the rest of our class marching in, and I smile over at Psy.

I don't know how I would have managed my semester without her.

"Psst. Hey, babe." She motions me over with a tired hesitance in her gaze. "I've got bad news."

"Do I need to sit down?" I tilt my head to the bleachers, where everyone else has begun gathering.

Her wry smile pushes me less at ease. "I'm... leaving for Fraixia tomorrow night. My dad's having an emergency and needs me there. I'm able to continue my classes over the summer next semester."

I exhale hard.

Great... just what I needed. Loneliness.

Biting my lip, the leftover orange juice from breakfast takes me out of the moment. "I'm bummed out, but... if it's an emergency, I get it. Just be safe, okay? I haven't been hearing a lot of good news from there."

"Oh?" She cocks a brow at me as if tip-toing on whether or not to be offended. "What news have you heard about my mother's motherland?"

I shrug. "Only that their gangs make a ton of cash kidnapping foreigners." Okay, maybe she should be offended.

She crosses her arms over her chest. "It's a third-world country, but like any other nation, they have their problems too." She sighs longingly as if looking at it over my shoulder. Wrapping her arm around my neck, we rock back and forth. "I'll miss you."

"I'll miss you too. Just come back as soon as you can so we can finish *The Walking Dead* together. I can't enjoy it without you." I groan, already missing her weird theories about how Rick *was* the cure for the zombies.

A minute later, the auditorium door slams open, revealing the tallest woman I've ever seen in person.

The coach stands, exuding an aura of strength and discipline. Her sharp jawline and piercing black eyes suggest she's witnessed battles on the field and in the trenches. She demands respect with a single glance as everyone stills on the bleachers.

Psyra and I plop down to our seats in unison.

The woman's blond pixie cut gives the image of a muscle-bound Tinkerbell, and honestly, I love it. Facing the ten of us, every movement she makes is deliberate and purposeful.

"Good morning, non-binaries, ladies and gentlemen. I'm Coach Tess, and today we will be teaming up for my personal favorite—Team Stick Ball."

A smile is born on my face. Oh, let's freaking go. I dominated this sport back in high school until it was replaced with lacrosse, which was the air-borne alternative.

This is a game essentially like hockey, but instead of hockey sticks, the players of each team hold short cotton-swap-like hockey pucks. There are cushions on one of the ends to prevent us from hurting each other, and instead of a puck, it's a soft pillowy ball.

Coach Tess points behind us as a student raises their hand.

"Pardon me, Coach Tess," the masculine voice interrupts.

I grit my teeth as I peer over my shoulder at the top of the bleachers. The coach smiles for once, facing Xalton. I was so stuck in my feelings I didn't even see him back there. "Yes, Mr. Kaiser?"

"Mind if I ask how the teams will be decided?" He inquires.

My Valentine's Virus

She adjusts her weight to one foot. "Certainly! You're getting ahead of me, but I figured we could have men versus women this round. Nothing sparks good competition like a battle of the sexes." She fists her palm with tamed giddiness at the prospect. "And for those not comfortable with that, flip a coin or pick the side you *vibe* with most," she shrugs.

A few scoffs and groans from behind us echo in the large space at Coach Tess's chortles and forced slang terms. She moves out of the way to reveal the equipment we would be using.

"You'll be playing for forty minutes. The highest-scoring team gets extra credit. Let's start with a ten-minute warm-up!" She claps and herds us into a line to commence jogging around the perimeters of the room.

Try as I must to ignore him, Xalton keeps up with me.

I frown at him, giving him the finger as he passes me. My heart clenches, and it drives me to wave goodbye to Psy so I can catch up and surpass his pace.

My speed quickens, and the rushing squeaks of my sneakers emit louder.

"On your left!" I warn in a mocking tone for him to move.

Xalton scoffs mid-jog, and he pushes more power into his steps to out-jog me. "On *your* left, Princess," he croons without panting.

I shove him with my arm so I can surpass him, but he's immovable. The force nearly makes me trip up, but it only pushes me further. "If you can't match my stride, maybe navigate the inner portion?" I tease.

The corner of his mouth rises into a snide grin. "Big words for someone who's about to come in second."

Minutes later, Xalton and I are neck and neck, overlapping the joggers with our sprints for victory. The squeaks of our relentless sneakers reverberate throughout the space and help me increase my velocity.

I overhear Grace, one of Melanie's cronies, hang back with Psy in the lap where we pass the rest of the students. "Are they seriously at it again?" She protests.

Psy snickers in response.

"It's not funny," Grace giggles. "Your friend shouldn't strain her lungs so hard. Can you ask her to slow it down a few notches? She just got discharged from the hospital yesterday!"

She gives Grace a side-eye. "You want *me* to get in the middle of *that?*" Psy gestures to Xalton and me, elbowing each other to get out of our ways.

His teeth grit in seething fury as I step over his shoes and overlap him.

"On your right!" I cheer.

Then I'm pulled backward. He yanks hard on the back of my shirt, and I flail for balance, only to end up pulling onto his shorts in my fall to the ground. I grunt, raising my head from the reflective floors, only to see his...

Oh...

Oh!

The coach's whistle echoes throughout the gym, pulling everyone's attention to her and not Xalton's family jewels.

Unafflicted, he casually brings his shorts back up, and I realize how long I held my breath.

Are men's privates meant to be that... intimidating? Fucker's packing a forearm down there.

Coach Tess sounds her whistle even louder, cutting into my freaking ears. Then I realize I'm the only one not paying attention to her. "Belle-Nuñez! You deaf?"

I roll my eyes, blushing halfway. If I wasn't, I am now.

Commander Tess pretends it never happened for Xalton's sake. "Got some ripe competition already. I love to see it!" she praises, rotating her arm at me to join the rest of the stretching circle. "I have a good idea of who I want the team captains to be." She winks.

Psy shawls her arm around my neck again but a little more aggressively. She yanks me near her onyx matte lips. "Did'ya have to

My Valentine's Virus

reveal him to the whole world like that?" she muttered low and somewhat taut.

It was a freak *accident.* "Oh yes. I *totally* wanted to have Xalton Kaiser's throbbing cock shown to me like *that."* I hiss through gritted teeth and cheeks, puckering with humiliation.

"Ugh, girl, you are *not* convincing," Psy snorts, letting me go.

As the coach goes on about the benefits of stretching, water consumption, and rest, I'm tentative too, but I glance back at Xalton.

He stands with his fanboys, wrapping an arm over his back to stretch his back muscles and glaring at me.

Like the complete child, I am, I make a suggestive stroking motion in the air above me, followed by a pantomime climax.

My gaze softens as he stifles his laughter, but it breaks into quiet hilarity. His sculpted cheeks shift into a deep red shade, and he's struggling to meet my eyes.

Once my hormones have their fill of the sight, I face forward as my chest flutters violently. Admittedly, it was all just lust before, but something's different. My chest feels light and filled all at once, eliminating any rage I've harbored for him.

As the realization sinks in, my eyes look everywhere and nowhere. *Fuck.*

The truth hits me in overwhelming waves. I'm in love with him. I know I always have, but the heat of competition was shielding me from sticking to it.

My chest tightens like it has a mind of its own. His permeating laughter is my Achilles' heel. I make a fist for my fingernails to dig into my palms until it hurts. Our conflict isn't over for me to be like this, and it's torment.

I'm losing all of my competitive edge from a minute ago. It fades into the background until the only thing that matters is him and the way he makes my heart race and my mind spin.

I feel sick.

Grace taps me on the shoulder. "Abbie, are you alright?"

"Yeah!" I nod, avoiding her green eyes. "Let's kick some *balls* around."

Psyra pinches the space between her slim brows. How is she putting up with me today? I'm usually at a reasonable eight, but my spazz-meter's soaring to a ten this period.

Everyone predicts the coach is about to use her whistle again, and we cover our ears for impact.

My team is a mix of familiar faces. We have Psyra Jean-Pierre, my bestie. Melanie Mayor and her friend, Grace Fry. And lastly, Hanna Nguyen, a red-haired girl who sprung into the gym last minute.

Xalton's team is comprised of himself, his fanboys Kevin Wu, Liam Baxter, Jaden Snow, and Gus, the Reliable.

Kevin, who stands at about the same height as Xalton, prepares the ball between our teams. He winks at Grace before the coach's whistle starts, and I charge in front of her for it.

Liam, a chocolate-haired Clark Kent thinks he can one v. one me as he grapples for control over the ball.

I push it forward and back, weaving it by his legs before my eyes land on Psy, running toward their goal and keeping eye contact with me.

Before I'm able to pass it to her, Jaden, a tanned blond-haired babe on defense, pivots in front of her and prevents my option to pass.

That's when I sharply check over my shoulder for Hanna, the new chick ready and open.

"Here!" She chirps, preparing her baton for the play. Her Crayola red hair swayed with the motion.

I don't hesitate.

I circle Jaden as he grinds his teeth, giving me a chance for a wide shot. Striking hard, the ball ripples over the floor and hits the end of

My Valentine's Virus

Hanna's baton, piloting it up in the air. Hanna loses control and locks up, but Grace sees it too.

Drool falls from the corner of my mouth. It's at the perfect height to knock straight back into the enemy's side and score.

Something overcomes Hanna as Kevin dives toward her, making her step back.

Grace takes over—it's her and Kevin now. Holding his staff like a bat, he fires it back to his team's side anywhere before Grace or Hanna can stop him.

What the hell?! It was two-on-one, and they *let* him have it! *What are they doing?*

The domino effect makes the other boys capitalize on Kevin's charge. The ball is passed back to Jaden, then to Xalton, who's gaining speed before I can intercept them.

I sprint down the gym, sneakers squeaking on the polished floors while I knit by the opposing players. Psy stays back on their side in case one of my other useless teammates decides to unthaw and fucking stop them.

Psyra showcases her bursts of agility. She maneuvers around the boys with quick footwork, as if dancing with the ball in the distance, waiting for us to catch up in time.

My heart races as I block Xalton, facing him during the game. His reinforced gaze causes my chest to seize up, conflicting with my desire to win.

Abusing the hiccup, he dribbles by me and thrashes the ball further away but close enough to keep on it.

Melanie raises her stick as Xalton aims and fires straight passed her. Nearing her head, the ball rotates, grinding against the net behind her, barely looking like an accident.

Undeterred in the goalie hoop, Melanie's stoic face lowers as she picks up the ball. Her powerful swing sends the orb soaring into the air, and the soft pillowy ball lands on the opposing team's side for Kevin to set it up again.

The whistle cries out. "Score: *boys!*" Coach Tess narrated.

Jaden and Kevin high-five, and I stare hate at the rest of my girls.

I stomp forward to Hanna and Grace. "You care to explain what the *fuck* that was?" I ask, sucking my breath through my mouth.

Grace rolls her eyes, crossing her arms over her chest. "Ugh. *Here* we go."

"You got something you want to say to me, Grace?" I cock a brow with my hands prompt on my waist approaching her.

"Yeah, bitch. You need to slow *down*. Not all of us want to risk injuring ourselves for a credit. This is only *P.E.,* not life or death—"

"What the actual fuck are you afraid of?" I spit.

Grace frowns, visibly shaking. "I'm not afraid of *any*thing. Back the hell away from me!" She leans against me, and her nerves break, causing her to shove me back.

My body tenses, but I keep my balance. "I am asking you for *this* energy for the next twenty minutes! Not the spineless cunts I saw a minute ago. Get your shit together. Just because they're guys doesn't mean they're stronger than *us*."

"What the fuck is she on?" Hanna grins at Melanie.

Psy hurries back over to my side. "Yo, babes. Check out the circle-jerk back there." She points her thumbs back at the boys.

"Men! Men! Men! Men! Men!" Kevin, Jaden, Liam, and Gus form a chant circle crouching over their stacked batons like a dumbass ritual. Xalton's leaning back against a wall, balancing the spinning ball on his middle finger while his other arm is crossed over his torso.

My shoulders raise and fall at the inferno of envy cooking beneath my skin.

I grunt and face the girls putting my hand out in front of me. "Get in on this," I order. Psy plants her hand over mine.

My Valentine's Virus

"Ooh. *Charlie's Angels* time. You bitches in?" She gives them a bubbly smirk they can't ignore.

Hanna huffs with an eye roll and struts over to us. "...fine." A smile previews on her lips. "I... I don't want us losing to *that*." She points back at the boys, still chanting louder and louder. Their deep voices echo across the stadium.

I glare over at Melanie, leaning her back against the wall with her arm crossed over her chest, nearly copying Xalton on the other end.

She swings her baton in her other hand. *"I'll* just be over here," she says, her head sloped to the side with a carefree smile.

My heart lurches, and then I eye both Hanna and Grace again. "No more *weak* shit. They're bigger, but we have power too. We have the *hips* and the *nerves,* and we're quicker. *Smarter* too. You feel me?"

"Damn straight," Psy scoffs with a devious grin, adding to the amplification of our squad.

"Let's quickly find out our strengths and weaknesses, alright?" I command, facing them. "I'm the fastest, strongest, and have great eyes."

"Don't forget *humble,*" Hanna glances at Grace, and we exchange hardy chortles.

"*Fuck* that." I come down from my stomach, filling with their comradery at my expense. "Psy?" I face her. "You have a gift for weaving passed them."

She nods with a cat-like smile. "It's just like in life, so?"

"*So,* for the next round, we're passing it to you, and I'll keep up if the ball slips free from you."

Psy gives me another nod of approval.

"Hanna, that ball kick you made was fucking perfect," I praise. "I need you to keep getting the ball in the air."

"Oooh, thanks. I'll try," she lowers her head, avoiding eye contact, but smiles.

It sparks my grin. "It's all I'm asking for, beautiful." I finally turn to Grace, nervously awaiting her turn. "Grace, your horizontal charges are immaculate. Lowering yourself to be aerodynamic, you're a genius and don't even know it."

She shrugs at me. "Yep. That... that's *exactly* what I did," she laces with a pinch of sarcasm.

I know they can't see their potential, but I do. "Grace, when you dive in for the ball, block the guy, and don't let him near us if we've got 'em," I instruct.

Grace moistens her lips. "Just say 'play defense?'" She shoots me an irritated smirk, but I know I'm winning her over. "I'll *see* what I can do."

"Great!" I beam.

"And Xalton is *mine,*" Melanie cuts in. She rotates her wrist, turning her baton into a slow windmill. She joins us, and I swallow what feels like a cotton ball. Melanie's red eyes remain on me joyfully but with a plumage of something I can't put together. All I know is it makes me uneasy and small. "Leave him to *me,* and we win," she promises.

My eyes catch Psyra in my periphery. I nearly lost my balance from how jarring her expression shifted. Her big, soft browns are sharp and small, like a grizzly bear before baring teeth.

"If we can get anything from this, guys," I break the hard tension that spurred from nowhere. "Is that we're capable of *anything.*"

Hanna makes a face narrowing her brown eyes at me. "Ugh. Too corny. Try again."

Grace takes her hand back and removes the phone she shouldn't have from her shorts to check a message.

The boys finish celebrating their Y chromosome with arrogant enthusiasm over their one victory.

When the round commences, Xalton and I share a charged moment. Our eyes lock onto each other in a silent exchange, leaving me wondering what's going through his mind.

Shattering the silence from all of us, a soul-shaking scream comes from Grace, and everyone's eyes jerk to her on reflex.

LEVEL FOURTEEN

ZONE_WARDEN

What the active hell is going on over there?

Grace, the silver one, hyperventilates while her hands shake, gripping her phone.

Coach Tess runs over and helps her to the bleachers so they can have a moment to discuss what happened. I can't hear them, but it doesn't take an expert to see she must have gotten unfortunate news.

Grace is dismissed from class a minute later, leaving the competing team down a player.

Coach Tess chooses not to blow on that irritating whistle for our attention. Our ears have had enough stimulation for the minute. "For the remainder of the period, just play your best, girls."

"What happened?" The ruby-haired girl asks on Abbie's team.

Coach Tess bites the corner of her cheek at the question. "It's not my place to say. Let's hurry this up. You only have twenty more minutes to earn your extra credit." She brings back the reminder as if it mattered more.

My eyes narrow at Abbie. Princess's pouty stance keeps my attention longer than appropriate, filling my chest with heat.

She still smells like citrus fruit. Her tight red tank top and black shorts highlight those impossible curves I can't keep my eyes off of. Despite better judgment, my mind roams down a dangerous alley. What I wouldn't give to press her body against a wall, trail my hands up her shirt, massage her breasts, and have her gasp in my ear from the invasion.

"'Sup, Xal-*ton!*" Gus breaks my eye contact by stepping in front of me. "Sorry about what happened the other day…" The rest of his words mute in my ear as if to protect myself from his stupidity.

It's not until Abbie's name leaves his mouth that my attention returns. My gaze sharpens on him, bringing me back to reality.

"Repeat that?" I order in a callus tone as I cross my arms over my core.

Gus takes a tentative step back, noting my sudden hostility. "Abbie agreed to help me study for our blockchain test tomorrow," he supplies. "I wanted to know if that was cool with you since you two seem… like an item." He hesitates on the right phrase to call us.

There's no other way to explain how hard I want to drive my fist through his pathetic face. I can practically hear it; his cries at the impact shattering against his nose, breaking cartilage as he goes down.

I take a deep breath through clenched teeth, but it doesn't cool the ragged mood I contracted from his words. The thought of him *alone* with my Abbie—no. She's not *"my"* Abbie. *Fuck.* I can't even place when I started referring her to that.

As much as I hate giving in to the tight coil of gripping envy, the idea of her knowing how much it bothers me rivals the ache.

"We're not together," I manage tightly.

My Valentine's Virus

"Oh, terrific!" Gus's expression beams like a child given full access to a candy warehouse.

Every muscle in my body squeezes to restrain myself from going berserk, but I can't turn it off. *Great.*

I squint my eyes back at Gus, high-fiving one of our teammates, and I slip my hands through my hair. He's not even her type. Is she *trying* to get me riled up over this?

Coach Tess figures our ears have had enough time to heal and rings her whistle again, long and loud enough so I'll be hearing it in my sleep. "Begin!" She waves at us to get back into position.

Abbie gives her frail team one more pep talk about how Grace's absence should only fuel them even harder to win. To win for her.

"Ain't happening, Princess," I boast in her direction. "The odds just aren't in your favor." My shoulders ease as she skips forward.

"I never *needed* them to be," she retorts, her gaze on mine. "From now on, we're not falling off." She points her thumb downward, and heavy chills march up my bicep. Her assurance is enough to have Satan bet on her.

Then I remind myself that this is the same little bitch who brought me to my knees through my monitor. My nostrils flare when I grit my teeth. *Don't. Hold. Back.*

Her eyes shift to concern in Psy's direction.

I watched Psy and Princess's interaction when she broke the news about her leaving. Psy has a good heart. I know she sees a sister in Abbie, so bearing the weight of her news cost them the game earlier.

The others couldn't tell, but Psy was the one that brought them down. Abigail just didn't want to criticize her friend.

Their distressed faces' looks were tight but now ripe with confidence since their captain brought them together.

Meanwhile, our idiots just shouted "men" a hundred fucking times, making me regret my gender for a minute.

♥

The game starts. Psy picks off the ball from Gus's fumble, and I'm in pursuit like a predator, keeping my baton gripped. I signal Kevin, our most competent, to stay opposite of me on the other side.

The girls rally near the center as Liam, Jaden, and Gus follow suit in case its direction changes.

I steal the ball from Psy's unbalanced hold during her dribbling, but Abbie glides passed Kevin, blocking him from receiving it.

My eyes fly to Liam running in front of Abbie, and giving me a chance to change receivers.

Psy is on me, but before she can take back the ball, I fire it back at Liam. He huffs, his long brown hair whipping back as he maneuvers the shot and proceeds to the goal.

Hanna secures her stance, taking a defensive role as Liam bares his teeth in his assured grin.

"Think you can stop *me*, cutie?" He teases the easily flustered redhead.

She pouts. "I *know* I can." Hanna's somehow able to punt the ball out of Liam's hold and into the air.

"*Let's fucking go!*" Abbie praises, backing up to predict the pass.

That's when Melanie stops babysitting the goal and dashes in. She strikes the ball mid-air as Hanna steps back, and it hits me square in the chest where my heart and my injuries once were.

My eyes widen, and my body stills.

It didn't hurt. It *doesn't* hurt.

The damn thing is made up of faux leather and stuffing, but my surgical scars may as well have opened up right then and there. My heart lodges into my throat, and I can't breathe.

A flash of memory from that day has me still, and before I can tell up from down, my hands are trembling. My mouth becomes dry as sand as the harsh scent of antiseptics overwhelms me in that minute.

A whistle calls out. Coach Tess raises her hands into a T for a time-out. "Everything okay, Mr. Kaiser?"

My Valentine's Virus

My glare rests on Melanie. I catch her crooked smile before she turns her back to me.

The rest of the game is an emotional grapple after another. My wounds ached at each glance at Melanie and Abbie.

She tried taking her from me and almost got away with it. I wasn't even a bad boyfriend to her. I didn't deserve what she did to me, but she set out to kill me.

It's getting harder to inhale again, and sweat leaks from my forehead. The invisible hospital scent gradually replaces with oranges and my vision returns.

"Xalton?" Abbie voices in my jog.

I didn't even notice her catching up to me. I look down at the ball, but she hasn't attempted to take it yet. "You don't even need the credit. Unhand the ball..." she swipes it from me with an untouchable precision. "...and move out of my *fucking path!*"

My eyes broaden as she steals the ball I was cradling between my baton and feet—as if predicting its direction. *Did she just?*

The ball curves at such an unrealistic angle that it flies ahead across the floor, and she catches up to it as if passing to herself and increasing her speed to regain power of the play.

She made up for her team's missing player by performing both roles. My jaw drops as her hunger for victory has me gaping.

The ball is pushed continually, and there's nothing Liam, Kevin, or Gus can do to stop her from scoring.

The redhead and Psy cheer the moment her ball kisses our net, bringing their arms overhead in unison as the whistle is blown.

"Score: *girls!*" Coach Tess calls.

Abbie exaggerates her strut back to her team, swaying her wide hips like she owns the court. Psy slaps her on the ass, and each ripple of it surges straight to my balls.

"Ow!" Abbie groans to the sound of Psy's laugh bubbling throughout the gym.

Melanie flips her long blond ends behind her shoulder, cocking her head at her team. "Told you." She narrows her eyes back at me, and my chest feels like it's filling with poison.

Hanna gives a round of applause, more to mock our team instead of celebrating. "Look at *that*, boys. We're *tied.*" She winks over at us with a flirtatious, teasing smile.

Awfully cute when they're full of themselves, and I have only one person to blame for igniting that fire.

Abbie sticks her tongue at me, and I form a fist at my side as the guys gather around.

My team doesn't have to say it. I already know I need to get my ducks in a row.

"Did you… *let* her have the ball, Xal?" Gus asks, tiptoeing in a sympathetic tone.

My jaw clenches in his direction, and it's enough of a prerequisite to have him back the fuck away from me. "Call me 'Xal' again, and I'll fill your gaming systems with so much malware your head will spin."

Gus's face pales, lowering from me like a sad dog. *"Jesus.* Sorry."

Jaden smacks Kevin's arm. "One of *us* should stay on defense. The Spanish chick only scored because no one else was guarding."

"Bitch, *you* play defense," Kevin rolls his eyes at him. *"I'm* gunning for her ass next round. Abbie's mine." His line lights something raw in me, and I point my baton at Kevin's head. With his lips pursed, he locks his eyes on me and gulps.

Staring him down with enough force, he remembers his place and blinks away.

"Abbie is *mine*," I stress in my correction and shoot a glare at Gus for no particular reason. "She's the ace. If she has the ball, back me up, but I'll be on her, and I won't let her take the winning shot again."

"Next round should be the end of it, everyone!" Coach Tess directs, pushing back her smirk at Abbie and the girls twerking their asses at us.

My Valentine's Virus

I especially want her to pay for *that*. I grin out of my restraint. Heat flares in my gaze on my prey in her tight-fitted gym attire. "You usually let luck determine how you win?"

She mirrors my smirk. "No luck here, baby. It's 110% willpower."

I tighten my stance, baton ready. "We'll see about that."

"Pfft—*willpower*," Psy scoffs at us, fiddling with her crystal necklace. "I'm the only one weaponizing *luck* here."

We discount her comment and start the final round the second the whistle echoes.

The ball is in Psy's possession, but before she can pass it to Hanna, Jaden dives in front of her. Nervously, Psy turns to Abbie for suggestions.

"Pass it!" Abbie orders anyway and gestures to Hanna.

Confused but willing, Psy hits the ball to toss to Hanna either way.

"It's *all* you, Hanna! Make mamma proud!" Abbie chants.

"Don't let her have it, Jaden!" I shout.

Hanna stiffens as Jaden and Kevin rush to her. She shakes her head, breaking away from her nerves, running in the direction at Psy's speed. The ball passes by Jaden's feet. *Fucking moron!*

She does something I didn't expect. Hanna charges back at Kevin and roars. She fucking *roars*.

Raising her baton, she bypasses Kevin's reach for the ball and performs her signature move.

It's in the air. At this point, anyone's ball, and we're already on the girl's end. Gus and Jaden are back on our side as defense. We just need Kevin or Liam to fire the rock to Jaden, who's closest. I'm currently blocked by Psy, but where is Abbie?

Kevin hits the ball over to Liam, but Abbie defends both of them while Melanie pretends to goalie.

"Pass it," I order. I don't care if he's closest to the goal. I can read what's about to happen just through Princess's sharp eye on them. But smart-ass Kevin ignores me. "Fucker, I said pass—"

♥

Abbie falls to the ground in her jog to a slide and punts the ball ahead, away from their position, and out of Kevin's hold.

Fucking wild. I'm not sure what I expected, but it sure as shit wasn't that. Everyone stills with their mouths agape, watching Abbie obliterate Kevin's ego with style.

Rushing back up, with skidded knees, she hurries to follow it.

"What the fuck, dude?" Kevin laughs in defeat.

I glare hate at him, and he rubs his neck, avoiding my eyes.

Liam runs to stop the ball from reaching Psyra, and I rush in front of her, stealing it back.

"Oh, come on," Psyra swears under her breath.

I attempt to make up for Kevin's misplay. I'm in Abbie's sights. Hanna and Psy chase after too. I glare up at Melanie, watching me intently as I aim and fire.

Bringing up her baton, she whips it so fast that her block seems like an after-effect, with only her hair movements proving she retaliated.

Unlike before, she gives a damn. I recoil when she fires the ball, but it aims back at Abbie.

She catches it in the air with her stick, and we're all on her now.

"Don't let her score!" Kevin shouts.

I sneer at Jaden and Gus, who have moved forward. *Who the hell told them to move from defense?*

Abbie's gaining on them, swerving past Liam and letting him trip on his own feet.

She borrows Hanna's maneuver from watching, bringing the ball in the air in front of her only to hit it forward and pass to Psy, who caught up.

She then, in return, passes it back to Abbie, flying by Jaden's crappy attempt to stop their exchange.

Gus, I swear, if you let them score. He raises his baton in front of him to protect his face and *not* the goal.

My Valentine's Virus

Psyra fires it and passes him straight into the net—a completely stoppable strike too.

Mother. Fucker. The whistle cries out, and I break my baton over my knee. Un-fucking-believable.

Avoiding Coach Tess's brow of disapproval as I toss the broken staff, I storm back into the men's locker room. Its darkly-lit ambiance casts long shadows that dance across the ornate wooden lockers. The air is heavy with a mix of musky cologne and the subtle scent of leather from the antique furniture scattered about.

I'm not upset over losing some pretend hockey game—not truly. The rush of witnessing Abbie's merciless beautiful moves was cinema. I overheard the way she orchestrated her team, like her personal chess pieces, each moving a step toward victory.

That glint in her eyes during the game, the sheer focus, concentration, passion, and the way her sexy brain worked to give her the best outcome had my chest fire with danger. Abbie manipulated the field, the boys, and her team. A shiver flies down my spine from my recap of her.

My reflection in the wall-length mirror is flushed, and my cheeks burn with embarrassment in my changing room. She defies every notion I thought possible about her capabilities.

Why am I constantly taken aback by the lengths she'll go to win? Why does her drive hit me with the force of a stampede setting my heart racing?

Again, she consumes my cause and has me questioning... everything. I'm sick of it. I'm sick of feeling one way when I need to be another.

I slam my locker shut, the metallic clang punctuating the bitterness in my eardrums. I incline against it for a breath. A rush of warmth fills me again at the prospect of Abbie's unrelenting need to not only survive but also gloat at every interval. It builds me up to beat her with even more intensity.

I'm not sure what I'll do when the time comes, and she's beaten me—not that it'll let it happen, but I need to retaliate. Zone_Warden makes no free threat.

My phone buzzes in my pocket, breaking my reverie. But before I dismiss it, my eyes grow wide at the name flashing on my screen: *Renee Kaiser*.

She never calls. Call? She never even *speaks* to me.

My pulse jumps to my collar as I answer on the third buzz. "Hello?" Caution paints my tone.

"**Xalton?**" The voice on the other end is feminine but textured, with a rough edge underlying its wariness. It's a voice I haven't heard since I was twelve years old.

"Mother?" My breath catches. The word is bizarre on my tongue, as if dust clouds it from years of misuse.

"**Yes,**" she swallows harshly on the other end.

"Are you okay? Where are you?" I breathe, struggling not to seem as desperate as I am for her focus as I did when I was a child.

"**I'm well,**" she clears her throat, but something nags at me to pry. She sounds ill, lost even. She replies with a forced cheerfulness that belies something darker beneath the surface. "**Did you receive your father's email?**" she prompts before I drill further.

My chest pushes hurt in my veins. I want to lie, but this is the only time she's reached out to me. "I haven't gotten the chance to respond to it."

"**Your father needs a response from you before the end of today,**" she states in a curt tone, as if there's more at stake than I can fathom. Like my existence has always been to be their bargaining chip. "**I figured I'd call to expedite your answer, my love.**"

I adjust the phone in my sweating hands. "Did he *make* you call me for that?" Try as I must, I can't keep the resentment from seeping into my voice, pain lacing each word.

My Valentine's Virus

"He's eager for your response," she deflects, her voice carrying a subtle strain.

My brows cramp at the center, and I lean against a surface. "And if I refuse?"

"Then a date will be *given* to you," her words drape firm in the air. Her loaded promise sends a shiver of hatred up my spine.

Her ultimatum halts time, and for a moment, the world narrows to a single name on my screen. The alarm I set to track Abbie during her study session proves its worth. I owe a strange debt of gratitude to Gus for being dumb enough to provide that nugget of info. The fact that she believes she can go on dates with her nemesis looming is the only thing that makes me question her intelligence.

"I refuse to accept. I refuse to attend," I supply, firmly, hoping she'll can understand my reasons.

"Listen, darling. Sometimes, you have to make sacrifices for your loved ones." Her rigid plea tugs at my heart.

"Do *you* love me? If you did, you wouldn't subject me to this nonsense again!" I lash out, the pain of everything from last year roaring free and too raw to shield behind pleasantries. "Why is this dinner worth more than your only son's peace of mind?"

The silence that stretches on the line weighs with unspoken truths that have gathered between us.

"Call me back once you've settled down, Xalton, darling." Her voice is both at arm's length and final. Before I can respond, she hangs up a second later.

"Wait—I" I grip my phone, desperation clawing, shredding at my throat the more time restarts, leaving me suspended in a sea of silence and betrayal.

It's been a minute since I felt this sting. I'm an idiot to think that after all this time, her cold shoulder wouldn't have this effect on me.

A glimmer of respite pulls me back to reality as Abbie's alarm vibrates for me again.

If I don't find an outlet fast, I'll take it out on this fucking building. Anger builds in me like a living, breathing phantom as I pace around the perimeter to calm it down.

It's no use. Exiting the changing room, I stomp into the quietest pair of boots I own. It's a good thing I know where my prey is for me to take my rage out on.

LEVEL FIFTEEN
PRINCESS_USER24

My girls rally, jumping, cheering, and hugging like we just won the lottery.

Psy and I imitate Hanna's precious battle cry from when she went against gorgeous and tall Kevin Wu. I'm over the moon about her breaking out of her shell.

We each break into thickening laughter, and Melanie even trades a few chuckles.

I peek over my shoulder for my rival, Xalton, as he heads into the locker room.

After changing back into regular clothes, my head tilts at Jaden, Liam, Gus, and Kevin approaching us from the other team after catching their breaths.

"Good game, guys! I mean girls." Kevin winks. I swear, he may need to get his eye checked with how often he does that.

Psyra stands in front of us. "You *too*. Thanks for a *good* game," she smiles, extra depth in her dimples for him. I cock a brow at her. Does my little Psy have a *thing* for Kevin?

Now that my ego is back in its resting place, I take a better look at the boys.

Kevin's lean with a cute button nose and dark brown eyes. He reminds me of the cutest member of a Korean boy band, but if I say that out loud, he'd have the absolute right to roast the hell out of me.

Now, Liam—he has the best, most beautiful brown hair I've ever seen on a guy. It must be dyed to look so chocolatey and moose-like. He's on the short side—around my height—with a gorgeous olive complexion. His muted blue eyes wander elsewhere, pouting like he's got a lot on his mind.

Then there's good old Gus and Jaden. Both are blond-haired studs, but Jaden strikes me as the smarter of the two. It's the glasses covering his bright brown eyes.

"I have an idea," Psy faces all of us. "Let's celebrate our victory over a few shots at the bar down the street," my little extrovert proposes. "Sound groovy?"

The boys grin collaboratively at her accent.

"The *grooviest*," Gus chuckles with a teasing hint.

"The Melancholy?" Hanna points her brows up at her. "Is that the big place behind campus?"

"The same," Psy confirms.

Kevin nods. "Sounds great. I've never been." He reaches into his pocket for his phone and leans closer to Psy.

Her face pinkens under her dark hue as he does, and I swear she tries to inhale him.

Liam wusses out, explaining he had to study all night, and Jaden has a modeling gig to run off to straight after class. After the boys wave us off and complement our sick war tactics, they pace away into their side of the men's locker room to change.

My Valentine's Virus

I look over and spy Melanie heading for our locker room too. I'm not too sure how I should feel about her.

Psyra did go into CSI detail about how she sabotaged the float I was clinging to in trying to get me killed, but I don't think there's enough evidence to support it.

She could have easily lost one of her hairpins by the pool, and Psy's no stranger to her active imagination. After all, we owe her for helping us win as much as any of us, and I'd feel weird excluding her from the festivities even if she does give off cold-bitch vibes.

"Oh, Ms. *Mayor?*" I sing out for her, and she gives me a once-over. "You're invited too." Maybe getting a few drinks in her will loosen her up more and make her seem less stilted and wicked.

She forces a quick smirk. "No thanks. I have other engagements to attend. Enjoy your little *party*, Belle-Nuñez." She flips her hair over her petite shoulder and saunters through the doors.

Welp. Can't say I didn't try.

Hanna wraps her arm around my neck and pounces on my back for an impromptu piggyback ride. "Girl, forget her. She's been tight-assed *all* game and maybe even her whole life," she adds.

Psy catches up with her arms crossed. "I'd steer clear of her. The psycho has demons hovering her shoulders 24/7."

I roll my eyes trying not to let Psy catch me do so. "You're able to see demons now?"

Psy perks her pillowy dark lips. "Always have, baby doll."

I shrug, keeping hold of Hanna, envying how weightless she is to carry as I escort them into the girls' locker room. Exiting in cleaner attire, I take a swig from my CRU-branded water bottle.

Xalton approaches me. Amidst the celebrating group of girls, as if suppressing the urge to act on his frustration, his night-green eyes narrow and ring my inner signals like a fire alarm in my guts. My jaw drops, and I still. The cold bottle in my hand numbs my palm. He's in all black, carrying a new jacket over his shoulders. He reveals black suspenders, his gray dress shirt, matte combat boots, and grayer cargo pants. A hunting knife in a dark holster discreetly rests at his waist. My throat dries even as I put away my bottled water.

When the other girls disperse, Psyra lingers, taking a brief opportunity to playfully tease Xalton about his loss in the game. Eventually, she joins the others for the head start of our bar hopping, leaving Xalton and me alone in the empty hallway.

His footsteps are quiet, but his heavy presence beside me deepens every nerve in my body to full awareness.

Without my consent, the memory of him setting those boundaries against me wearing the jacket plays back in my mind. I don't care if he tries to intimidate me. I just don't want him playing with my heart.

I turn from his direction, but he circles me, and I'm forced to give him attention. "What do you want?"

His tired eyes rest on me, and I avoid his face. "You played exceptionally well," he states. "Your skills were both frightening *and* exciting." He hikes into me until my back is to the wall.

He doesn't disclose the latter, but I offer a curtsy, accepting his snarky praise.

"You…" I start, but somehow, my breath keeps losing me.

I forgot how intense he is up close. I'm reminded of how his fingers felt when we met. I still can't replicate the orgasm he gave me when I'm in my bed. Damn him.

"You… Would… would you mind it if I…?" What am I even trying to say? He made it clear we aren't friends. I shouldn't even think about asking him what I want to say.

He cups my chin to raise my lowering gaze to his. My eyes drift to his airbrushed lips, and he brushes his thumb against my chin. "What is it?" He asks in a low husk. His touch is like my soul is taking a warm bath.

I swallow and smile for a quick second. My knees dip slightly, remembering the power his touch has on me. "I want you to come with us to celebrate tonight," I supply, my lip wobbling out of my control. I

My Valentine's Virus

stiffen it with a bite, and I grunt. "I'm inviting you *outside* for fun with a group of new friends," I clarify. My speeding heart beats faster at his unreadable, trained expression. "Something *your* nerd-ass wouldn't know about."

He shows me his perfect white teeth in his laugh. My eyes nearly roll to the back of my head from the silk of his voice stroking my eardrums. "I'll take you myself," he grants before letting me go.

"Hey, Abbie." An outside voice makes me clench. Speeding to the right of Xalton's bicep, I find a blond blur coming to greet us. Gus waves, and my eyes rover back at the break of stoicism on his face.

Slowing a blink of irritation, Xalton sneers before raising his arm to block his approach to me. He pinches my chin in a tender but quick manner before leaning away. "Your time belongs to me, Princess. Remember that," he threatens in a tight whisper.

I ignore that for now. "Hey, Gus." I wave back sharply. "I'll be with you in a minute, okay?"

Gus nods, putting his hand down and props against the wall to scroll through his socials or something.

Xalton leaves before I can offer any retort. Maybe it was a bad idea to invite him. The bliss from winning so hard must have damaged my senses, but there's no going back now.

Gus escorts me to the library, and for the hundredth time, my breath is stolen by the beauty of this campus.

It looks like the library of my dreams, or at least an improved version of it. This place is a cathedral of darkness.

Obsidian doors stand sentinel while the scent of aged leather and rare incense permeates the space. Dark mahogany shelves loom like guardians as I distract myself from Gus's path toward the front desk in the center.

Hypnotized by the high ceilings, I slowly spin. Bookshelves point my gaze upward in the direction. Its gothic arches, and stained-glass windows, where red and dark paintings of abstract gargoyles adorn some kind of battlefield. Fiery red and inky black merge in a timeless clash.

Dim evening lighting filters through, casting a glow on velvet-upholstered furniture and monuments, creating a gorgeous hub.

I pass a stone fireplace roaring and casting shadows on the carpets, mirroring a group of students in a study circle.

My widened eyes trace each book spine, each shelf.

Despite the university's dark pool theme being one of the hurdles to my rescue, it was still pretty. It makes the most sense for a library.

"Careful, Absters. If you open your mouth any wider, a moth will soar right in," Gus remarks. Having to come back and get me, he whizzes back toward the front desk.

"I reserved a room for us on the left," Gus reveals, motioning me ahead of him to analyze while he checks us in like it's a restaurant.

It's impressive.

We're given an entire hall full of private rooms meant to be used for an hour. If any more time is needed, we can hit a button near the door like a timer, and the door will unlock.

The keycard clicks against the door, and he opens it. Our private room spills into view with rows of bookshelves stocked with textbook copies from our course on the ready. A wide rectangle mahogany table sits near the door, displaying a cornucopia of unused school supplies.

The sign above the frame reads it's soundproof, and I can see how that comes in handy when you need to block out the world for hardcore sessions.

Before entering, I catch a glimpse of Liam in the right room beside ours. He was the quiet guy who rejected our invitation to The Melancholy. Liam mumbled something about finishing his lessons for the day, but as I squint at him inside, I find he's doing anything but.

A hefty headset leans over his shoulders, and he lifts his chin at me in acknowledgment. He's rank grinding into the virtual world of... *League of Legends?* Ew.

And he mains *Yasuo* of all people—I should break into his room right now and ruin his match before he continues the reign of toxicity.

My Valentine's Virus

I adjust the slipping strap of my bag over my shoulder as Gus unlocks the door to our room. "What do you think the odds are of logging into Liam's game and ending up matching against him?"

Gus shrugs, having caught him in my line of sight. "You play League?"

"...no," I trail, narrowing my eyes away from him and my cold past. "Not anymore."

"Cool," he smiles. "Who was your main?"

I swallow. "...guess."

He rubs the hairs on his chin. "You strike me as an *Ahri* player."

I'm flattered, but no. "Riven," I supply. "Her, or Dr. Mundo."

He strokes his beard, and I notice it's coppery in this light. "My *second* guess. I definitely should have picked a *Top* laner."

My brow rises. "You?"

"Oh no, that shit's for nerds," he flashes a sardonic grin, exposing his deep smile lines. "I'd rather spend my time on something more beneficial—"

I cut him off with an accusing laugh. "Yet you *know* the characters!" I blurt.

He snickers, pulling up a seat for me, and I accept. Hanging my bag on the table's hook, I find our primary Blockchain books were already set out for us.

"What's your definition of *'beneficial?'*"

"Charity work," he drawls. Ooh! He's rich *and* gives back? Dad would want me to bring this one home. "My little brothers play it," he continues. "I can't stand it," Gus bemoans as he gets himself settled.

I know we're both lying about how we feel about the game. It's okay.

"Speaking of family, what's going on with you and Xalton? Is he bullying you or something?" That's got nothing to do with that, but let's see where this goes.

"Is he bullying me—*no,*" I fumble, trying not to sound as offended as I am. "I suppose that's what it looks like from your perspective. But if anything, I'm *his* bully. I've already taken his lunch money and talked jive about his mother," I flip a page.

"Ha, no way," Gus does a double-take from his page to mine before frowning at his answers. I helped correct and offered him advice on question six.

I'm genuinely impressed by Gus's second impression. He was giving me heavy "fuckboy" energy. Now, he's treating me like a person and not a pair of honkers with legs.

"Thanks," he grins. There's a genuine regard in my tone that warms the selfless part of my heart.

I blush, grinning smugly as something in the corner of my eye pulls me away. My eyes narrow thinly toward the back area, where the light can't touch. I swear I just saw a glint of something behind one of the shelves.

"Let me know if you need help with that guy. I've noticed him following you around campus the minute you leave for other places. Just because he saved you doesn't mean you owe him anything you're not willing to give him."

Genuine remorse fills his expression, and he fishes out his phone. Swiping the screen open, he shows me its contents.

"Here. He doesn't know, but I've been recording him in the act. This is a battery-powered camera, and he can't hack into it. I can go to the police with it and help with your statement as a second witness. I don't mind walking you places either."

"Oh, you don't have to do any of that," I say. "I've—" I rest my hand on his shoulder. "I've got it handled. If I'm being honest, I have feelings for him, but he's…" Her jaw clenches slightly. "He set his boundaries and told me he wasn't interested," I sigh, my shoulder sagging with the motion. Not that his actions match his words--but still. I'll respect it.

He gives me an odd look that urges my clarification.

My Valentine's Virus

"He *is* a stalker, though," I continue. "You're right about that. But I deserve it. I'm holding something that belongs to him. Or at least *he* thinks belongs to him."

"So, you love him?" Gus's brow arches. The question hangs in the air like a lava bubble.

"Yes."

Admitting it out loud after his concerns is like falling into a vat of needles.

He chuckles at my bitter unrequited pout, and it skewers both me and my pride. "What's there to like? I mean, he's tall but *horrifying*. If you ask me, he's overdoing it at the gym, but I don't doubt you can handle yourself." I roll my eyes, but he continues. "Abs, don't think you're alone. I'm sure Psy's got your back too."

I cover my face with a hand away from him. "Thanks, Gus. Can we move it along here? I didn't want this to turn into a whole thing. We're here to focus on you." I extend my arms into a light stretch, easing comfort back into the space.

"Sure," he chirps. I guess he found my anxieties and spared me by adjusting his seat. It screeches, and he returns to his textbook. He nods and taps the eraser side of his pencil at the next problem.

While digging into these books, I actually find a few lines of code I've never memorized and hankered down on being the best tutor Gus has ever seen.

After I instruct him to practice fictional problems, he slides his large headset over his ears.

While he fixes his playlist, I recommend I return my textbook to the back shelves. I may as well look up the ones for next semester for a heads-up.

I adore the unprepared looks on the professor's faces when they realize how much more I know. It feels like cheating. If I can't find a rival amongst my peers, it has to be their masters.

It's darker back here. The fluorescent lights are lit more over our table in the stretched front of the room, leaving the bookshelf aisles in this dim void in the back. I understand the need for there not to be a window, but it's eerie as hell.

I sigh, the physical strains of the day beginning to set in. Every muscle in my body aches as I stroll to find the textbook's spot. Grunting, I bend to rub my sore knees and am reminded of Grace.

She may have been right about going too hard today. But it was worth it to see the veins in Xalton's neck pulse in his annoyance.

A sinister smile breaks out on my face, releasing a fulfilled chuckle. I check back with Gus, and he hasn't moved. *Good.* I smile. *It's nice when men do what I say.*

My body stills and the hairs jutting up my spine elevate at the perfect aisles bathed in shadows ahead of me. I know it's stupid, but I need to explore it. I got to make sure a demon isn't hidden in one of the alleys by chance.

Returning the book to its seat, my tingles only prickle against my neck the further back I go. My steps slow, and my ears are open.

I may have played too many video games in one lifetime, but if they've shown me one important thing, it's to *always* check your perimeters.

What are the chances of anything of value being back here? There was a school attendant here setting everything up before we entered, and I caught only a sliver of them leaving before handing Gus the keycard.

I inspect the corners of the aisles, both empty. With only three more down to go, my mind races with paranormal thoughts the more I walk.

Psy likes to dabble in that witchcraft stuff. Maybe when she's in the dorm by herself, she summons portals or some shit, and one of her "entities" found this place for shelter?

I exhale at the idea. They'd probably be everything she'd dreamed of. Smirking at the thought, I envision some muscular demon with four arms and a ten-inch cock.

My Valentine's Virus

Inhaling harshly, I check the middle corners of the aisle, and my shoulders ease. Nope. No sexy creature-thing. One more aisle to go.

I jump ahead, checking forward and back to more vacuums of darkness, and my goosebumps warm over. Accepting my imagination is getting the better of me again, I turned back to the study session.

When reaching for my pocket, a hand extends behind me and squeezes around my mouth. My eyes fling wide open, and my heart drums a mile a minute. A wall of muscular heat presses against my back and my chest runs cold with panic. An entity yanks me back into the aisle—*an aisle I confirmed was empty!*

Before the bookshelf blocks my view of Gus, he continues his studies, deafened by his headset.

"Don't scream," the deep timbre of my abductor's voice heats against my ear. Soft lips brush against the rim.

Glancing down, I recognize the combat boots Xalton wears, and my chest heaves with a deep burn. I grunt, my frown deepening before I can break his balls in seven different ways.

His other hand glides beneath my shirt, smoothing up to my breast, releasing a shudder from me along with my strengths. The flat surface of his thumb strokes my peaks in agonizing circles. Xalton grips me tighter against his suffocating body, and my panicked gasp has him shield my mouth harder. His other aggressive hand cups and massages my breast like he's trying to force sounds from me. The peak hardens between his fingers, and he molds it around his thumb.

My face runs hot, and my body tenses as the sharp, sweet sensation surges downward.

"Come on," I pant through my nose. He feels too good on contact. Too much. The son of a bitch has me alone back here, and my pussy weeps with the idea of what he'll do to me back here. The swoon from my lips muffle between his fingers. All he has to do is touch me, and I'm butter.

I opened a fortune cookie earlier during lunch, and it read, *"Do not give defeat an easy way out."* Abiding by *that*, what's left of my commonsense scans for options.

How did he even do this? I checked every freaking aisle, *front to back*.

Xalton arches my neck back to have me peer into his pine-colored gaze. My lip quivers without order finding myself consumed in the dark forest of my nightmares as he pillars over me.

Heat fills his eyes with mine as he slides his fingers passed my lips. He strokes my tongue, and when he brushes against my teeth, every ridge of his smooth fingertips finds my drool.

I'll bite—

"*'Anything I want,'* you said," he purrs, cutting off my racing thoughts. My drunken words from that night weaponize off his tongue, and my pussy throbs from the lust in his voice.

At the end of my backward trip, I raise my leg, knocking over a few books, and he releases my breast to grab my thigh.

I hold my breath when his arm wraps around my waist as he pulls me over his lap.

Leaning over the AC vents, he locks my knee near my head, wrangling in his arm. The draft pushes up my skirt, and its iced air slaps against my privates, exposing just how wet I can get with sixty seconds of fondling. Great. It's not that I can help it. He's had a spell on me since I can remember. But seeing him in magazines and having him touch me is a different avenue.

"Hush," he tsks in a quiet voice. "What do you think your date will do if he sees you this way? With your legs spread *wiiide* open in another man's arms," he teases. Xalton whips out a blade from his side. The gleam from it fires panic behind my eyes. Not because I'm scared of him. But because it means he must have heard the embarrassing shit I told Gus earlier. *Fuck, I hope he does kill me!*

He gives me a pocket of space to breathe. "He's not my—"

My Valentine's Virus

"*Shh...* Princess," he quiets, slowly gliding the soft edge of his knife up my inner thigh. My breath hitches with my throat knotting at the cold touch near my entrance. "I don't want him hearing the *shameful* sounds you'll make when I fuck that needy cunt of yours." He caresses my ear with his lips, hot and sending chills to my exposure. "You really had me worried, you know?" He susurrates and nips the fat of my ear. Slowly tugging on it, a shooting thrill ignites beneath my skin. My knuckles whiten, and my chest heaves at the sting. I'm a puddle when he's near me. Every muscle I've honed weakens beneath his touch. "As if death could keep you away from me," he scoffs.

His harsh words from before throb in my ears like a headache.

"*...We're not friends. I don't even like you... Don't parade around in it like I'm your boyfriend. It's disgusting...*"

A cold tear carves from my eyes, and the sick bastard runs his tongue up my cheek. I shudder in his hold as his blade smooths under the band of my underwear. Tugging, it tears the right banding, and he pauses at the other side of my hip for the other.

"*Beg*, if you want me to stop," he says tightly.

I grunt in his hold, shaking my head. "Gus will hear—"

"*That's* what you're worried about?" He scoffs before ripping my underwear like it's parchment paper. The shredding pitch echoes across the aisle like a symphony of my exposure. My heart pounds behind my face, and he folds his knife away, easing his hold on my jaw.

"You're *such* a dickhead," I manage, but I cut myself off from the heated caress of his hand spreading up my thigh. Relentless shivers course through me like rapids taking me to those fantasies I had back in the auditorium.

"Yet, you can't get enough of me."

I stiffen as he presses his face to my side. I bite my cheek feeling his damning smirk. My inner protests hide the moment his thick finger slips between my crease. He traces my sensitive bud immediately, and my face heats to my ears. My hips buck for more before he's even started.

"Always this wet for me, Princess?" He rumbles in my ear. My embarrassment peaks, making me headbutt him, but I miss.

He sways right, using my momentum to spread my legs farther apart. My left thigh props over his, and he doesn't waste time. His thick fingers ease into my pussy. Sliding slowly in and out of me, my chest boils with his sensual motions.

He focuses on my face as his movements quicken. The moment I stop struggling, his thrusts speed up, stealing a moan from my sealed lips. I swallow, unable to ignore the lewd echoes of my arousal. His thumb teases my clit, the manipulating strokes only adding gas to the fires of his insatiable petting.

My walls clench as a climax threatens me. I whimper, and he sinks his teeth into the curve of my neck. My head falls back, and I grip his thigh. Every muscle clenches as I come undone. Eruptions of aftershocks power through my body from head to toe as darkness encapsulates me.

I surrender to the blissful abyss swallowing me, and in the throes of the jaw-opening release, stars glitter behind my iris.

"That's my girl," he praises, coating the side of my neck with aggressive kisses. "Come *all* over my fingers. Let me taste you again."

"Uhhn....!" I squeeze between my hard breaths. My heart pounds hard in my chest, and my body trembles in his strict hold. Waves of precious release fire from me, and I'm *blinded* with need.

I whip my leg from over him to close, but he wrestles me back before I can maneuver free. I struggle to catch my breath as he swings me around like his personal fuck toy.

His ability to react to my turns makes my brain do summersaults mid-breath. I'm a goddamn blackbelt. He shouldn't be able to counter me with casual rhythm in such a tight space.

Smirking at my pinching expression, he crouches between my thighs. My leg hits the bookshelf, and I pull back. He leans me against the vents and spreads my thighs wider.

My Valentine's Virus

My legs wrap around him, but before I can brace myself, he buries his face in my pussy. He cups my butt like a seat. My skin spills between his fingers, and he hoists me high, where my head peaks over the bookshelves.

My stomach drops to my tailbone. Up here, the screech of Gus's chair grabs my attention. He rises and turns to see my flustered face.

He lowers his headset around his neck before locking eyes with me. I heave while Xalton's heated tongue darts and laps my sensitive skin. I wince when he captures my clit between his teeth, dangerously teasing the nerve with his tongue.

The jackass doesn't care.

My attention jerks back to Xalton, his eyes filled to the brim with heat while he slurps and sucks my pussy like a starving maniac.

I have no words—no, I have several.

It's like he doesn't care that Gus is coming here. His wet slurps and hard sucks threaten to give us away, and he groans into me despite it all.

When I try pulling him off, he doubles down, and my muscles tighten. Sharp bliss bleeds into me, rivaling my anxiety. My eyelids become heavy, and I grip the fabric of Xalton's hoodie as my climax slams into me with the force of an ox.

"*Ahh—*"

"Abbie? You good?" Gus asks, hauling me back to my doomed reality.

"*Fuck, fuck,*" I pant heavily, barely hearing him. Xalton increases the pressure, making my head hit against the wall for support. "Ugh—" Rushed breathing vibrates in my voice as I stifle a burning moan. "Y... *yes,*" I whimper, my ears boiling when he finds another sweet spot to torture. *Gus will see us,* my eyes beg with Xalton's.

A finger slips inside of me again, zapping all thought from my brain. With aggressive laps, it's like he's eating my pussy off the bone.

My walls swallow around his pumping fingers, and he releases my clit with a suck. Not being able to cry out is impossible. My face is hot to my scalp, and a moan breaks from the corners of my lips.

Fiery need brims through my eyes as my hands dive into his silky groomed hair. His perfect sleepy green orbs rain over me, ruthless and with no hint of moving away.

"I *can't...*" I squeak at him. Gus's footsteps approach, and my ears throb. Xalton lifts his crooked nose to me, dragging his wide tongue up my slit savoring every taste.

"Get *rid* of him," he growls, and a muscle ticks in his jaw. "I'm nowhere *near* finished with you."

My eyes roll as he continues. Gus nears, an aisle away and I don't know if I'm in the mindset to trick him. If he catches me like this, it'll be a struggle to look him in the eye again, and Xalton's grip is unrelenting.

A haggard breath escapes me as I grow dizzy. The bookshelves close in around us as I ascend from the crux of a juicy orgasm greater than before. So much so, I might let Gus see if it means reaching a portion of it.

"You *sure?*" Gus pries further. I want to bite his goddamn head off. The only thing saving me is the song *Supernova* by Within Temptations blaring from his headphones.

"I'm..." I draw in a quick breath. *"I'm coming."*

The muscle in Xalton's jaw clenches again, somehow lapping around my clit faster.

"Stay... stay right *there,*" I ache as cold bliss overcomes me. In the deafening chorus of the song, the heat in Xalton's eyes on mine has me spiraling.

There's a crack in my will to fight, and filling those breaks is his essence—his bourbon aroma, his intensity, the tension hidden in his pupils, and his immovable strain.

My Valentine's Virus

Barrages of release hit me, and my body screamed out to me in a flurry of hunger. He knows exactly what my pussy craves somehow, and I lose this fight every time.

Gus stills, arching a brow from my stifled groans—I'm at least hoping he can't hear through his blaring headset. "Are you crying?"

"C-can you get me a bottle of water from the *café?!*" I hurry out. Xalton inserts another finger and slows a thumb over my sensitivity with tight, deliberate strokes.

"Which brand?" Gus nods.

"Oh *God*—the *good* one—" I pant.

He nods. "Cool. I'll be back."

The moment his steps recede and the door clicks closed, I glare at Xalton.

Shivers course up my spine at the devilish glint in his eyes. My chest aches from how hard I breathe.

He lowers me down, and I lean against him as my knees wobble. He takes my wrist and spins me to face the wall. Hovering over me from behind, the scent of my arousal is highlighted in his breath.

"Do you plan on staying a virgin or sacrificing your body to me? I'd love to see your bloodstains paint my cock." He grips my jaw, forcing me to face him.

"Don't," I warn, gritting my teeth with finality.

He smiles, releasing my jaw, but his other arm keeps me pressed against his hips. He pushes me to bend over the unit while he slides his bottoms down against my ass. When he pulls me harshly against his burning erection, blood roars in my ears.

My eyes widen, and my core throbs as he strokes his impossible girth firmly against my entrance.

Is he just going to take it from me? Before I protest, he draws my free hand to feel his cock, and my jaw drops. I struggle to turn, but he grips me in place with his broad arm so as not to see him. Facing the wall and propped over the vents, I bite my cheek as I stroke from base to tip.

♥

A tight groan shudders through him. He's coated in thick precum. Using it as a lubricant, I pump his cock once, twice, and three times.

His grip on me tightens as his dick pulsates against my palm. He falls over me, his hand palming the wall as his breaths harshen. *"Fuck*, Princess. You feel incredible," he moans. Every ounce of resistance I had melted from me like butter. *His voice.* I could listen to it for eons.

I'll do anything to keep him groaning.

He slides the length of his cock up and down my wetness, spreading our emissions between my thighs like lube.

"X-Xalton—"

He doesn't penetrate me, but a nervous squeal comes from me anyway. His girth slits between my thighs in a ruthless thrust. My pussy clenches over his length as it massages my clit from the other side.

Wet humping, he slides me around his dick, and my hips grind for more.

A stifled moan breaks from him, and he grips my waist. Pulling my ass against him with a smack, he forces me in place so I can't move. He sighs, giving me a moment to catch my breath. "You told him you love me," he brings up in a tired voice. His hips begin to piston, sawing his cock against my center.

My chest tightens, and his thrusts jab through me at a sharper pace, lengthening my gasp.

"No," I rasp, shaking my head. "I... I said what I thought he wanted to hear—"

He grips my jaw, arching me back. I face his heat-filled gaze as his balls slap my thighs. He thrusts. "I'm your hero." Thrust. "Your *adversary*." Thrust. "And you *love* me." Thrust. He whispers against my neck.

"I don't," I pant.

"You do." Thrust. "What changed?" Thrust.

My Valentine's Virus

"Your …*jacket*," I mutter between breaths of his excruciating propulsions.

"You can wear the damn jacket, just say it."

"I can't! I hate you! All you do is *fuck* with my head! Everything about you feels like a fantasy."

He grips me so hard I almost believe he's going to snap me in half. My arms tremble, and I grip the edge of the AC. "I woke up covered with it. I searched for you to let you know I wanted to let Elysium go."

Thrust. "For fuck sake, Abbie," he breathes, a break in his tone. "You can say it."

"I love you," I admit, my head dropping in defeat.

Xalton grips my hips tight against his stomach, and a deep grunt rumbles from his hold. Come bursts from his crown, coating the vents under us. His erection throbs between my thighs, and every pulse hums through my skin in our fading storm of pleasure.

Panting, Xalton closes his eyes, releasing me and tilting his head back. He heaves behind me like he just finished a marathon. "I love you too," he utters. He runs his hands through his scalp like he's fought a hundred battles against the notion.

I snort. "*Now* who's lying? You were going to kill me when we met, remember?"

He smiles at me, dripping with certainty. "I fail to see your point." Leaning to my chest, he flashes his brows up to me.

"Heh. You're a psycho."

"It takes one to know one, Princess." He swallows and brings up his pants to fix.

"When…?" I press. "It couldn't have been just now."

The flat of his cheeks bleed pink. "…when we met online. I just didn't want to admit it."

He's a masochist. Everything I've said online could be summarized as a series of slurs for men like him. I can work with this.

♥

I grin with a spark of challenge in my eyes. *"My* crush was first," I badger.

"Ugh, shut up," he laughs, the pleasant hum of his rasp weary and lilting. He shakes his head at me as if knowing he's going to regret his decisions later.

Xalton angles to swipe my marred underwear off the floor. Shoving the black strands of fabric into his pocket like his reward, he flashes me a wounded look. After I turn, unable to keep a straight look in his eyes, I rub my elbow and lower my head. "Release Elysium," he states with finality.

"Okay." Moisture slips to the crux of my knee.

"I'll… text you before you leave the grounds." He lowers his forehead to touch mine. "I stole your schedule, so you can't escape me." He lifts my head to his face and captures my lip between his. Kissing firmly, he pulls my tongue to meet his.

I moan from the sensitive brush of his mouth, sweeping with the rhythm he had me come to.

His face heats over me, and my lungs fill with the delicious scent of orange juice I catch on his breath.

My cheeks ache in his tender hold once he separates from me. He runs his fingers into my scalp and slightly tugs so I face him. "You make me want to scream. You're as stubborn as The Plague, and all I dream about is wringing your tiny neck." He inhales my hair, stroking my scarred eyebrow. "But I'm glad we met. Face to face. My little rival," he grins.

My smile matches his, stretching more as I absorb his sweet words. "You're so weird. And quit calling me your *'little rival.'*"

"Princess, then?" His brows lift with his question, rubbing his temple against mine.

"…I like Princess… *'My Abbie'* too.

My Valentine's Virus

"My Abbie...?" His smile pours heat into me, leaving my skin boiling. "'My little rival' works just for me." He releases me fully and strides to the exit, taking all of the warmth from the room with him.

As I stand with the books for company, the weight of the room alters. Seconds later, I received a text message and noticed the "unknown" text assigned itself as a contact.

 [Xalton]: I love you. You beautiful psycho ♥

My brows lift at his emoji, newfound warmth swelling in my chest. Oh, what the hell did I get myself into?

LEVEL SIXTEEN

ZONE_WARDEN

I'm lost in the world's most pretentious library, stalking its pewter avenues of shelves and book covers in the blissful aftermath of my haze. Heated cedar fills my lungs. I nearly trip, the air-conditioned space rivaling my sweat. If I cared an ounce of what these trust-fund babies thought, they'd think I looked ill, smiling at nothing.

My heart beats, having grown three sizes today like it discovered the true meaning of Christmas.

"She *loves* me," I mutter into the book spines, the phrase falling entirely foreign on my lips.

She *loves* me. The effects of my little rival's confession echo through me with a force strong enough to bring me to my hands and knees. The doomed version of me days ago would scoff at the novelty, but those three words alone were ample enough to shatter the remnants of my resolve. Fuck. I haven't had a release that satisfying in… ever.

My Valentine's Virus

I'm still reeling over her checking each aisle while I stood inches from her in her blind spot. I made the allure of the room too great to ignore. I still don't know how I kept my composure with my dick bending with need once she was certain the coast was clear. I got to indulge in her taste again, and I'm hard envisioning how wet and tight she felt. I'm not sure how I controlled myself from impaling her. I came the hardest I ever had, snug between her plush thighs.

I cover the lower half of my face and groan from her lingering scent on me. I'm on new grounds with her now and want to stay like this for a while.

She loves me. I needed to hear that more than I thought. I needed *her*. Abbie's hold on my mind blossoms into a euphoric biochemical that swells inside me long after being with her. It's akin to helium from how weightless my footsteps feel.

"She loves *me*," I repeat, under my hopeless hypnosis. I run my finger through my hair as power leaves my veins. I submit. It feels too good.

The echoes of her sultry moans repeat in my head, making me dizzy with want all over again. I could fall asleep to those sounds. Even the odd ones she makes—her annoyed huffs, her frustrated grunts, her cartoonish gasps, and her precious fucking whimpers. I'm in love with that demon, even if she lured me back into hell.

My throat dries when I find the hands of a clock overhead. Typically, at this hour, I'd be home. Brooding. I'd fixate on every word Abbie sent during our online scuffles like they held the keys to her demise… or her heart.

The corner of my lip lifts, reminiscing on how driven I was to murder her at the start. I knew I was gone spending those sleepless nights studying her like she was the final test, holding the reigns of my ruin. I was aware of how I plummeted to the maws of my obsession. It engulfed every ounce of my attention. Sleeping and eating became afterthoughts. Nothing else mattered but one-upping her and being in front of her somehow. Even physically. I didn't care. I *don't* care. I knew everything I did was wrong—the stalking, breaking, gambling with my traumas, and harassing the shit out of her. I savored every second of my secret high. As long as I got close to her, nothing else mattered.

I should have accepted how I felt the moment I stilled from her dark silhouette wandering the halls. When I sunk my teeth into her supple skin, ecstasy I've never known eclipsed my murderous wants like a cleansing.

Those nights of teasing her online brought about an undead hunger taking me to a zombified mental state. And if I *were* a zombie, I'd stalk her with the fever of *Nemesis* from *Resident Evil 3*. If *she* were a zombie, I'd fuck her decaying brains out while she consumes me all over again.

I don't know if reincarnation theory is feasible, but my soul will chase hers until the end of time. I'd throw my pride, my money, my body—everything I am into a volcano if it meant I could live inside her head like a virus. How she's done to me.

I need Elysium back, but I know if she hadn't seized it the way she did, I still would have made the journey out to pester her.

Abbie fixes her skirt through the window of her study room, and my chest pounds hard. I fell for your little dare, Princess, and I don't regret anything about it. *Ugh*, if I weren't carved like a Greek prince, this whole ordeal would be creepy. Gus saunters in with their water bottles unknown to the balance his absence has gifted me.

A click from Abbie's private room yanks me back to reality. Her face is still red from her ears and chest, and I smirk, knowing I'm the cause of that. I look forward to our group date.

When she steps out, she locks the door behind her without her tech, and I wait until she's out of view.

A nefarious smirk pulses on my face as I tsk. *My little rival doesn't know?* What an embarrassing slip-up. Fishing out my handheld from my side, my fingers work against the screen on autopilot, and after it buffers, the door clicks open. The school's locks all run on Wi-Fi, locking down

My Valentine's Virus

the campus with the press of a button in case of emergencies. It's easily the most brain-dead security risk I can think of.

I'm past fighting with myself over how I burn for her, but that doesn't mean I'm letting my little rival off the hook for everything she's done. If Abbie wants my Number One spot, she'll have to earn it like I did. I'm sure she wouldn't want it any other way.

Liam, one of the douchebags who helped me lose to Abbie's team, passes by as I approach Abbie's door. I nod in his direction. Not sure why. I don't want to be seen by him right now. He exits his private room with his laptop cuddled in his arm like it's his firstborn.

"Good to see you, Xalton *Kaiser*," he sings, arching his arm overhead for a high five like I'm one of his boys. I'm not. But he hasn't pissed me off entirely, so I comply. "Where are you heading? I can walk with you," he proposes.

A better idea flickers to me as we chat, taking up space in the empty corridor. "I'm killing time before The Melancholy," I offer, and his brow lifts.

"*You're* going to that? Shit." He runs his fingers through his scalp, his L'Oréal brown hair slinking through his appendages. The kid is wasting his life being at this school when he could be modeling for Vogue or whatever. "Now I have to attend."

A frown threatens to crease my face. "Wouldn't that interrupt your spree of playing terrible games?" I add with little flavor. Abbie invited him to hang out with her, and everyone out of the goodness of her heart, yet this piss-stain can't be bothered to show up for a minute. I take a deep sated breath, willing patience to cool my chest.

I need to calm down.

"Didn't think anyone could see that," Liam chuckles wryly as the shift in my demeanor grows hostile.

Taking a drag of my cigarette, I wrap my arm around his little shoulder, pulling him close to my side.

"Are we allowed to smoke blunts on campus?" His body tenses from the smoke wisping from my breath as I adjust him toward Abbie's room.

"No," I say curtly. "Do me a *big* favor, Liam, and take this." I fish for the USB stick about the size of a fingernail from my pocket and hand it to him. I adjust the burning plant in my mouth, inhaling the charred serenity it provides. "Go to room four and stick this into the shitty laptop inside—the neon green. You don't need to do anything else."

Liam glances at his palm and quickly at me before eying the door with Gus exiting again. "Oh… 'kay. Sure." I sense his hesitance, so I pat him on the back as more of a shove toward it. "Uh, the room might be locked—"

"You'll figure it out," I yawn. Raising my arms overhead for a much-needed stretch, I await the night I have planned with my little rival after my virus goes through.

Liam nods, moving forward with the conclusion of my scheme.

I wait out the rest of my free time in the library, hacking Abbie's computer through my tablet. I lean by the printers as their rhythmic beats of my revenge stutter through the space. My screen accesses Abbie's files and personal data with ease from the direct entry, but while stalking through her files, something odd about her mother's death has me pausing.

I blink rapidly, reading off the death certificate, her will, and how her father earned himself a sizeable amount from charity. Her mother's death doesn't make sense. The cause of it in the online paperwork seems altered. I've forged so many fake government documents that spotting them has become second nature to me.

Not only that, it lists more than one.

Here, we have Ana Belle, who died from blunt trauma to the head. The other states she was rushed to the hospital and then died in the E.R. from heart failure. Her medical records don't list the procedures done that should have come up in these reports, but they don't. It's like they've been erased or never input into the system. But why?

My Valentine's Virus

My heartbeat slackens as every background noise mutes to my ear. *Ana Belle. Ana Belle.* The name sounds familiar, like a lost song whose lyrics tease on the tip of my tongue.

I continue typing, scrolling, and looking up my family's list of prior charities from the year Orion crashed through the East Coast.

My device almost slips from my grip. I freeze by the words appearing on my screen. Abbie's family name appears at the top of the page in a list my father helped that year. It was purely for tax benefits, but… what are the odds?

I smile, heat filling my chin and forehead. When I was a kid, my father told me to pick a name out of a jar, and Abbie's family name was on it. The thought of a younger, neglected me being *that* close to having met her even back then makes my head tilt back in astoundment.

My soul really does follow hers.

My lip part as I continue my shameless file rifling.

In middle school, Abbie created an artificial intelligence all on her own. Every time I learn more about her sexy brain, my cock tries to uppercut me. So, she named the device after her mother. I put Abbie's private details aside to continue scanning her mother's suspicious files. Reopening the tab on Ana's death, I deep-dive into realms I can't fully conclude.

My hands remain stuck on my screen re-reading the hidden info this entire time. This is a secret, so… Shakespearian, Abbie wouldn't believe me if I told her. Swallowing hard, I close my laptop screen and accept it as is.

It's not my secret to tell. Especially knowing that if Abbie knew the truth about her mother, it'd get her killed.

This news would have been everything I would have needed from her since the start of our contest. But things have changed. The idea of Abbie being hurt or murdered now would be like falling into a pit of poisoned spikes. So, I must do everything in my power to keep the secret safe from her. Deletion of my finds across the board should finish within twenty-four hours.

It's what's right.

My Valentine's Virus

[Part II]

THE FINAL BOSS

LEVEL SEVENTEEN
PRINCESS_USER24

I wish I could email my younger self. I'd assure her she was always right in not stifling her skills. Anything less than that was a scam.

Emerging from the restroom, I saunter back to the library and exchange texts with Psyra every other step. I get lost in the fog with my replies, though, my heart teetering as everything *Xalton* fills my brain.

I feel like a lovestruck teenager again, hard simping over the sad and sexy tech stallion on the cover of UTN magazines.

"*He loves me,*" I mutter, still finding this all hard to believe.

Sighing, I do my best to ignore the wedgie my bikini bottoms insist on giving me. I still at my flush reflection on the floor, and I stop to examine the smile gracing my face. Dammit. I can't stop thinking about him or how hard he came through my thighs when I told him I loved him.

My Valentine's Virus

"You can't do this!" a woman shouts inside the auditorium, jerking my steps near its entrance. My pulse quickens, and I examine the voice, which sounds a lot like Grace from P.E. I pinch my brows as guilt mounds inside me. I still haven't thanked her for saving me from the pool that day.

My feet whisper against the floors as I arrive to eavesdrop.

The more they speak, the more I determine it *is* Grace. But who is she talking to? Is this connected to why she missed our game earlier?

I keep my ears peeled when I remember the mirror keychain I stole off Psyra's dresser tucked in my breast pocket. I found it this morning when I was searching for the necklace she fondles all the time.

Opening it, I spy Grace's platinum-white hair in the heavily dark surroundings inside its reflection.

Careening it further, my eyes narrow at Melanie standing on stage with her arms crossed. No one else is around, but I suppose the headmaster's daughter can enter any room she pleases. What are they doing here?

"I believe I can do whatever I please," Melanie states with a finality that brooks no fight. "I *warned* you about getting in my way."

Poor Grace's pale skin is flushed, and her expression is wide and wet with panic, like she witnessed a murder. Grace's heartbreaking cries pierce into my heart and leave me hollow. I don't mind going toe-to-toe with Melanie if it means my savior stops sobbing, but I can't barge in unless I have more information on what's up. I school my features, waiting despite the thickening tension growing.

"You're sick in the head!" Grace sneers. "Like I was *ever* going to let you get away with homicide!" her voice trembles. "You should be *thanking* me Abbie survived the shit you pulled!"

A thunderous slap resounds throughout the auditorium seconds later, and it throbs in my ears. My breath catches when my hand clutches my heart. Melanie retracts her hand, and a tight scowl mars her usually stoic features.

"Keep your voice down. What's done is *done*." She points to the doors, and a piece of me shrinks inward.

Grace's cheek swells while her hate-filled green eyes burn at the tyrant. "You can't—"

"*Go*. Pack your bags and get the fuck off my campus," Melanie orders. "You're officially trespassing."

Tears continue streaming down Grace's face. My heart tears from each one, a whine of hopelessness bleeding through. She sprints so clumsily that she rushes right by me without noticing.

I inhale the air-conditioned space as my thoughts are interrupted. Melanie's maroon-shaded eyes meet mine through the mirror.

A smile curves on her lips, the creepy act heightened by how criminally well she wears it. She's always given me the sense that she was unhinged, but this moment adds more to my whole theory.

"I take it you… *overheard* most of that?" she calls out to me in a rectifying tone.

My cue.

"Most of *what?*" I mirror her stance and cross my arms too.

Rolling her eyes, she descends the stairs on the side, each step echoing around the space like a threat. "*Good,*" she croons. "Let's *all* pretend I'm not out to get you and that we *like* each other."

"Want to tell me why you tried *drowning* me?"

"I *did* drown you, first of all," she snorts, holding back a laugh. "My, *my*, you got over that revelation quickly." She eyes me from head to toe. "I expected the indomitable Abigail to strike a pose and declare, *'not so fast. I'm handing you over to the police!'* How *big* of you."

I cringe at her cartoonish perception of me. In the week we've been forced into proximity, what makes her think I'm anything like that?

"I've survived death before… experienced better attempts, too," I scoff, surveying her new form of hoofs and horns in my mind.

My Valentine's Virus

She cracks another grin at my response. "Sure. And to answer your question, it's really because you're an unkempt slut siphoning my Xalton's time." She examines her manicure. "It's disgusting."

My brows shot up. "Not as disgusting as doing all of this over a guy! You're really that small of a person? Newsflash, bitch. That doesn't warrant murder—"

"Aw, it does in my world, little piggy," she interrupts me as if my reaction is boring her. "And something of this nature is bigger than *you* can perceive. Simply put, you're in our way, and I'm dealing with it accordingly." She rotates toward the door. "My soul has *always* known his. He doesn't *know* we belong to each other yet, but he will. It's written in the stars, not that expect you to understand." She tosses her hair behind her shoulder, delusion ebbing off her like an aura. I hold back a burning urge to gag.

She did not just tell me she's "*fated*" to be with Xalton like some recurring lover's fantasy. Right? This cannot be real.

I've read the room the way Xalton looks at her. How his face pales from the sight and mention of her. I sensed there was something traumatic there, but I didn't know how to bring it up or even if I should have.

"What did you do to him?" I ask, baring my teeth on reflex.

Melanie eases into me with a knowing smirk, I would pay cash to hit. "What *didn't* I do to him?" I glare at her as if she's sprouted two more heads. "Well? Go on," she shoos me toward the light. "Run to my mother, *my* man, or the board. Sue me. See how far you get. See what unfolds during your little stay here," she dares. "As far as I'm concerned, you're already out of my hair." With that, she strides past me and disappears into the hallway.

I should've pulled her by the extensions and broken her face. I should've tripped her the moment she passed me. I should've done a hundred things, but the whiplash of all she said was so delusional—so insane, I figured I was daydreaming everything.

♥

Melanie's footsteps fade, and I stand there in the dark expanse of the auditorium. Parts of me are waiting for her to reel back and laugh at how this was all a stupid joke.

But no. There isn't one. She was dead serious. The tormentor of my tormentor is wealthy, has connections, believes Xalton is hers, and could jeopardize everything I've worked for to get here.

My sneakers drag down the hall as my palm rubs my temple. How do I handle this rationally?

The weight of her words linger around my ears, leaving a searing bitterness in my mouth.

Sure, people face Mr. Death every day, whether it be heart failure or farting in front of a crush, but Melanie is too close to my stuff. The idea of watching my every step, knowing she has the power to boobytrap the fucking hall, makes my jaw clench.

I've made it halfway across the country, and I love this school so far. I don't want to go back until I'm finished with why I came here.

Glancing at Psy's mirror keychain in my hand, I keep it as a memento to remind me of how little I truly know about the people around me. Melanie's confession was only part of a larger puzzle painting the connection of Xalton's distress.

I take a steadying breath and shake off the unease sinking beneath my lungs. Her getting to me is what she wants and the last thing I want right now. The memory of Grace's tear-streaked face tugs at my thoughts, but I push it aside with the promise I'll check on her later.

It's Psy's last day before leaving tomorrow, and I don't want to waste it getting caught up in Melanie's nonsense. I need to clear my mind and find some normalcy in this chaotic day, or my night could be at stake.

This is far from over, but dwelling on Melanie and her kind of crazy isn't helping me. I loosen my hold on Psy's little mirror and pocket it.

My Valentine's Virus

The sun has shifted in the skies above in the corridor, casting a warm golden hue across the dark campus as I march back to the library.

I find Gus in our study room cradling a water bottle for me. After the remainder of the study session, we give each other our farewells. Warmth fills my heart with the knowledge that I've made a difference for him. The moment I'm met with a revving engine outside, my euphoric pat on the back yanks free.

Several yards in front of me is a sleek black motorcycle with Xalton astride it. The white Elysium logo on his black helmet brings back my smirk, and he cocks his head up at me. Several students passing by spare him several glances as I approach, struggling to look and reel back my obvious excitement from seeing him riding it.

I approach the most beautiful motorcycle man has ever made. I never doubt Xalton's tastes, but this bike is a dream—even if I've never been one for motorcycles. It's a panther on wheels. All black paint glistens under the sunlight. The body is sculpted with smooth lines, allowing pure beauty to break through.

The obsidian wheels, the chrome accents on the exhaust and handles—this motorcycle isn't just a motorcycle; it's a work of art. Xalton's helmet follows my eyes as I refuse to look away from it.

He retrieves a second helmet from the compartment, and I notice a much smaller one inside. It can't be any bigger than a toddler's head. There's a story there.

"Fancy a ride, Princess?"

A thrill blooms through me at his playful question.

"I can't ride that."

He swings his head down in disappointment before shutting off the engine and climbing down. He advances to me with that mysterious aura surrounding him, amplifying that rugged confidence he effortlessly holds. It feels more so when he has something covering his head.

My core tightens while my heated gaze devours his large masculine figure. Can he stop being eye candy for fifteen minutes?

He hands me his spare helmet like a bouquet of roses, and my face tingles. "For you."

"I said no."

"Did you?" His covered head tilts with a mischievous glint. "I'm a little deceived, considering your eyes say otherwise." His pernicious grin sprouts behind his face shield. "First time?" He arches down to my eye level as if to remind me how much bigger he is and could easily lift me over his shoulders while I kick and punch. "You nervous?"

"I'm not!" Heat lashes from my cheeks. "They're not exactly what I'd call safe, and I wouldn't be the one driving it. Not that I know how." I gesture at the potential hospital expense on wheels. Before I continue my lecture, he rolls his neck and fits the helmet over my head.

With protesting arms glued at my side, I stop in front of him like his angry mini-me. "Xalton!"

He chuckles darkly at my pouting and lifts the chin of my helmet to bonk ours together. The moment he rests his gloved hands on my shoulders, my tension heals faster than it arrived. "Princess, The Melancholy's a few blocks away. You'll be fine," he assures. "Trust me. I won't let anything happen to you that isn't directly *my* doing," he adds, his deep voice pirating a semblance of comfort.

My lips purse before I try pushing him. He stands firm as if he were being shoved by a squirrel with a jar stuck to its head. "Is that supposed to make me feel better?" I grunt, continuing to shove him even with my feet skidding on the grass.

His erotic laughter sends shivers down my spine and makes my pussy blush—a response I don't think I'll ever be fully used to. "I thought you were a *badass*, Abbie." He secures my helmet tighter.

"Being a badass and being *stupid* are two different things."

My Valentine's Virus

Ignoring my concerns, he scratches his hand against the back of my neck like I'm a stray and guides me to his bike. "Get on, or I'll duct tape you to the seat," he casually threatens. Xalton's hand extends for mine, and I huff in surrender. He straddles his chair like a pro and yanks me behind him. The immediate closeness is unexpectedly intimate. The wall of his back is warm and soothing.

He presses into my chest and stomach when I inhale his rugged scents. The leather seat booms beneath my thighs, and my heart shoots to my throat at the engine's nightmarish growls.

"Don't be shy," he instructs. "Wrap your arms around me tight. I can't have you flying off."

I nod and give in his guidance, but a question still nudges me before we drive. "Why is there a toddler-sized helmet in your compartment?"

His body tenses in my arms. "You saw that, huh?"

I shake my head, wanting to take it back. "If it's a secret, I don't need to know—"

"It's for Dice," he confesses. Who or *what* is Dice? "My raccoon. He accompanies me sometimes and naps in there while I run errands."

Picturing Xalton with any kind of pet—let alone an illegal one—doesn't fit my perception of him. I like finding out more about him, but I can't even picture it. "You're fucking with me."

His chuckle fills the air in a harmonious rumble as he tests the engine. "Always."

Perched on the motorcycle's rear, my arms find their spot around his stomach. The engine's purr resonates, sending specs of adrenaline through my skin.

We sweep through the sun-drenched streets of our opulent college town. The hard winds caress my veins, giving me an endless cascade of goosebumps. The contours and warmth of Xalton's torso brings me to a reassuring place. There's a depth of his promise of protection in the whirlwind, with each grip of my fingers against his taut stomach. I can't tell if he's tensing his body on purpose or if his body is always this firm.

A dark truck in the avenue to the right screeches on its brakes after ignoring the stop sign. My eyes widen as my heart pounds and render my chest numb. I dig my nails into Xalton's jacket as I wince, preparing for a possible crash. Anxiety becomes a living, breathing entity bunkering beneath my skin as regret fills me from ever giving up control again. Why do the people of this town ignore that specific Stop sign?!

Xalton's shoulders lower when he switches lanes at the last second before the van can ram into us. The driver brakes mid-way, catching their mistake, but my nerves delay like an annoying wasp in my ears.

The sensuous hum of Xalton's engine weaves through the air like a roaring steed. I focus on my breathing while we soar under the green traffic light and through an empty lane.

I want to get off. I hate this!

My arms shiver as I struggle to will my nerves to relax. Nothing happened. I'm fine. Inhale.

In the breeze, my nose finds rich coffee from the tucked-away café mingling with kabobs from outside stands infused with spices. As we drive on, the coffee is replaced with delicate floral fragrances that grace the pathway and melt away my invisible fears. The quilt of scents around town is like a love letter to the town itself. I exhale as my body calms.

Architecture flits past like a scene from a dream while the cobblestone streets echo a gentle vibration. My eyes close as I'm whisked away by the beauty of Main Street.

Navigating the heart of the town, our bodies move as one, pairing with his motorcycle's every command. In fleeting seconds, my uncertainty melts into an intoxicating thrill. Tension leaves my body, and I glance up at Xalton, keeping his face glued to the stretch of road in front of us. My senses link with the beating of his calm heart under my fingertips—like I'm holding onto his soul as he guides us.

My Valentine's Virus

Xalton slows down as the traffic light transitions to a mute yellow and swivels his head at me. "You good?" His raised voice cuts through the motor's purr. I can't see what he's doing with his right hand, but not a second later, the traffic light adjusts from red to green.

I nod. When he faces ahead, a wide smile conceals under my helmet. His gloved hand warms over mine as I clutch his stomach. The gesture ignites my heart and bathes my skin in a blush.

I wish this moment wouldn't end so soon. The minute it does, I don't know if I'm capable of going back to how I felt before being with him. I'm finding it harder to compare the Xalton in real life to the terrorist online.

This was a great idea, after all. Because nothing in the world compares to this.

Our journey leads us inside a vibrant bar despite its name. It's sandwiched between two closed businesses, and the transition from outside to inside is transformative. Music pulses, and people around my age dance with abandon to the catchy beats.

My expression beams as we absorb the atmosphere. Strangers smile and nod as they pass us, and the bartenders behind the counter laugh as they slide drinks across the surface to customers to the beats.

Xalton and I take turns scanning strangers' faces until we land on our small group near the back. Thanks to Hanna's red hair lighting up the room, we're able to find everyone dancing in the center.

Taking Xalton's hand, I lean against the bar beside them. Catching the busy bartender between finished orders, I wave. "A pint of honey bourbon, please. No ice."

Xalton's brows slant at my order, eliciting a grin from me. "Slow down, Princess. The nights only started."

"Did I guess your brand right?" I bite my lip, holding back the smile.

"*You're* wonderfully perceptive," he taunts. The minute my drink lands in front of me, he swipes it off the counter and wolfs it down without a flinch in sight. Mmm... my father would hate him. The sharp sweetness of it surrounds him again like he's been refilled.

Sticking the glass back against the counter, he leans closer to me. "I'd prefer something tangier." He faces the bartender when they come to collect his glass. "One pint of orange juice with ice, if you'd be so kind," Xalton requests, and seconds later, I have it in front of me. He tips the bartender, the register chimes under the music, and they return with his change.

I chortle at his subtle jab at my go-to. The thick citrus envelopes my lungs as he wraps his arm possessively around my shoulder.

We lean against our stools, cheering and laughing as Kevin challenges Liam to a dance-off. Pulsating music surrounds us like a warm blanket.

Several drinks of my spiked orange juice later, I note the alcohol starting to get to me. This is nice. His arms feel like a home after a long day. It's like nothing can go wrong in his embrace. My shoulders sway to the additive rhythm around us as blue and red lighting coat Xalton and me in an aura of intimacy. Heat saturates my pours, thinking back to his hand on mine during the ride here. I tilt my head back, resting it against his chest, and he lowers to give me a longing kiss on my forehead.

"I didn't peg you as a lightweight," he teases with his drowsy smile.

"It's the... temperature. Nothing else," I bite back. My eyes fall into his pine-green gaze, giving me every ounce of his attention. Something hard presses against the small of my back.

"You're beautiful under any light, you know that?"

"Oh?" My face is melting under it, but I accept the compliment. "Thanks."

My Valentine's Virus

"Based on the scar above your eye, my initial assumption was you were a regular drinker or someone who picks fights in bars."

I laugh at his imagination, then slam my hand on the counter, shaking our empty glasses. "*Great* assumption. But no. It was a gift from Hurricane Orion when I was five. The bastard wrecked our house and landed me in the hospital."

His expression whitens, and his brows pull downward. "My condolences."

"It's *fine*," my voice stumbles. Geez, his face makes me wanna cry. There's a sting of tears near the corners of my eyes, but I swallow my emotions before speaking. *Please suppress, Abigail.* Let's not start wallowing in the middle of the bar now. It's been decades. "It's not like *you* were the tree that fell and killed my mom," I still, unable to take my inside thoughts back.

Xalton's brows knit with further sympathy before he wraps his arms around me into a tighter embrace. I hide my face in his chest, and I'm reminded of the issue I pushed aside.

I lift my chin, falling into his examining pupils again. "Hey... Can you tell me what happened between you and Melanie? If it's not too much of an ask."

His shoulders drop while his nostrils flare as his head jerks left and right across the space. My stomach runs cold as he rotates us to face the counter. "She threaten you?" he questions, his jaw ticking like a bomb.

My eyes roll. *I take it her trying to drown me doesn't count?*

"Recently, I mean," he corrects, reading my expression.

"Well, she insulted me with this awful *Sailor Moon* caricature, then monologued about how you two are *fated* for one another." I look less disturbed than I'm feeling. "I want to kick her ass for how she keeps calling me 'little piggy,' but I want to graduate with this school's name on my certificate more." I trace the rim of my glass as impatience burns a hole in my heels.

Xalton heaves a long sigh and the once fun atmosphere tenses. His fingers drum on the bar top before he parts his lips again. I still at how his hand trembles before resting it at his side. "I hate discussing her, but—" He takes a moment to rectify himself before facing me again. "My parents. Promised me to her. With no inclusion of my say."

My brows lift at his reveal, and my heart thuds in my ribcage. "...You're... *betrothed?*"

"No," he hisses. "God, no—Her mother seeded the idea of us together since she was in diapers. Of course, Melanie believes she owns me." He grits his teeth as he speaks, and I'm impressed I'm even getting this much out of him. "My parents adored her, but the situation was a curse I kept trying to get rid of. When I tried, she stabbed me eight times and punctured my heart. I laid there on the floor choking on my blood, unsure if I was going to live or die."

"What the fuck...?" My voice shivers, and my calculating expression falls. Tears begin pooling in my vision, blurring his form, and my eyelids itch.

Xalton finds the guilt breaking my masked expression and strokes the side of my face. His soft caress freezes over the tension in my muscles but only slightly. I keep his hand here, squeezing him tight. "I'm pretty sure I just ruined our night. Alcohol gets me weepy. A much sober-er Abigail would have been able to keep her composure."

The image of his full-cover bathing suit flashes behind my eyes. Now I understand it was meant to hide his scars. Agony bobs in my throat as I hold back drunk tears.

"Abbie?"

The idea of someone close to him turning on him like that is inconceivable. Had I known earlier, I would have torn her apart with my bare hands East-Coast-style.

"Abbie."

My Valentine's Virus

The memory skips forward to the way he paled during the stick and ball game. My stomach squeezes more. I realize I inadvertently baited him back to his tormentors. I forced him here, and to make matters worse, I helped Melanie believe she was the cause of his return. Her earlier nonsense about thinking they were *fated* makes sense now. Well, not entirely, but it's my fault. Her misguided belief that his return was because of her. Hell. No. She can't take my credit.

"Abbie?" Xalton's voice pierces the cloudy haze of my regrets before his arms swallow me again. Warmth floods my racing thoughts. "It's fine."

"It's *not*," I whimper. "... It's my fault. You did all of this because of me. You escaped. You escaped, and I brought you back under your abuser's radar—I am *so* sorry."

His face tightens, and he lowers his head to mine. "You didn't make me do anything I couldn't handle, Princess. I knew which school you were attending, took the flight, bought my parents' old house, and moved everything to hunt you down. Nothing was going to stop me from annihilating you." His lips linger over my scar. "Except I fell for you from the start. I didn't even know what you looked like; I knew you were mine." He kisses me again.

My heart sinks with each word, and I nudge him so I can reach my drink. The weight of the situation presses into me, and grappling to avoid the coming storm of crazy seems less realistic the more I process.

"Opal's daughter is like a wolf on meth," Xalton says. "When she sinks her teeth into something, she doesn't let go. But as long as I'm around, I won't let her get to you." He bumps my forehead against his, and my drifting vision returns to his. "I promise." He leans in to kiss me, but if I don't correct him now, I'll break out in hives.

"I'm not afraid of her," I assert. "I'm afraid for you, but next time—just let me handle her. Got it?" He chuckles at me, unsure if I've threatened him or am applying to be his protector—maybe both.

"Of course." His eyes darken in amusement, pairing with his dangerous smile.

Our gathering finally caught the attention of Psyra, Kevin, Hanna, and Liam. They begin converging toward us. The boys carry Psy and Hanna piggyback, and judging by their lazy gestures and dreamy gazes, these whores have been having fun without us.

As they join us, Xalton and I simultaneously spot Psyra's annoying necklace now adorning Kevin's Adam's apple. We avert our eyes while we're greeted, and they ask if we've been enjoying our party of two.

Drinking in unison, our brain waves connect in this moment of silent camaraderie.

Liam waves at Xalton again, and Psyra keeps giving me a thumbs-up for some reason. Hanna's attention wanders to the rest of the bar while riding Liam.

My date lifts his finger for Kevin's attention. "I'll give you a hundred grand for the necklace," he says straight-faced.

Kevin's smile lowers. "Uhh... No. Psy gave it to *me.*"

"Two hundred grand," Xalton offers.

"No," Kevin doubles back. "You can't buy me, Xalton. I don't care who you are." He's so real for this. Kevin offers a kind smile though a muscle pulses in his jaw like he's offended to even part with it. I would have jumped at that offer—anyone would.

Xalton and I have been in this unspoken contest to see which of us can steal Psyra's lucky necklace, but every attempt has been a failure. You see, we were suspicious at first, but Psyra might be a legitimate witch—or mystic like she told us.

We try to humble her for her own good by pretending she's just devoted to the role-play. When I first humored her, I brutally chalked her up as a theater kid, but Psy's proven it to us. We've been trying not to freak out about it ever since. Keeping her as our little secret has welded this other bond between Xalton and me.

My Valentine's Virus

"Fair enough," Xalton smirks, lowering his hand to Psyra like a mock surrender.

"Will you stop?" She scoffs at their back-and-forth auction, and I cut in.

"She's trained Kevin well," I tease, nudging my darkly dressed date.

Psyra lands between us, and I nearly pass away from the flames of strawberry rum, breathing out of her. "I promised I'd be a good wingman!" she blurts.

"You alright?" I ask. I've never seen her this zooted before.

"No."

I hold up three fingers in front of her, and my throat dries as she drops her hand on my shoulder. The rumbles of her bowels churn, and I raise my hands above my head to brace for her vomit, only to hear the chortles of a very drunk witch.

"You should see your face!" she cackles, pointing at me like a goddamn child.

I shake my fist. "When are you leaving for Fraixia again?"

"Stooop," Psy whines at me. "Okay."

"Okay?"

She smiles. "Okay," she huffs. I promised I'd be Xalton's wingman," she chirps again, and I give Xalton a questioning look.

"When did you say that?"

She snorts. "When he snuck—"

"I appreciate you, Jean-Pierre," Xalton laughs wryly, raising his glass to interrupt. "But my little rival's already confessed her feelings for me."

My friend's eyebrows raise, and a smile I've never seen from her blinds me from here and tomorrow. *"Oh my god!"* She erupts, her mission to break the sound barrier, it seems. "Is this your first *date* then?"

I narrow my eyes at Xalton, and Kevin swoops in to save me. Literally. Psyra's princess-carried by the man of muscle, and spins where they're lost in a sea of dancers.

A clear shot glass stands between Xalton and me now as he cradles the shimmering amber liquid under the neon lights.

Xalton smirks. "This isn't our first date."

"We don't need to rush anything," I say, hidden behind my empty glass, slurping at the rim for air inside.

"Really?" His brow arches before stepping closer to me until my back is pressed against the counter's edge. Heat blossoms on my face when he cages me with his massive arms. His face hovers to my neck and his lips graze against the side, somehow having time cease functioning.

"Yes," I confirm with a swallow. I close my eyes as flames engulf me in his silken graze, the effect of the alcohol hiking my sensitivity. "I'm fine with taking things slow." His perfect smile chills near my ear.

"You mean you don't fantasize about joining an *internship* under me? Get invited to a Christmas party with the hopes of me getting *so* tipsy…" His hand trails up my thigh, causing my sharp breath. My eyes widen as he rests his head beside mine. "…that I run my hand up your skirt?" His voice rasps, and my muscles tense. "And I ram my cock inside you *all* night at some lounge?"

I gulp my stuttering heart before facing him. My nostrils flare, and my cheeks pain cramp with rage. "You read my fanfiction—?"

"I read your fanfiction," he validates, further launching me into a downward spiral of doom.

He won.

My chest violently drums as he pulls out a stapled, rolled-up packet from his side pocket. If that's what I think it is, I should run now! The workings of time renew, and I set my glass down before making my escape. Xalton's arms cage me in tighter as he flips to the first page of my damnation.

"*Please*, no!" My lip trembles.

My Valentine's Virus

"Don't fidget around so much. You're pathetic begging is making me *painfully* hard," he groans into the back of my neck. "I'll fuck you right here, and I won't care who sees," he purrs.

"If you read it, I'll end you, Kaiser! I wrote that *before* I realized you were overrated." Despite his warning, I squirm and strain to keep my emotions in check.

His devious smile persists. *"It was a crisp winter's day at Kaiser International—"* He rests the side of his face against mine as I writhe, a prisoner of my own making. His nose brushes my neck. "Can you tell me why you made me a pilot in this universe, or is that up to the reader's interpretation?"

"I can't fucking *stand* you!" I shout over the music. I snarl at the counter, and he snickers as I fall apart in his grip. *"How* did you access my—" Frowning, I recall leaving for the bathroom in around twenty-ish minutes. My eyes narrow into tight slits. I made sure the door was locked at the library. *The library... He never left, did he? Why did I assume he left?* I had to clean up the mess we made, and I left my war machine unattended. Could he have broken in—? My eyeroll confirms my acceptance. *Of-fucking course he did.*

He whips out a blunt from his pocket. Removing his dragon-shaped lighter, he kindles the end without paying it any mind. "You thought you could take a swing at the king," he taunts, voice drenching in ego.

I raise an eyebrow at his lackadaisical gaze, challenge simmering in my frown. "I take this also means you have everything on me, huh?"

"*Every*thing," he susurrates. A ripple spears through my chest.

I... lost. I don't feel as wounded as I should be. I mean... I *was* close. I just needed a few more hours.

"Ready for another game, Princess?" he proposes before dark berating thoughts consume me.

I moisten my lips, examining his face. "I've handled everything you've thrown at me."

The corner of his lips quirk. "That's my girl."

A. DARANG

LEVEL EIGHTEEN

ZONE_WARDEN

The fiery atmosphere crackles. I'm uncertain if it's the cheap booze or the nocturnal ambiance, but the way Abbie's big brown eyes lay into mine keeps me hard. Now I know what a werewolf feels like, wrestling with myself so as not to paw at her all night.

Knowing I have the power to hurt her like how she's threatened me has my dick pulsing against her addictive curves. As if reading my thoughts, she closes the gap between us. Precum slicks down my shaft the more her body grinds against mine.

I pay no mind to Liam taking her manuscript in the corner of my eye. His eyebrows lift, examining the front page and understanding what he's reading.

Blocking the moonlight peeking in from the window, I hover over Abbie's small frame. Her lower lip trembles identifying the lust burning in my gaze. I capture it between my lips, and a chill ascends my neck as I savor the sweet bloom of bourbon off her lips.

Our dominating caresses warm our bodies, and our eyes lock again. The music swells around us, and in the heart of the bustling club, something chaotic ignites between us. Our lips collide in a fusion of kisses. Her lips are quivering nectar, and I lose myself tasting her.

After a minute of scraping my teeth against her, arching her face to deepen our kiss, Jean-Pierre's whistle cuts through the air.

We exchange heated pants with the remainder of our public setting, but my gaze doesn't leave hers for a second. The muscles in my throat strain to swallow while each cell of my body regrets separating from her.

"Your place?" I suggest, my whisper dripping with need. Red paints her cheeks, and the beautiful hue of her skin shows even if she looks like a giant blueberry under this obnoxious purple light.

"Yes," she whispers back. Her nervously willing smirk has me biting back a groan.

I take her hand, leading her outside to a tight, empty alley. My skin crawls from not tasting her, and I need to remedy this now before I lose it.

The last glance of our group is of Hanna leaning in to read the manuscript in Liam's hands. His shoulders tighten in a blush, and she circles him like a curious bee.

With only the echoes of chanting crickets beneath the moonlight, it's somehow less tight than when we were inside. I snake my arm around Abbie's waist, lifting to spin her in front of me. I nearly slam her back against the brick wall, and she grips my collar, yanking my head to orbit hers. I trap her mouth in a rough kiss.

Our lips collide in a feverish storm brewing between us. Abbie's drunk kisses are a tempest of desires with no space left for subtlety. Her taste is both intoxicating and sweet. She cloaks her heated thighs around my back. Her hips grind into me, and each flow of her perfect fucking body has my cock whirling with need. I crane her head back to deepen

My Valentine's Virus

the kiss, and our tongues dance with a raw hunger. My fingers tangle in her hair, pulling and gripping her closer as if I'm trying to wear her.

This is far from a tender kiss. It's a tornado of fire that threatens destruction. I need her in my lungs more than oxygen, and my chest tightens coming to that revelation. My lips slope to her neck, leaving a trail of warm kisses.

Breathless and lost, I savor Abbie's pants, and my hand grips up her soft thighs to squeeze her ass. My balls tighten with her skin spilling between my fingers. Her hooded eyes spark with that flame I adore, prompting molten fire in my veins.

My heart thunders against my chest, and my arousal begs to fulfill her precious little fantasies.

Our tongues wrestle for dominance like there's no tomorrow. My fingers explore, and I snap at the thick strap that dares to get between me and my favorite meal.

"Bikini bottoms?" I laugh and lick my lips. Savoring in her flustered, woozy expression, I fondle her in her nod. She's too cute not to kiss and touch all night long. "This may be the last night I get to torture you." The pad of my finger circles the soft bud under her skirt and through her swimsuit.

"How do you make me feel so good?" Her breathy moans compete with the crickets' cries, and I need to lean.

I rest my forehead against hers and search for my motorcycle near the street.

The night commences, and we make it back to her dorm room. I barely remember the distance between our last kiss and this one. All that matters is that I enjoy her for longer.

Crawling on top of her on her bed, the hinges whine beneath my weight, and I slide her orange bottoms off.

After her tenth orgasm using my mouth, my fingers, and dirty talk, I reached a point where sleep overwhelmed my desires.

♥

"I'm not having sex with you tonight," I state, slowly brushing her hair into a mess as she lays on my chest. Tangled in each other's arms, our breaths gradually steady. "We're both drunk, and I want you with 100% clarity when I fuck your lights out."

A smile lifts her face. "Maybe I'll be the one fucking the light out of you? Didn't you ever think I'd be amazing at it?"

Both my brows rise from the sheer audacity of her words. This nerdy fucking virgin.

"I'll know it when I see it," I humor. Cupping her chin, I give her a lengthy kiss and then peck her again on her scarred forehead. "I'm about to pass out. Will you be here when I wake up?"

She blinks twice at me as if it's not apparent. "Xalton, this is *my* place."

Is it? My eyebrow curves and I arch my head to survey my surroundings. Inside my little rival's lair are her treasures. Oh.

Video games, posters, and medals earned from the most random of sports adorn her green walls, and a handmade bookshelf sags beneath the weight of her dated computer science textbooks. The worn spines tell me tales of late-night sessions on how she'll best the universe. Over it is a gold-framed portrait of a Latino gentleman with a thick dark beard—presumably her father. Randall's beaming with pride alongside a younger Abbie, and a smile tugs at my lips at her smug little face posing at the camera. She has a short tomboy haircut, and her bangs swept over her eyes. My smile increases, knowing I would have bullied the shit out of her, and she'd probably do the same to me.

Her side of the room speaks volumes about her that I couldn't see the few times I've broken in.

"So it is," I rub between my eyes, and she smiles into the arm she's using as a pillow.

"It was your idea—I guess you are smashed."

I sigh, struggling to recall when we got here and how long time has passed. "I ripped you away from your friend. I hope you're fine with that," I admit. The unease of that slowly flickers in. Psyra is leaving tomorrow morning… I mean later this morning. It's got to be somewhere after midnight now.

Abbie rolls her eyes through her captivating lashes. "She's going to spend the night over at Kevin's. She texted me after we left."

"Poor Kevin. Does he know she's leaving in the morning?"

Abbie stills, her eyes fixed on a spot in her ceiling. "I… don't think so. And what do you mean by 'poor Kevin?' He's a big boy. He can handle the girl he just met leaving for a few months."

"He was already acting weird over her. I offered him two hundred grand for the choker, and he asked me to swan dive off a cliff."

Abbie's angelic laughter fills the space, and my heart flutters with warmth. "I don't think it's like that. He might just hate you."

I smirk, dropping my head against the pillow. "No, I'm right. Certain aspects about people; I know about, Princess. He was handing out dirty looks at both of us when she'd talk with us. He's possessive of her already, and they *just* met."

She rubs my chin. "I have faith in Psy. If anything goes wrong, she'll just hex him."

I reach for one of the cactus-shaped pillows and cover her face with it. She pulls it off, then smacks one and then another at my face.

"Be careful with these. I'm borrowing them," she groans.

With a slow smile creeping across my face, I reach for one. Her lips pinch as darkness surrounds her gaze. I reel the pillow back in a pitcher's stance.

"Are you joking? We're about to sleep—" Launching it at her, she ducks, and it lands by her competitive mushroom-picking medallion hung on the wall.

It only swings but heat blazes in her eyes anyway.

She tries her hand at throwing it back. "What happened to being tired?" she bemoans.

"You're tired? I can tell."

♥

"Ha, fuck you!"

My grin flashes.

We settle our score with a heated pillow fight. Catching our breaths, we collide against her bed, and she shimmies closer in my arms. When she takes her spot against my chest, my heart blossoms at comfort.

A few minutes later, Abbie snores soundly, and I watch her blissfully. She's the sweetest lullaby. I close my eyes with the promise of tomorrow with her.

Morning arises, casting a soft glow through Abbie's orange curtains. The birds outside sing a song of serenity. I stir from my deep sleep, and my smartphone buzzes on Abbie's nightstand. I reach for it and meet a red notification. My heart leaped to my gullet, throwing my eyes entirely open.

The screen displayed an urgent alert from my security cameras back home. The police are present at my doorstep, peeking through my downstairs windows. My mind races through each possibility of their snooping. Of course, they could be here for a plethora of reasons. The blackmailing and cyberstalking, money laundering, terroristic threats, cyber espionage, a ton of malicious code distribution, fun unlawful intrusion, possession of hacking tools, and even the raccoon I've been harboring. The alert hangs in the air, leaving my stomach stirring at my impending doom. Sweat beads on my forehead and my hands, and I wonder if Abbie has anything to do with this. It is her last day of my threat, but would she betray me purely for the prospect of winning?

A huge part of me believes so.

The wall of trophies by her side lays out a testament to her insanity, clearer in the light of day. Perhaps she turned me in her drunken haze, or she mapped this whole thing out since our encounter. I shift, finding

My Valentine's Virus

her sleeping form beside me, and my body stills, watching her chest rise and fall.

The siren wins…

Whatever the case, I need to drive back before they break in and gather all the evidence, and they need to put me away for life.

I massage my face, rolling over in search of my clothes.

Her roommate's decorative pillows litter the floor, and my heart begins to break pieces of itself at the sight.

I had a great time, I just figured she did, too. This isn't the first time I've felt this terrible. I lived through that, and I'll live through this too. I should be fine. I should feel… fine.

"Anybody home?" An officer voices at my cameras, nabbing back my attention.

"Good evening, officers," my voice rasps in irritation at my watch. "Unless you have a warrant, refrain from illegally spying on my premises."

Five or so blunts flicker their ends beneath my helmet. I speed toward my address with burning eyes and inflamed lungs. Despite the flaming betrayal coursing through my veins, I'm holding out from succumbing to heartbreak. Thanks to this distraction, my adrenaline-fueled ride ends when I brake into my driveway. My heart races at the scene in front of me, and my tires screech in protest.

Four officers surround me. A symphony of clicks plays through the space as they ready their firearms. The flashing blue and red lights cast an irritating glow in my retinas, painting the scene to make me look as bad as I feel. I can't help smirking. This was the ending I gambled with before I even met Abigail.

They close in on me, my pulse echoing in my ears as I raise my hands in slow motion.

The lead officer steps forward, his tone firm but respective. "Xalton Kaiser, you're under arrest for blackmail and extortion. You have the right to remain silent. Anything you say can and will be used against you in a court of law. You have the right to an attorney. If you cannot afford one, one will be provided for you."

Interesting. I didn't think they still read Miranda's rights in the West Coast. It felt like a cute novelty you'd spot in movies.

I lower my hands, letting the blunts fall to the ground, and raise an eyebrow at the officer.

"We'll need you to come with us to the station for processing."

They lead me away, surrounded by flashing lights and the fading scent of ash.

[Xalton]: Well played, Princess.

LEVEL NINETEEN

PRINCESS_USER24

[Unknown]: Your stalker has been arrested. It's what scum like him deserves.

I reach under my comforter for my phone on the nightstand. Drunk Me may have left clues for Sober Me to survive today. "Who is this…?"

My eyes flutter open, greeted with soft morning light filtering through my curtains. My head throbs in protest of consciousness, giving me a cruel reminder of last night. Most blur together in my memory as I groan.

I can't figure out what this mystery message is about. Got who arrested? I've had around eleven stalkers this year.

My vision clears as a series of notifications light up on my screen. The air swims cold in my tightening chest.

The news reports I prioritize for when "Zone_Warden" does anything is a jab-punch at my ribs, each one announcing the same unbelievable result:

Xalton Kaiser A.K.A. The Notorious Zone_Warden Arrested On His Property.

An image of Xalton in handcuffs, being escorted by the police, takes up my screen, and I zone in on his pale face. His eyes are red and tired, but there's something of a smirk there.

My chest pounds, thinking back to his text when he ditched in the middle of the night.

He's wearing the same clothes as last night.

 [Xalton]: Well played, Princess.

This wasn't me. Or was it? My brow creases, trying its hardest to form a brain cell. Vertigo spins my room causing my stomach to heave. It interlinks with my headache as I sit up and scroll through the articles. My escalating heart pounds inside my skull. The words haze while I struggle to process what the fuck I'm reading.

Could I have hit "send," submitting all of my evidence against him to the police in my blackout? I hold my head in my arms, tangling my hair in my fingers.

My hands tremble as I grip my phone. Tears sting and threaten to emerge, and I wonder if he can talk to me after this. Will he be... okay? I swipe my tears back to prioritize what might have happened and who this unknown sender is.

A knock on the door makes me jump, and I shove my phone under my pillow.

"Abs, you up?" Psy's voice yawns on the other side.

Oh no.

My Valentine's Virus

How am I going to break it to Psyra? There's a chance she may even already know. I look over to her empty side of the room. She's already packed away her crystals, clothes, and books, but her pillow is flat against the floor.

A stabbing pain pierces my chest, remembering my nice time last night. The feel of Xalton's perfect mouth on mine while his aggressive tongue battled mine fills my veins with fire.

"Y-yeah, come in," I manage, my voice cracking.

The door creaks open, revealing her in Kevin's loose black T-shirt over her uniform. Her usual up-do is let down in a cascade of caramel and brown braids down her back, and I couldn't help noticing how naked her neck is as her shoulder reveals.

"You don't look so great," she groans in a sleepy voice without easing me into the truth. "Long night?"

I force a weak smile, hating how the innocent question feels like an accusation. Her stare prompts me to accept it as just that. My smile drops at Psy's pinning brown eyes. "Something like that," I swallow.

Psyra's eyes darken under her lashes. "You hear the news. About Xalton?"

My heart tugs at the mention of his name, but I manage to say, "Yes."

"He's always been a mystery, but this is..." She pinches the space between her eyebrows. "He was really Zone_Warden?"

I give her an odd look, my head tilting with my brow raised.

She grimaces at my lack of response. "Those questions you asked me at the start of our friendship... were it all... to get ahead of him? I was your little pawn in this? Why couldn't he tell me? I would have—" She hesitates and crosses her arms over her chest. Her eyes finally meet mine, as if her mind is being made up. "I would have been on his side."

My breath catches, and my hands shake again. The warm spirit Psy revolving around her makes the air around me even colder. So cold, I think I can see my breath. "Psyra—"

♥

She raises her hand. "Don't lie to me," she snaps, bursting her bubbly persona into that business tone she uses with her father over the phone. "Just don't," she urges in a casual warning.

"Okay," I huff. I found a thread leading from Zone's account to you. You were one of the first accounts he linked with, and statistically, I meant you knew each other in real life. So, I followed you. I copied your classes, and it worked well because we had a lot in common. We hit it off instantly, and... I wanted to stay friends." I groan, unable to bite back, my information pouring through like vomit.

She stares me down for over a beat, and I pale. No matter what happens, I'll know I'll be okay, so why am I so... out of focus? So outside of myself. I sigh, keeping her gaze, and she shakes her head. I swallow and break the silence.

We need answers, clarity—anything that can help me understand what happened. "I know it's hard to believe. But I didn't rat him out."

"Why should I believe you?" She questions like a professor. Business Psyra is a whole other person—it's even in her stance. Confidence drips in her every sharp posture.

Well, she does have a point.

I barely believe myself, but my twisting gut knows Drunk Abigail wouldn't do this—not after the night we shared. We dove into our pasts, our dreams, and our fears. With every word exchanged and every touch we shared, I realized how essential we were to each other in this short week of games. Sure, he threatened my life, but a fierce part of me was convinced he was changing his mind.

I had everything I needed to win but delayed sending the email to authorities. I didn't do it. Hell, my alias isn't even attached to most of these articles.

My mind drifts back to our interactions, the games we played, and the connection sealing between us. There's more to Xalton's arrest than what I'm accusing myself of.

My Valentine's Virus

Our relationship is complex, but that's why being with him was so magnetic. We get each other and match our insanities but at the core. I know if we went through our deal, we would both be left rotting inside. Things can't go back to the way they were between us, but I can at least try to make it right.

"Let's pretend I believe you—" Psyra clears her voice, her usual self breaking through the walls of her distrust.

I focus on Psy's distant expression. "Who else is close to Xalton that's as hacker-savvy as he is?"

Psyra's face hardens, and her eyes slowly kindle into that look I caught once during our team's circle. At Melanie.

My eyes broaden. "She's still stuck on him—enough to murder me. What could she get out of him being arrested—?"

Psyra's eyes are close to dropping from her head. "Xalton never leaves his house. With him not there, she—" She works a swallow, and we connect the same brain cell.

"She could gain access to his servers—the files he has. The ones he's compiled on me and my family."

Psyra snatches her absurd car keys from the counter and wheels her suitcase bag ahead. "I'll drive," she asserts.

"Don't you have a flight to catch?" I remind.

She throws a scoff my way as we rush to lock our doors and flood into the hallway. "Catch a flight, or catch a murderous psycho?" Her hands balance like a seesaw at the options before me. "It's not much of a contest."

ZONE_WARDEN

I hop off my motorcycle with my palms to the officers as I proceed. One bounds my arms tight behind my back, and cold handcuffs slap tight around my wrists before it all runs gray. My soul drifts from my body, watching myself go through the motions like good television.

They throw off my helmet, I'm pushed into their vehicle and driven off my property. There's a flash of light, but at least they let me take a glimpse of my mugshot. My hair is messed up and I look as dry as I feel.

I'm shoved into a tight cell, and it's more constricting the moment another guy waves at me like he's forced to. He introduces himself as Jim before making space. Jim smells familiar to me though. A bit too much like Dice after he wakes me from his nights of partying in the trash. I'd hose him down while I smoke and the little devil would showcases his dance moves to the water in my backyard.

Jim hugs his large arms against his chest as if he were a nude dame in his white tank top, slippers, and Valentine's Day-themed boxers. Sweat coats his bronze skin and he's about as happy as I am about having to share the space.

He's certainly having a better day off than I am, I roll my eyes in my frown, catching the sightline of the officer behind his desk. "I need a phone call," I order.

It takes a minute—around a-fucking-hundred of them before a response. My stomach turns for me to try and vomit from the sewer odor. It doesn't help how in these hellish hours of the best high of my life, I'm forced to hold an audience to Jim struggling to convert me to Christianity.

Every other minute between my disassociating, I had to make peace with who I had to call. For help.

I'm approached by a guardsman to be escorted to their only phone and wait, staring at the silver buttons for answers. My fingers work in my grumble.

It's unlikely they'd respond.

The news about my arrest could have gotten to them by now.

I wait. Each ring whizzing in my mind like a hurricane of shit.

My Valentine's Virus

"Son?" His curt voice answers.

"I need help," I sigh.

"Seems like we've helped you enough," he replies with an edge in his tone like he's rehearsed it.

My heart twists in a violent motion, plunging me into a sobering ache. I come to terms—no. I *really* focus on my father's place in my life, my past, my present, and future within seconds.

He's a good person—more honest than most. Lawrence Kaiser is an upstanding member of society, he gives back to communities and the ones over, he's never late to doctor's appointments, he greets everyone, and treats regular people like he's the main character of a cheesy sitcom.

But he's not a good father.

His only redeeming character to me was that he was around and it wasn't enough.

He showed me how to tie my shoes corporate-style, shave, how treat women, speak to crowds, arrange my suits, and how a man in our tax bracket must behave at all times. He was there, but never present. Being my father was more like an assignment to him and I'm aware there are worse experiences to have as a son, but I don't think I've ever seen my father laugh before. Not when I'd beg him to take me to movies or family outings that felt like chores.

I grin as madness seeps into my bones. I don't think the bastard has... ever liked me. "I'm in holding. I'm your son. I'm asking you for your help."

He sighs, and I know what will happen the moment it does. It doesn't prepare me for the slam of hurt caving into my chest though. The phone clicks, ending the call from his end. I go through the familiar pain throbbing in my chest. When I'm high, the pain is a vibration, loud and echoing.

The thought of contacting Abbie only increases my misery, so who else do I have that hasn't let me down?

"Xalton Kaiser?" The teller calls my name and I shuffle to face them.

"You're free to go for now. Sign here." She hands me a form and I read the statement for a beat.

An officer unlocks my restraints and over her shoulder, I find a familiar tuff of blond hair with an irritating smile.

"Xal-tone! You look exhausted—like, more than usual," Gus strides in with his hand in his Varsity jacket pockets, the other raising to greet me.

I groan, keeping my hands to myself and instead offer a patient grimace. "You?"

"What do you mean 'you'? We're friends so I figured, I'd help you out," Gus inches back, seeing the glint of fury in my gaze. He averts his short attention span over to Jim still in the holding cell. "Isn't that your jacket?" He points back and I motion him away from the scene.

"What the hell are you getting out of this?" I stretch my shoulder. "In case you haven't noticed, I'm not in a position to pay you back. At least not for a while," I laugh, then straighten. "And we're not friends."

His lips thin. "Aren't we?"

"Most definitely not. Your confusion is not my responsibility—"

He breaks out into laughter and I grit back my teeth, trying not to let my fist fly into his young face. Ever since I caught Abbie drooling at him for a tick, I've hated him and anyone who looks like him.

"Abbie's influence made me do it. I'm not after anything."

Her name in his voice makes my stomach tighten and images of her flash behind my tired gaze. Her bitten quivering lips, how her pulse raced beneath my touch when I kissed her. How soft her hair felt gripped in my fist and how her mind was completely wiped when I whispered obscenities in her ear. Her perfect blushing face. Her fire. I gulp down the memories like candy, sweet but fleeting.

The hard sting of sunlight strains my eyes as we leave the police station behind. I've been there all night but thankfully it wasn't over the weekend, or I'd be stuck with Jim. Who knows. He could have

My Valentine's Virus

convinced me to join his little cult at that time—especially in my state of mind.

I found out a lot about my scruffy friend against my will. He's from the same town I lived in over in Maine and ended up here after his girlfriend dumped a pile of trash on him when he got home.

She accused him of cheating, when really, he was just stuck at work and his phone had died. She then got him arrested for trespassing.

His end-of-the-world thoughts reminded me of my own, so we talked it out of him by tossing ideas and working on his life goals.

One of them is opening a restaurant. I promised him when I got out, I'd wire him two hundred grand as an investment loan, and we shook on it. It'd sure be easier to reach out to him if he had a phone number or an address, but I know my capabilities. I'm able to find anyone.

PRINCESS_USER24

I'm accompanied by Psyra's tense silence on the ride to Xalton's place. It's hard to tell if she's upset over missing her flight, her parent's reaction to it, or the betrayal. She brakes, and I could have hurled forward if it wasn't for the seatbelt digging between my chest.

"What the fuck—?" My frown lands on the bug-eyed driver.

"They're taking Dice!" Psy blurts out, cutting me off behind the wheel. She unbuckles like a mad woman in the center of the road. "Stop!" she shouts, running out of the car to a dark-paneled two-story house in the clean street.

This is Xalton's place? This is the type of residence I pictured my mother always dreaming of. It has sound air, black wide streets, and perfectly spaced sidewalks with a floral planter every few yards. A woman in a fur coat and her large dog pause their walk to stare at Psyra, held up by a bearded sheriff.

She gets into a screaming match, and something in the sheriff's eyes triggers my protective instincts. I push Psyra behind me and have the man shoot his argumentative glare at me instead. "What is the problem?"

"*He* is!" Psy speaks out.

The uniformed man cringes at her voice. "As I told your mouthy friend here, there's nothing you can do, and you need to leave the premises. We have a warrant for the goddamn rodent—"

"Dice is a Carnivora!" Psyra cuts in.

He pinches the bridge of his nose as if coaxing himself to calm down, but it doesn't work. "Get out of here!" he roars, transforming into an animal by lunging for Psyra. She screams and runs behind me. I work his gun free from his holster like second nature, and my mind syncs with my actions—*shit. Shit. Shit!* With the constant training I had before college, disarming someone was part of the practice. *But* my muscle memory failed to register this is a goddamn sheriff.

I arch a brow, but I need to make this appear like I did that on purpose and keep up the act. Raising the heavy pistol to his head. The ASPCA representatives caging Dice In the driveway halt their steps.

"I *knew* you were a badass!" Psy praises before stomping toward them to rip Dice's cage away from their hands.

I maintain my composure, holding the sheriff at gunpoint while he nervously swallows, recounting his faults.

Psy was being yelled at. Dice was in danger. I moved. It is what it is. It's not like things could get any better, so I stand with this role for now.

Psy liberates Dice from his cage and quickly acquaints him with the backseat of her car. I step back toward her SUV with the gun still training on the group.

Retreating into the front seat, I slam the door shut as Psyra accelerates into the street.

My partner in crime gloats in Creole, her laughter echoing in her Caribbean accent. Dice grabs her tumbler with his nimble raccoon hands and drinks from the straw, like he's a human trapped in a raccoon's body.

My Valentine's Virus

Glancing back at Dice periodically, I remove the bullets from the handgun, adrenaline subsiding at the sight of his charming, masked face.

"So, this is Dice. We finally meet," I mutter, then extend my hand for the fluffy thing to sniff or inspect or whatever, but he swiftly darts down to retrieve the gun from my lap. A brief tug-of-war ensues as we wrestle for control of it. The gun slips free, and he hops away to the furthest seat as I lurch for it.

Psyra scoffs, keeping her focus on the road. "Aww… Let him keep it. It's empty anyways."

"Yeah, that's not the issue here," I protest. Amusement settles in while I watch him wave it over his head, imitating me from earlier. "Where did Xalton get this raccoon?"

Psyra shrugs with a derisive *I dunno* glance.

LEVEL TWENTY
PRINCESS_USER24

It's been over a month since Xalton's arrest. Not being able to see him has done great work keeping me up at night. I've been skipping my free breakfasts at Cupid's. My stomach knots every time I look at orange juice, and it's extended to eating overall.

My studies have suffered because I have spent time and energy figuring out who this person who's been texting me is. Who put Zone away?

I tirelessly scanned the Dark Web for evidence, but no one knew who we were dealing with. The current Number One spot falls to me, but it repeats in my head like a dirty taunt. *I didn't win our contest.*

True as Tuesday, there's someone out there operating right under my nose. I've been giving myself bald spots over the lack of leads. *Number One hacker, my ass.* I often wonder if Xalton would have been able to figure it out. …Or we might even find them together if he could talk to me.

The UTN story that exposed him as Zone_Warden painted a bullseye on his back. From what I've gathered, he's been getting hit with death

My Valentine's Virus

threats by faceless criminals after being doxed. My organs twist in every direction learning how he's under house arrest *and* might be in danger.

He doesn't have anyone in that house with him. The police confiscated all of Xalton's servers and phone—all of his tech, and he has no internet either. He's probably gone psycho by now and not in his usual way. The web of challenges I initiated got him stuck in here in Oregon. My involvement has given him nothing but pain. It's my fault, and I'm not sure how to face him.

As for Psyra. I'm unsure if she's forgiven me for using her, but she's holding Dice during her flight back to Fraixia. Campus life hasn't been the same since she left. It's like her being around was Melanie's deterrent. Not that I needed her protection against her, but I've noticed the dramatic shift.

She and her cronies have been giving me and everyone else their all.

I find her cornering Hanna, one of the first years I hung out with, framing her for being in the auditorium without faculty permission. It's an expellable offense.

A year ago, someone set fire to the auditorium in the night, and the culprit still hasn't been named. The district chalked it up as an accident, but ever since, stricter rules have been applied regarding students being inside facilities without a faculty member present.

Melanie wanted to set her straight and make an example out of her.

The poor girl was tricked into going inside, led in by Melanie and her crew because she called her out on some nonsense. I didn't want what happened to Grace to happen to Hanna. My pride wasn't going to let that happen a second time on my watch.

I approached Melanie, and Hanna ran off as I instructed. A week later, campus security took everything in my dorm out to the curb. Finding all of my belongings and things I treasure in the dumpsters like that had my hands trembling beyond my control. Insurmountable blinding fury flanked me, and I couldn't stop it.

♥

I couldn't stop trembling like I was vibrating from reality. All the gold medals I've earned throughout my life were covered in muck. The books I spent countless nights memorizing were sprawled out like a crime scene to literature.

The framed limited-edition pre-order posters of games I obsessed over with are wet, glass shattered, and torn. Glowing neon pieces scatter across the space in a vulgar nightmare. My stomach plunged to my throat when I discovered the portrait of my dad lost under a mountain of circuitry that used to be my war machine.

My knee shook with murderous ambition. I knew exactly which class Melanie was going to, and I searched. I found her striding along on campus next to her rat-faced friend. Hatred spreads through me like a pandemic. I began my march.

I lost my scholarship and can't even change it back with a few hacks. I lost my walking good-luck charm, Psyra. I lost Xalton, my maverick, my rival, my heart. And I lost a piece of me I didn't think I'd find while attending this school. All because of his crazy ex.

Meeting her halfway, I used that notion to fuel the charging punch aimed at her face in the walkway. I caught the Big Bad Wolf strutting it out with her rat-faced friend.

She flinches from my hit, and I savor it before the puta tumbles backward. "Bitch!" I spit, cocking my shoulders back and falling onto her. She tries crawling backward, a semblance of fear flashing in her maroon eyes. "You got me expelled?!" My right hook lands, her satanic head whips to the side, and blood gushes from her nose. "You broke my *computer!*" I hit her again when the rims of my eyes itch.

Melanie raises her fist to strike at me, and I let her bruise me if only to ground the inner pain clawing to be freed of me. "You got Xalton arrested!" I reel my fist back, but before it lands, I'm thrown.

I land pressed against a stout tree. Skidding against the grass, I grunt from the buckling pain in my back that echoes to my skeleton.

Who is that?

My Valentine's Virus

Grunting for breath, I struggle to my feet, and my vision blurs as another woman runs up to me with chaos in her gaze.

My chaos isn't fucking done.

She's the same height as me but more muscular. She ties up her long brown hair and reveals a constellation of fake freckles dotting her nose.

She's in my way, and I'm not finished hurting yet.

The other girl pounces for me while Rat-face hurries to check up on her mistress. I shift to the side, ready for another attack, but without my knowing, a third chick of their group comes out from hiding, and they proceed to jump me. A flurry of limbs blinds me, and I can hardly tell what's up from down. Hatred whirls within me like a flaring storm.

The kicks and jabs feel like they last for an eternity. My arms and sides shield my bruising face. My ribs crack up, and something foul is smeared into my hair. It smells! *Is that shit?!*

My world spins, struggling to hold my balance while I'm flat on the concrete. Fighting to breathe, I cough and writhe for oxygen. Soreness thrums to the beat of my racing heart.

Coppery fluid fills my mouth, and I spit right on Melanie's shoes.

Her head drops, glaring at the mess, and her fists shudder at her side. "Hold her steady!" She grunts and whips her attention to the ground, searching for something.

My vision is a haze in my grapples. It becomes too much, and I'm stuck under the weight of three awful bitches.

Her brows lift, landing on something before returning. Melanie returns, hauling a boulder, her arms are straining to carry. Managing to raise it high over my head, she grins while I grunt.

I can't even curse her out before she K.Os me.

Her wicked grin is the last thing I see. Without hesitation or reluctant speech, a miracle happens. A blond blur from the corner of my eye charges at Melanie, knocking her to the ground like a linebacker.

her friends jolt up to their feet.

My eyes widen at the jagged edge of the rock falling toward me. Rolling away at the last second, the fracture of the impact has my heart throbbing in my skull. Gus races away from the horde of dangerous women chasing him.

Melanie brushes herself off while giving me a once-over. When my legs limp, a low smile carves on her face.

She doesn't move where she stands, but I fall over on my knees. I struggle with my sprained ankles as her sickening expression burrows a hole in my stomach.

I need to get out of here. I have nothing left.

Limping takes me to another relentless realm of torture. Coughing, I drag my feet to the bus stop clutching my side. My ID card still works, thankfully.

This would have been somewhat manageable if only one of my ankles were sprained. No one else is on the bus this early. The driver in his navy suit is half-asleep and refuses to argue with me about sending me to the hospital. Instead, he's settled on driving someplace off-route. I miss the sound of A.N.A.'s voice when she freaks out over traffic. She's gone too. My life's work smashed in a second.

My neck aches, shifting at the dark two-story house on the foggiest side of town. Panic seizes my chest when the first drop of rain falls against my ride. I teeter from the exit, and the sky drops a hundred thousand rain shards that scrape my bruised skin. Each droplet has my heart throbbing, and it plummets with the crashing of thunder.

I whimper. My swelling eyes refuse to blink. With rushing breath, I fall to my knees, just… accepting I have to army crawl. My jaw clenches at another deafening strike from the sky. Every muscle in my body tenses until I don't feel pain anymore.

It's not natural how my body reacts to this weather, but all that trembling tells me, *the clouds don't give a shit who they affect.*

Storms like these are my constant reminder of how merciless nature can be. High tides don't care if you're a toddler. They'll swallow you

My Valentine's Virus

without effort. Winds don't care whose mother they take; they take without prejudice. Earthquakes don't care what nations they destroy or the lives they break. They take.

It's more to me than just rain. It's my grim reaper.

My battered knees scrape the stone floors to the last place I expected to end up. What's left of my momentum knocks on the large dark door, and my chest swells at footsteps quickening behind it. My throbbing eyes drift to his shoes, and I struggle to swallow the ball in my throat. His right ankle hangs a monitor around it with an irritating red light.

This phrase has haunted me for decades. I promised myself to never say this—never be like my dad. Never ask. But dammit, I've missed him, and it's been a shitty fucking day.

"Help me, please," I beg as tears rain down my face.

Xalton's face is unshaven. The sleepless shadows beneath his eyes have grown, and I find the turmoil rooted in them. Pain clouds his eyes when he sees my battered skin, but despite it, a flicker of his warmth shines through.

"Princess…?"

LEVEL TWENTY-ONE

ZONE_WARDEN

My servers have been taken into custody by Homeland Security. My pull from interning at the CIA has them prevented from seeing harm.

I stalk around the ruins of my office, my chest clasping and twisting inside the space it once occupied. My office lacks the comforting hum that helped break the eerie silence of my house. I've lost a huge part of my soul. It becomes harder to breathe the more my mind wanes on losing the internet.

It was my outlet, my work, and how I kept in touch with my sanity—it made me who I was.

Without it, it's hard to breathe right. I lean my hand against the wall as the other holds my chest. *This is only temporary, you drama king. Breathe.*

Staggering back to the bed, my vision distorts. A fog, the cops didn't seize my medication. I flame the end of my blunt and fan the air around me.

My Valentine's Virus

The smoke is dark, hanging above with deep curves that remind me of Abbie. Pain bleeds in my chest.

I have no way to contact her. Who knows what Melanie has planned if I'm not watching over my Abbie?

Abbie needed the win *that* badly.

I knew I'd regret giving my heart the reigns. You sappy fucking organ. *All* you're supposed to do is pump blood to my body and *not* steer me to annihilation.

My brain wanted to experience the answers for itself. I did, and in response, my parents disowned me. They lied, saying it was to minimize the death threats coming their way from my foes. But, hey. If they can't handle a few disembodied pig heads on their doorstep, who needs them?

I keep up my calisthenics training. Just because my heart and mind are going doesn't mean my body has to. I didn't make it to the front of UTN five years in a row for my intellect.

I throw in a few hours of Muay Thai refreshers in case there's another break-in during the night.

With a towel, I wipe the sweat from my forehead before approaching the shower. My muscles throb and relax as I scan the house.

It's too quiet with Dice gone. It's like the ruins of a madman's depleted empire, and then I remember I'm the mad one. I'll miss Dice, though. His absence has each room giving me the silent treatment. I pause at the hole in my wall, gravitating me. The memory of him popping his little masked head out covered in dust makes me smirk, and my eyes ache.

I sit at my wheeled throne, passing the time before I shower. I remove my headset, rest it inside my drawer, and pick up a pencil beside it. I take the battered end and jam it into my ankle monitor. They saved the itchiest one to shackle to me.

After showering, I reach for my razor blade and shaving cream. I lift my head mechanically and swipe the fogged surface to reveal the man in the mirror—the ghost of Number One. My expression hallows.

♥

I'm not even sure who I'm looking at.

The rain against my windows is the background echo of Xalton, the fool who let his heart rule. The rain matches my mood hauntingly.

I glide my fingers through my hair, taking a moment to absorb the cleansing droplets. Inhaling over the sink, I drop my shoulders and stretch my neck. *It's not like I'll be going outdoors. I'll skip shaving for the time being.*

No meetings to attend, no more emails... it's freeing. I don't mind moping all day and love not leaving my house.

My security monitor pings, alerting me that something is creeping toward my doorstep. When I check the screen, my chest squeezes. Air fills my lungs spying her familiar black hair, half straight and wavey. Abbie's on her knees at my doorstep with blackened bruises coating her olive skin like tasteless graffiti. The flickering fire in her autumn-colored eyes had been put out. She's shivering.

Storming down, I glide down the railing without stopping and fling open the front door.

"Help me, please..."

"Princess...?" My chest swells at Abbie's deteriorating sight. A whiff of her stings my eyes like burning sewage. A wet crimson line drips from my seizing hand, and the sting breaks my tense haze. I've been gripping the pointed door accessory so hard the edge sliced me.

"Who fucking did this to you?" My blood runs hot, and it's stifling.

Clutching her side, Abbie shivers as the rain overlaps her.

I frown when the lightning strikes, revealing her injuries. *She can't stand.* Her nostrils flare wide open when a gunshot of thunder propels her into my arms. I swallow her against my chest, holding my breath before I carry her upstairs.

Kicking open the bathroom door, I rest her in the center of the tub. My girl examines the area while I fetch an array of bathing supplies from my housewarming gifts. She frowns in protest when I run the faucet.

My Valentine's Virus

"Stop. I'll do it myself—Get out—" her voice rattles, but I ignore her even when she blocks my hands. The bottles spill into the tub, bobbing up and down in browning water.

My stare is vacant when she slaps my arm again and again. I continue reaching for her top, and she punches my wrists. I gaze into her eyes as each drop of water echoes our pain.

Something close to rage trickles from me after her last punch. I break, gripping at her shirt and tearing it in two. She grunts, covering her chest with her hands as I reach for her skirt next. The roar of the faucet rages when I unzip her and toss the rags into the trash bin beside me. Abbie stands calf-deep in brown water. My eyes rove over her black lingerie. Soaking, she tries pushing me away as I yank off her underwear. Her defiance mirrors in her eyes when her bra hooks are next.

Forcing her arms down, I pin her shoulders back against the tile. I snatch the nozzle and spray her hair on the strongest setting. Piling shampoo, soap, the salts, *everything* falls into the tub as I dig out the shit in her hair.

Confusion lingers in her eyes as I go into autopilot. Her movements tire as she still fights with me when I check her injuries.

Welts, scrapes, and bruises take up the side of her breasts, ribs, arms, hips, and legs. She has two black eyes but nothing a blood thinner can't assist with.

Exhaling deeply, I wish I could exchange her pain with mine. She lowers her head, but I lift her chin and massage her hair with more soap. I repeat this until the awful smell fades from the woman I love and I rinse it all away.

I then wrap her in my thickest towel until she's a calmer burrito. With another, I cover her head, tasseling her hair inside and lifting her in my arms. I rotate out the door with her eyes captive in mine.

"My med kit's downstairs," I break the silence in my rasp.

In my kitchen, I suture her gashes and manage her injuries in silence. I plug in the hair dryer, and the mechanical whirring fills the space.

Her waves of gorgeous black hair fly around until her soft hair dries.

I haul her up again and note the exhaustion in her eyes when I return to the stairs. My steps creak from our combined weight as I bring her to my bed. She sits on the edge of the king-sized, and I search my walk-in closet for a shirt to cover her.

Yanking out a Minecraft shirt, I pull it over her head before placing her arms into a thick sweater. Her big brown eyes peer at me through thick eyelashes, and I kiss the scar on her eyebrow.

"You're sleeping in my bed. I don't have anywhere else to put you this late," I announce, rolling her back into my arms.

"Can I not stay in one of the other rooms?" she nudges my ribs with her elbow.

"There *are* no 'other rooms.' You can check for yourself. They're storage. It's been that way since I adopted Dice. He would have destroyed my shit if I didn't put them away."

Her eyebrows fiddle in annoyance. "Then... Let me take the couch—?"

"It's destroyed. *Also*, thanks to Dice. Any other suggestions?" I'm legitimately open to knowing. My ego craves it, like medicine.

She mutters a swear in Spanish as my grin stretches. "Where... do you have your friends sleep when they come over then?"

I lift my brow at her odd assumption. "I don't let *other* people sleep at my house."

She bites her lower lip as if remembering I'm a goddamn shut-in, mostly. "...I'll take the floor then," she huffs, but I'm not convinced, nor would my ego let a beaten woman writhe on the hardwood.

"As if I'd let you. If you're that uncomfortable, *I'll* take the floor."

I catch a glimpse of her rolling her eyes as I pull the bedding from her. "How *noble* of you."

"Furthest thing from it." My jaw tightens at her sarcastic voice. "You look so pathetic, I want to lend you the high ground for once in your sad life."

My Valentine's Virus

The air surrounding her vibrates, and my hidden grin increases.

She pats the bed's surface, inviting me to lay beside her. I relish her eye-avoiding pout before I pull the comforter over us. She haggardly shifts, and my stomach squeezes, hearing her pained grunts.

A moment of silence stretches before she groans again. "Hey... thank you."

I ignore her, but a minute later, Abbie's gentle snores caress my very soul, and I'm able to close my eyes.

As much as I was ready to sculpt a plan to get back at her, finding her the way I did was just short of reinvented pain. The defeat in her eyes—a defeat I didn't cause, was too much. It differed from the jubilated glint in her eyes when I showed the airport erotica at The Melancholy.

That was when I tasted what *true* victory was. That loss was invigorating, but this loss was a stark opposite.

A terror.

I want to win against her all the time, to savor moments like that night at the bar—not the ones where her being is shattered for me to repair—and I would repair.

I'd do it again and again because she meant more to me than I was ever prepared for. I just wish I accepted it sooner.

Abbie's arms drape over mine before my mind can inspect the turmoil in my heart. She brings me to a dreamland with her, and I'm more certain of where she lies within my heart. Without fighting it this time, I relax in the waves of her warmth.

LEVEL TWENTY-TWO

PRINCESS_USER24

I wake to the relentless shivering of my bones. Tears streak down my face as thunder rages outside the windows of… Xalton's room? Squinting in my sit-up, a sharp pain aches into my sides—a harsh reminder of my lost control the other day.

Crawling to Xalton's door and begging him for help—*I wasn't hallucinating that?* I reached out… and I'm okay. I'm breathing. I'm alive. I'm safe.

I gaze down at the sweater I'm wearing. It's three times larger than me, and beneath is another shirt I don't recognize. Xalton's breathy snoring beside me resonates with my soothing pulse, but guilt tugs at my heart.

He did this. My eyes water as the memories come back to him carrying me indoors. He thought I snitched on him, and I consistently mentioned I would. He still took me in from the storm. I gave him

My Valentine's Virus

bruises while fighting against his help in the bathtub. He bathed and clothed me despite it. To make matters worse, I rich-shamed him for not having a separate room for me. I drop my head, running my finger through my scalp and rubbing the embarrassment plunging through me.

My hands shiver, and I hesitate to wake him. His dark hair swoops over his forehead, and I grab my wrist to prevent it from fixing it back so I can enjoy his sweet face. He looks so disarming when he's asleep. He needs it more than most.

His beard gives him a rugged side I want to capture for my private collection. The shadows under his eyes remind me of when I first fell in love with him.

He was on UTN magazine, looking like he'd never slept a year in his life. He was disheveled in a sexy way but dripping with misery behind those eyes. To societal standards, he wasn't on his best game that day. His fake smile shined through it, and I glimpsed at a man who needed to face the camera despite the war raging behind his mask. I found myself admiring that. The mysterious tortured tech mogul. How could I resist?

I can't bring myself to wake him, but I hate how every cell in my nervous system is reacting. The thunder crashes make me shrink, smaller than I force myself to be. My heart insists on racing through my breathing exercises—in and out, in and out. But it still aches in my chest, and my shivers don't waver.

I wish I were better. I wish I could just shake it off like I shake everything else, but this one thing always gets me. Shimming from his hold around my waist, his thick arm grabs me and pulls me into his chest.

"Where are you going?" he asks, his tone drenching with exhaustion.

"I…"

"You're shaking," he acknowledges before sitting up. His examining gaze heats my face, and he fixes my hair from it. "You're not cold. Talk to me."

"Wh-why did y-you take care of me? I ruined your life," my teeth chatter.

♥

Emotion crashes behind my eyes like a great distraction. I can't tell him I'm scared of the rain, so I let my waterworks trail down my cheeks. "I'm... I'm sorry—"

He takes my head between his large hands and leans over my face. "I was disowned by my abusive family, and it's illegal for me, an introvert, to leave my house." His gaze softens. "You did me a huge favor."

I blink a tear away. Wiping them, I pray he continues talking so I can have more time to deflect. He sits back, with his analyzing pupils still, tilting his head. "My servers being gone is a throat punch but nothing I can't adapt to. Besides, I've been catching up on my reading and started working... on a novel to pass the time."

I snort. "Heh... knowing you, it's p-probably an autobiography about how g-great you are."

A smile stretches on his face at my antagonistic tone. "... want to read it later?" He releases me before laying back down. "I mean... It's not a well-written fanfic about me railing you in a cockpit while our plane goes down, but—"

"*Okay!*" I grit. "I'll l-look at it."

"Later—you're also deflecting. Now, tell me. Why the trembles?"

"I'm just malfunctioning, is all. It's like an allergic reaction. Happens all the time." My rumbling teeth clench in my attempt to will my nerves manageably.

"It's not an allergic reaction I've ever seen," he theorizes, his eyes never leaving mine. The black sky illuminates for a millisecond before the smashing of thunder rings throughout the space.

Wonderful. I've activated his CIA mode. There's no avoiding that. I sigh so sharp, I'm sure he feels it. "As if your minimal mindset is the standard of verifying allergens."

His brows wriggle, and he smirks in amusement. Leaning in, he gauges me further. "You're hiding something. And by the insults, I'm *sure* it's something embarrassing. Did you wet the bed? You should know I'm not ashamed of your accidents on me."

My Valentine's Virus

"You—" I cut myself off with a snarl. My expression pinches as if I'm about to hiss, and his abdominals tighten with laughter. Heat trickles into my face, and I wait until we've both calmed.

The sinister storm rumbles, piercing through the silence, and I'm urged to speak.

"D... do I really have to t-tell you?"

He keeps his eyes strict. "Yeah, or I'll eat you out and give you a reason to keep quivering." *That's not the threat he thinks it is—*

I take a deep breath, cutting off my thoughts.

When I part my lips to speak, the truth won't leave.

Xalton caresses my cheek, his pine green eyes flicking from my lips to my shivers. "If it's tough, speak it slowly... I have nowhere else to be."

"I... I'm a-afraid... of."

A thunderstrike crashes against the window, causing his room to brighten like a flashbang. The crack of violence has my heart fist in my skull before I tumble into Xalton's pillow. He unlatches me from it and has me squeeze his broad chest instead. He strokes my shoulder, and he hushes me, whispering to me in a doting timbre. "It's alright, Princess. You're safe. *Breathe* for me, please. In and out. In and out, alright? You're safe. I've got you. I got you."

My nails digging into his skin lessen with his strokes. His soothing voice and the racing of his heart lessen my nerves, but I still shake. I exhale as he raises my head to him.

"It's the thunder?" he surmises.

"S... Storms," I wheeze, willing my tight muscles to stop *moving* their own. I grit my rattling teeth.

He sits me upright, his deep gaze resting in mine like he's seeing me for the first time. "It's just your Achilles heel, Princess. Everyone has one. It's normal."

I scoff at his attempt to make me feel less like a freak. It's working. I adjust my hair behind my ear. "What's yours?"

Xalton stares at me for a beat as if it were obvious, but his fearful swallow breaks the staring contest. "Wait here." He rolls his eyes and shifts out of bed.

He closes his thick curtains, ending the crippling light show, and opens a drawer. A pair of black headphones come into view in his hand with his Elysium logo stickered on the shells.

Meeting in front of me, he fixes them against my ears, and my eyes widen at the sheer silence. Besides the voices in my head, I can't hear a single thing. I snap my fingers in front of me to confirm, but the action is muted.

Tricking my body of the storm's passing, I beam at him, and my muscles slowly relax.

Xalton's lips move to speak, teasing me with his devious grin, and I nod. He lifts one of the ear folds. "I'll take that as a 'yes.'"

I don't know what I agreed to.

He presses into me, and my shivering surges between my legs. His eyes narrow into a boiling gaze before stealing a kiss from me. His warm hand presses against my back as he eases me against his bed.

He deepens the kiss. My heart jumps when he crawls over me and tugs the end of my shirt up.

A hot shiver rattles through me as Xalton parts my knees. He rests his smooth lips against my pussy, having me gasp.

Second later, a lo-fi melody plays through the headset, and his tongue slides up my slit.

This is... nice.

My body's shivers lessen but jolt from his more fervent licks. My eyes shut, falling into the sensation of his warm lips kissing my clit. Teasing, licking, swirling, and sucking.

My head cranes back as I sink further against his pillow. When my hip jerks, he yanks my hips against him with ravenous strength. Going from delicate tongue strokes, he focuses on the exhilarating spot that has

My Valentine's Virus

me writhing. I prefer this pace over him treating me like some wounded houseplant.

My eyes flash to his perfect dark hair, and I slip my fingers through them. The warm strands fire bliss through my fingers in his ruthless sucks. *"Fuck...!"* I moan, my head craning back, and he only increases his pressure. *"Ugn—"*

His finger enters my pussy with the same quickness of his tongue against my clit. He only gets better at this, and my sanity slips having to come to terms with this. *I belong to these fingers,* his cavernous gaze tells me. Gripping my hips tighter, he doesn't give my G-spot time to recover, and my stifled cries hum throughout his room.

"Fuck! Ahn!" My toes curl, my muscles clench, and my mind frees itself of coherent thoughts. *"Please."*

His deep groan vibrates into my pussy as he strokes the perfect spot turning me into a puddle of feral need. I grow deaf to the soft hymns in my ears and breathing is an afterthought.

I fist the sheets under me, grinding against his face coming and shattering on his tongue and fingers. Gasping, my eyes close as strays of static ecstasy linger. Then I notice Xalton looks almost... disappointed.

"No waterworks this time?" he mutters, licking his lips and fingers. I nearly climax again at the dominating sight of him. "I guess I'll have to try harder."

My eyes devour his form as I get to my knees. He gets off the bed, and the erection tenting in his sweatpants holds my attention.

A heated thrill skirts up my spine as perverse ideas birth between us when he talks. "Xalton...?" I interrupt. "Can I see your dick?"

♥

LEVEL TWENTY-THREE

ZONE_WARDEN

I'm at war with invisible demons who know I'll break at any second. "Not your best idea, Princess," I advise and clench my jaw. I face the door. If I leave now, I won't jump this injured woman. "You're healing—"

"I just want to *see* it," she adds, crossing her arms. Her breast spill against the collar of my shirt, and my cock burns with desires I shouldn't further entertain.

I pinch the bridge of my nose, my raging battle endangering my composure. "Why?" I badger and cup her chin to face me.

"I… want to… try sucking you off," she says. The dense lust flaring in her bright brown eyes prey on mine, shattering my resolve.

My throat bobs, and I slide my pants down. My cock dips up in front of her, pulsating like it has its own heart. Abbie's pinkening expression

My Valentine's Virus

matches my throbbing tip. Her brows lift a bright glimmer of intrigue in her autumn-colored eyes.

"Oh, my god…"

My brow cocks at the hint of drool cornering her mouth.

"It's so big…and veiny."

She eyes my length, tilting her adorable head while she uploads it to memory. My smile amplifies by her amused scientific expression.

"Don't be frustrated if you can't take it all in," I urge.

Abbie holds my cock in her hands, and my pupils dilate. My stomach tightens as she pumps my shaft. I rest my hand on her shoulder when agonizing desire has me lean my head back and groan. *"Fuck, Princess…"*

Her palms are warm and soft like a feather. It's like a million angels stroking me at once. Her big eyes glitter from my reaction, and her tongue darts out, licking and caressing my tip with her lips.

She takes her time, rubbing me, and a low groan vibrates from me, my body aching for more.

"Abbie," my teeth grit, and she gently takes me in, passing her lips. My cock reaches the back of her throat, and my heart roars in my ears. *"Fuuck…!"* Her pink tongue licks the sides of my balls, and my hand slides through her scalp. "Christ," I hiss. Her eyes water and her mouth hitches to gag before I yank her back by her hair. I pant from the blinding sensation as heat pulses in my face and chest. "Why… did you… do *that?*"

She rolls her eyes. "You challenged me."

I smile through my annoyance at her for misreading me. "No, the fuck I didn't," I breathe, wiping my awe. "I wasn't—I wasn't teasing you when I said—"

Her hair slips between my fingers, and my protests are lost when her mouth plunges around my cock again. I am struggling to breathe right. Her gag reflex is like a suggestion to her. *"You're so fucking pretty,"* I groan, my voice aching with need.

Abbie's cheeks hollow, sucking and stroking my cock in hypnotic motions with her head. My balls tighten as my eyes roll to the back of my head. Abbie smirks, plucking my dick free with a lewd slurp.

Nearly trembling, I glide my hands through her hair, petting and aggressively kissing her face. *"Explain. How* are you so good at this?"

"Is it supposed to be hard? I only watched a video tutorial on it." Her eyes glance away from me while red fills her cheeks. "...I got curious." I know the one she's talking about and grin.

"When'd you watch it?"

She lowers her head, hiding behind my erection. "...none of your business."

My smile heightens, leaning into her. "Was it after you saw it when you yanked my pants down in your class?"

Her swelling expression is my answer. "You're so full of yourself—"

"And I'm *right.*"

She half smiles, playing with my dick like a toy, and it's not. In her state, it's a weapon.

"I want to keep going until you finish," she rasps before wrapping her lips around my crown and gliding me back in. When she strokes, sucking me like a flawless fit, my mind boils to a euphoric haze. My body shudders, my breaths haggard like an afflicted bull, and I groan so deep from the sensation I find stars. "You feel so fucking good, Princess," I praise.

A weak groan rips through my lungs as she increases her speed. *"I'm c... coming ughh,"* I grunt, and my release fires with the torque of a shotgun.

My knees buckle, and come leaks from the corners of her lips. I ease my cock free, and I'm breathless. My vision still fogs, but her gulp pulls me to the pornography of her licking the corners of her lip. *Fucking lord...*

I had no idea what I was dealing with. If I knew she could recite poetry on my cock like that, I'd have given her my soul ages ago.

My Valentine's Virus

"How was it?" she asks, finding me struggle to return to this dimension.

Leaning over, I take her face in my hands and kiss her.

We kiss for what seems like hours.

I fondle and caress her breasts, getting higher and higher to the feel of her in my space. Her smooth curves keep my every attention, and I can't stop running my hands through her hair. I'm immediately hard again.

"Let's stop," I propose. My heart ricochets in my chest. "Before I forget you're injured and fuck you unconscious."

She pauses as if debating in her little head if she wants me to or not, but I cut off that line of thinking.

"You're *traumatized*, baby. Sleep," I urge.

She pulls the comforter over her head. "...okay. You're right."

"Good girl," I susurrate. A warm smile heats my face, so I reach over and kiss her again. "I love you." Lying beside her, my eyes shut of their own accord, and I sleep as soundly as I ever had.

My neighbor helped me call an ambulance to have Abbie examined at a hospital. She argued against it, saying it would bring ugly accusations to me if a criminal had a beaten woman leave his house. Her health meant more to me than my credibility, so I won that argument.

Nothing happened to me.

I was sure she just didn't want to leave my side. I couldn't join her when the ambulance hauled her down the street, taking my heart with her. I contacted the state's best criminal attorney, and they helped plead my case and get my devices back.

She was brought home to me after she was cleared. Her ribs weren't broken, but they were severely bruised, along with her ankles and other sets of injuries I already patched up. We've been playing house for several weeks since then.

Abbie's wounds have fully recovered, and she's been helping decorate my "depressing" house when she can. I bought her a better laptop than the shitty green one she was attached to. Together, we helped revive her AI, A.N.A., and she's been organizing the used Amazon boxes that are piling up.

I love having my Abbie around. When I'm in my house now, it always smells like orange-scented candles and autumn. I love waking up to the sight of her timid expression like I'm her fantasy in the flesh. It does wonders for my ego. The odd citrus scent of her on my pillow and my clothes remains, and it's difficult not to groan in delight.

Taking care of her is the highlight of my day, especially when her face lights up from my cooking. We threaten each other like a pair of unhinged frat boys during video games, and I tease her until she's red from rage or some colorful perversion.

I find all her buttons. Pushing them is my favorite hobby. She's my everything, despite me *losing* everything, I know we'll be okay because I've never been better. I've never really had a friend like this with whom I could let go. I was lonelier than I thought without her.

LEVEL TWENTY-FOUR

PRINCESS_USER24

In the middle of the night, I wake in a pleasant haze. Hunger swarms me all at once, twisting my stomach until it's dry and feral. Rolling to my feet, I find my situation dead asleep on his side and debate waking him just to feed me. *I don't want to be a bad houseguest, but if I don't eat something now, I'll die,* my stomach convinces me.

I nudge Xalton's shoulder, but he doesn't wake. His blissful low snores cease to an end, but I'm pretty sure an earthquake couldn't wake him. I caution my steps and search downstairs in the kitchen.

Opening the stainless-steel fridge, my tired eyes adjust to the light. In its center, a beautiful array of cooked shrimp with red sauce sits. I pry the container open and pluck the shellfish in my mouth. The briny sweetness of the sea cascades over my tongue. *"Mmm…"*

A blush tickles my cheeks at the pile of shells I leaned to the side. Gathering them, I close the fridge and search for a trash bin, but there isn't one in sight. Xalton's always taken my trash, so I never knew where the bin was.

My brow lifts as I open the lower cabinets with my pinky, careful not to drop the shells.

Before giving up and turning on the lights, something shiny opens in the dark kitchen corner. A little robot opens, revealing its trash bag, and I toss the shells. Even his trash bin is electronic? *Ridiculous and unnecessary.*

I drink a glass of water, leave it in the sink, and scurry up to Xalton's room. When I open the door, I find him staring at a handheld screen with a growing smirk on his side of the bed. "You're awake," I chirp.

"Yeah…" he drawls distantly.

I crawl into bed and wrap my arms around his chest until I find what he's looking at. On his screen, a recording of me jumping up and down after biting into the shrimp plays on repeat.

My face cramps, and I shrink. "You saw that, huh?"

A rumbled laugh leaves him, and I fidget with embarrassment on the inside. "You always do a little jig every time you eat. It's fucking *adorable.*"

I watch myself jump back when his trash bin finds me in the stumble of darkness.

He rests his device on the nightstand and shifts to embrace me. Kissing every inch of my face, heat surges throughout my stomach, and I squirm from the overdose. I exhale, the butterflies filling my guts as he gazes into my eyes.

"Hey…" My face heats the more I speak. "…I want you."

His brows rise, and this time around, he's open to hearing me. "…alright."

My Valentine's Virus
ZONE_WARDEN

"Why are you a virgin?"

My question hovers between us like a fart, but I'm not ashamed of it. It's natural we expose hard questions before traversing certain paths together. Being her first is romantic on paper, but it gives me more to consider. I'm not small by any definition.

My last sexual encounter was with a short-haired brunette named Ellie. She had a contagious warmth in her smile. She'd go out of her way to find me, pull me away from meetings, and kiss me like it was the last time she'd ever see me.

I was recovering after isolating myself from my near-death experience with Melanie. A few of us from the Elysium conference shared drinks at the bar's lobby nook, and I was getting out of my shell. My employees' faces lit up every time I'd speak, and Ellie would swoon, cradling her chin and longing at me with her intense gaze.

She invited me to her hotel room, and the moment we were alone, our bodies collided like meteors. We consumed each other like hungry beasts taking turns stripping each other, kissing each other every other second like our lives depended on it.

The moment she unlatched my buckle, my cock freed, and she froze.

The look of genuine horror in her eyes still haunts me. It was like she was hired to slay a Basilisk.

I thought I did something wrong and asked if she was okay. Ellie confessed she couldn't continue and shared a heart-wrenching tale about a traumatic event she had with a guy around my size. She mentioned how he wouldn't listen to her when she begged him to stop. He ruptured her cervix, and she needed to be rushed to the ER for surgery.

My whole body winced at her tale, and my blood was boiling with rage that someone she entrusted hurt her like that. I'm no stranger to abuse from an ex or the frustrating hospital visits that accompanied them, so I thanked her for being transparent with me.

I held her on the hotel couch during the movie she picked out. When we moved to the bed, Ell felt stiff in my arms. It was like she couldn't get comfortable. I kept assuring her *we* were okay while the movie played on in the background of her uncertainty.

I hesitated to ask if I could have done more for her, but I froze up too, and remained quiet the rest of the night.

The next morning, she was gone, and she blocked my number. I couldn't give it another thought because I had a plane to catch. Dwelling on it would have compromised my meeting with Elysium's partners.

I hoped Ellie was alright and that she'd be able to find peace if she ever got to leave her traumas behind. I figured she might have forced herself into dating to get over her fears, and something about my dick backtracked her. I was happy I got to savor her company, even if it was fleeting.

Abbie's tight cunt barely takes my finger, and I was pushing it when I plunged two inside at the college. I'm not upset she's a virgin. I'm terrified.

She licks her lips, hesitating to respond. "It just… never happened for me," she says. "My focuses were on other things. It's not like I haven't been curious about sex. They make good vibrators, and that's satiated me until… this point. I… don't really know how to answer your question."

I lean into her and feel her temperature rise the moment I do. "What do you think about when you touch yourself?"

She swallows, and a soft pant leaves her breath. "…you."

"Me?" I susurrate, my ego slowly replacing my fear.

"Mhm. You take… really nice photos."

I smile. Who would have thought the UTN Article would be the catalyst for our situation? I was forced into that interview, and it was the

My Valentine's Virus

same day I'd been dumped. I remember how depleted I felt during those photos. Dead eyes, sunken cheeks.

"And what am I doing to you in those *filthy* little fantasies, Princess?" I trace my hands over her thighs and stroke my thumb over her dewy slit.

Her face reddens, and her cheeks light up like a nightlight. I take the shell of her ear between my lips and don't let go until she answers me.

"This... and more."

The more she keeps her response, I apply pressure to her clit as it soaks around my thumb, kneading in firmer intervals.

"Ahh..." her voice breaks between her lips, and I chase the spot I ran through.

Her breathing escalates, and I lean her against my pillow without stopping. Resting my warm palm over her abdomen, I increase my speedy strokes to elicit those precious sounds from her.

"Xaah... Xalton...!" her eyes beg for me not to stop. *"I'm coming...!"*

Her thighs tense beneath my hand. She's so easy to read, it's intoxicating. No—it's addicting. The way her eyes flood with sin overwhelming my senses, is all here for me to decipher. Like code in the form of a goddess, Abbie's magnificent opera of wails have my cock pleading to fuck her stupid already.

Precum leaks from my dick like a warning. Her head tilts back, and I grit my teeth to stifle a groan. "Eyes on me, Abbie. Eyes on your 'fantasy.'" I press her sensitive bud, and her body jerks, shuddering with every slow stroke of my finger. As she teeters between pleasure and release, I kiss her. My tongue forces between her lips in search of her sweet tongue, and it fights with mine. Separating, she gasps, and I kiss aggressive trails down her neck, her collarbone, her breasts, and her stomach.

She makes a discernable gurgle with her voice. "I'm... I'm sorry my nipples aren't all cute and pink."

I raise a brow at her, the only hint of insecurity from her I've heard since the start of our tryst. *Where'd that even come from?*

I tilt my head, gesturing with a glance at my mostly dark-colored room. "I hate pink, you fucking dork." I kiss her breasts and pull the rounded peak between my lips. "Are you on birth control?"

She nods. "It manages my periods—yes."

My jaw ticks, a primitive part of me regretting I asked, but this is best.

I part her thighs, her throbbing center pulsing for me. I stroke my length once, twice, using pre-cum as lube. My gaze heats as she watches with starvation. The look fuels danger in me, and I don't know if I can control it.

"P…put it in," she asks. "…don't go easy on me either."

"Don't push me, little rival."

I push inside her tight heat, and she moans in my ear. She grunts an adorable huff, and her fists pat my shoulder blades. "Stop teasing. Fill me all the way, I can handle—"

"Fuck," I breathe, a cruel smile hinting at my lips. I give a full, slow thrust, and her body rides away before I yank her hips back until I'm fully seated inside her. I moan in her mouth as she whimpers. Her walls squeeze my cock with a death grip. I pepper her with kisses. "You're doing so good, Princess." Kiss. "You're fucking perfect." Kiss. "Every inch of you is perfect." Kiss. "I love you." Kiss. "I *love* you."

A tear rolls down her face, and she smirks, nodding with me to continue. "I love you too. …keep moving… It's feeling better."

I wrap my hands around her neck, plunging my tongue into her mouth. I shield my face to her neck. "Your tight cunt is paradise." I continue filling her, and her moans rage against my ear, but I want her to deafen me with her siren song—her hungry cries of bliss. I've ached for this since her bratty text sent my world into an obsessive tailspin.

"You're taking my cock so well, Princess." I grip the sheets on both sides of her, my muscles tightening as my balls slap against her ass. My grunts escalate to pained moans, and I can't hold back.

My Valentine's Virus

Abbie's eyes roll to the back of her head, and a roar shatters through my chest, burning everything in its path. I pull her hips tight against my cock as I spill into her. My release barrels through me with the force of a tsunami.

"Fuuuuck...! Unnh...!" My charging hips decrease their speed as a deep groan tears through my chest. My blurring gaze resides in Abbie's, and my knees give out. Landing over her, her body draining me of my come.

She passes out in my arms, and I embrace her until sleep follows.

LEVEL TWENTY-FIVE

PRINCESS_USER24

Blind to the time, thanks to the dark aesthetic of Xalton's room, he and I were knocked out until noon. He cleaned my thighs in my sleep, which was sweet of him, but I couldn't find the energy to wake up and kiss him.

He goes back to sleep, pulling me against his chest, where his heartbeat lulls me to sleep. This is bliss. There are no obligations, no places to be, no adhering to the clock. Only the harmony of his strong arms possessing me while we sleep.

He slides his large hand up my stomach to my chest. Fondling my breast, I find how sensitive my skin is during my snooze. He knows exactly how to touch me, like I'm an open book, and my movements are chapters for him to savor. "Good morning, Princess," his husky voice vibrates, and I feel it in my soaking core. His other hand takes over, squeezing me as the flat of his thumb against my peaks in agonizing

My Valentine's Virus

circles. His finger buries passed my entrance, and his graveled voice groans into my ears.

I moan at his penetrating touch.

"I love how wet I make you. Your sweet cunt was *made* for me, Princess," he growls.

A moan flares between my lips. He lifts my thigh in response and rubs his morning wood against my crease, teasing my body like his personal gamepad. I groan, the thrill of his touch taking me as much as he wants *when* he wants. I bite my lip as his crown slips into me. Slow at first, and then he thrusts himself fully. My eyes heat, and I shudder when my walls cave around him. I feel every ridge of his veiny cock filling me.

He hits that spot that makes me see colors I can't image on my own, and their arrays are light, dark, and beautiful.

My body begs for more, and he provides it without hesitating. More. I need more. I come around his cock as another climax follows. My speech is gargles, and I can't discern up or down as he thrusts with absolute madness.

A sheen of sweat coats him, and his abs tightening has me delirious.

With a glowing smile on my face I pass out again. Waking hours later to breakfast in bed. I groan, wiping my eyes to a large tray in his arms, and his cheeks dust with a blush. My eyes draw to the orange juice on his tray and cinnamon fills the air from the stack of French toast and syrup.

We briefly spoke about his house and his parents a few days back.

I hate Xalton's father for everything he's put him through. His mother included. Though I didn't know them, I feel like they could've done better. It's not like they didn't have the funds to afford therapy. This whole debacle has me appreciating my father more. I love our relationship. I can talk with my dad for hours about everything and nothing.

Now I'm wondering if he'd even like Xalton. Knowing Dad, he'd ask him a million and one invasive questions, uncaring whether Xalton would lean away. And knowing *Xalton*, he would turn the whole conversation into verbal chess.

After we finish eating and cleaning up, Xalton goes downstairs to check the mail. A text message sent from Psyra announces her safe travels throughout Fraixia. A weight I didn't know I had lifts off my chest. *Good, she's still talking to me.*

I miss Psyra. She's like a walking crystal emitting nothing but good vibes and a quiet deviancy. In her selfie, I notice an unfriendly mug of a man hovering by her with his arms crossed. I practically smell the cologne through my screen from the suit he's wearing.

The man beside her is built like *Spider-Man's* Miguel O'Hara. He has a full head of dark hair, towering beside Psyra like a bulky unapproachable watchdog. I can only assume he's the bodyguard her mom hired during her time there. I stare at them like an artist critiquing an asymmetric piece of abstract art.

How are they going to work together? They're like night and day. Either way, I'm content with someone working overtime to keep up with her. I know I've been holding her true nature back, but I can't help but look at her sideways whenever she brings up her hobbies.

I don't want to diss her, but I'll heal later. Putting topaz crystals inside a computer does not improve its efficiency!

 Sister From Another Mister: Landed yesterday. Dice is fine. Still healing from the trauma of the plane landing.

She's so dramatic. I roll my eyes, and my heart aches at her stilted update.

She found out I was using her and still hates me. Maybe hate is too strong for Psyra, but she's not acting like my amiga anymore. Do I even have the right to ask her if she and I can continue this? I'm not even sure if we'll see each other again. A hollowness churns inside of me, hesitating to send my text.

My Valentine's Virus

 Hey, Psy. I want to know what I can do to fix our friendship. I'm sorry about what I did. When I get into something, I lose all sight of everyone else. I didn't think about how u felt, and I regret it. I miss u. I miss watching shows with u, waking the dead, partying even when I didn't feel like leaving our dorm. I miss ur clinginess, suffocating girly fragrances, and ur reality-bending conspiracy theories. Ur the only real friend I've ever had, and I'll always look back on how I betrayed that. Please let me know how I can win u back again. I mean every word, but I understand if u wouldn't want to hear from me again after all of this. I wish u luck on your trip. Be safe.

 Sister From Another Mister: Give me time to reflect. I'll get back to you when I'm ready.

I sniffle, knowing it could go either way. And if I do lose her forever, I'll still be fine. I won't forget how I ruined things, but in case I'm lucky enough to find another like her, I won't repeat the same mistake. Who am I kidding? Psyra's one in a billion.

 Me: While ur at it. Plz. What happened to Tex?

 Sister From Another Mister: About that…

Between texts, a crash rings from downstairs and breaks my reverie, following another. And another.

My heart catapults to my throat, and I hurry out of bed. "Baby?!" Is someone breaking in again?

Xalton flings the door, and I'm nearly pushed back by the force. His eyes, once calm dark green fields, are now unsettling storms. He looks possessed, but the whites of his eyes are red, giving him away.

My racing chest aches to see the wounded man beneath the torrent. "Babe, are you crying?"

What happened between now and when he left? A flicker of pain lingers as he glares at me like a bull on a rampage. Lifting me by my waist, he swings me into the hall.

"I'm locking myself in. Don't reach out no matter what you hear," he threatens in a wobble.

I give him a patient look. "I understand. It's a full moon tonight, isn't it?"

"You think this is funny?"

"In a cosmic sort of way, yes." My brain autopilots to *SpongeBob* references, fully aware this isn't the time. "Wh-what's happened?"

"Don't worry your pretty head, Abbie. I'll be fine." He shuts the door and leaves me with uncertainty for company.

"Abbie?" No... I'm "Baby" or "Princess." ...I really like "Princess."

I scamper downstairs, following the concerning commotion. The vase from the table is in bits and pieces in the corner.

The robot trash bin opens, spooking me as usual, even in daylight. Next to the discarded eggs and shrimp shells inside is a crumpled letter. I fish it out by the edge and stretch it, examining its contents.

It reads that Xalton's mother passed away in her sleep yesterday.

To my precious son, Xalton.

My heart aches with regrets as I write my final words. I've distanced myself from you your entire life, withheld my presence and my love, not to punish, but to spare you.

The moment you came into my world, I knew love like no other. You were my small, soft, defenseless, and rowdy baby boy. But with that love came spiraling fears.

I'm very sick. I've been sick—for longer than anyone could have guessed it. Not that I'd let you notice. I made a choice when you were a baby.

My Valentine's Virus

After Lilly, my mother, and your late grandmother passed, I couldn't see the world straight. It destroyed me, Xalton. After we buried her, I was never the same person. So much so, I wished my mother was never in my life so I couldn't feel the crushing weight of her absence.

I wanted to protect you from that pain.

My gift to you.

I know in my heart this hospital bed is where I'll meet death.

As I reflect on this letter, I see in real-time that the chasm between us was a big mistake. I should have filled it with you instead of living the remaining years of my life and pushing you away. For that, I hope you can forgive me.

I wish I could rewrite our story, but I need you to know my love for you has always been there.

- Renee Kaiser.

She confesses how she's been fighting an illness her doctors couldn't assess and thought it best to keep Xalton at arm's length to protect him from the news of when she would die. It was undetermined when she'd pass.

Xalton's father kept this from him. She kept this from him. His relatives kept this from him.

They didn't even ask if it was what he wanted.

My hands tremble at the unimaginable fury he must be going through.

It wasn't the best option at all. Xalton's heart is broken, and I don't know how to restore it.

A symphony of crashing jerks my attention upstairs.

I swiped Psyra's lock-picking keychain as a memento from her nightstand a few weeks ago, but I didn't think I'd be using it. I gear my way up to Xalton's room and break in.

His rage-filled eyes meet mine, and he rushes toward me.

My gaze widens, but I steel my dangerous reflexes and have him reach for my neck. He slams me against the wall, and I grunt from the dulling sensation. His eyes are shrouded with ferocity, a danger I've only seen when we first met in CRU's hallway.

"I know... what happened," I barely manage, wrapping my hands over his wrists. I'm allowed a pocket of air to breathe, but he doesn't let me down. "You're right to feel this way."

A muscle pulses in his jaw, his complexion tinted red. "The *bastard* took her off life support—something I didn't even *know* she was on!"

"We can talk—" I gurgle. He releases me, and I rub my throat. I hate seeing him in a terrain of agony so deep that I can't reach him. He bangs his fist into the wall, and blood scraps his knuckles.

"I don't want to talk! I want to kill him!" He seethes, turning away from me, and my legs move on their own.

I wrap my arms around his back, fully aware he could snap my spine like a gingerbread man. "That won't bring your mom back! And you shouldn't be like him by taking his life."

"Like you're such an expert." He wriggles to untwine my hug, but I refuse to let him go. "And why not?!" He pulls me off and grips my arms against me. "I was going to kill you. You would have been my first. Then I was going to stab Melanie in front of her cunt mom and maybe burn that *fucking* campus to the ground!"

"But you didn't!"

A vein pulses in his jaw as his labored breath heaves. "Careful, little rival. Who says I still can't?"

"Do it then. You won't," I snarl like it's a dare. "Pussy."

A low, sinister laugh rumbles from him, madness overwhelming his senses. He takes a deep breath, and the vein throbbing in his jaw eases. Raising his head, he moistens his lips, towering over me until I'm back against the wall. "...Call me a pussy *one* more time—"

"Pussy!"

My Valentine's Virus

He steals my gasp with his lips crashing against mine. A moan creaks from me as he squeezes me against him, his lips envelop mine in firm, hungry motions that has my core writhing with wants. I try having the electric sensation settle, but it escalates around me like I'm drowning in him.

His bourbon scent fills my nostrils, blanketing my lungs and leaving me gasping for more.

"I'm going to fucking ruin you." He pulls my arm and throws me against the bed. Forcing me to bend over it. He thrusts his erection inside me with such ferocity my vision immediately trickles with stars.

The sweet spot he teased me the other day is as sensitive as it was before, and he keeps slamming at it.

I yodel into the mattress like I'm sinking. *Oh my God.* Angry Xalton fucks at such careless intervals. He's not as patient as he was the other times. He's rough and isn't wasting my time with his kisses and foreplay.

There's no sign of mercy or stopping the way his hips smash into me, his cock warring in my pussy. He grips my hair, pulling my head back so I can see him. Power flows in his dominating glare at my oblivion, and I come like Niagara Falls.

He doesn't stop.

Time doesn't exist, but it's been over an hour. I've come too many times to count, yet he keeps thrusting like a machine with infinite power. I don't know if I'm moaning in English, Spanish, or gibberish.

"Raahh Fuuhh fuuuuck!" My muscles squeeze, and my voice aches from my howls.

My next release splashes him like a ruptured pipe. Xalton's fists clench the side of the mattress, and he grunts and strains as his sweat drips over me like summer rain. His rippled abs tighten against my back, and he lays over me, panting for air.

I nudge him because he's heavy. "You're crushing me," I mumble against the sheets.

"Good," he huffs. Rolling over, he runs his hands through his hair.

The air between us is lighter, an in-between feeling from before and after his tragic news. I can work with it.

"I'm sorry I snapped at you."

I roll my eyes, pleading with him not to do *this* part of the conflict. "Quit treating me like I'm some delicate flower. I can take you on any day of the week," I taunt.

He fights not to smile. "You're incorrigible."

I swing my arm over his shoulder and pull him in for a weak hug. We remain like this until one of us decides to move or speak. Neither of us do. We lay in silence, and I roll over finally, a prisoner of our thoughts.

"I'm... gonna shower," I rasp, rubbing the back of my neck. His gaze lowers. "I want you to join me."

His brow raises, and I take his hand no matter his answer.

"Come." Pulling him off the bed and out of the dark, I lead Xalton to his bathtub. I have him sit inside it with the hot water running through the lower faucet as I rub a washcloth along his sculpted back. I envy and admire his muscle's girth.

Xalton shudders a few minutes in. His stifled cries make me swallow the bitterness of my heartache. I lay my head over his, and my ears focus through the roar of the faucet.

I kiss his forehead and the side of his face as I do. Wrapping my arms over his shoulders, I rest mine over him, and he unravels beneath me. His every shudder sends spikes to my heart, and I don't know what to say to stop it.

"You're mine," I mutter.

Come on, Abbie. He's probably more upset over his mom's death and his dad being the reigning *king* of douches. I swallow and try again, stroking his shoulder. "She made her choice out of love for you, baby. I sort of get it—I mean... The pain would have hit either way. I *hate* it, but... I'm here for you."

His cries, trembling under my grip.

"I'm here," I repeat.

My Valentine's Virus

Xalton exhales and reaches to twist the faucet off. He doesn't speak to me for the rest of the bath or much over three days.

I've been in his state of mind before—being so crippled from the inside, you can't even speak. I don't take offense to it since he still holds me close at night. He kisses me between chores and works like I'm the comet in his orbit. He fucks me after I catch glances of his body after his showers.

I was finally able to cheat the system and get our internet despite his criminal record, which is under investigation.

With Xalton's help, our ideas bounce off each other to solve who actually busted him. We mapped out the reasons why it couldn't have been Melanie. She took advantage of the situation, but she wasn't the director. Nothing connects to her.

Xalton's eyebrows furrow as he looks at my monitor. He looks like a hundred ideas are filtering through his mind, and I'm his fangirl again.

"You say they've been texting you randomly?" He asks. "Like they have their eyes on you?"

I nod, handing him my phone. "Take a look. It's been creeping me out."

[Unknown]: URGENT: Skip ur P.E. course tomorrow. U have a target on u.

[Unknown]: Zone_Warden has been arrested. It's what scum like him deserves.

"Good girl," Xalton praises, wrapping his arm around my waist in a possessive hold. I melt. His brow lifts from a hesitant frown like he solved the answer, but he pales, and his robotic CIA mask appears. "It's a great thing you didn't respond to them."

He parts his lips to speak but moistens them instead.

My head lifts. "What is it?"

"Nothing." He blinks away from me. "We'll keep searching."

LEVEL TWENTY-SIX

ZONE_WARDEN

If I could go back in time, I'd have my mother shoot me in both kneecaps instead of jotting her final wishes through postage. I would have cried less.

The atmosphere of the funeral home isn't as solemn as I expected. Attendees are adorned in their black clothes, while visiting my mother's corpse before the funeral commences. My family pay their respects to the open casket. Peaceful music plays from speakers above, reflecting the shimmer of life Renee Kaiser once exhibited.

Everything she poured in her letter was the furthest from the truth.

The few times I'd seen her on her social media pages, she would brag about her Peloton, blog about the organic fruits and veggies she'd grown from her garden, and be active in her community by offering free

Our call months ago made me suspect something was happening, but she wasn't in the headspace to speak with me. Or... rather, *I* wasn't. I wish I had fought harder to see her. But there's no use weighing regrets on myself when it was already out of my hands.

It's time to put her to rest and begin new chapters of my life without her neglect looming over me.

I stand back to Abbie, who waits for me in the crowded pew with my estranged family members. After aiding to place my mother's casket on display, I search for Abbie. Melanie and Opal Mayor are in attendance, on the other side of the sizeable gathering.

Abbie reaches for my hand with a sympathetic gaze, and I rejoin her on the bench. I shift, glaring over my shoulder at my dad in a gray suit that undoubtedly cost him a mortgage. I understand he's canceling his gala. Shame. I still have *my* date.

Since I last saw him, his demeanor has seems smaller to me. It's been over a decade. I don't know what to make of him anymore. He doesn't seem all that distressed and most likely has been gearing up for this since I was born.

I face forward when someone from my mother's side gives the sermon. Once the front projection shows a slide show on my mother's life, I grip Abbie's hand in mine. My intestines twist and pull the more I learn about her through the familiar man's speech.

"Renee Kaiser was a decorated Greek chef who enjoyed the pleased faces of her customers."

One of the images shows her short blond hair shimmering. Big green eyes fill the screen, brimming with life. I have her crooked nose and subtlety. I exhale, unable to find the tears I had this morning.

Abbie's thumb strokes mine, and my organs detangle. My little rival has been at my side through my grief, and I can't thank her enough for putting up with my demons. I'm grateful to her for not giving up on me.

My Valentine's Virus

I'm thankful she's delusionally strong and stubborn. I lick my lips, gazing at her, pretending to listen to the man I didn't recognize, who was my uncle, until a third into the ceremony.

The more my mind wanders, I fiddle with her left hand. The naked spot on her ring finger grows obscene to me. I lean in to give her a lingering kiss before rising from my spot.

"Hey, I'm going to step out for a few minutes. Will you be okay by yourself? Uncle Damon could listen to himself talk for hours, and he's just getting started."

She nods without pressing. "Take your time. I'll be here questioning whether to smile at your family or be cool and neutral."

I humor her with a low chuckle. "Stay precious. I'll return shortly." I leave the grounds before driving to the nearest jeweler.

The closer I got to my destination, the warmer my face grew at the thought of my purchase. I walk inside and pace the counter until a clerk approaches, noticing my eye for size five engagement rings. I asked the jeweler if they could custom-make one for me and I'd pay any price as long as they had it done right away. An hour later, it's done. It's perfect and everything I hope Abbie will cherish forever. I picked the design myself, knowing her favorite colors and rebellious aesthetic.

A chill of crippling regrets sticks me from nowhere. I pace the shop as nausea swells in my stomach. There's a fifty-fifty chance she'll say no. She will, or she won't. I pinch the space between my forehead. I don't want to think like that.

I return to the function. Pressing through the crowds of family members who try stopping me for a brief moment, I find Abbie automatically in the crowd, only to see she's arguing… with my father.

"Abbie?" I hurry to get in front of her, facing my dad. "What's happened? What did you say to her?"

My father snarls at me. "Xalton, is *this* the type of woman you keep in your company?"

I lean into him, heat beyond my control raging to my throat. My vision throbs, and my nostrils flare at his tone for her. "What did you say to her?" I demand again, unuttered threats gnashing between my teeth.

Abbie pulls my arm. "Nothing I couldn't handle, babe. Your dad needs to know he's a piece of shit for *everything* he's put you through!" she roars like a lioness before a prowl.

My dad huffs, gesturing at her with a trembling finger. "Everything *I've* put him through? You have no idea of the countless messes I've had to endure because of his existence–?"

"You stupid *pendejo!* He's your fucking son," she shouts. My father raises his hand to strike, and darkness reigns control over me.

Whack!

The room becomes an orchestra of gasps when my father goes down like a bowling pin into his brothers. I pull my fist back, flailing off the phantom pain.

Blood roars to my ears, and I heave. Abbie barrels her fists at my side, but I gesture for her to stay behind me. "I'm not a tool for you to use when you remember I exist."

"That's right, bitch!" Abbie boosts, like my personal hype-woman.

I put my trembling hands to rest in my pocket, shrugging off my nerves like a boxer. Abbie locks her arm in mine in support.

"And don't ever talk to my fiancé that way."

"Yeah, he... what?" Abbie stumbles before raising a brow at me.

My father and my uncles toss me a similar look, and everyone else who is listening follows suit.

I face her, examining her gaze, burning a hole in my side.

The fists at her side uncurl, and her luminous brown eyes shimmer at my affirmative stare. I take a knee, and my aunts' gasps fill the space.

My father frowns, his rage bouncing off me like I'm in protective armor.

"Abigail Belle-Nuñez," I say.

My Valentine's Virus

Several phones and cameras rise from the sea of people catching eye to the turn of events playing out in front of them.

"A thousand 'fuck yous' if this is a joke," Abbie adds. My gothic queen stands straight, the sparkles of her tight-fitting dress highlighting those dooming curves that captivated me in that college. "Xalton...?"

I remove the black velvet box, burning a hole in my pocket. Opening it, I reveal a ring that matches her: a black gold band encrusted with diamonds. At its center, a blinding ruby that can be seen from space clutches the ring.

"Will you be my wife?"

She exhales harshly in a quick nod. "...I guess," she squeaks. Tension leaves her face as I slide the ring onto her finger. She leaps into my arms, and my arms consume her against me.

"Nooo...!" A shrill voice screams out from the abyss of heads. Pulling our attention, Opal Mayor drills through the crowd with Melanie being yanked along. "Xalton Julian Kaiser!"

Abbie glances at me. *"Julian?"* she mouths.

Part of me wants to carry my future bride over my shoulder to escape before she goes off on a useless tirade. But that would ruin the next phase of my day.

My eyes narrow into slits as Opal swings her vile offspring in front of me.

"Tell her what you found, dear," Opal demands, between clenching teeth.

I cock a brow at Melanie and then remember she had access to my files at one point. My eyes open as if a car crash begins unfurling.

Melanie clears her throat. "Before you accept Xalton's proposal, little pig, know he's hiding something very detrimental from you, which I dug up from his hard drive."

The information that threatened Abbie was deleted weeks ago... unless.

Abbie raises a brow to me. "What is she talking about?"

"About your mother. Ana Belle, was her name?" Opal's daughter smirks, glaring at me like it has any effect.

The moment Abbie's mother's name leaves her lips, flames lick in her eyes. She cracks her knuckles. "I don't care what you've got to say to me, bitch. I still owe you for that beatdown your friends gave me, and I'm not about to hold back on your hag of a mom either." She points at Opal, but it holds no power.

"*Ooh*. Big feelings," Melanie retorts carefully inching behind her mom and maintaining her smirk. "Are you sure? Family *is* the most important thing at the end of the day, isn't it? Don't you want to know all about your mother's whereabouts this whole time?"

I list a thousand and one death threats at the devil's daughter in my pupils. Melanie smiles at every one of them like a poem.

"...what?" Abbie's eyes turn to mine for clarification, and a heavy sigh heaves from me. "What is she talking about? Her whereabouts? Her grave?"

"No, little rival," I say.

"Don't *'little rival'* me—what is she on about? I want to hear it from you." Her lower lip quivers, and my chest tightens at the worry in her frown.

I lick my lips, understanding where this is heading, but unable to face away from her. I stroke her shoulder slowly like I'm trying to coax a cornered panther.

I wasn't ever going to tell her. Cradling her limp and lifeless body after she drowned that day was a world-shattering ordeal I refused to entertain ever again.

But I know Abbie.

I know how she'd rather die than have me discredit her, and a part of me owes her that sliver of trust, even if it breaks me all over again.

"Ana was never dead," I strain. "Your parents faked her death."

LEVEL TWENTY-SEVEN

PRINCESS_USER24

"Why—wh… why would they do that? How long have you known this?" My voice wavers as I press him for answers. He shuts his eyes slowly, working up the will to explain.

Melanie raises her hand to interrupt. "Because your mom is the hacker *above* Number One. She's an assassin for a deep-state rebel group," she explains.

I scoff. "You're fucking with me."

"I wouldn't about *this*," he sighs. "Do you remember when I told you about Student X? How there's *always* an invisible member in digital lists? That same invisible code applies to the hacker board. If *I'm* Number One, that makes Ana Number *Zero*."

Number Zero…? I stare at Xalton for an aching minute. A headache burns at the back of my skull, and I can't look at him anymore.

not able to reach out to me? Countless questions spin in my head like a curse.

I've sometimes delved into unique conspiracy theories, but this is the one that's breaking my reality.

"How *long* have you known?" My voice breaks. *After everything we've been through.*

He monitors my gaze in his trained way. "...Since before The Melancholy."

My shoulders sag. A tear slides down my face. The weight of his betrayal seems limitless. "And couldn't you tell me?"

Xalton's eyes plead with mine as he inches closer to hold me. I sneer, pushing him, and his jaw muscle tenses. "It wasn't *my* secret to tell you—if you knew, baby, your life would have been in danger. I wanted to protect you from that knowledge." He glares at Melanie, who checks her phone like a bored teen. "Someone threatened to dox your mother, putting you and your dad on the map from her enemies. *Violent* enemies. She faked her death, went into hiding, and your father had your family relocate. Hurricane Orion made a decent cover... and your dad is a convincing actor."

I rip the engagement ring from my finger since it's a taunt to me now. "Here," I hand it to Melanie and look for my chain purse.

Her eyebrows lift in amusement and stick there. Eying the ring, she raises it in the light before Opal snatches it.

Picking up my bag, I give Xalton a final glance. Betrayal reflects in his moldy, green-colored eyes. He knows better than God how I feel about being looked down on. A raging beast pounds and pounds inside my face before I jerk toward the exit.

Twenty minutes have passed. The memory of stomping to the nearest bus stop is a blur of heat and flurrying calculations. My feet throb, and my ankles grind against the gorgeous black heels serving as a reminder.

My Valentine's Virus

The bus is running late this evening, but if I don't get on a computer right now, I'll detonate.

My mom is alive. *My mom is alive.*

All this time. All those years robbed of her corny smile. All those heart-wrenching motherless Mother's Days, my prayers for her soul's safety at her gravestone, and not a *single* letter received. She would have found a way to reach me.

The bus slows to a halt, and the familiar driver who aided me when I was injured drops his jaw.

"Abbie, that you?"

"Who else would I be?" I joke humorlessly. Stepping inside to a varied group of people, I land in my seat. Some staring, some gawking, and even leering.

The minute I get home, I'll find her. I never thought I had to or would have done it ages ago. My head drops in my hands as the bus's mechanical whirring commences, transporting me away from town.

Where the hell are you, Mom?

ZONE_WARDEN

I wonder what being a serial killer is like these days.

Abbie wouldn't be happy with me entertaining these thoughts, but I fear she won't be talking to me anymore. The expression she directed at me was familiar—the same disgust from when I told her her beloved dish was referred to as *"the cockroaches of the sea."* I didn't mean to tell her that. We were deep diving on YouTube, and it slipped out.

I almost fear for the world I envision in my killing spree. Why should any of these people go to their homes and sleep happily when *I* won't have the luxury anymore? The one woman able to see me in my darkness, has left me with it to lean on.

Common sense returns from its break, and I remember I still had something worth living for. Revenge.

I give my signal, and several officers I set up throughout the funeral home approach to slap handcuffs around Melanie and her mother.

This was supposed to happen earlier, but I didn't expect Melanie to still have a bullet left to fire at my relationship.

Abbie is reckless, but we've both survived Melanie before, and we can survive her again.

"What is going on?! Do you know who I am?!" Opal searches the area for her husband, but he sneers at her with impatience. She lands her terrified gaze on me, and I inhale it, soaking it in like a sponge. "Kaiser! What did you do?!" She shouts as she's being hauled into the back of a police van.

Sure, a part of me wishes I killed her, but I'm trying to be a better man.

"I found my mother's health records the night I learned of her death," I charm, leaning against the vehicle's exterior. "You've been poisoning Renee's Garden." I cock a brow when Opal's red face pales. I nod, my fist clenching against the hood. "I borrowed the live cam footage of the street camera near her yard. You've been visiting at night and spiking her garden with poison."

Opal starts jerking and kicking as officers wrestle her away from my sight. "No! I don't deserve this! It should have been me with Lawrence! Not the *whore* from next door!" She screams, wailing and flailing in her handcuffs like a spoiled toddler.

I wish Abbie was here for this live-action drama. She would have loved it. My father stands dumbfounded like the dumb founder himself.

His nose reddens in his distant look, but I'm not sure for whom.

"How could you do this, Xalton?" he sighs, facing me.

I frown. "Excuse *you?*" I scowl.

My Valentine's Virus

He exits the funeral home, leaving me disgusted for answers. I face everyone else in the room, eying me, and smile genuinely at their disturbed faces.

I don't owe my dad anything, including my cares, and my uncle has been waiting on stage for everyone's attention to return to him. I give a gentlemen's bow and leave the room while fiddling with the ring in my pocket. Without a second glance, I give my final farewell to the Kaiser's forever.

PRINCESS_USER24

"A.N.A., play *'Youth'* by Daughter."

"**Playing!**" my digital friend DJs my music into my headphones.

I've been staying at a luxury hotel for a few nights while I worked this out. I found time to yell at my father over the phone, and he sighed, struggling to explain everything. He said he would need to send me an encrypted explanation. That's when I knew this went deep. My father doesn't even know how Bluetooth works.

After opening his message, I discover how the orange didn't fall far from the orange tree. As it turns out, my mother *also* loved tormenting dangerous criminal hackers on the Dark Web since before I was born. Knowing she might have been on the sidelines of my wins warms my nervous system.

My body stills, recalling what Psyra told me after one of my nightmares.

Was Mom watching over me this whole time? I figured Psy was just... being Psy. Would she be proud of me or repulsed about my involvement with Zone?

It's taken me plenty of sleepless nights to find her, and it became a lot easier with the combined knowledge of what I picked up from Xalton.

He's taught me so much in the span of a few months—things I kept freezing up on. I'm almost grateful—no. I'm being a brat. I *am* grateful for him. Hell, if it wasn't for him, I probably would've never known.

The light in my room reflects the image of my forehead's scar against my laptop screen. It's been a few days since its received a kiss from him. My heartaches in a flicker, making my typing fingers freeze up every other keyword. Xalton was always kissing my scar. It was one of his millions of wordless ways to let me I was his and he was mine.

My throat tightens but before emotion overcomes me, my screen reveals the information I've needed.

And just like that, I found her. I just needed a push in the right direction.

[Unknown:] Hey, sweet girl. We need to hash some stuff out face-to-face.

What if this isn't her? It could be one of her rivals who's found me, pretending to be her. I could get kidnapped and used as a bartering chip, possibly getting her exposed—or. I watch too many movies.

I shove my phone screen away once I'm tempted to reply. Xalton's words about not responding to the message whisper in my head: *"It's a great thing you didn't respond to them."*

I stare at the untraceable contact with fatigued eyes.

I'm sent an image of my mother if she were alive today.

Long dark hair reaches her waist, fair skin, and my bright brown eyes. She has smile lines near a dot by her chin and captivating curves I'm relieved I inherited.

Snot fills my nose and my lip wobbles. When I fight the urge to break down, my eyes burn.

Hands shaking, I type, giving her my location. We set up a time to meet—just her and I. Whether this is her or not, I'll fight out of it and troubleshoot from where she *would* be.

My Valentine's Virus

Tears slip down my face. In my imagination, she looks different from the corpse. The texted pic of her raising her arm and flexing her bicep fills out the rotting image of her I had all this time. Mom. *My mom's alive.*

I stand out at the time of our meeting, in the open of the hotel lobby I've been staying at. I have one of Xalton's knives in case my meeting turns into something I'd regret but not be caught unprepared for. He gave it to me as an anniversary present. I also have a taser and muscles built for destruction.

A woman smells of oranges, and the scent immediately steals my attention. She has long, swaying raven hair as she saunters through the sliding doors. I slowly approach her, an inviable force pushing me.

"… Mom?"

She drops her handbag, her eyes fixed on mine, and her face squeezes in a blurry pink tint. "Baby?"

My inner walls break down as I bolt to her. It's like a scene from a movie. I'm a lost little kid again while she embraces me. We both collapse onto the navy lobby carpet while the world walks around us.

She lifts me by the shoulders, memorizing my face with each breath. "I knew that EctoPhantom capture *had* to be you!" she chirps. Mom shuts her mouth with gloved hands in an adorably flustered manner. My cheeks heat, figuring how proud she must have been. Had I known she was my number one fan, I would have given her a more chaotic show.

We caught up in the corner of the lobby, but she explained that her time with me must be short.

"Duty calls overseas. I found the time to meet you between flights and check up on you. I was already at risk coming here, but." Mom shrugs. "I decided I had enough." Her head sways in a doting manner.

My mom is a badass virtual hacking warrior who *slays* bad guys for a living. The more I think about it, the more I'm about three steps away from following in those footsteps. I hold my head high as my face cramps from all the smiling.

It's amazing how much of her I've absorbed even miles apart. By the way she's basking in me, she couldn't believe it either.

Despite my elation, there's still this hollowness eating away in my heart that's plagued me for days now. I huff, willing the issue to emerge while I have the time. "*Both* of you lied to me—including my boyfriend, *Mom*. How did you think that would make me feel?"

Mom takes my hand, closing her eyes. "Honey." Her eyes carry no guilt but sympathy hems within them. "If there was another way I could have gone about it, I'd have taken it. As harsh as this sounds, your feelings couldn't be prioritized over your safety. *Our* safety. Understand? You were a child–a *huge* show-off too. You're always talking about your victories and gambling. Asking you to keep our secret wouldn't have worked."

She's right. I'm annoyed, but it doesn't lessen my betrayal. "Were you ever going to see me again if I hadn't tried finding you?"

Her nostrils flare. "Ahh, yes. The second half of my visit." She gives me a sterner look that has my stomach falling to my butt. "That was very dangerous of you. Honey, I've been watching over you for years. I never needed to reach out. You were doing wonderfully without me. I cried many nights but couldn't be with you or Randall. I was at my lowest. I turned to alcohol, then I reminded myself—like I have time and time again; I did it for *you*."

I glance at the ceiling for the nearest security camera or anyone who looks slightly suspicious.

She chuckles. "Don't break your neck looking for invisible bad guys, baby. My team has disabled the cameras and background searched everyone in here."

Huh. "Okay, Mrs. Smith," I taunt, but really, I just became my mom's biggest fan. *She has her own team? Ugh, I want that.*

"When you showed interest in *that* school, who do you think helped push your application to the top of the scholarship boards? They would have seen your father's name and employment status and tossed it into

My Valentine's Virus

the trash. I even got wind of some students at the school causing issues, and I got worried. I looked into this Melanie girl, and she... *she* has a lot of feelings about you—"

"Oh, you were *stalking* stalking," I pitch by mistake.

She shushes me. "I only wanted a peek to know if you were fitting in college, okay? I stumbled on how she was dragging your name on her Tic-Tac account."

"It's Tik-Tok, Mom," I correct.

She gulps her water, and a frown creases her brows. "Did you receive the protected messages I sent you? She was vague about her post, but she... I saw something inhuman in her eyes. It's something I find daily in the eyes of killers who maim innocence like an average Wednesday."

My brows raise. "That was you?"

She snorts at my guilt-ridden expression. "Yes, dear. Then I got bored and investigated that boy you've been antagonizing only to find weeks later you're dating?"

"Mom?"

She pats my hand, smiling more every second. I never thought I'd see her corny grin again. My chest is so... full. I wonder if my great-grandparents are still alive somewhere, too, avenging the galaxy.

"Thanks..." My gaze drifts to my feet. "I've been... avoiding him over this."

"Aww, baby." She adjusts my hair behind my shoulder and then helps to fix the stands in front of my scarred forehead. "Don't miss out on that because of my issues. That isn't fair to you or him."

"He kept my secret. He wanted to keep you safe. That's love, my love. Give him another chance. It's... my fault anyway. I shouldn't have interfered."

"Yet I'm glad you did. You brought us both together in the end. I love hacking because of you and... hm."

I roll my eyes, blushing halfway while recalling Xalton's face. I've been isolated and arguing with myself to respond to his texts. "I'll think about it, but… Can't I be with you? We can be a cool mother-daughter hacking duo. I *did* just become the world's number one recently."

Her lips purse. "No, baby. Even being here right now is a risk." She fixes my hair again behind my ear. "Thank you, though. Be safe now. No more challenging criminals online. Don't turn out like me, understand?"

"I'll think about it," I repeat with a sigh. She looks back at me with a radiating smile every other second until she disappears beyond the corner.

I call a ride over to Xalton's place. It'll take over fifteen minutes for them to arrive, and that's enough time for me to run upstairs to gather my things. Regret stabs me with each step downstairs. I check out of the hotel. I open the car door with my head down, unable to face the driver during the ride.

I open my phone and read through Xalton's messages, but ultimately, needing to send my own.

 [Me]: I need to see u, baby. I'm sorry.

I arrive at Xalton's front door in the evening but notice his front cameras have been removed. Bile churns in my stomach as I open the lock with Psyra's keychain, and swing open the door.

"Xalton?" I call out into the dilapidated space. Pieces of bubble wrap and wads of packing tape are everywhere, but everything else is gone. The living room doesn't have a ruined couch or a coffee table anymore. Our video game posters are gone, leaving only the tacks as evidence of where they once hung.

My quick, shallow breaths wisp through space. I shuffle upstairs, and the rest of my stuff's gone, too. Adrenaline roars into my ears enough to make me stumble. Resting my hand against the wall, I search the line of texts I sent him, including the one I gave him as I was riding to get here.

Would he have fled the country?

My Valentine's Virus

Sitting in front of his doorstep, my hands shake, gripping my phone as I crumble into myself. The idea of never seeing him again makes me want to dive off the nearest cliff. The reality of not returning to Xalton constricts my voice now that my search for mom ended.

Three dots appear on my screen, indicating he's responding. I hold my breath until impatience swims through, and I tap his little character on my screen.

 [My Fantasy]: If you can find me, you can do whatever you want to me.

END GAME
ZONE_WARDEN

[Ell]: Hey, X. You have time to talk? I have something I want to get off my chest.

I glare at the random text from Ellie consuming my screen. Wildly convenient of her to choose now of all times to unblocked me.

As I nurse my hangover, the raw stench of bourbon sticks to my jacket. I'm aware enough of my mental state and refrain drunk texting something I'm sure I'd regret.

Maine has some of the best bars in the country—one of the reasons I first moved to the state. It's quieter than The Melancholy, a place for people my age to relax after a long day—and my day's been very long.

I lost my mother, I lost my Abbie, I've lost my mind. My liver may as well go next.

I meet with Jim, the man I bonded with behind bars inside the autumn-lit bar. He raises his groomed brow at me like I should be the poster child for sobriety.

My Valentine's Virus

And I look at him like I forgot I invited him.

I try my best to keep my promises. Once my charges were lifted, I lent him the two hundred grand, and he began his restaurant empire.

I needed a friend, so, like any sane man with end-of-the-world thoughts, I wired him cash to fly over and teach me about Jehovah.

I need something to believe in. I don't give a shit if it's reincarnation, moon magic, aliens, or affordable seafood entrées. I need a new grip, or I'll fall into an abyss I can't go back there again—not when I've made it so far from there.

"Hey," Jim urges. He stands around my height in a red and black leather jacket like he's *Batman's* Jason Todd. I'm just happy he's wearing pants this time. Dark jeans eat up his legs like pythons being shoved into cowboy boots. Jim smacks my arm and pulls me off my bar seat. "What are you doing?"

"I'm living, friend. How's your family's business doing?" My eyes barely focus on his groomed baby face.

Jim pinches between his brows, and watching how he cools himself down is somewhat amusing. His shoulders raise and lower, and he breathes hard before gesturing at me. "I didn't fly all the way back to Maine to talk about that."

I raise my brow. "Why not? Something going down?"

He scoffs. "No, Xalton. I'm here to get you down from the edge. We're here to talk about *you.*" He exhales. "The same way you did for me."

I rest my glass against the counter and lean over my knees. "Alright. I'll listen."

"Now, when you think of the word 'God,' what does that mean to you—?"

My phone buzzes before he gets cozy in the seat beside me.

 [Wifey:] I need to see u, Xalton. I'm sorry.

I could have handled that better. I was biblically enraged and u were trying to protect me. Don't do that anymore? Idk. I'm incredibly sorry You'll always always mean more to me than you'll ever know

"Oh…" My brows lift as daylight is born in me. I pat Jim on the shoulder twice—once to alert him that I've got to leave and the second to shut him up. "I…" I face him with a devilish smirk. "You did it, Jim. I'm saved. Praise Jesus. Hallelujah. Merry Christmas." I nearly lose my balance, but leaning against the door handle saves me.

"Why are you like this?"

"Christmas is a Pagan holiday!" I tease just as I shut the door behind me.

I meet up with my driver around the corner with a smile hidden beneath my scarf. Making it back, I whir the door open, slapping my keys against the counter, and read Abbie's long-winded questions and threats. I snicker like an idiot after I send her my demands.

 [Me]: If you want to actually earn the Number One spot, Princess, you've got to find me this time.

 No flirting for hints 😊

 [Wifey]: I will find u, and I'll cannibalize ur flesh.

"Heh." I grin at her colorful response. I can't wait to marry this woman.

PRINCESS_USER24

My Valentine's Virus

Xalton wheels his bike into his garage, and I sink inside my rental car around the corner. I'm in a woodsy suburban town, and the house with the darkest exterior is where I successfully hunted down Xalton's cyber footprint.

Heart pounding, I fling open the car door and proceed up the driveway to retrieve him.

"Hey." I open my posture with my hands in my coat.

His helmet tilts, all confused, and I honestly don't have the patience for his coyness.

"Well? I found you. Can we talk?"

He points at himself like he's mute. "Uh… with me?"

Wait a minute. I raise a brow at the man in Xalton's helmet and home. I recognize his cameras, and they rotate slightly.

The man removes his helmet, and my heart drops to my feet. "Oh, you're not…" My face heat up, so I stop explaining and look around. "Xalton!" I shout into the abyss. Snow falls from atop nearby pine trees, scattering across the driveway.

The man before me laughs and motions at the front door. "You must be Abbie!" He puts his hand out for me. "Nice to finally meet you. I'm his roommate, Jim. I've been looking out for him."

Rage and crankiness vibrate through my pores. I leave Jim hanging, and I know I'll feel bad about it later, but I'm not in the mood to be a human at the moment. I haven't slept, I haven't eaten, and I haven't spoken to another creature for weeks.

"Where is he?" I exhale.

He gives me a wry smirk before glancing over my shoulder. "Don't worry. Your creepy husband's close by. Don't worry."

A second later, a hand wraps around my mouth, and a strong arm wraps around me. Pinning my arms against my side. I bite back my panic until the scent of bourbon and leather fills my nose. "I'm right here, Princess," Xalton purrs into my ear. "Care to see your castle?"

I'm whirled away from Jim as my mouth uncovers. "Put me down!" I kick. He retorts with deep torturous laughter against my ear. He releases me and rubs the back of his neck.

"You really found me."

Frowning at him, my fury washes away as something overwhelms me. My chest untightens, and my lip trembles at his face.

He's got a splash of color, letting me know hasn't been locked away in his house. He still has a beard, which I love. And his eyes, those gothic forest eyes, are as healing as ever.

I have him again, and I beam.

"Xalton."

He gets on his knee and removes his ring from his pocket. "Let's give this another shot."

My foot taps, staring down at the perfect diamond-encrusted gold band and a ruby the size of my ego at its center. I push my lips to the side, fighting back my elation.

His brows raise purely, and I'm about to break.

"Don't take this personally. But I don't marry losers," I let out with a humorous grin.

He tilts his head at me. "Well, you're *already* married to me, and I don't either."

I moisten my lips. "I already accessed the clerk's offices…"

His smile increases. "I know."

"Fuck you. You knew nothing!" I spout.

He laughs before removing the marriage certificate from his back pocket. "I keep telling you not to underestimate me," he says.

I wrap my arms around his waist, and he embraces me against his chest. He runs his fingers through my hair, and a sensation of home trickles through me. "I missed you," I hum. "You're on my mind every day. I'm so sorry."

My Valentine's Virus

"Me too, baby, me too." He fixes his hold, arching my face to brush against his. "I understand you more than anyone. I'm happy you made it."

It's disturbing how fast a month can sneak by. I wrap my hair in a towel after taking a cold shower. Relocating to Maine with Xalton was easier than I thought. My Number One tattoo—*my first tattoo* wraps around my thigh, which is fully healed and ready to show off on our honeymoon trip to Spain. It's my mother's home country, and I've wanted to visit since I was a little girl.

Xalton sits up, his PJ legs propped against the bed while his eyes draw up from his laptop screen.

"Good morning," he greets, and I lean for a kiss before passing him.

His phone vibrates across the counter, and he asks me to check it for him while he works on his laptop.

I squint at the suspiciously *feminine* name appearing on my husband's phone. "You have an Unknown text from an… *Ellie?*"

His brows wriggle with a mix of confusion and then exhaustion. He runs his hand through his hair. "What's it say?"

"She says… she hated what happened between you two and was going through some stuff. She wants to give you guys another chance if it's still on the table." I flatten my lips, a challenging smirk quirking them. "What are we telling Ellie?"

Xalton snickers at my pinching face. "Tell her I'm genuinely happy she's feeling better, and then block her number. I've got to get this software update for A.N.A. sent before our trip."

I skip the clothes and crawl under the comforter beside him. "I realized something recently. You were right."

His eyes gravitate toward me, and he pulls the top of his laptop down. "Go on."

I smile at his devilish smirk, growing while I delay my response. "Not everything is a... contest. I've made room in my heart for you, too," I smirk in the least sappy way possible.

His shoulders open up as he turns to caress my chin. "You promise?"

"I do." Heat kisses my cheeks, and I thank him for helping me see my life in a healthier light. This is my finish line. I don't really need to challenge everything. I'm right beside him and the happiest I've ever been.

On the brink of it all, I understand it's not about winning or being number one. It's the people you compete with, the bonds that mend in our different paths, and how we make others feel.

It still feels great trampling over those in the way but doing it with Xalton is even better.

He sees more in me than I ever could from my pedestal. Even if I'm not in a Goddess-of-Victory mood, he loves me over everything, and I'm grateful for it. I want to give him everything, and even if I end up a busted shell of what I once was, he'll still hunt down the crumbs of me.

Since I first laid eyes on him in a magazine. Even then, I knew I'd be chasing him, baiting him, and admiring his essence forever. Shining strong together makes us the real winners, and I couldn't have asked for anything more.

ZONE_WARDEN

I may not have lived out my serial killer fantasy, but I found my permanent outlet in something else.

My precocious wife told me it was her dream to visit Spain. I don't think I listen well when she gets into her babbling, so instead of visiting,

My Valentine's Virus

I bought us a villa near the ocean. It has an outside garden, and we have a couple of chickens and plan to expand.

I go out more and even have a bit of color. Abbie spends her days helping me, hiking landscapes, and taking time away from our hacking. We still get heated over video games and matches that will last an eternity. We take martial arts together, and I introduced her to Wing Chun. The minute she got the hang of it she uses it against me every time. I love her and all the oddities of her fiery spirit.

She pushes me to unachievable points of advancement. Although her anxieties have been better controlled, I still find that opponent in her eyes.

We don't hack as much as we used to, but our services are available online for those who can find us.

The women who attacked my Abbie, Cassiopeia, Jacqueline, Janice, and Melanie were found stranded on an island after two months.

They were found shaken up and emaciated but alive. From what I overheard, when Melanie tried manipulating them into cannibalism, they found God or something they *think* is their God. They made up a whole new religion. I couldn't have set that in motion better if I had written it myself.

I still keep in touch with Gus. He's a genuine person, and we've formed a charity for farmers across the U.S.

My memoir became a best-seller the moment I was relieved of my charges. I was guilty on all counts, but it's not my problem if people underestimate me. If I were stranded on a desert island, I could build an entire computer, so what made them think I needed the Internet to hack?

I set myself free from the faulty prison systems. It isn't like they'll be able to find me now.

Opening the sliding door to our jungle-like backyard, I find Abbie sitting beneath the shade of her small orange tree. The warm breeze runs through my hair as I watch her type away on her laptop. Our chickens,

Data and Nugget, pick at the floor beside her while the stray black cat who greets us every day curls under Abbie's palm.

"Abbie," I approach with my hands behind my back.

She lifts her head, and I reveal a heart-shaped array of jumbo shrimp.

"Will you be my Valentine?"

A stifled laugh snorts from her, causing her laptop to fall from her lap and startle her pets away. She accepts the gift and raises her arms so I can join her. "Kiss me," she orders.

I smirk and take her face into my hands for a deep embrace. The only thing left I have to accomplish is living the rest of my life with this amazing woman at my side. From now until oblivion.

My Valentine's Virus

MY PROTECTOR'S PROMISE

Featuring Psyra Jean-Pierre and Marco Rosario is coming soon.

Please enjoy this teaser.

Spell One

Texas

If keeping my insane family from falling apart is like moving mountains, then I've already proven I can do the impossible.

When turquoise water shimmers across the plane's window, I wince. Yellow sands come to view, and a knot in my belly tightens.

Fraixia was a secluded island nation once, and now it's home to over 22,000 souls. *That island.*

I was the fool who thought she could escape it.

Most take a gander at our warm, beautiful beaches and think, *"Wow, honey, this sure is a perfect vacation spot."*

And to that, I say—wrong! Dead wrong. Thanks for playing! It's like a Venus flytrap, my personal hell disguised as a tropical paradise. I grew up here. I'm *still* growing up here, and there's no out. Foot down, I told my father I was leaving this *sauna* to pursue a computer science degree.

Nine freaking years later, I'm back for the *third* time like an overused joke. And for what? To translate for him because he's too busy to learn for himself?

The plane does that stupid dip it does for attention, and we dive. The floor trembles beneath my sandals, and the prickling terror I've buried for hours shoots up my spine. I turn away from the ocean's view, but it does little to ease my nerves.

Unsticking myself from the leather seat, I massage my temple. *This is what I get for keeping promises.* My forehead aches, but I don't want to process right now. *I need... I need a drink, maybe a drink and a half.*

Moments pass, and my medicated attention sways to my phone. When the plane crests, my eyelids fly open. Everyone on the flight strains against their seatbelts, and my heart races a mile a minute in the rough drop. Sweat coats my palms in a flash. My fingernails dig into the armrest while the other grasps my companion's hand in a death grip. When my phone falls to my lap, I grip it between my thighs. *I just need to block everything out. I've done this a hundred time, yet it doesn't stop my body from behaving this way.*

"I *hate* planes," I say, grinding my teeth behind a smile.

"Really? I couldn't tell," quips Brock, the man we hired to hold my hand.

I envision the wing of the plane has been shredded into a bushel of coconut trees, and perhaps it's about to crash inside the volcano. Maybe our pilot's too shy to mention it. At least, that's what this *feels* like.

Brock squeezes my hand, and the speck of comfort grounds my racing thoughts. Solidifying my connection with reality, I ignore my delusional inner voice screaming how *we're all going to die.*

I coax my drumming heart from not flying out of my tits, and my face cools a degree. *Deep breathing, Psyra. You got this! Your brain just hates you. Trust you're safe, and everything is okay.* The plane finally wheels into the airport, confirming the hard part is over. I rub the back of my neck and release this poor man's palm.

I've got to hand it to Mom, Brock was a good pick. He's a temporary bodyguard from an *Uber*-styled app I designed freshman year. I was inspired to craft it for people who generally have a rough time. I figured it'd be nice to choose from a list of capable applicants to have around for backup—someone you can genuinely trust, even if it's for a brief time. Though, I should admit I didn't expect my mother to push my own app on me.

Hands like Brock's give off lore of a man who's lived a modest life with woodworking or *any* adorable hands-on hobby.

He flails his crumpled hand to clear it of my phantom squeezes, then my phone vibrates. A deep-throated groan escapes us both from my Lady Sovereign ringtone. Needless to say, it's no longer my favorite song. Brock shifts away, and I narrow my eyes at the blaring screen. I answer it before fully debating how much energy I have left to communicate. I don't have much really, but she's my—

"Let me guess," Brock grumbles mid-stretch. "It's your mom again?"

"You guessed right. I wish I had a prize to hand you," I drawl, swiping up and revealing Maggie's adorable round face. Brock snickers, grateful his client matches his sarcastic spirits, I assume. I flash him a courtesy grin and face away for a bead of privacy.

Fixing my smile, I examine Mom as she pulls back and exposes her background. Beneath the shade of a wooden canopy airport bar, she leans against a cedar counter. The gentle breeze from the shore a mile away plays with the strands of her pink straw hat.

Aww. She landed before me? I share a modest pout. *Texas is closer to Fraixia than Oregon is, I guess.*

My mother has been a human commercial break every thirty minutes. She's fully aware I can't answer mid-flight. I'm not sure how to explain that I was convinced if I didn't focus on the plane, it would fall from the sky somehow. Life likes to play games with me, and I want to be on the lookout.

Uncertain I even answered her, Mom lowers her sunglasses, pouting at the screen. Her pink neon cardigan and leggings could rival the sun—they're so intense. It reminds me of my brother Phil's high school graduation.

She wore a *Crayola* yellow sweater with gaping orange spots. Phil scoped us out in the stadium-sized crowd immediately and complained. His dopey classmates couldn't stop roasting her, and it ruined the whole event for him.

I sneer at the memory behind my smile. *How was it my fault she left the house dressed as SpongeBob?*

Mom's always been a fashionista, yet somehow, *I* got blamed for everything. But if there's one unspoken rule in our household, it's to never *ever* criticize Mom's tastes.

"Hi, momma~" I sing.

"Hi, baby!" Mom squeaks, bouncing with giddiness. **"Oh!"** She manifests an enormous crystal blue margarita. **"Look what *I* have."** It sweats in her long-manicured hands as she offers a celebratory *cheers* at the camera. **"Isn't this such a great color? I'm renovating the guest bathroom with this exact shade! Do you like it? Your dad says people will be stopping by our estate more often now, so I've been refurbishing the *whole* house."**

Have mercy. Now, I'm extra jealous. I can practically taste that blue baby through the screen. *Ooo—with the lime garnish and ice?* I hope it tastes like the fruity ice pops I loved as a kid, only *sinful*.

Mom giggles at my drooling reaction as I pay her no mind. **"You like it?"** She tests it's weight, tormenting my thirst even more. **"Your brother is in the restroom, so I was able to sneak off and nab this fun drink. Where are you? You haven't posted anything on your timeline."**

"We're just landing," I grit in my thirsty haze and adjust my braids. I know why she called. She wants to lecture me about how I need to document my journey to her more. I've been trying to step away from the social media scene. Gaming too. Anything involving a screen, really. Exhausting doesn't even begin to explain this trip from Oregon to the Caribbean, but I'll live.

It's just that dear old dad called me the morning I missed my flight. When his name appeared on my phone, I was ripping out hairs. I just *had* to answer it. It's a special kind of mental state when you already know someone's bullshit's about to fly. When it hits you, all you're left with is a steamrolled heart to work with.

I remember it as if it took place minutes ago.

My heart pounded against my chest like an angry neighbor, but I raised the device to my ear anyway. "I can explain…" I swallowed a knot and recounted the events in vivid detail.

I didn't do anything wrong. It was a severe emergency. My dweeb of a friend was sent to an American dungeon. Animal poachers were seizing his familiar, and I couldn't stand back and watch that happen. Especially not when I know how important Dice is to him. That little raccoon saved his life during a bad break-up.

I weaved through the motions of his rant. **"You're making me look foolish,"** he rumbled, out of breath just to force the words out. **"I can't even tell you how disappointed I am with you for not being capable of doing the simplest task."** Of course, Dad dismissed the entire thing in his classic patronizing tone. He made me feel as though his situation was an adult matter… and I, his dumb kid still, remixing excuses.

My heart bled residual pain as my vision blurred to nothingness. His assistants murmuring in the background brought me back, and my fist shook.

How neat! He's already undermined me in front of my new co-workers. Returning from the reverence, my teeth grit and my muscles tighten in real-time. *Can't wait to look forward to that after thousands of miles.*

Folding my arms, I huff in a private grumble. I still haven't gotten an apology, but I'm not gasping for one.

There's been a rift between us ever since, and like always, *I* have to be the one to make up. *I shouldn't even show up at all—Maybe I can watch him choke on his food at dinner.* The dark thought sparks my deviant smirk, and the overhead stereo fills a buzz across the space. It announces we've landed seconds later, and the tight air fills with a symphony of clicking seatbelts and thuds from overhang compartments unlocking. Many travelers stand to shuffle ahead. While everyone retrieves their luggage, Mom continues her virtual lecture, I didn't sign up for.

Brock snorts and gestures for my attention. "Man, am I glad my mother wasn't this clingy," he muses as he reaches for the pet carrier beneath my seat.

Dice hisses, causing Brock to stumble back into a group of startled bikini models in the aisle. "Son-of-a...!"

I reach to haul Dice's carrier myself, giving an empathetic coo at the cage. My friend's familiar is under my care until everything is situated and I can return him. "You *scared* him... *booo,*" I bemoan. The moment I'm between them, the baby-shaped raccoon tilts his masked marks to me. His big obsidian eyes sparkle like the perfect little angel he is.

Brock pins my temporary pet with a venomous sneer. "The *fucker* spooked me first! Where are my sympathies?"

Travelers squeeze around him, and I pet his soft head through the cold bars. "Check back when you grow a *cute* little robber's mask," I tease.

Brock takes the bags off my hands, and we vacate the tight space. We each throw nods of courtesy and *thank yous* at the beautiful flight attendants standing to the side, but a glimpse of my irritation flickers at the pilot. *Fly smoother next time, lunatic. I might be the only one alive who loathes the Wright Brothers for the audacity.*

The sun rays above pierce through the skyline inside the airport lobby. In our transition across the sizable space, I can breathe on my own again. Warm buttery pastries from one of the vendors by the entrance envelop our lungs. The floors clap with distant flip-flops, ocean waves a few miles away crash against exposed rock, and the laughter of seagulls echo around us.

My stomach twists, having a full-on allergic reaction to what's considered paradise.

Psyra & Marco's Story:

Texas (Psyra)
I've learned to fight my battles, build my shields, and never need saving.
Then Marco crashed back into my life, still carrying the same fire that burned me. He says he's here to protect me. But I've also learned not all promises can be kept.

New York (Marco)
I've spent my life defending others, atoning for sins that will never wash away. But Psyra doesn't need another betrayal.
I failed her once. I won't do it again.
Not even an unforgiving island, our duties, or the ghosts haunting her will stop me from proving some promises are forever.

ABIGAIL BELLE-NUÑEZ

XALTON KAISER

THANK YOU FOR READING.

I want to extend my gratitude to everyone who supports my writing. Your encouragement means the world to me, and if you leave a review, I will mention you in the acknowledgments of my next title! Stay updated on future projects and madness if you like. I also like to draw art of my characters sometimes. You can find them anywhere here including how I make them.

Facebook (The Literary Universe of A. Darang)
Twitter/X (@AuthorA_Darang),
Instagram (@Author_ADarang),
TikTok (@AuthorADarang)
BlueSky (@adarang.bsky.social)
Please join my mailing list @ http://www.ADarang.com

Feel free to give a shout-out or your thoughts on the stories even if you have general beef. Don't hesitate to reach out.
Warmest regards,
A. Darang.

[SCAN ME (QR Code)]

ABOUT THE AUTHOR

A. Darang is a New Yorker powered by 49% chaos and 51% sugar. She writes for romantically inclined nerds, goths, and tomboys who crave the unexpected.

When she's not crafting stories, A. can usually be found binging shows, devouring novels, gaming, or sketching, and hyping up strangers ♪

But don't let the squishy face fool you: A. has a dark side. By nightfall, she transforms into a masked vigilante. She lives blissfully in her tower, hoarding houseplants with her sweetheart and goofy pet sidekicks.

www.ingramcontent.com/pod-product-compliance
Lightning Source LLC
LaVergne TN
LVHW011945060526
838201LV00061B/4208